P9-CJC-261

THIS BOOK IS FOR **BROOKE SANDEJAS BOLTON,** WHO ENTERED THE WORLD WHILE WE WERE MAKING IT.

K. B. AND C. A. B.

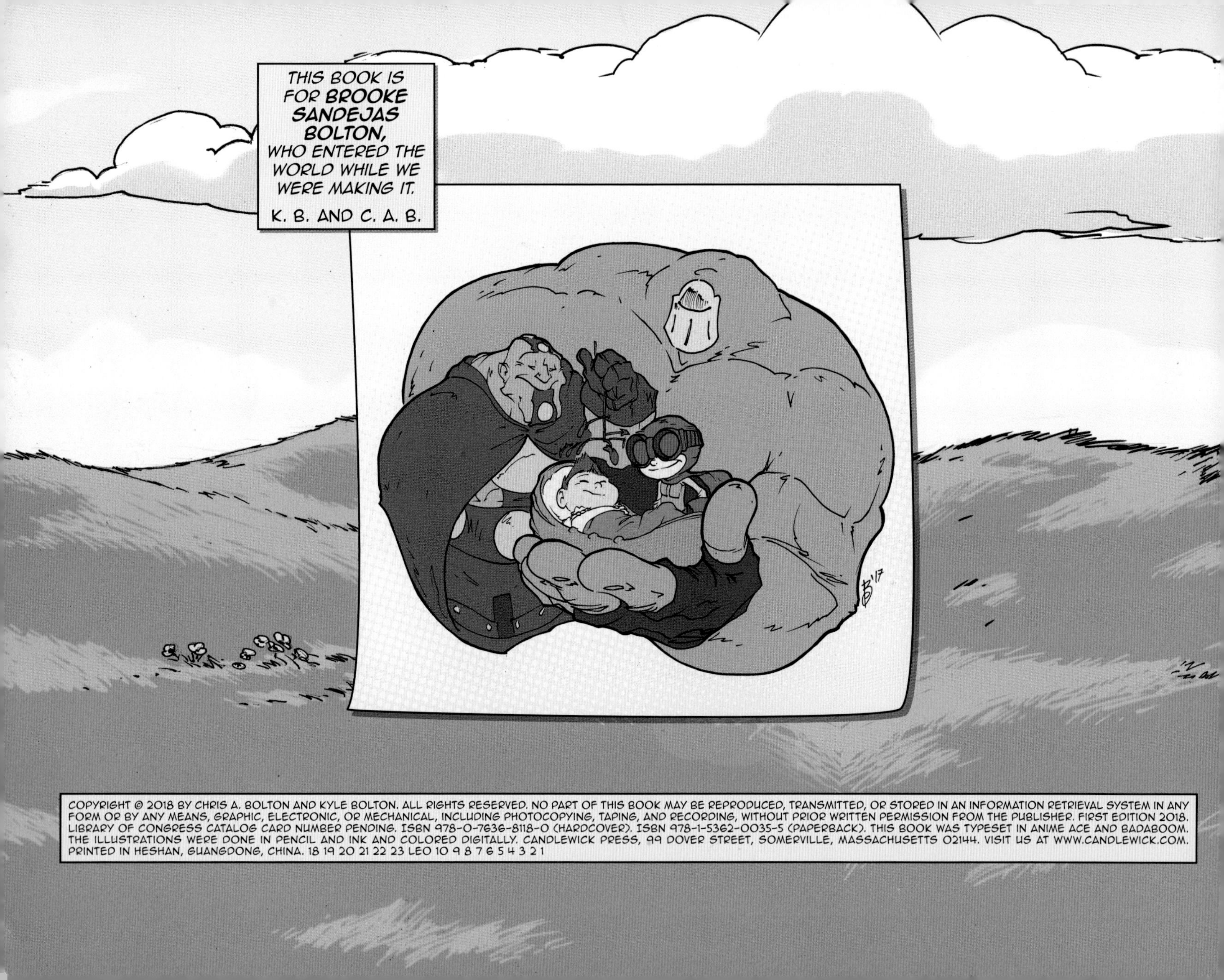

 FIRST EDITION 2018. LIBRARY OF CONGRESS CATALOG CARD NUMBER PENDING. ISBN 978-0-7636-8118-0 (HARDCOVER). ISBN 978-1-5362-0035-5 (PAPERBACK). THIS BOOK WAS TYPESET IN ANIME ACE AND BADABOOM. THE ILLUSTRATIONS WERE DONE IN PENCIL AND INK AND COLORED DIGITALLY. CANDLEWICK PRESS, 99 DOVER STREET, SOMERVILLE, MASSACHUSETTS 02144. VISIT US AT WWW.CANDLEWICK.COM. PRINTED IN HESHAN, GUANGDONG, CHINA. 18 19 20 21 22 23 LEO 10 9 8 7 6 5 4 3 2 1

SMASH
FEARLESS

WRITTEN BY **CHRIS A. BOLTON**

ART BY **KYLE BOLTON**

COLORS BY **JUSTINE HERNANDEZ**

CANDLEWICK PRESS

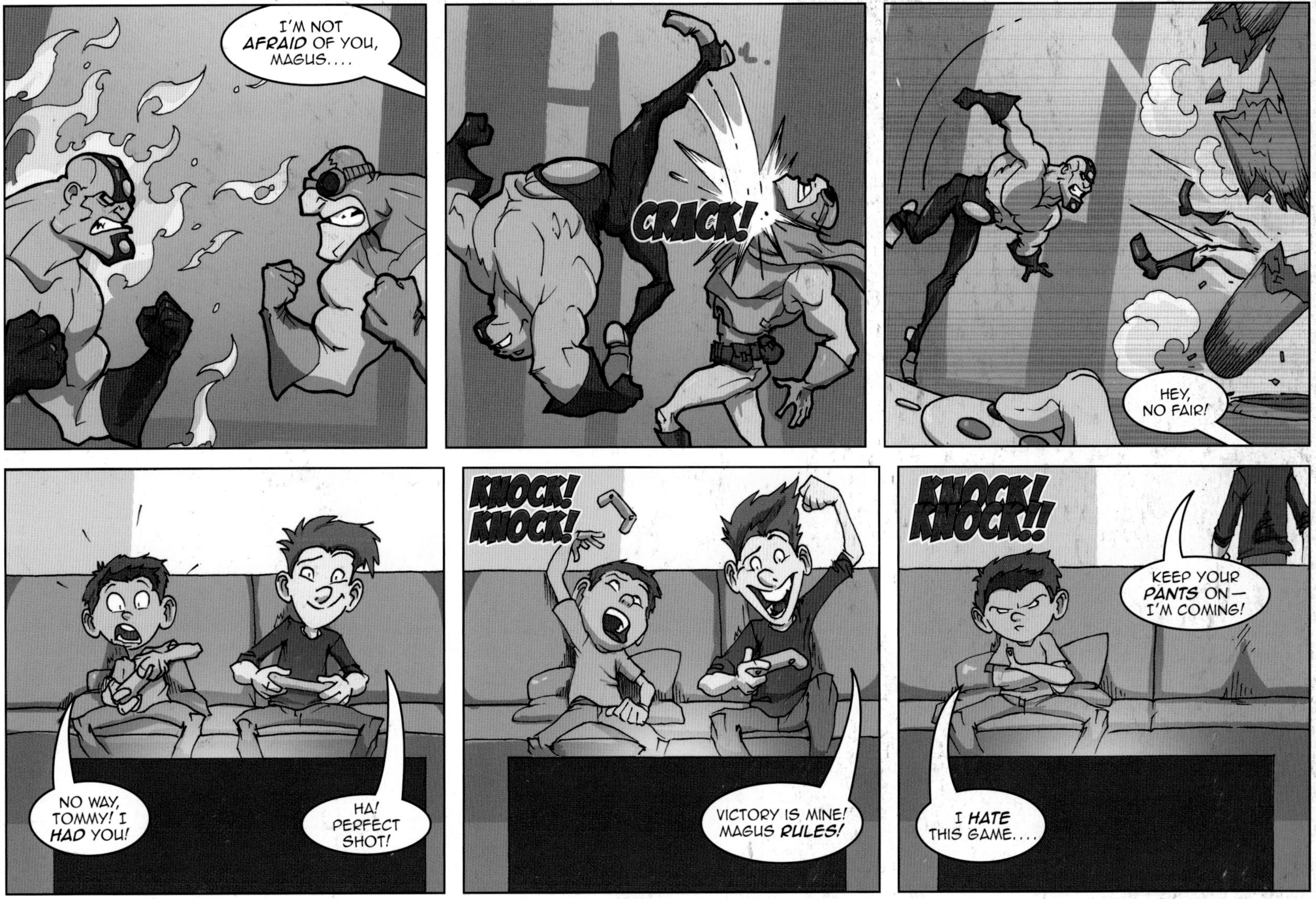
I'M NOT AFRAID OF YOU, MAGUS....
CRACK!
HEY, NO FAIR!
NO WAY, TOMMY! I HAD YOU!
HA! PERFECT SHOT!
KNOCK! KNOCK!
VICTORY IS MINE! MAGUS RULES!
KNOCK! KNOCK!!
KEEP YOUR PANTS ON— I'M COMING!
I HATE THIS GAME....

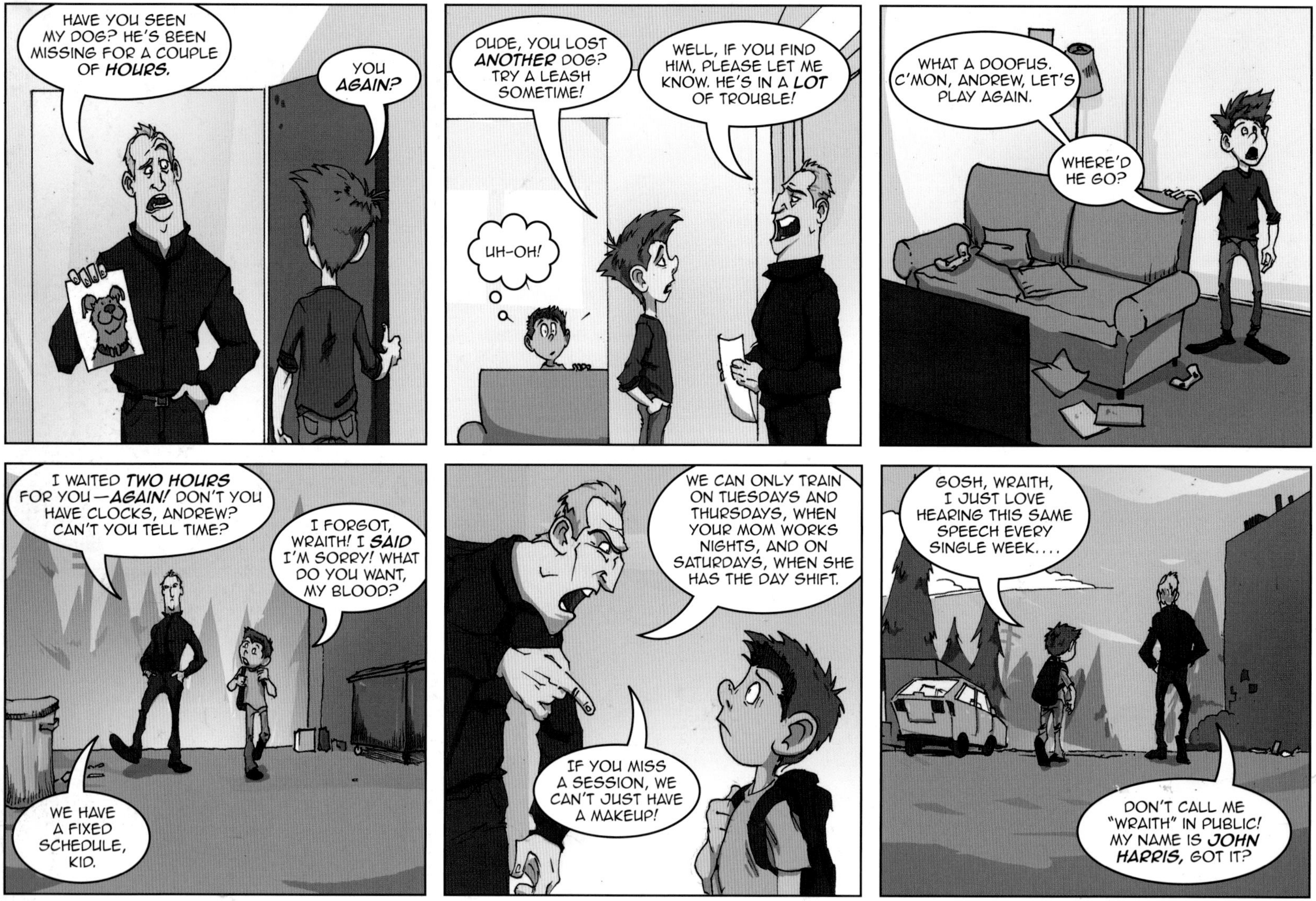
HAVE YOU SEEN MY DOG? HE'S BEEN MISSING FOR A COUPLE OF **HOURS.**
YOU **AGAIN?**
DUDE, YOU LOST **ANOTHER** DOG? TRY A LEASH SOMETIME!
WELL, IF YOU FIND HIM, PLEASE LET ME KNOW. HE'S IN A **LOT** OF TROUBLE!
UH-OH!
WHAT A DOOFUS. C'MON, ANDREW, LET'S PLAY AGAIN.
WHERE'D HE GO?
I WAITED **TWO HOURS** FOR YOU—**AGAIN!** DON'T YOU HAVE CLOCKS, ANDREW? CAN'T YOU TELL TIME?
I FORGOT, WRAITH! I **SAID** I'M SORRY! WHAT DO YOU WANT, MY BLOOD?
WE HAVE A FIXED SCHEDULE, KID.
WE CAN ONLY TRAIN ON TUESDAYS AND THURSDAYS, WHEN YOUR MOM WORKS NIGHTS, AND ON SATURDAYS, WHEN SHE HAS THE DAY SHIFT.
IF YOU MISS A SESSION, WE CAN'T JUST HAVE A MAKEUP!
GOSH, WRAITH, I JUST LOVE HEARING THIS SAME SPEECH EVERY SINGLE WEEK....
DON'T CALL ME "WRAITH" IN PUBLIC! MY NAME IS **JOHN HARRIS,** GOT IT?

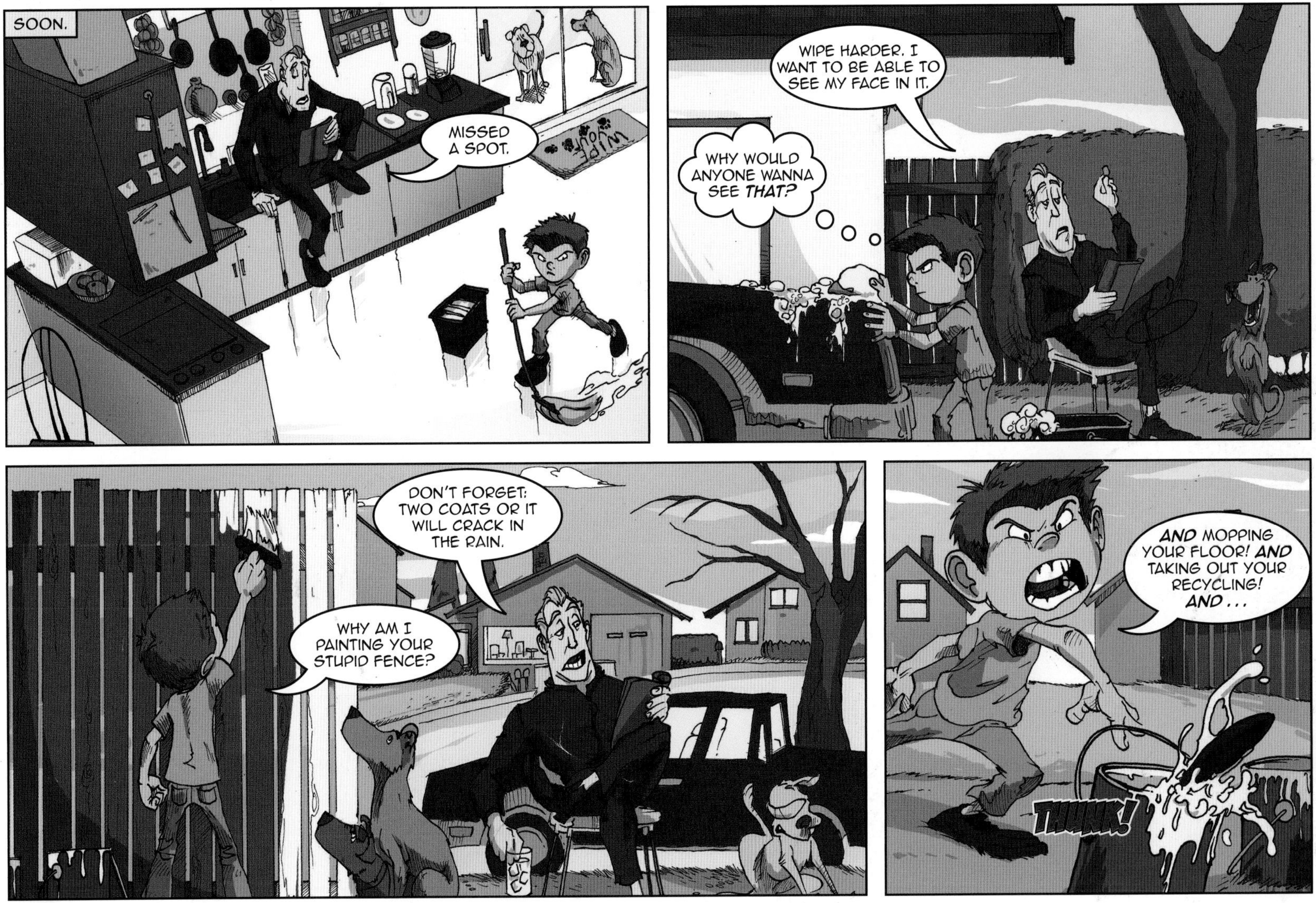
SOON.
MISSED A SPOT.
WIPE HARDER. I WANT TO BE ABLE TO SEE MY FACE IN IT.
WHY WOULD ANYONE WANNA SEE THAT?
DON'T FORGET: TWO COATS OR IT WILL CRACK IN THE RAIN.
WHY AM I PAINTING YOUR STUPID FENCE?
AND MOPPING YOUR FLOOR! AND TAKING OUT YOUR RECYCLING! AND . . .
THUNK!

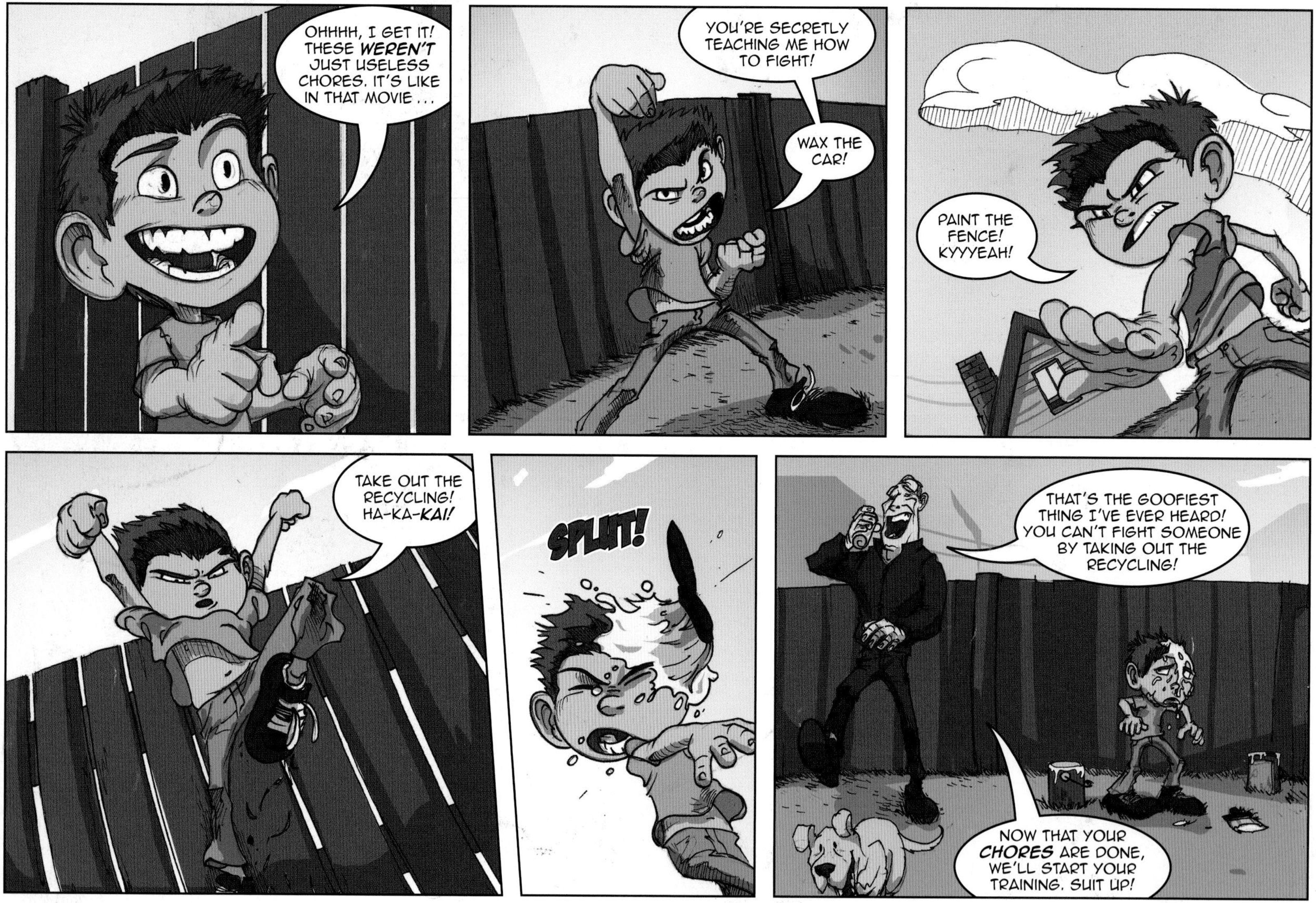
OHHHH, I GET IT! THESE *WEREN'T* JUST USELESS CHORES. IT'S LIKE IN THAT MOVIE . . .
YOU'RE SECRETLY TEACHING ME HOW TO FIGHT!
WAX THE CAR!
PAINT THE FENCE! KYYYEAH!
TAKE OUT THE RECYCLING! HA-KA-*KAI!*
SPLUT!
THAT'S THE GOOFIEST THING I'VE EVER HEARD! YOU CAN'T FIGHT SOMEONE BY TAKING OUT THE RECYCLING!
NOW THAT YOUR *CHORES* ARE DONE, WE'LL START YOUR TRAINING. SUIT UP!

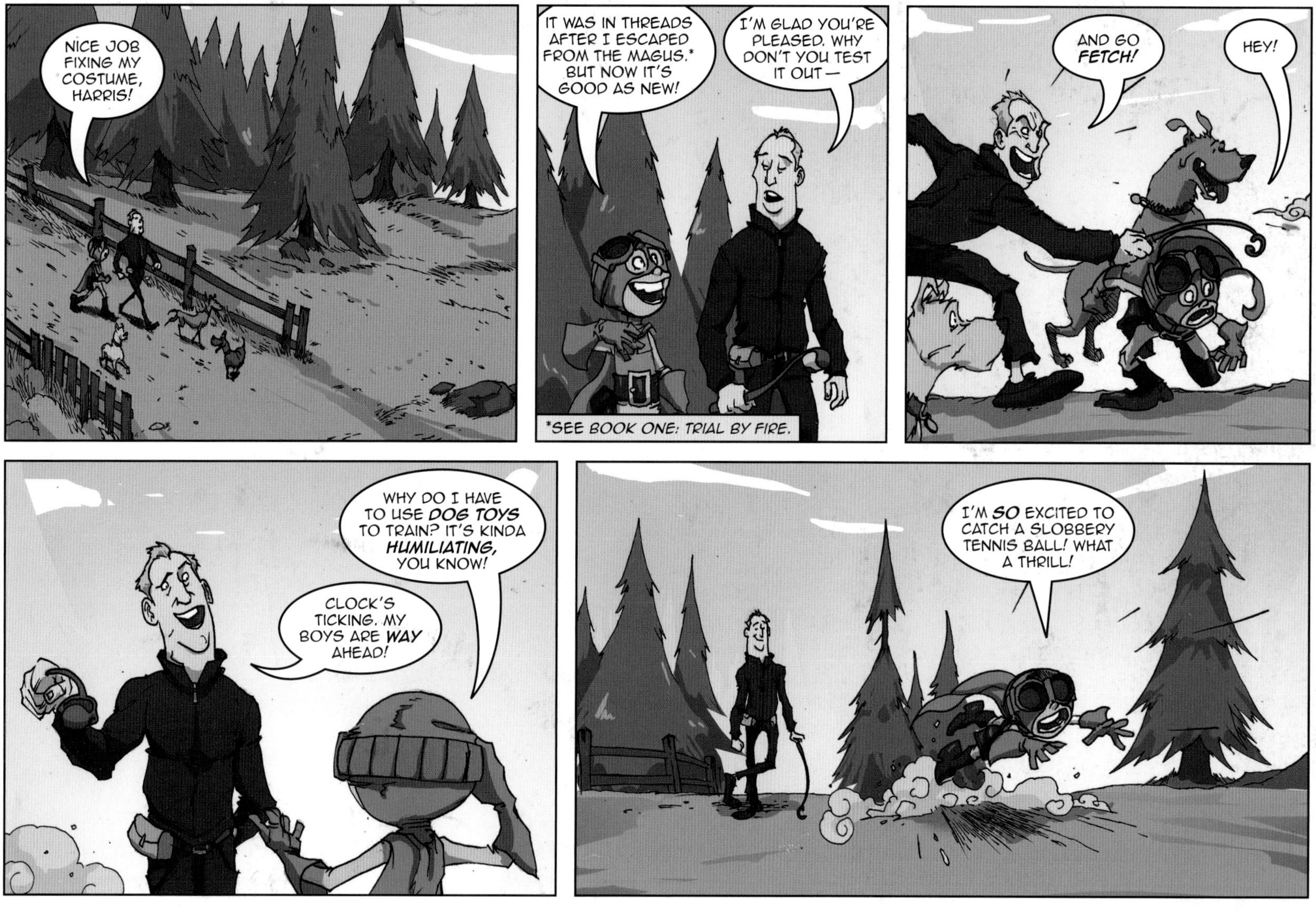
NICE JOB FIXING MY COSTUME, HARRIS!
IT WAS IN THREADS AFTER I ESCAPED FROM THE MAGUS.* BUT NOW IT'S GOOD AS NEW!
I'M GLAD YOU'RE PLEASED. WHY DON'T YOU TEST IT OUT—
*SEE BOOK ONE: TRIAL BY FIRE.
AND GO FETCH!
HEY!
WHY DO I HAVE TO USE DOG TOYS TO TRAIN? IT'S KINDA HUMILIATING, YOU KNOW!
CLOCK'S TICKING. MY BOYS ARE WAY AHEAD!
I'M SO EXCITED TO CATCH A SLOBBERY TENNIS BALL! WHAT A THRILL!

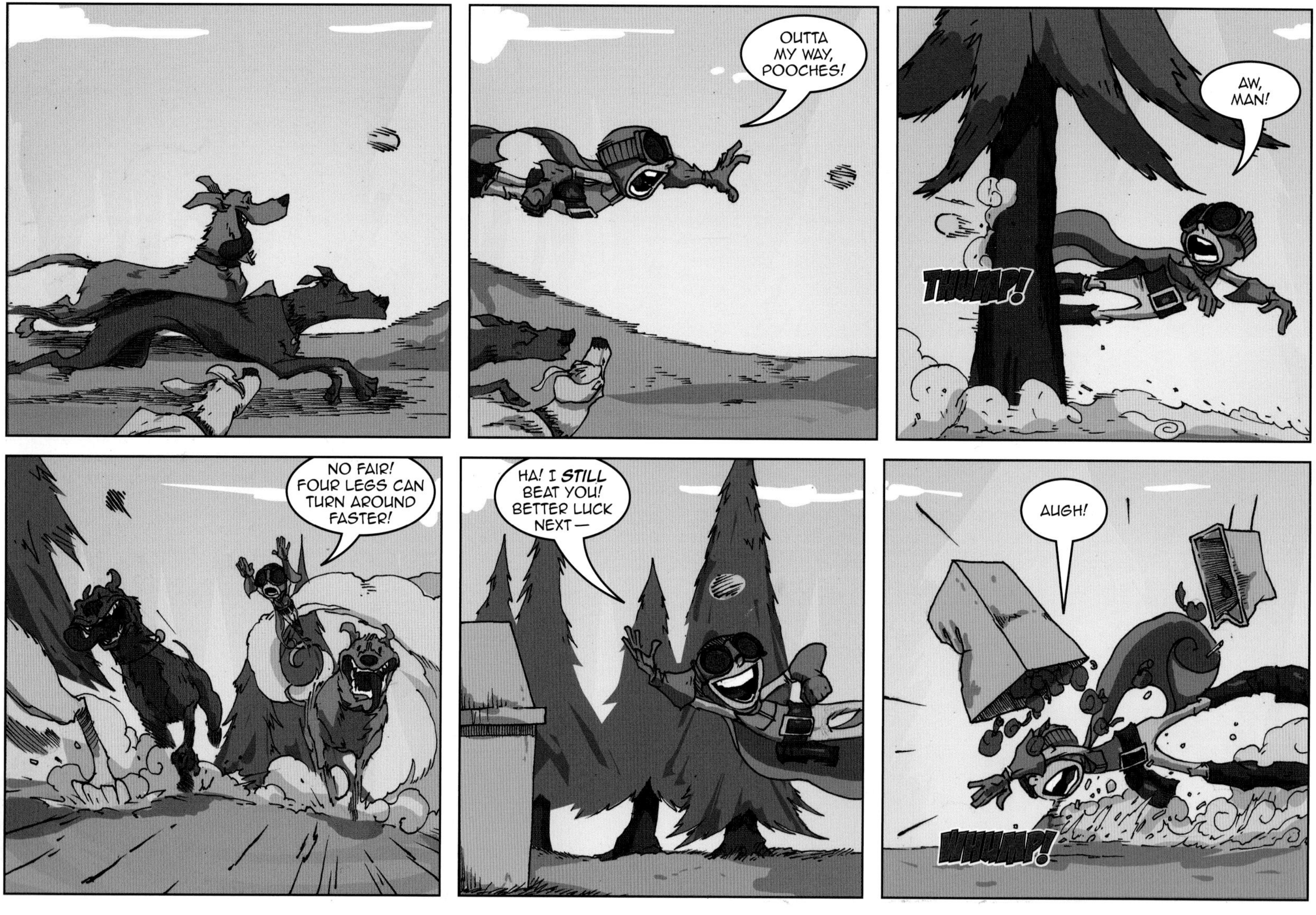

OUTTA MY WAY, POOCHES!
AW, MAN!
THUMP!
NO FAIR! FOUR LEGS CAN TURN AROUND FASTER!
HA! I STILL BEAT YOU! BETTER LUCK NEXT—
AUGH!
WHUMP!

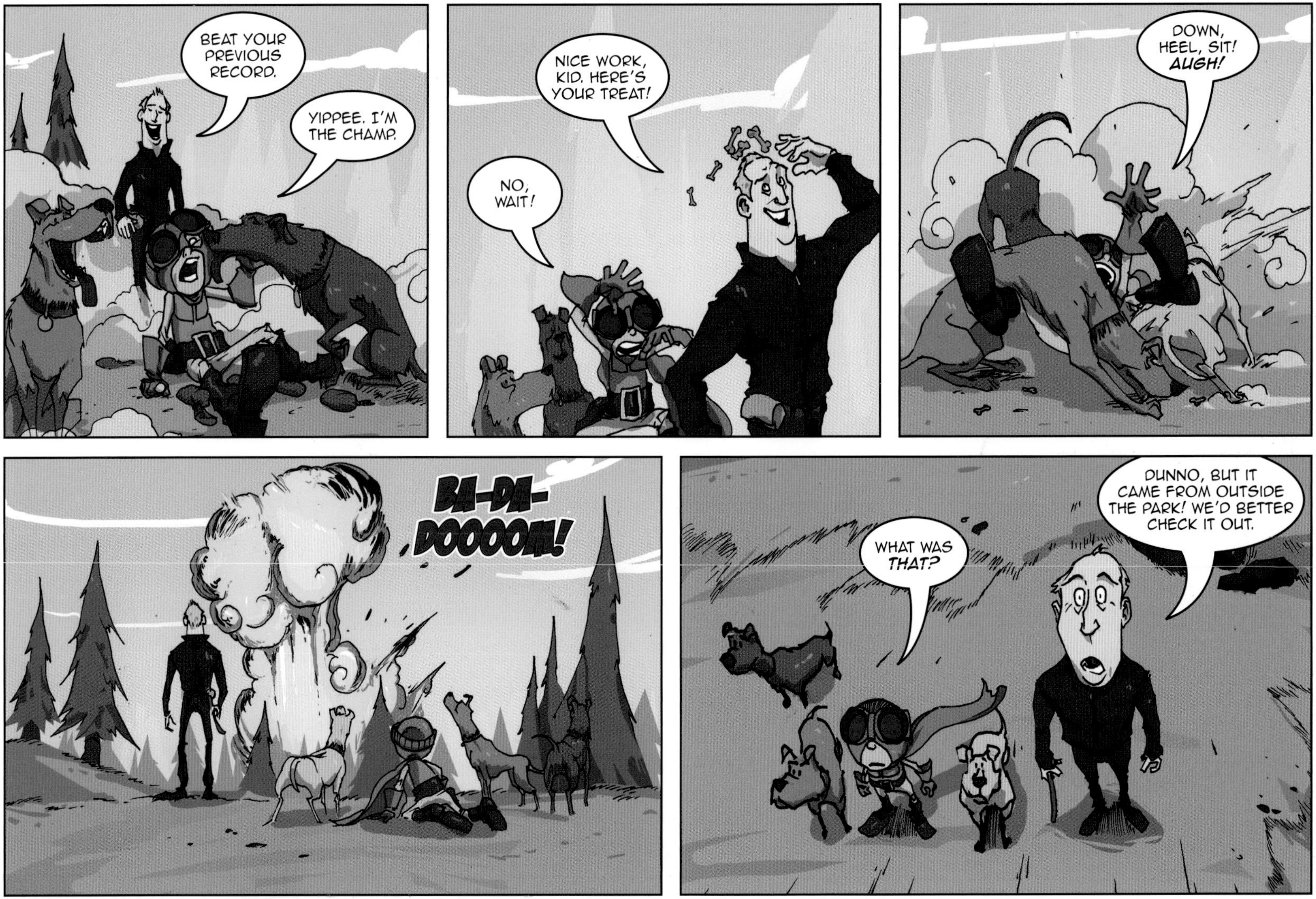
BEAT YOUR PREVIOUS RECORD.
YIPPEE. I'M THE CHAMP.
NICE WORK, KID. HERE'S YOUR TREAT!
NO, WAIT!
DOWN, HEEL, SIT! *AUGH!*
BA-DA-DOOOOOM!
WHAT WAS *THAT?*
DUNNO, BUT IT CAME FROM OUTSIDE THE PARK! WE'D BETTER CHECK IT OUT.

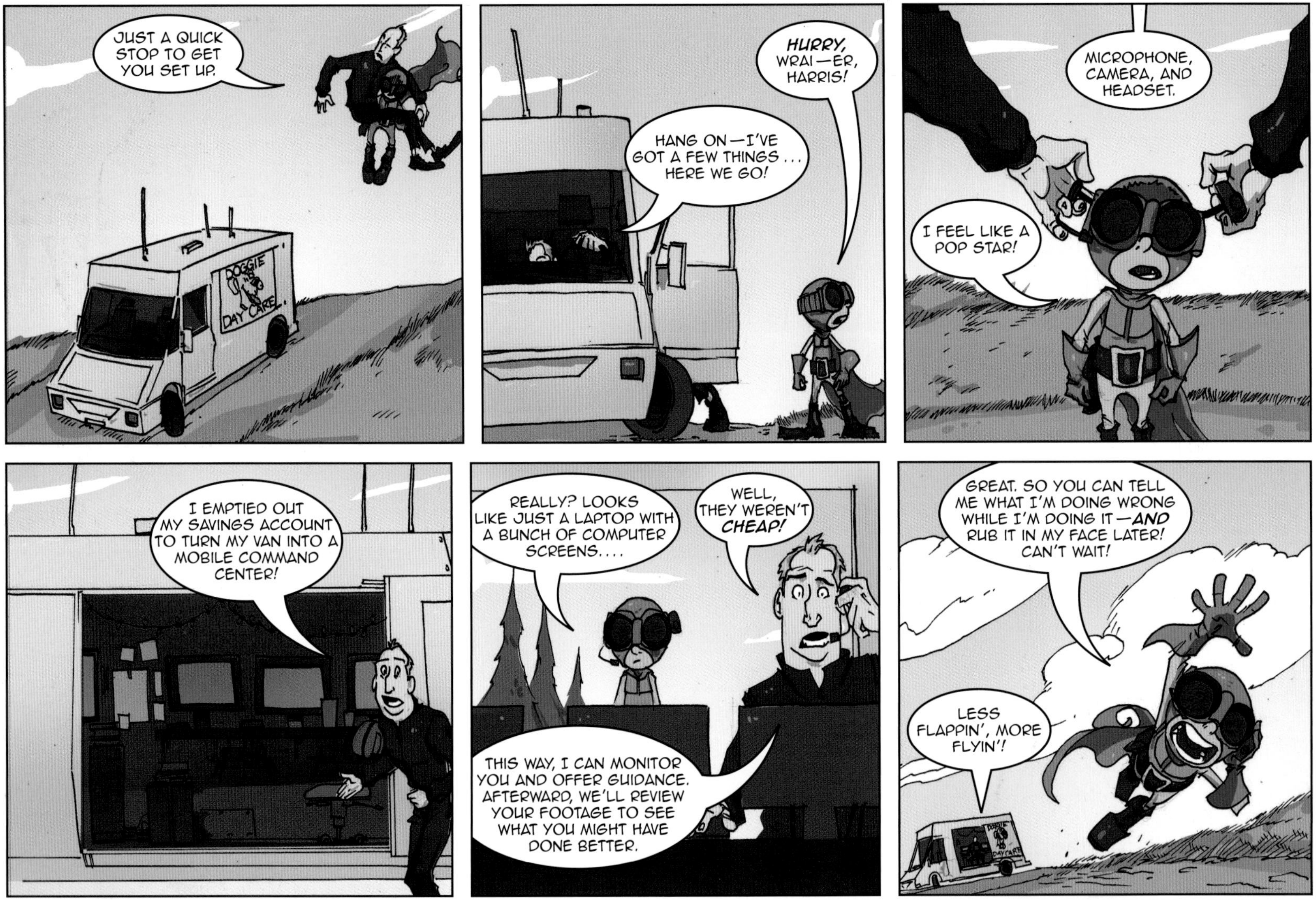
JUST A QUICK STOP TO GET YOU SET UP.
HURRY, WRAI—ER, HARRIS!
HANG ON—I'VE GOT A FEW THINGS . . . HERE WE GO!
MICROPHONE, CAMERA, AND HEADSET.
I FEEL LIKE A POP STAR!
DOGGIE DAY CARE
I EMPTIED OUT MY SAVINGS ACCOUNT TO TURN MY VAN INTO A MOBILE COMMAND CENTER!
REALLY? LOOKS LIKE JUST A LAPTOP WITH A BUNCH OF COMPUTER SCREENS. . . .
WELL, THEY WEREN'T *CHEAP!*
THIS WAY, I CAN MONITOR YOU AND OFFER GUIDANCE. AFTERWARD, WE'LL REVIEW YOUR FOOTAGE TO SEE WHAT YOU MIGHT HAVE DONE BETTER.
GREAT. SO YOU CAN TELL ME WHAT I'M DOING WRONG WHILE I'M DOING IT—*AND* RUB IT IN MY FACE LATER! CAN'T WAIT!
LESS FLAPPIN', MORE FLYIN'!

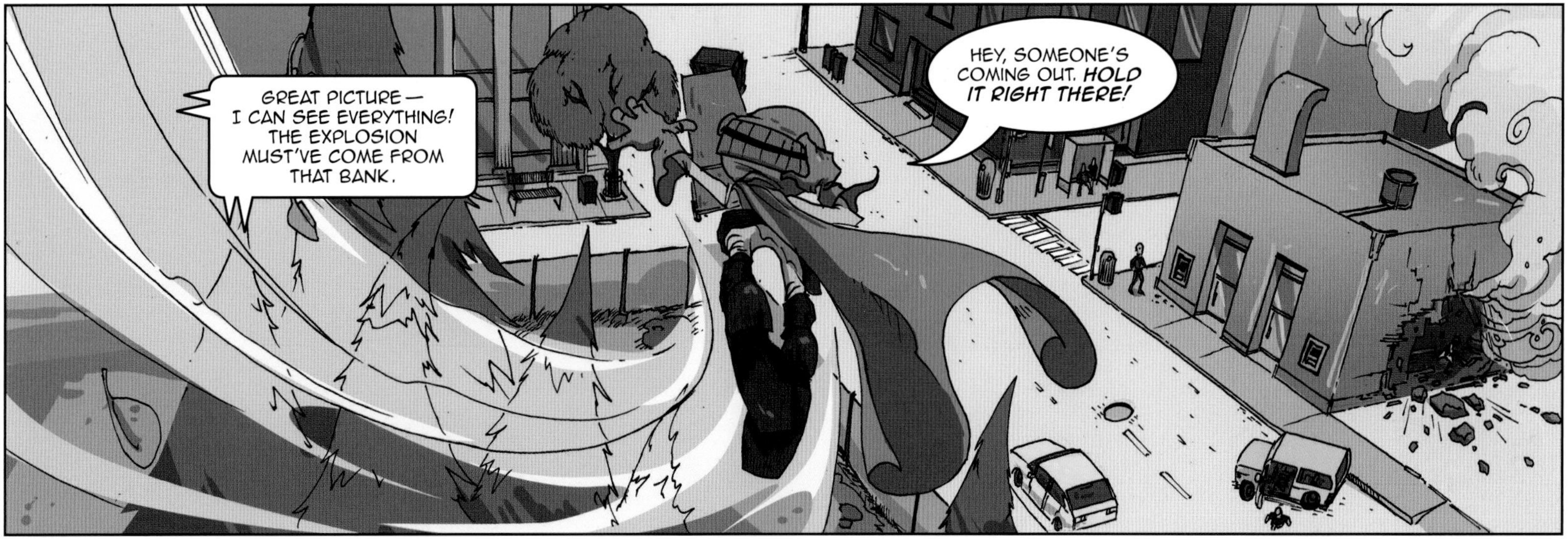
GREAT PICTURE— I CAN SEE EVERYTHING! THE EXPLOSION MUST'VE COME FROM THAT BANK.
HEY, SOMEONE'S COMING OUT. HOLD IT RIGHT THERE!

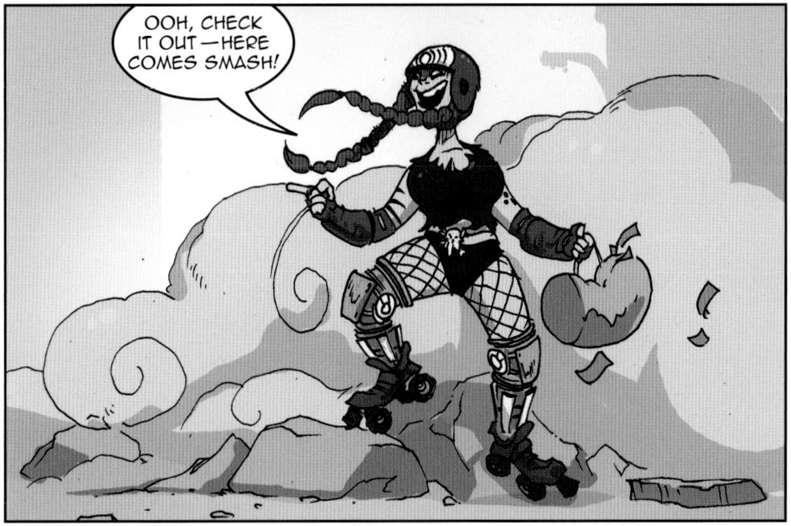
OOH, CHECK IT OUT—HERE COMES SMASH!

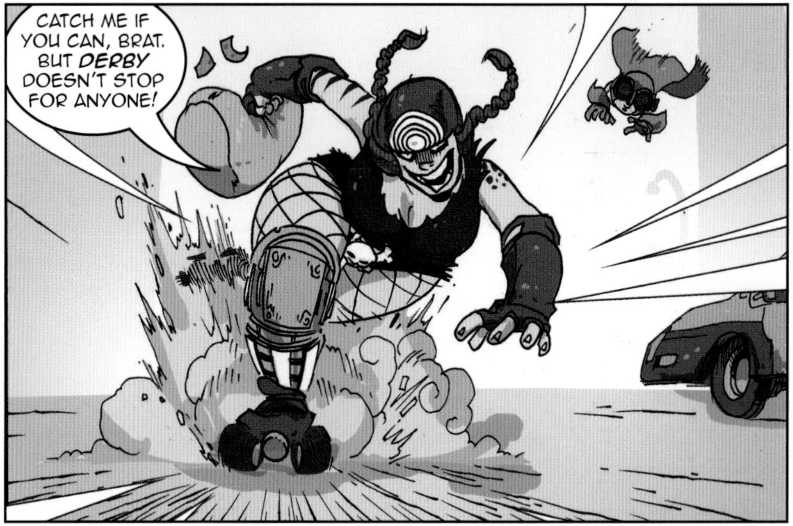
CATCH ME IF YOU CAN, BRAT. BUT DERBY DOESN'T STOP FOR ANYONE!

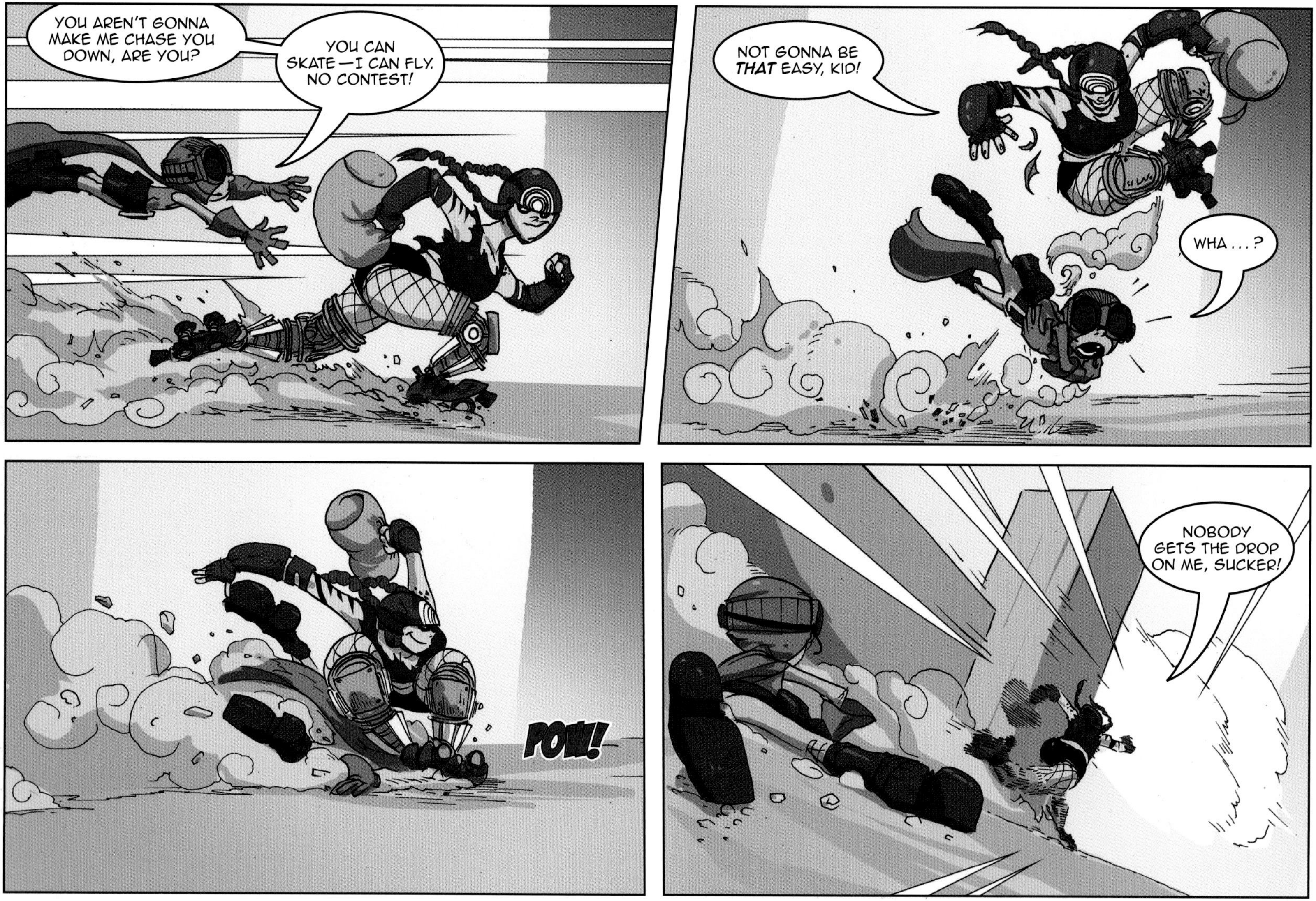
YOU AREN'T GONNA MAKE ME CHASE YOU DOWN, ARE YOU?
YOU CAN SKATE—I CAN FLY. NO CONTEST!
NOT GONNA BE THAT EASY, KID!
WHA . . . ?
POW!
NOBODY GETS THE DROP ON ME, SUCKER!

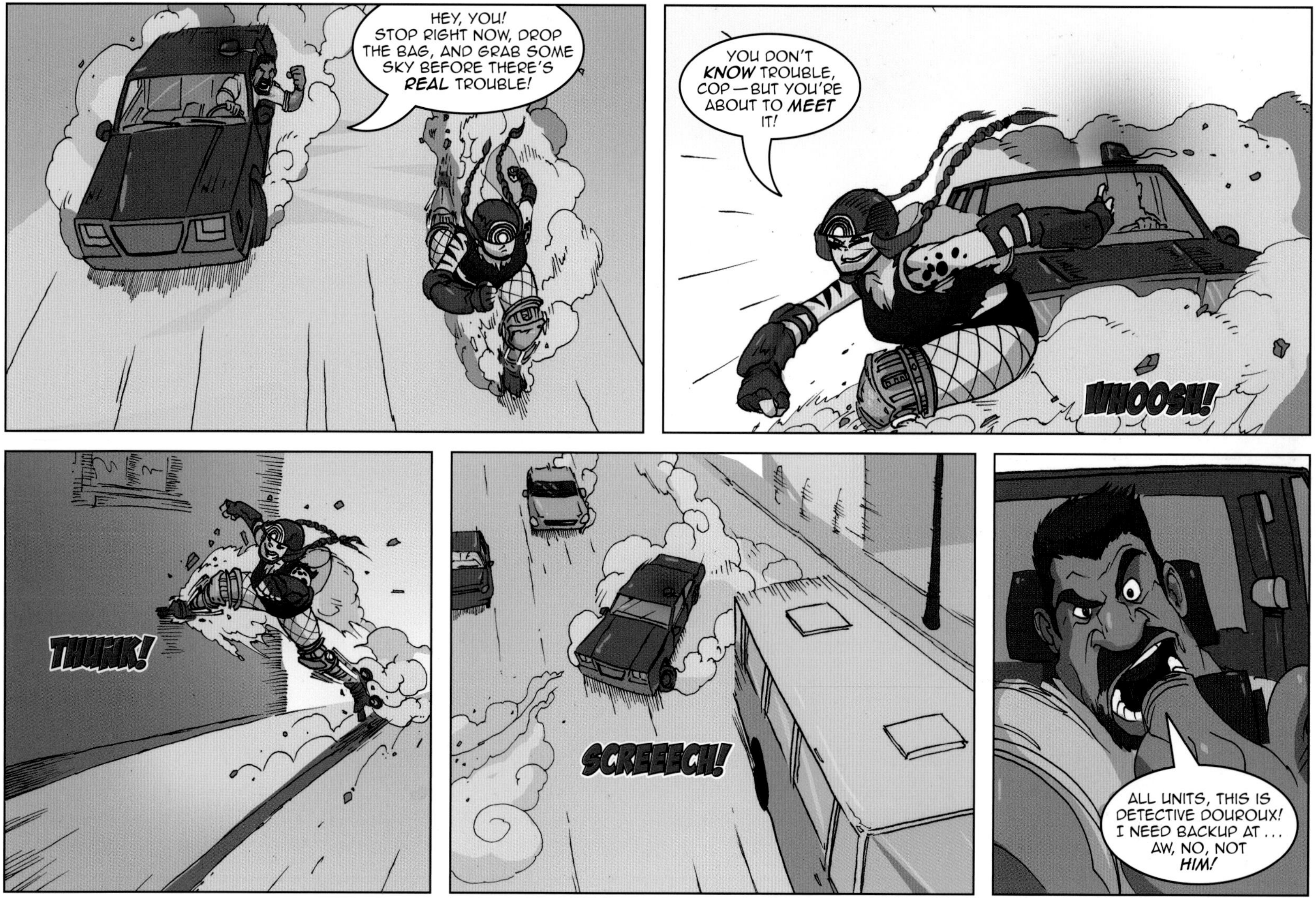
HEY, YOU! STOP RIGHT NOW, DROP THE BAG, AND GRAB SOME SKY BEFORE THERE'S REAL TROUBLE!
YOU DON'T KNOW TROUBLE, COP—BUT YOU'RE ABOUT TO MEET IT!
WHOOSH!
THUNK!
SCREEECH!
ALL UNITS, THIS IS DETECTIVE DOUROUX! I NEED BACKUP AT . . . AW, NO, NOT HIM!

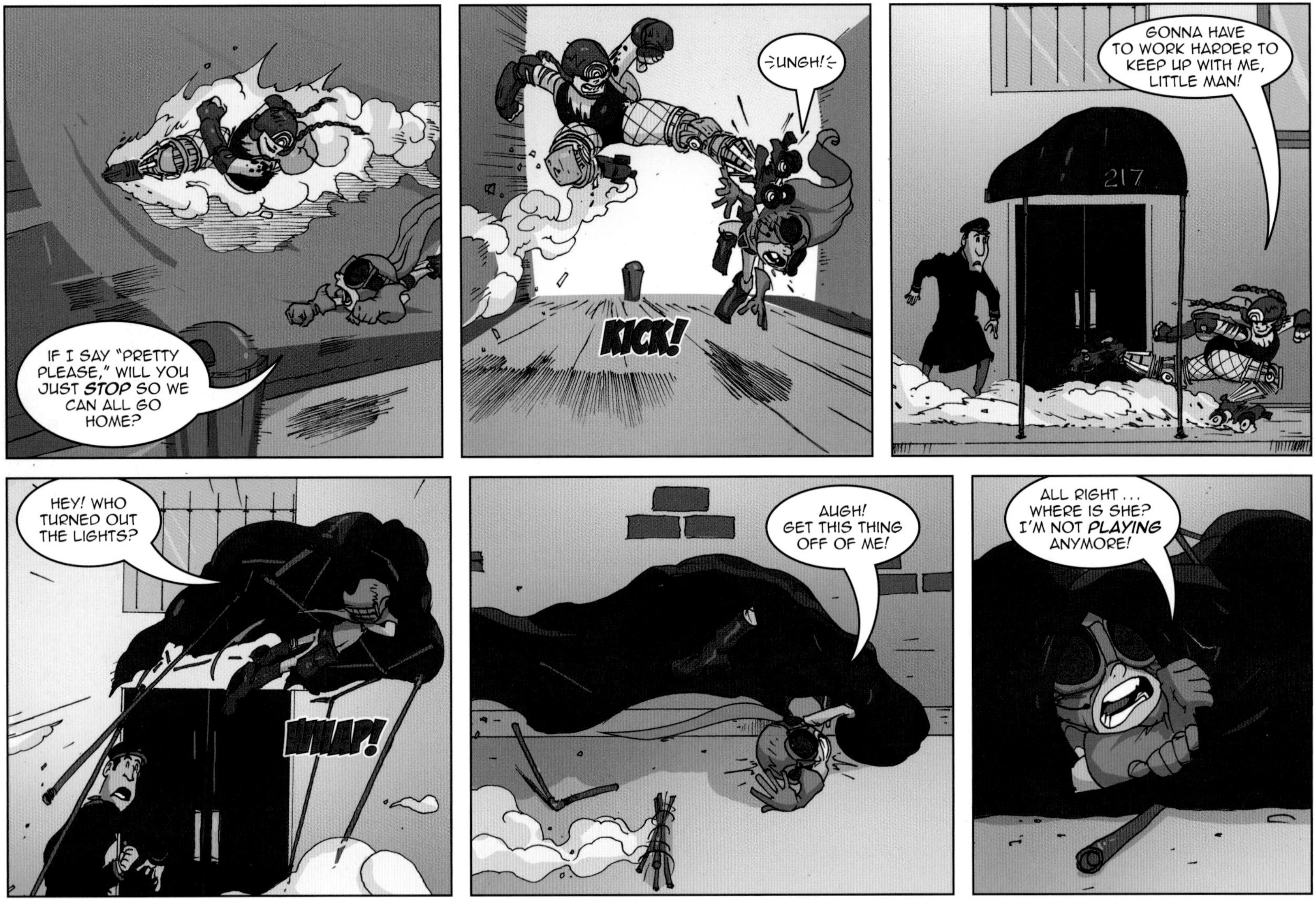
IF I SAY "PRETTY PLEASE," WILL YOU JUST STOP SO WE CAN ALL GO HOME?
UNGH!
KICK!
GONNA HAVE TO WORK HARDER TO KEEP UP WITH ME, LITTLE MAN!
217
HEY! WHO TURNED OUT THE LIGHTS?
WHAP!
AUGH! GET THIS THING OFF OF ME!
ALL RIGHT . . . WHERE IS SHE? I'M NOT PLAYING ANYMORE!

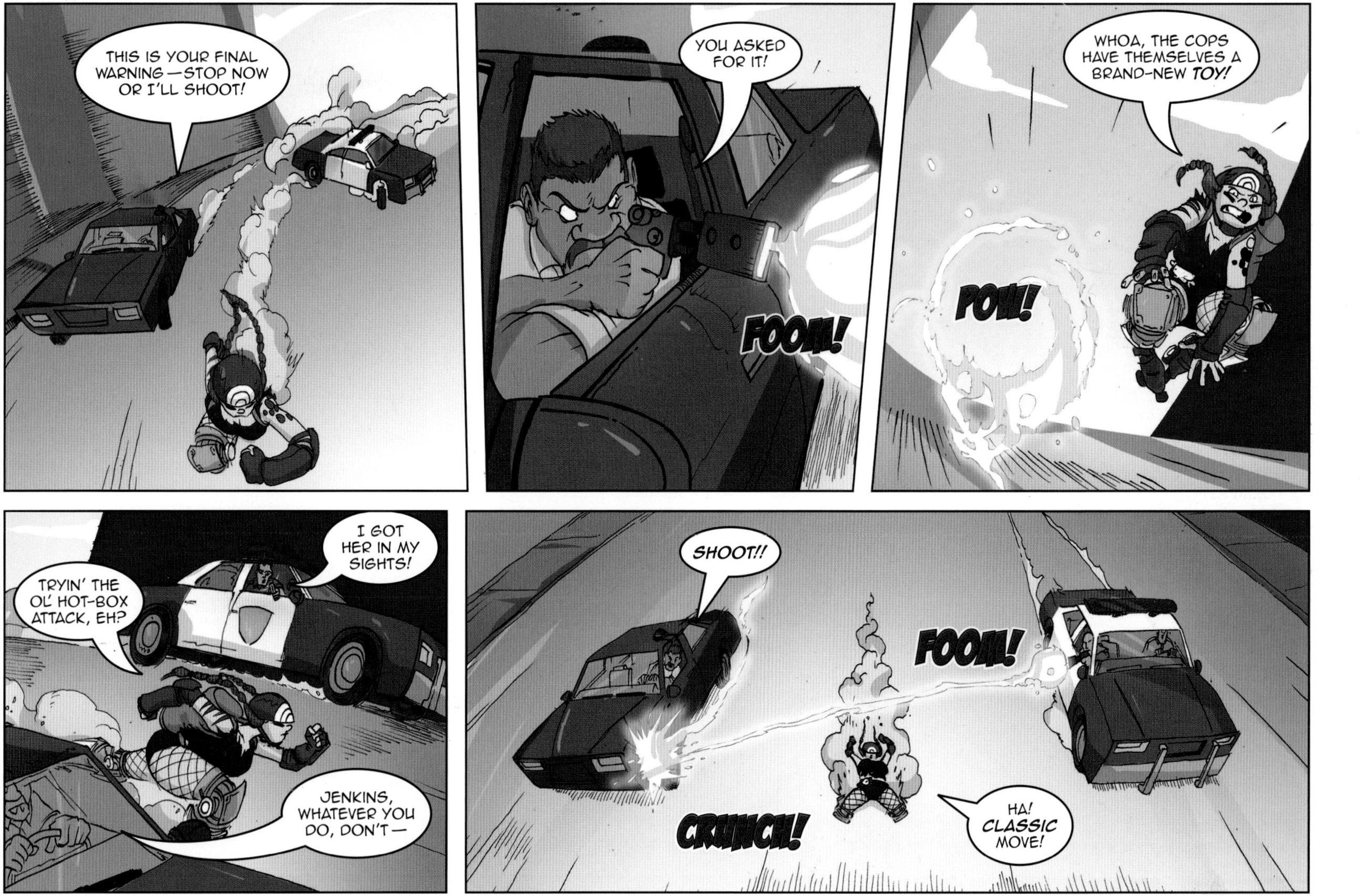
THIS IS YOUR FINAL WARNING—STOP NOW OR I'LL SHOOT!
YOU ASKED FOR IT!
FOOM!
WHOA, THE COPS HAVE THEMSELVES A BRAND-NEW *TOY!*
POW!
I GOT HER IN MY SIGHTS!
TRYIN' THE OL' HOT-BOX ATTACK, EH?
JENKINS, WHATEVER YOU DO, DON'T—
SHOOT!!
FOOM!
CRUNCH!
HA! **CLASSIC** MOVE!

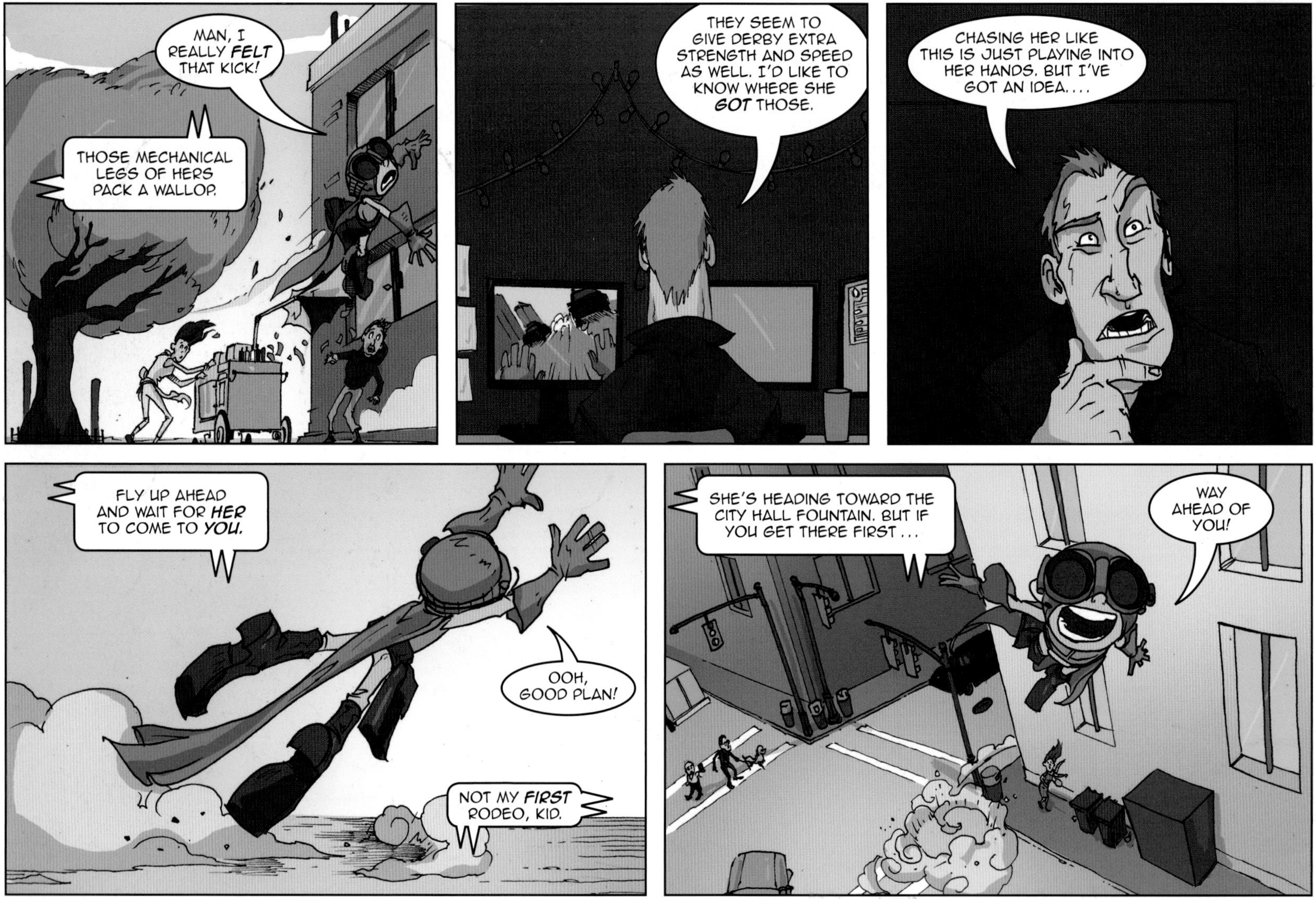
MAN, I REALLY FELT THAT KICK!
THOSE MECHANICAL LEGS OF HERS PACK A WALLOP.
THEY SEEM TO GIVE DERBY EXTRA STRENGTH AND SPEED AS WELL. I'D LIKE TO KNOW WHERE SHE GOT THOSE.
CHASING HER LIKE THIS IS JUST PLAYING INTO HER HANDS. BUT I'VE GOT AN IDEA. . . .
FLY UP AHEAD AND WAIT FOR HER TO COME TO YOU.
OOH, GOOD PLAN!
NOT MY FIRST RODEO, KID.
SHE'S HEADING TOWARD THE CITY HALL FOUNTAIN. BUT IF YOU GET THERE FIRST . . .
WAY AHEAD OF YOU!

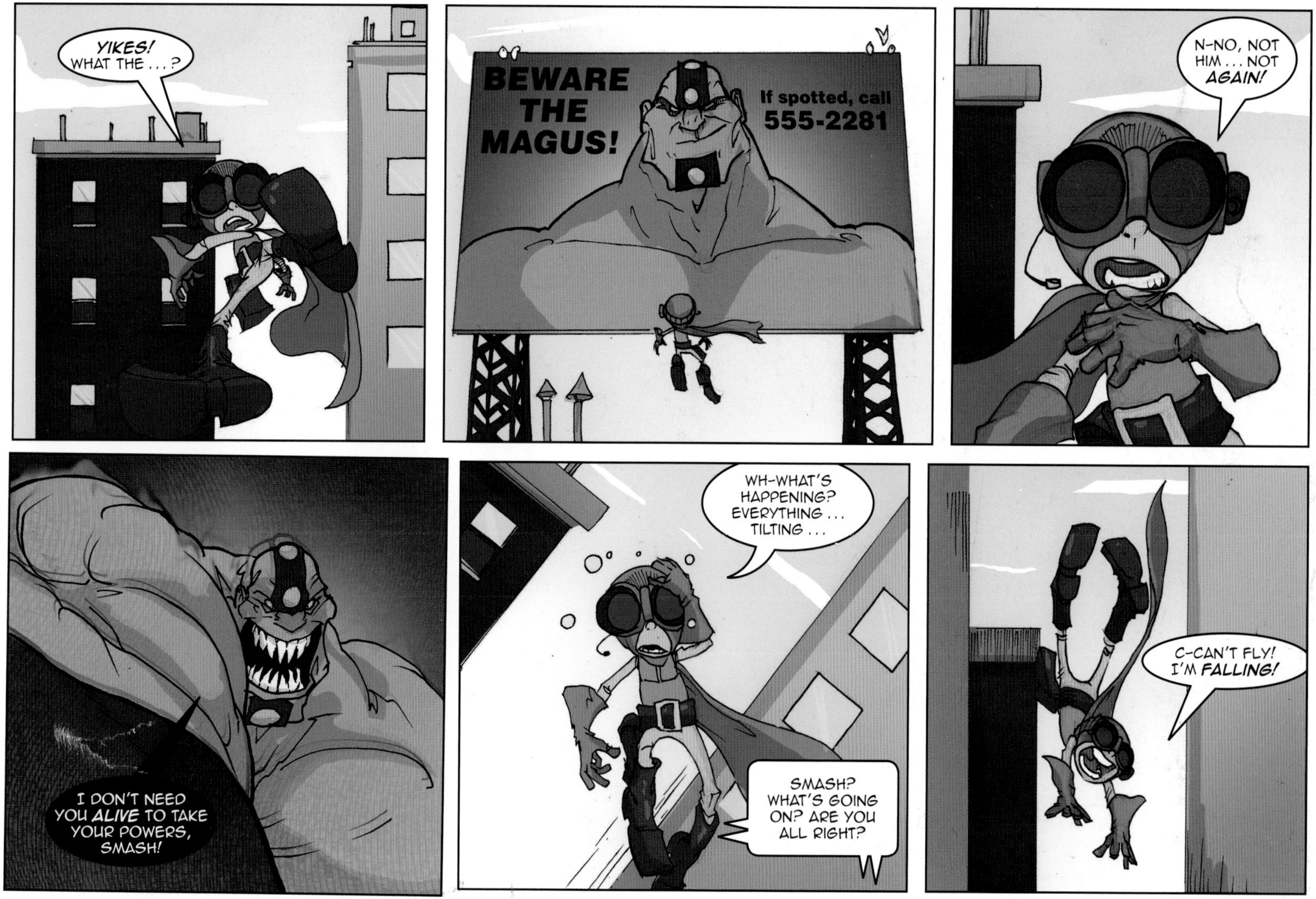
YIKES! WHAT THE . . . ?
BEWARE THE MAGUS!
If spotted, call 555-2281
N-NO, NOT HIM . . . NOT AGAIN!
I DON'T NEED YOU ALIVE TO TAKE YOUR POWERS, SMASH!
WH-WHAT'S HAPPENING? EVERYTHING . . . TILTING . . .
SMASH? WHAT'S GOING ON? ARE YOU ALL RIGHT?
C-CAN'T FLY! I'M FALLING!

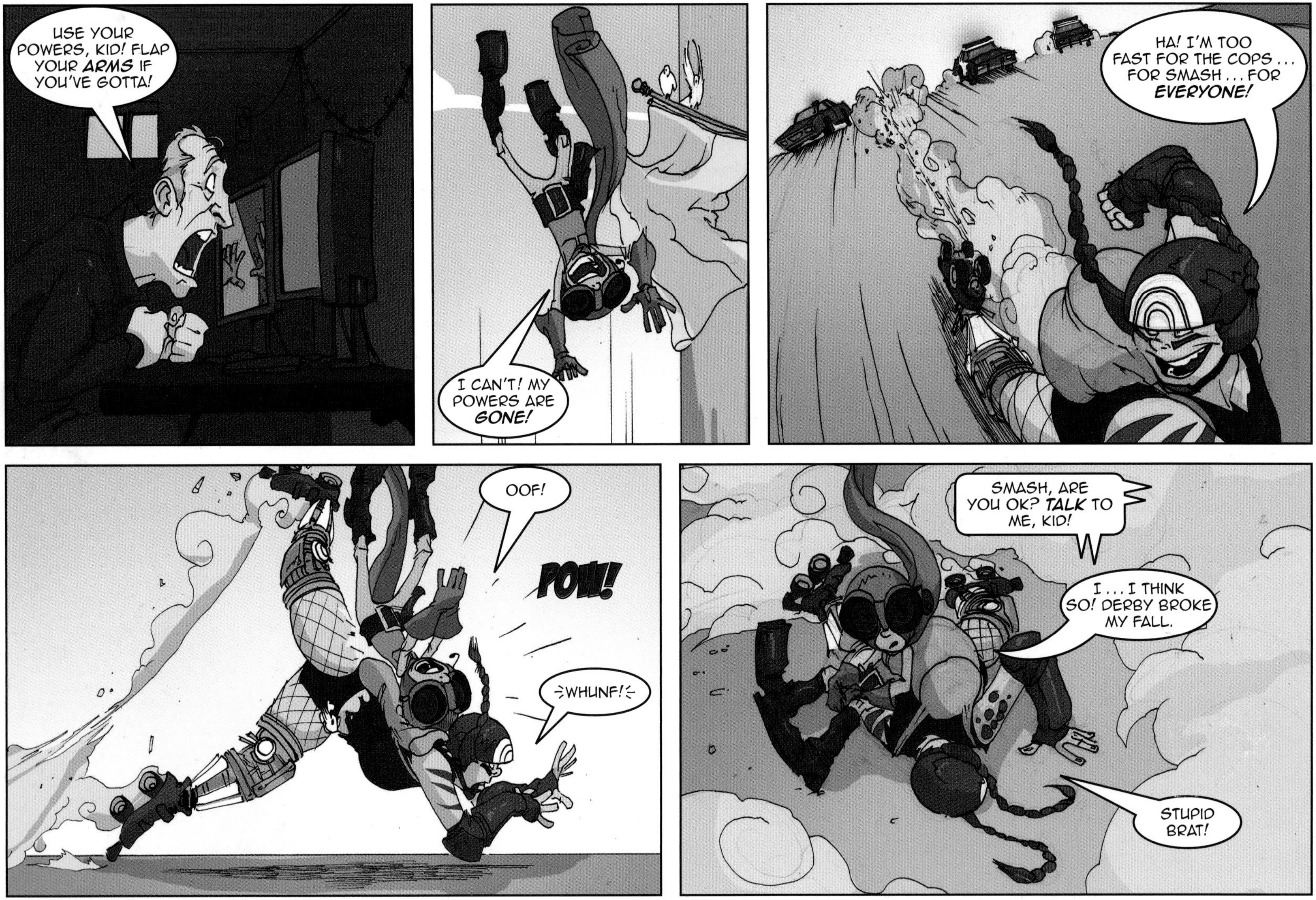
USE YOUR POWERS, KID! FLAP YOUR ARMS IF YOU'VE GOTTA!
I CAN'T! MY POWERS ARE GONE!
HA! I'M TOO FAST FOR THE COPS . . . FOR SMASH . . . FOR EVERYONE!
OOF!
POW!
WHUNF!
SMASH, ARE YOU OK? TALK TO ME, KID!
I . . . I THINK SO! DERBY BROKE MY FALL.
STUPID BRAT!

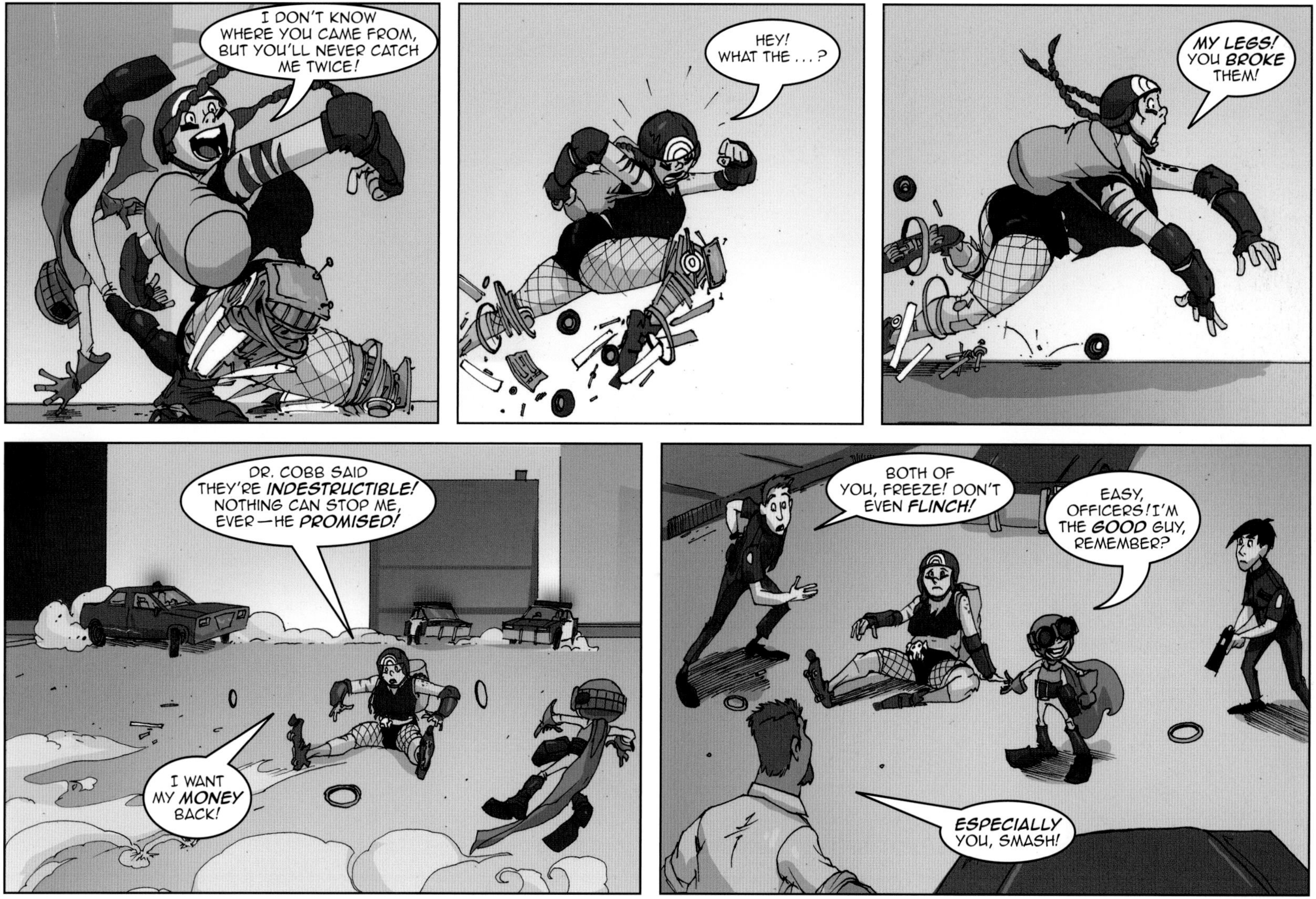
I DON'T KNOW WHERE YOU CAME FROM, BUT YOU'LL NEVER CATCH ME TWICE!
HEY! WHAT THE . . . ?
MY LEGS! YOU BROKE THEM!
DR. COBB SAID THEY'RE INDESTRUCTIBLE! NOTHING CAN STOP ME, EVER—HE PROMISED!
I WANT MY MONEY BACK!
BOTH OF YOU, FREEZE! DON'T EVEN FLINCH!
EASY, OFFICERS! I'M THE GOOD GUY, REMEMBER?
ESPECIALLY YOU, SMASH!

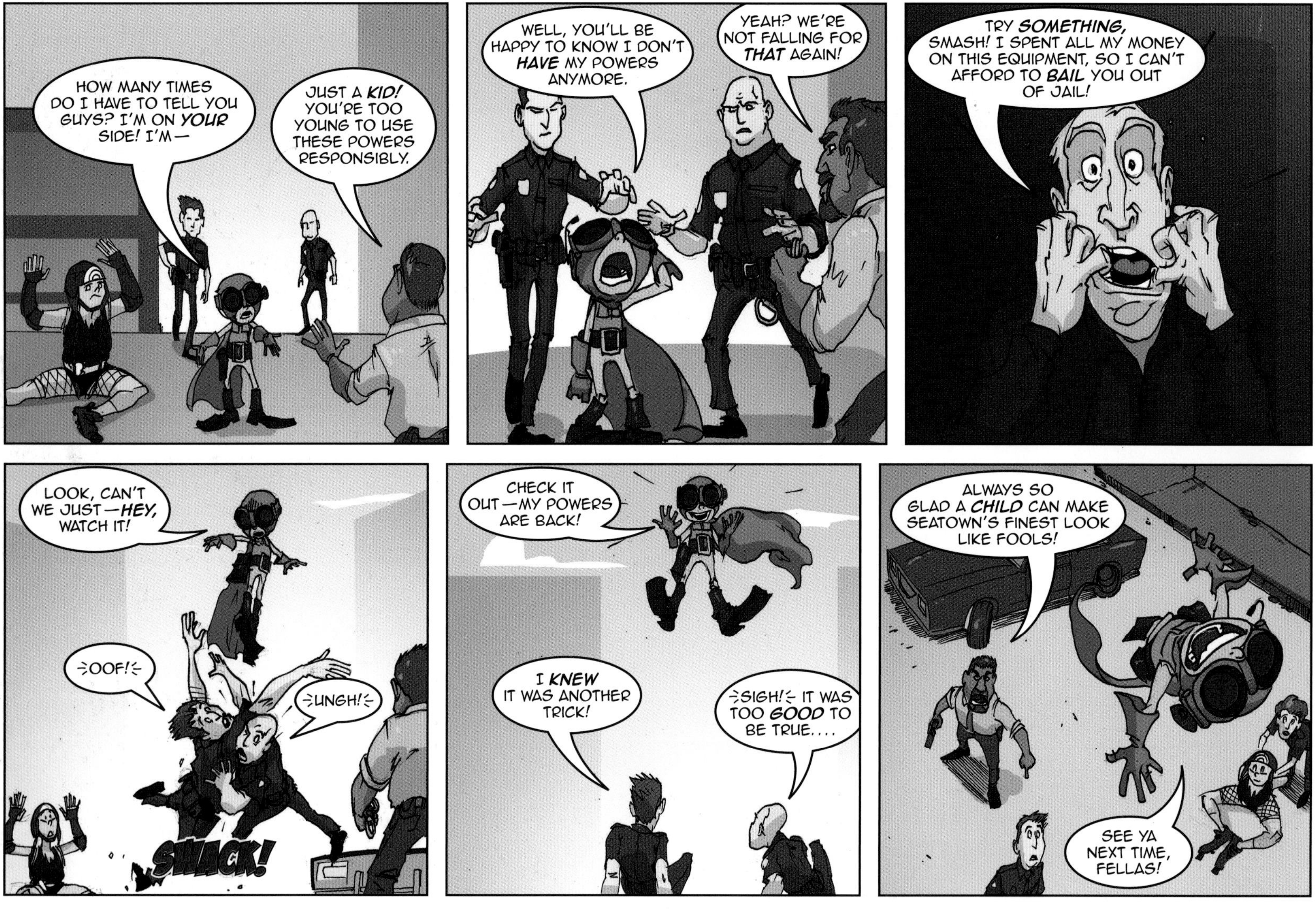
HOW MANY TIMES DO I HAVE TO TELL YOU GUYS? I'M ON YOUR SIDE! I'M—
JUST A KID! YOU'RE TOO YOUNG TO USE THESE POWERS RESPONSIBLY.
WELL, YOU'LL BE HAPPY TO KNOW I DON'T HAVE MY POWERS ANYMORE.
YEAH? WE'RE NOT FALLING FOR THAT AGAIN!
TRY SOMETHING, SMASH! I SPENT ALL MY MONEY ON THIS EQUIPMENT, SO I CAN'T AFFORD TO BAIL YOU OUT OF JAIL!
LOOK, CAN'T WE JUST—HEY, WATCH IT!
OOF!
UNGH!
SMACK!
CHECK IT OUT—MY POWERS ARE BACK!
I KNEW IT WAS ANOTHER TRICK!
SIGH! IT WAS TOO GOOD TO BE TRUE. . . .
ALWAYS SO GLAD A CHILD CAN MAKE SEATOWN'S FINEST LOOK LIKE FOOLS!
SEE YA NEXT TIME, FELLAS!

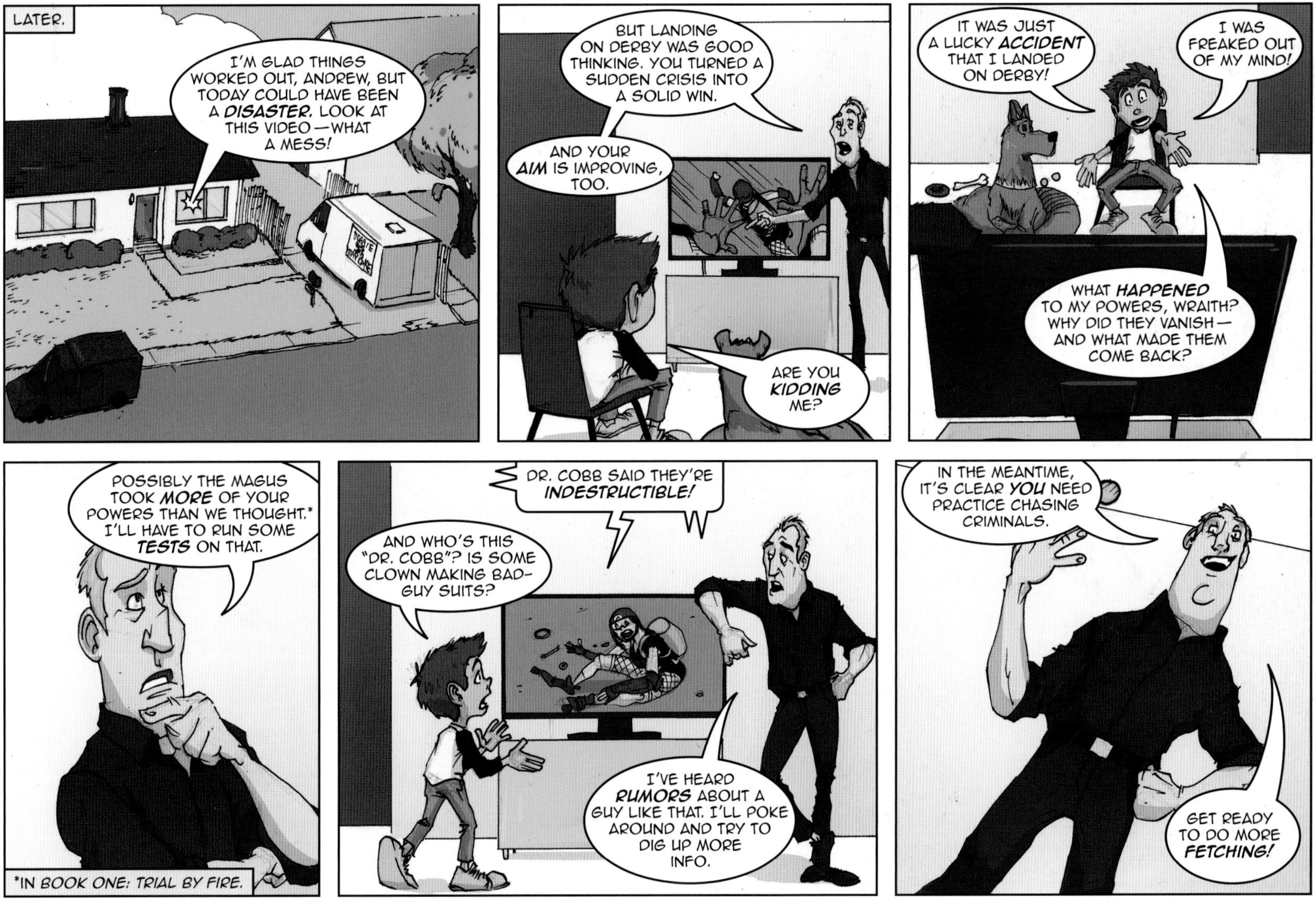
LATER.
I'M GLAD THINGS WORKED OUT, ANDREW, BUT TODAY COULD HAVE BEEN A DISASTER. LOOK AT THIS VIDEO—WHAT A MESS!
BUT LANDING ON DERBY WAS GOOD THINKING. YOU TURNED A SUDDEN CRISIS INTO A SOLID WIN.
AND YOUR AIM IS IMPROVING, TOO.
ARE YOU KIDDING ME?
IT WAS JUST A LUCKY ACCIDENT THAT I LANDED ON DERBY!
I WAS FREAKED OUT OF MY MIND!
WHAT HAPPENED TO MY POWERS, WRAITH? WHY DID THEY VANISH—AND WHAT MADE THEM COME BACK?
POSSIBLY THE MAGUS TOOK MORE OF YOUR POWERS THAN WE THOUGHT.* I'LL HAVE TO RUN SOME TESTS ON THAT.
*IN BOOK ONE: TRIAL BY FIRE.
DR. COBB SAID THEY'RE INDESTRUCTIBLE!
AND WHO'S THIS "DR. COBB"? IS SOME CLOWN MAKING BAD-GUY SUITS?
I'VE HEARD RUMORS ABOUT A GUY LIKE THAT. I'LL POKE AROUND AND TRY TO DIG UP MORE INFO.
IN THE MEANTIME, IT'S CLEAR YOU NEED PRACTICE CHASING CRIMINALS.
GET READY TO DO MORE FETCHING!

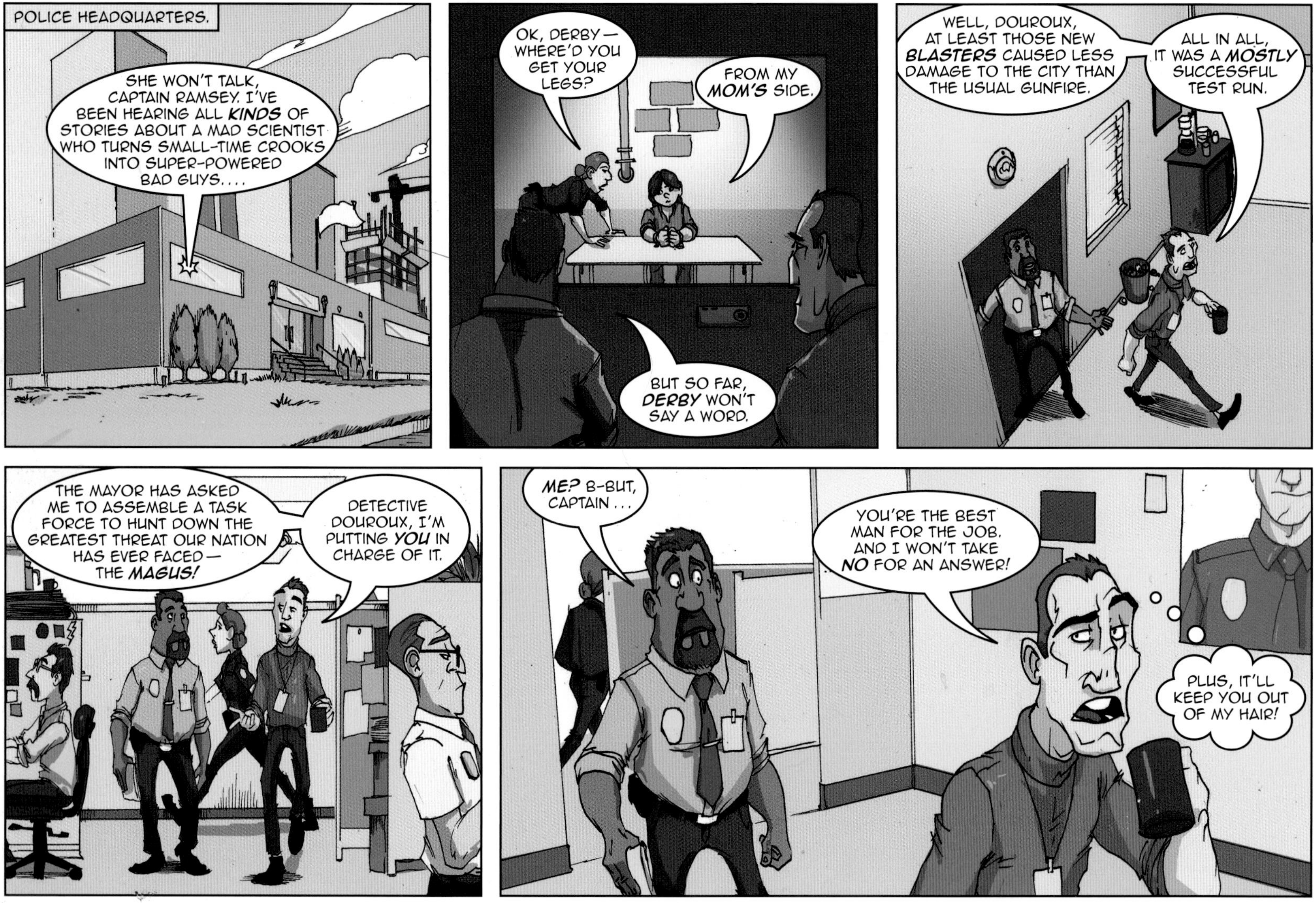
POLICE HEADQUARTERS.
SHE WON'T TALK, CAPTAIN RAMSEY. I'VE BEEN HEARING ALL KINDS OF STORIES ABOUT A MAD SCIENTIST WHO TURNS SMALL-TIME CROOKS INTO SUPER-POWERED BAD GUYS....
OK, DERBY— WHERE'D YOU GET YOUR LEGS?
FROM MY MOM'S SIDE.
BUT SO FAR, DERBY WON'T SAY A WORD.
WELL, DOUROUX, AT LEAST THOSE NEW BLASTERS CAUSED LESS DAMAGE TO THE CITY THAN THE USUAL GUNFIRE.
ALL IN ALL, IT WAS A MOSTLY SUCCESSFUL TEST RUN.
THE MAYOR HAS ASKED ME TO ASSEMBLE A TASK FORCE TO HUNT DOWN THE GREATEST THREAT OUR NATION HAS EVER FACED— THE MAGUS!
DETECTIVE DOUROUX, I'M PUTTING YOU IN CHARGE OF IT.
ME? B-BUT, CAPTAIN...
YOU'RE THE BEST MAN FOR THE JOB. AND I WON'T TAKE NO FOR AN ANSWER!
PLUS, IT'LL KEEP YOU OUT OF MY HAIR!

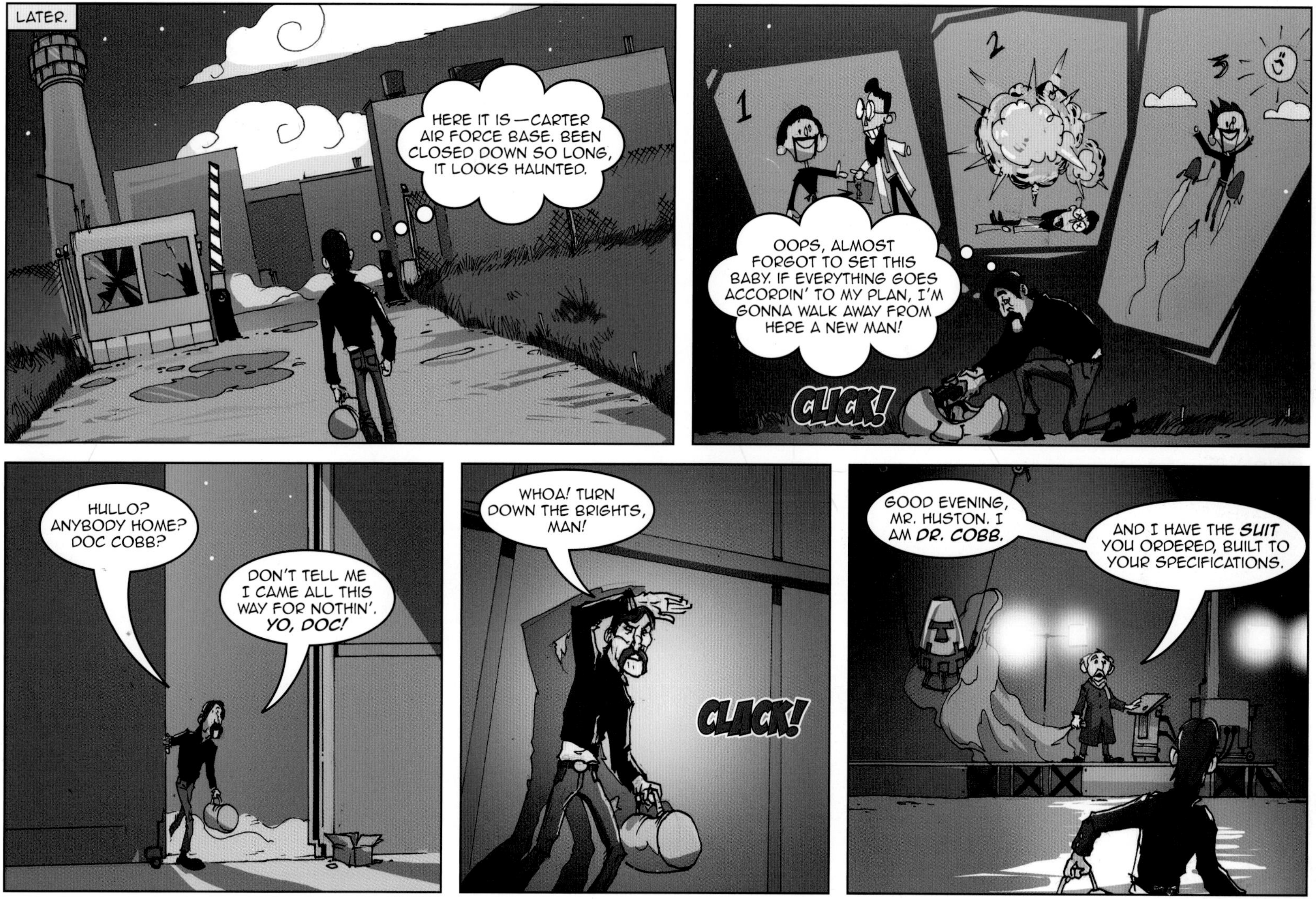

LATER.
HERE IT IS—CARTER AIR FORCE BASE. BEEN CLOSED DOWN SO LONG, IT LOOKS HAUNTED.
OOPS, ALMOST FORGOT TO SET THIS BABY. IF EVERYTHING GOES ACCORDIN' TO MY PLAN, I'M GONNA WALK AWAY FROM HERE A NEW MAN!
CLICK!
HULLO? ANYBODY HOME? DOC COBB?
DON'T TELL ME I CAME ALL THIS WAY FOR NOTHIN'. ***YO, DOC!***
WHOA! TURN DOWN THE BRIGHTS, MAN!
CLACK!
GOOD EVENING, MR. HUSTON. I AM ***DR. COBB.***
AND I HAVE THE ***SUIT*** YOU ORDERED, BUILT TO YOUR SPECIFICATIONS.

PRESS THE BUTTON ON THE **RIGHT** GLOVE, AND A BURST OF ENERGY FIRES FROM THE POWER PACK. PRESS THE BUTTON ON THE **LEFT** GLOVE TO BRAKE.

FOOM!

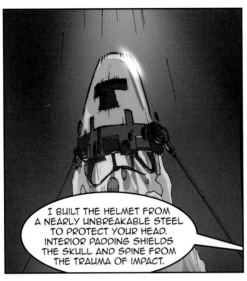

I BUILT THE HELMET FROM A NEARLY UNBREAKABLE STEEL TO PROTECT YOUR HEAD. INTERIOR PADDING SHIELDS THE SKULL AND SPINE FROM THE TRAUMA OF IMPACT.

HOT GRITS IN THE MORNIN', DOC! IT LOOKS EVEN BETTER THAN YA PROMISED!

⇒KOFF⇐ I AM PLEASED THAT YOU'RE PLEASED. NOW, I HAVE PROVIDED THE MERCHANDISE . . .

⇒KOFF⇐ I TRUST **YOU** HAVE BROUGHT MY PAYMENT. ⇒KOFF⇐ IN FULL!

WHAT'S TO STOP ME FROM JUST TAKIN' MY SUIT AN' WALKIN' OUTTA HERE?

I DON'T RECOMMEND IT.

HAVE YOU MET MY ASSISTANT . . .

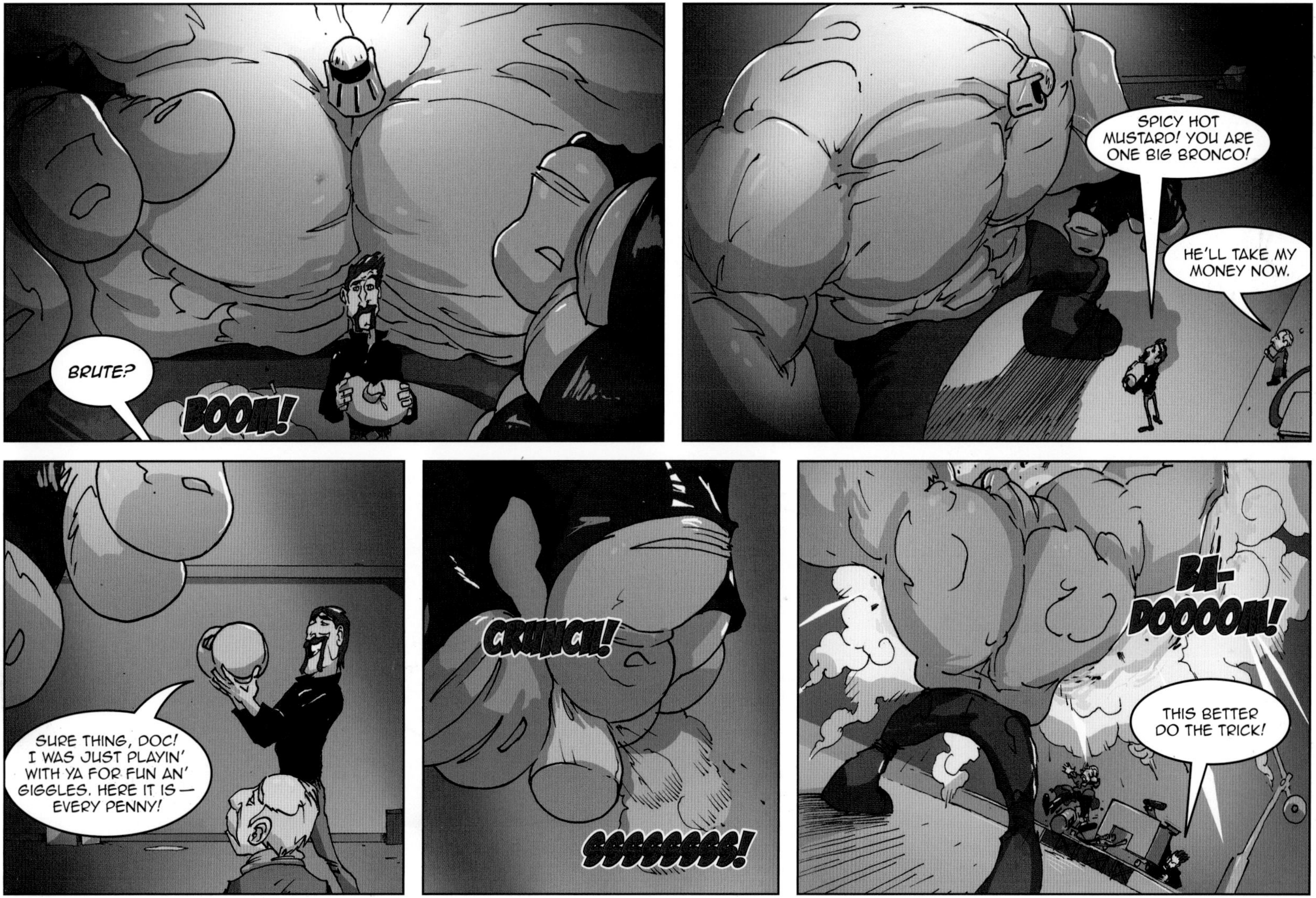
BRUTE?
BOOM!
SPICY HOT MUSTARD! YOU ARE ONE BIG BRONCO!
HE'LL TAKE MY MONEY NOW.
SURE THING, DOC! I WAS JUST PLAYIN' WITH YA FOR FUN AN' GIGGLES. HERE IT IS — EVERY PENNY!
CRUNCH!
SSSSSSSS!
BA-DOOOOOM!
THIS BETTER DO THE TRICK!

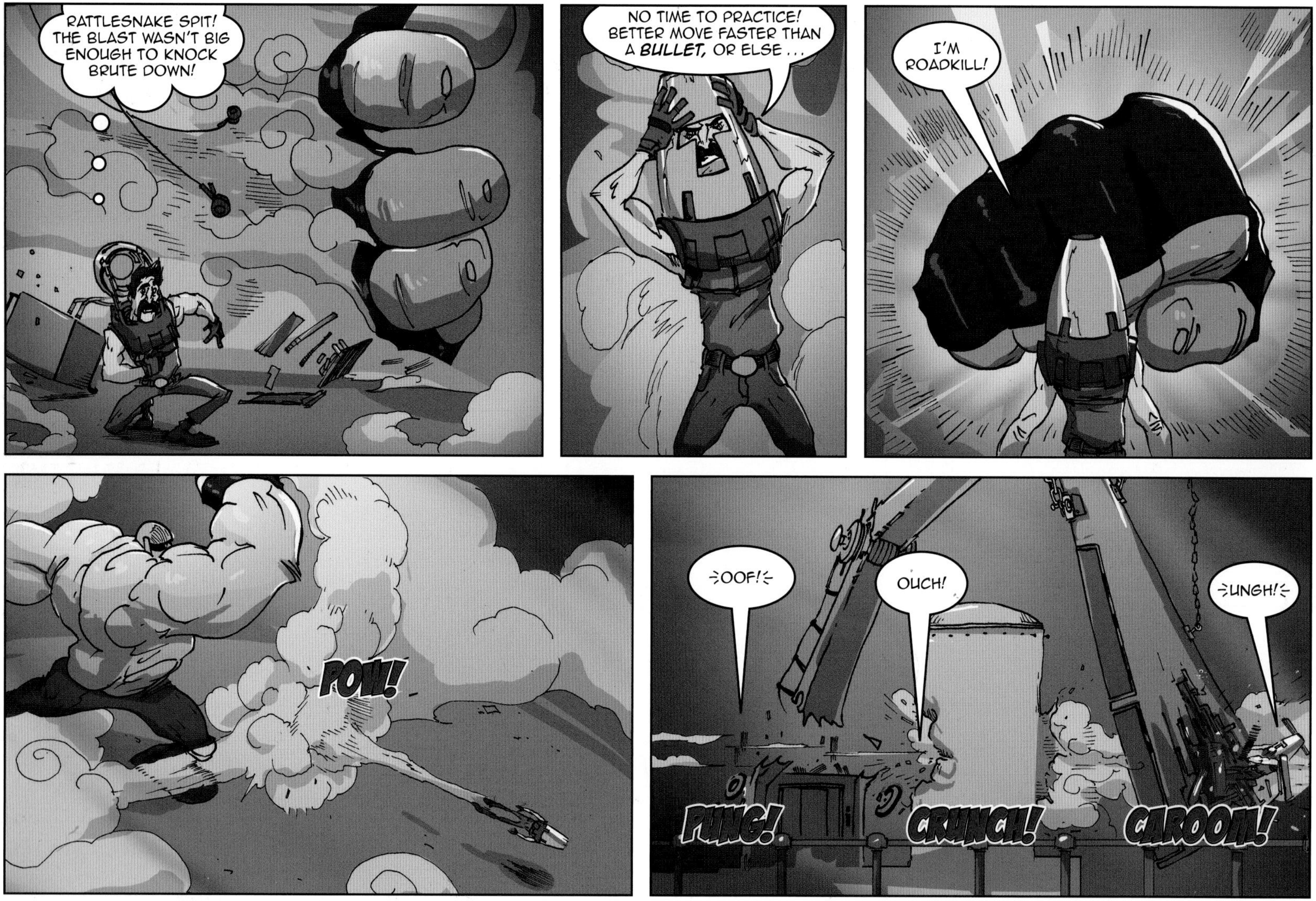
RATTLESNAKE SPIT! THE BLAST WASN'T BIG ENOUGH TO KNOCK BRUTE DOWN!
NO TIME TO PRACTICE! BETTER MOVE FASTER THAN A *BULLET,* OR ELSE . . .
I'M ROADKILL!
POW!
OOF!
OUCH!
UNGH!
PUNG!
CRUNCH!
CAROOM!

CRASH!

GAH!

I'M ALIVE!

THIS SUIT IS THE ANSWER TO MY PRAYERS! NOW I'M BADDER THAN BAD— I'M *SUPER-BAD!*

UH, BUT HE'S SUPER-*BADDER!*

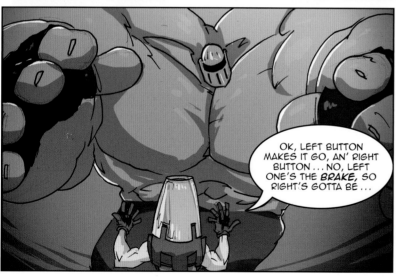

OK, LEFT BUTTON MAKES IT GO, AN' RIGHT BUTTON ... NO, LEFT ONE'S THE *BRAKE,* SO RIGHT'S GOTTA BE ...

YAAAAAAA-HOOOOOOOO!!!

FOOM!

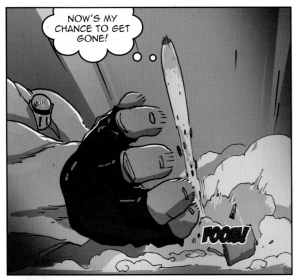

NOW'S MY CHANCE TO GET GONE!

FOOM!

WHAM!

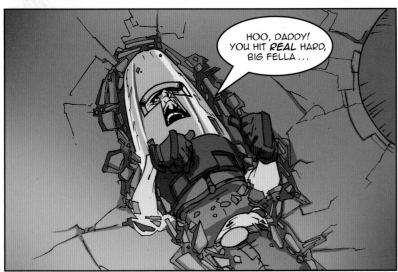

HOO, DADDY! YOU HIT *REAL* HARD, BIG FELLA . . .

LET'S SEE HOW HARD *I* CAN HIT BACK!

FOOM!

CRASH!

NOW I'LL FINISH HIM OFF . . .

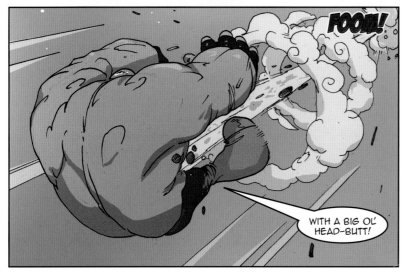

FOOM!

WITH A BIG OL' HEAD-BUTT!

FOOM!

AIR BRAKES!

BOOM!

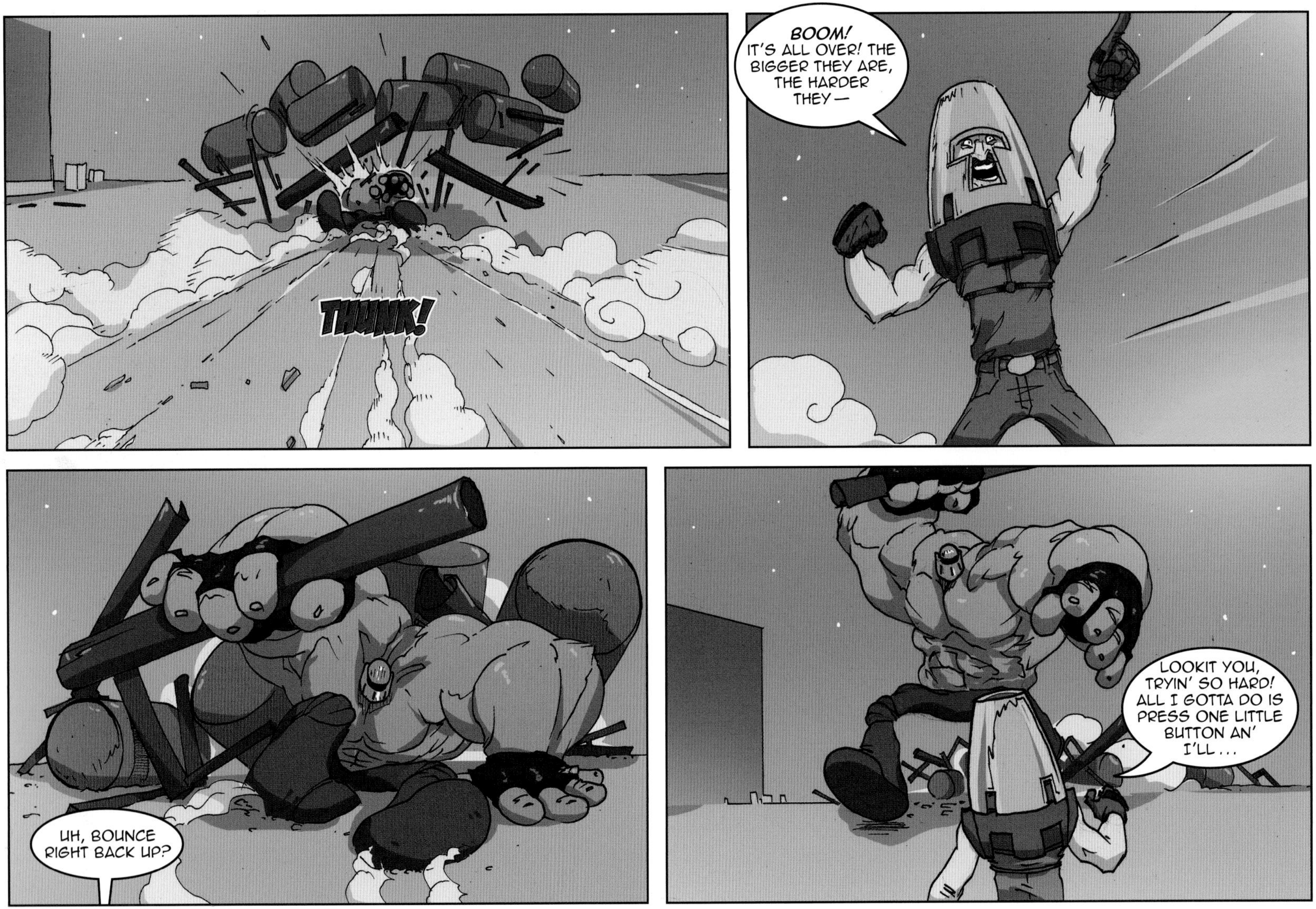
THUNK!
BOOM! IT'S ALL OVER! THE BIGGER THEY ARE, THE HARDER THEY —
UH, BOUNCE RIGHT BACK UP?
LOOKIT YOU, TRYIN' SO HARD! ALL I GOTTA DO IS PRESS ONE LITTLE BUTTON AN' I'LL . . .

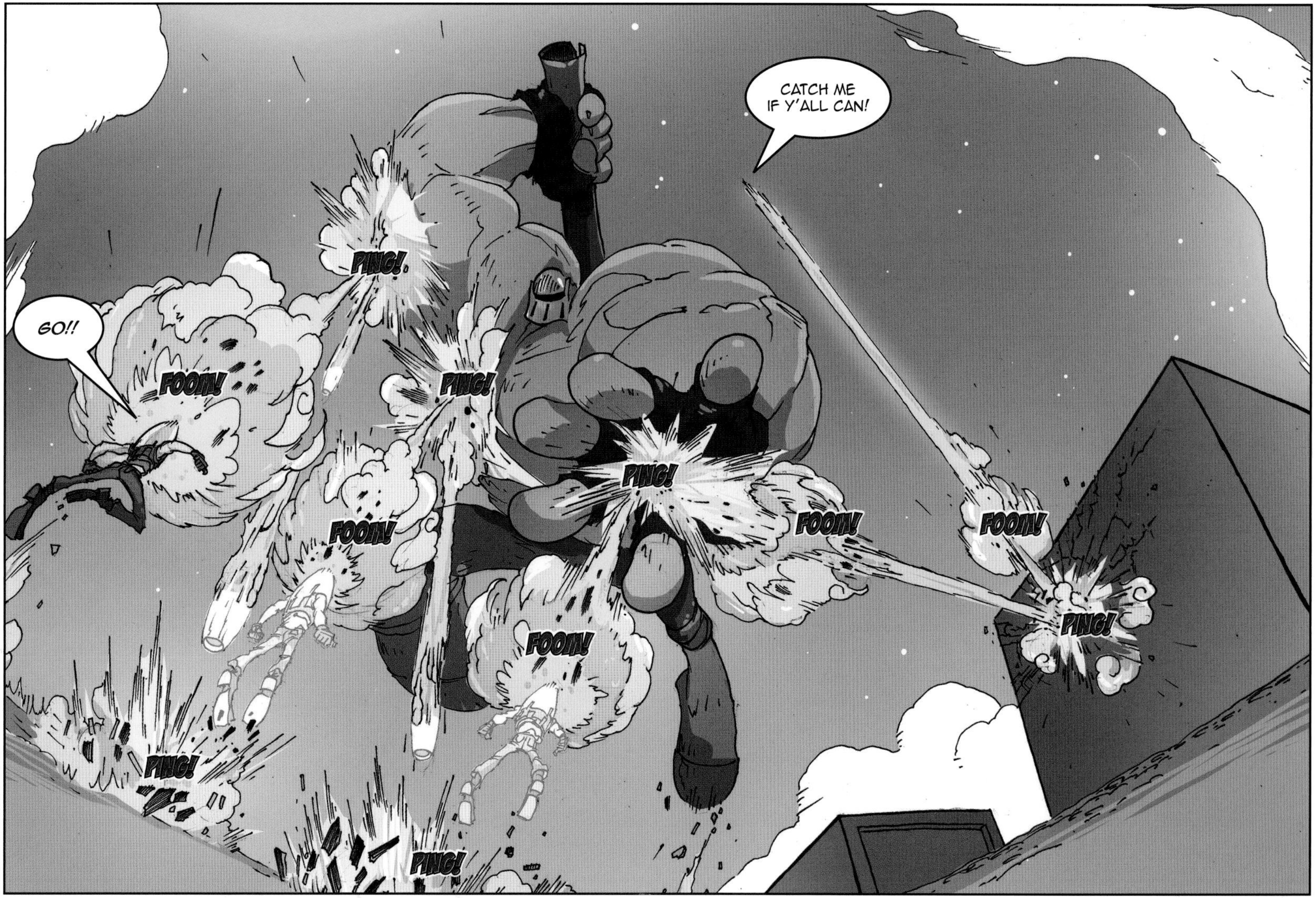
GO!!
CATCH ME IF Y'ALL CAN!
PING!
FOOM!
PING!
PING!
FOOM!
FOOM!
FOOM!
FOOM!
PING!
PING!
PING!

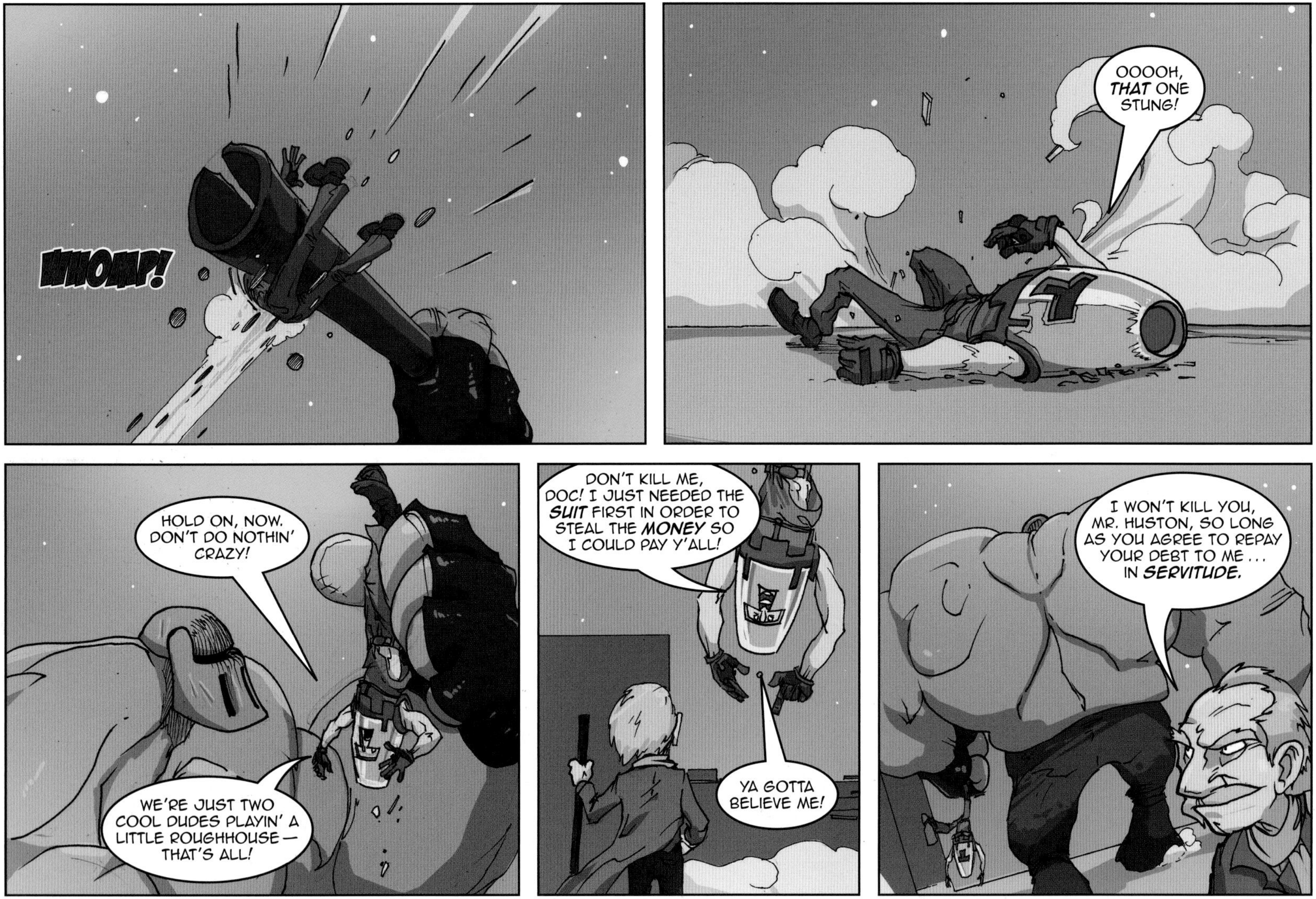
WHOMP!
OOOOH, THAT ONE STUNG!
HOLD ON, NOW. DON'T DO NOTHIN' CRAZY!
WE'RE JUST TWO COOL DUDES PLAYIN' A LITTLE ROUGHHOUSE — THAT'S ALL!
DON'T KILL ME, DOC! I JUST NEEDED THE SUIT FIRST IN ORDER TO STEAL THE MONEY SO I COULD PAY Y'ALL!
YA GOTTA BELIEVE ME!
I WON'T KILL YOU, MR. HUSTON, SO LONG AS YOU AGREE TO REPAY YOUR DEBT TO ME . . . IN SERVITUDE.

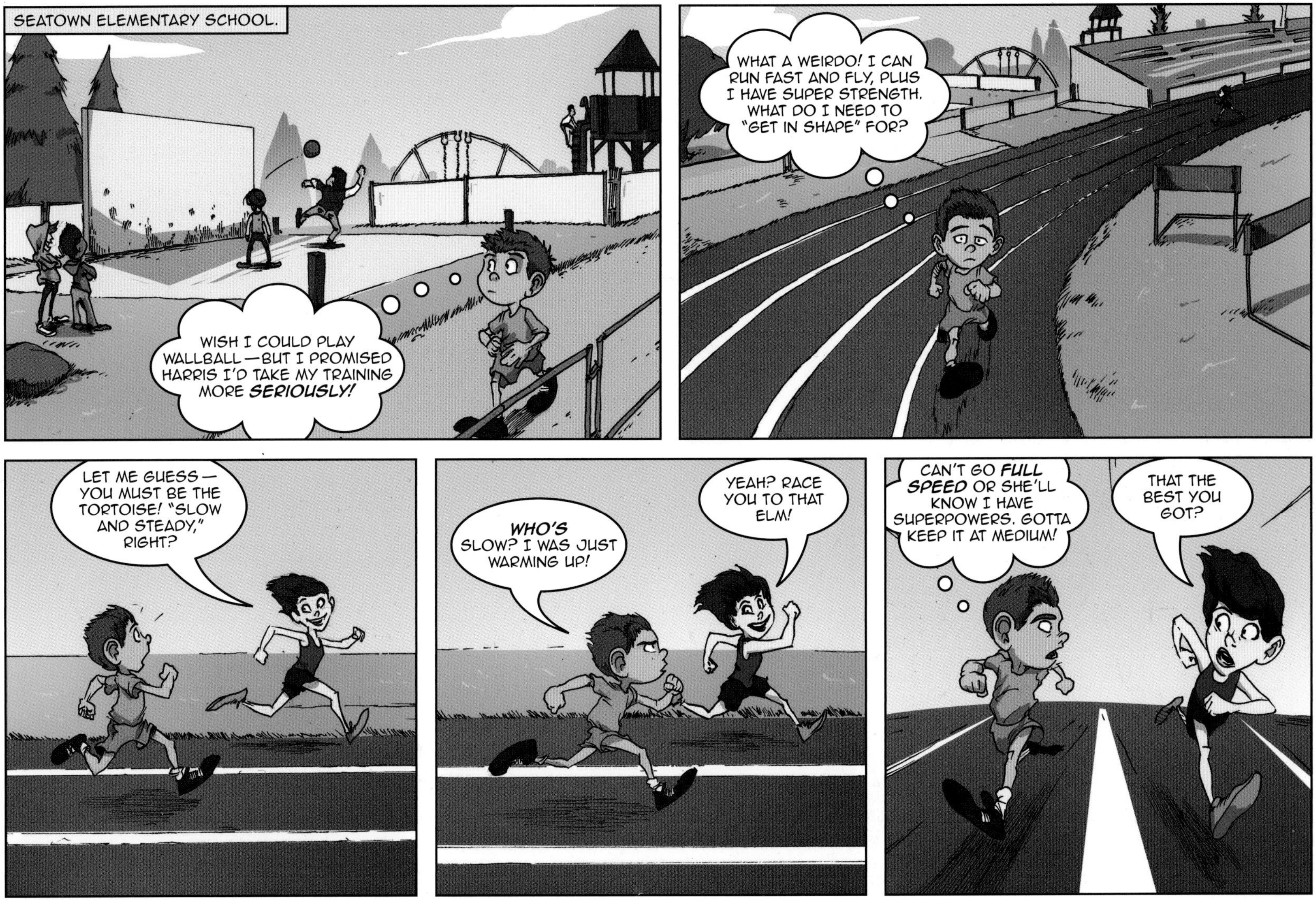
SEATOWN ELEMENTARY SCHOOL.
WISH I COULD PLAY WALLBALL—BUT I PROMISED HARRIS I'D TAKE MY TRAINING MORE **SERIOUSLY!**
WHAT A WEIRDO! I CAN RUN FAST AND FLY, PLUS I HAVE SUPER STRENGTH. WHAT DO I NEED TO "GET IN SHAPE" FOR?
LET ME GUESS—YOU MUST BE THE TORTOISE! "SLOW AND STEADY," RIGHT?
WHO'S SLOW? I WAS JUST WARMING UP!
YEAH? RACE YOU TO THAT ELM!
CAN'T GO **FULL SPEED** OR SHE'LL KNOW I HAVE SUPERPOWERS. GOTTA KEEP IT AT MEDIUM!
THAT THE BEST YOU GOT?

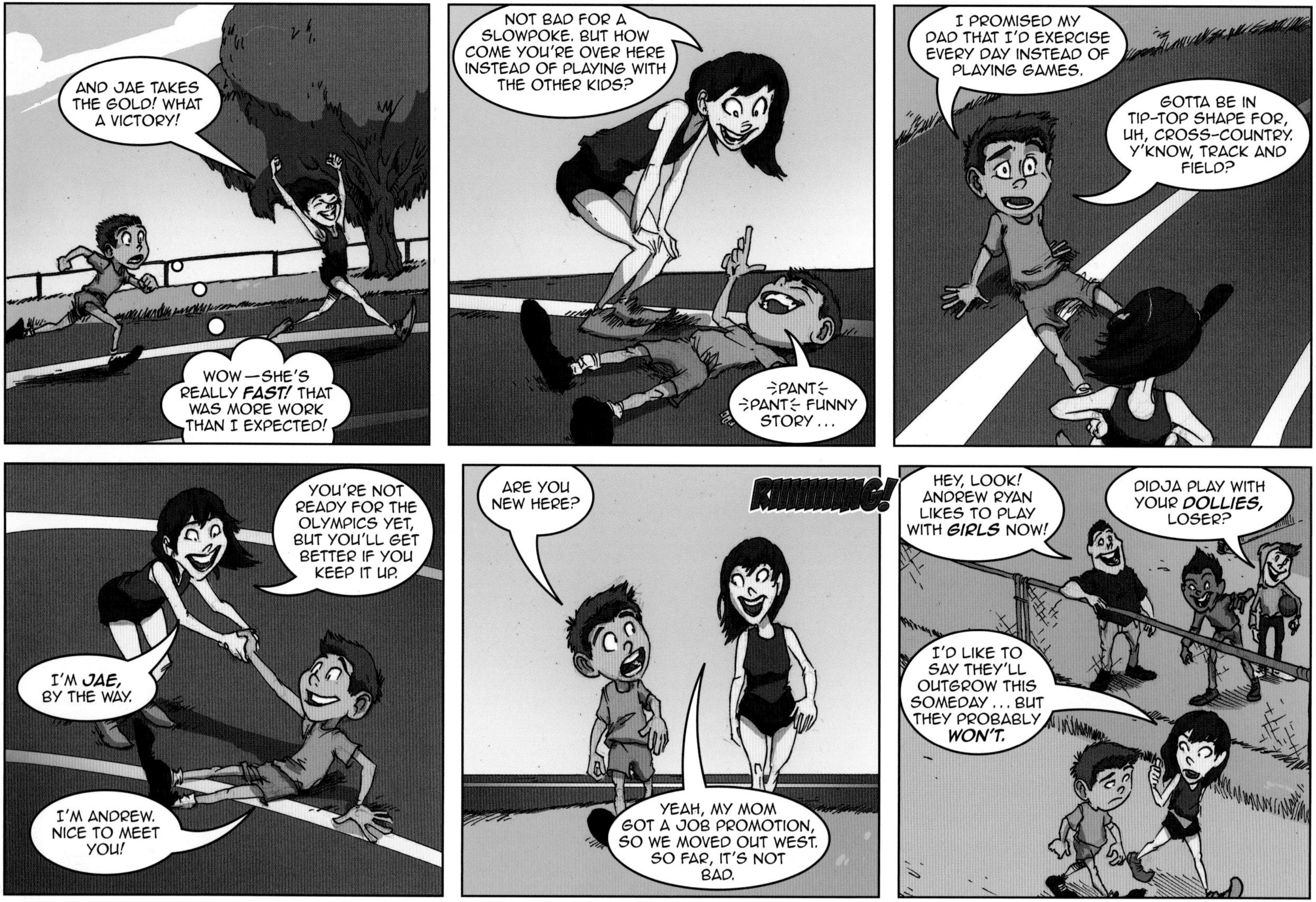
AND JAE TAKES THE GOLD! WHAT A VICTORY!
WOW—SHE'S REALLY FAST! THAT WAS MORE WORK THAN I EXPECTED!
NOT BAD FOR A SLOWPOKE. BUT HOW COME YOU'RE OVER HERE INSTEAD OF PLAYING WITH THE OTHER KIDS?
PANT PANT FUNNY STORY . . .
I PROMISED MY DAD THAT I'D EXERCISE EVERY DAY INSTEAD OF PLAYING GAMES.
GOTTA BE IN TIP-TOP SHAPE FOR, UH, CROSS-COUNTRY. Y'KNOW, TRACK AND FIELD?
YOU'RE NOT READY FOR THE OLYMPICS YET, BUT YOU'LL GET BETTER IF YOU KEEP IT UP.
I'M JAE, BY THE WAY.
I'M ANDREW. NICE TO MEET YOU!
ARE YOU NEW HERE?
YEAH, MY MOM GOT A JOB PROMOTION, SO WE MOVED OUT WEST. SO FAR, IT'S NOT BAD.
HEY, LOOK! ANDREW RYAN LIKES TO PLAY WITH GIRLS NOW!
DIDJA PLAY WITH YOUR DOLLIES, LOSER?
I'D LIKE TO SAY THEY'LL OUTGROW THIS SOMEDAY . . . BUT THEY PROBABLY WON'T.

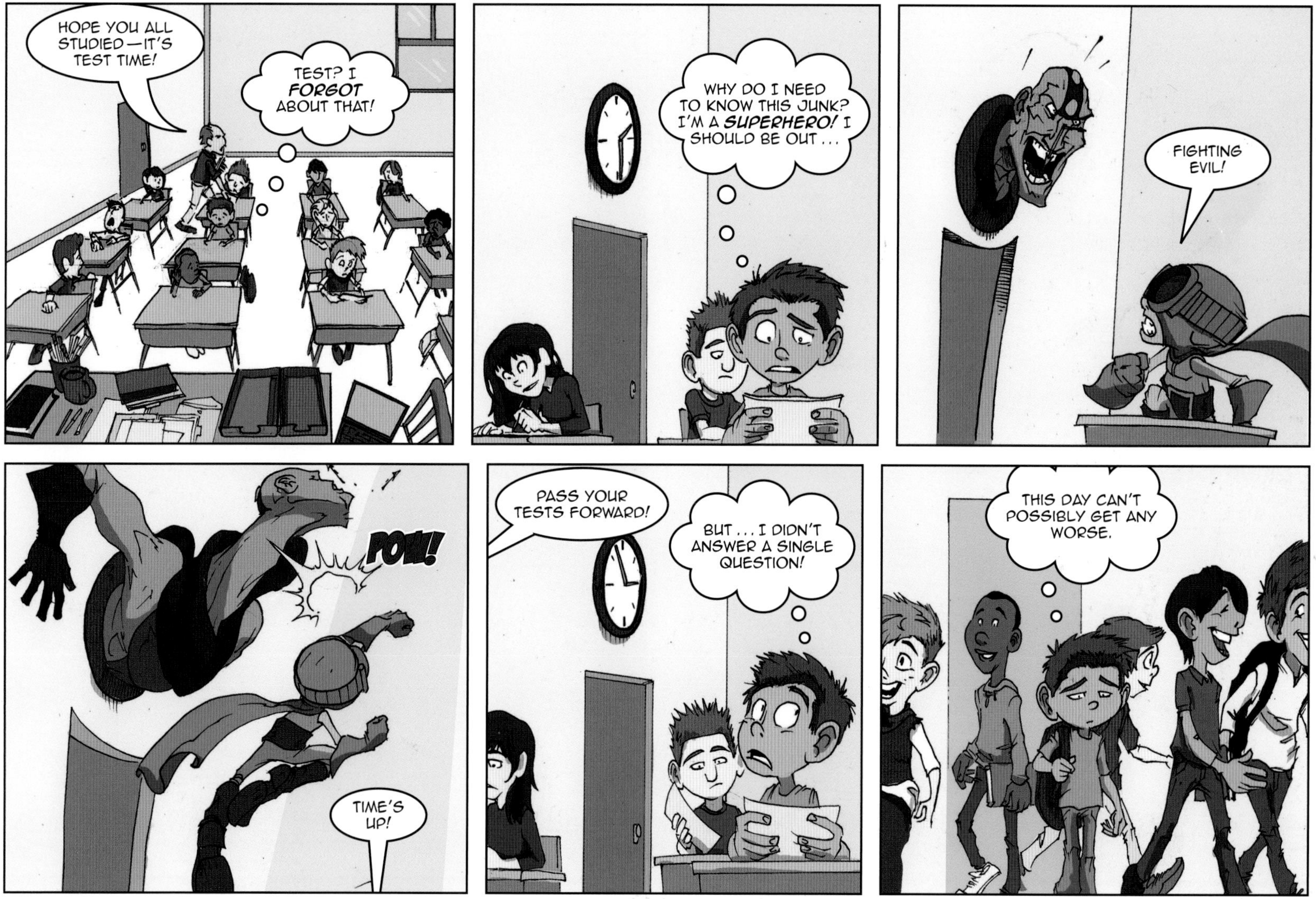
HOPE YOU ALL STUDIED—IT'S TEST TIME!
TEST? I **FORGOT** ABOUT THAT!
WHY DO I NEED TO KNOW THIS JUNK? I'M A **SUPERHERO!** I SHOULD BE OUT . . .
FIGHTING EVIL!
POW!
TIME'S UP!
PASS YOUR TESTS FORWARD!
BUT . . . I DIDN'T ANSWER A SINGLE QUESTION!
THIS DAY CAN'T POSSIBLY GET ANY WORSE.

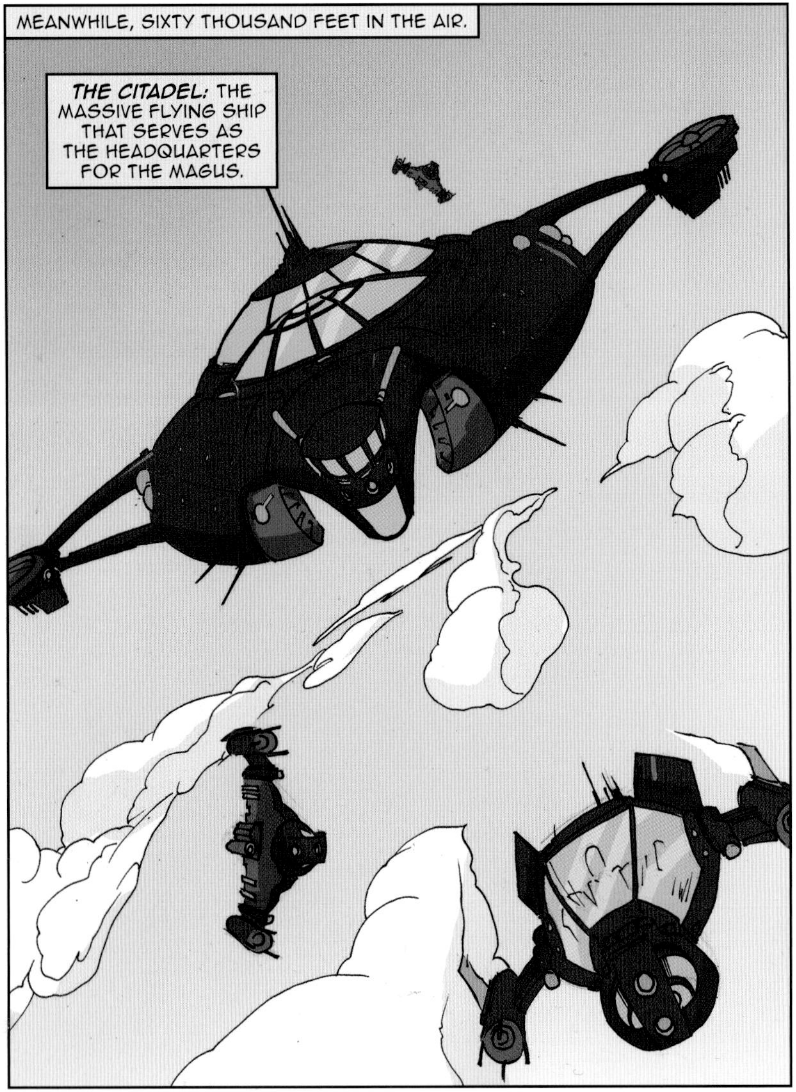
MEANWHILE, SIXTY THOUSAND FEET IN THE AIR.
THE CITADEL: THE MASSIVE FLYING SHIP THAT SERVES AS THE HEADQUARTERS FOR THE MAGUS.

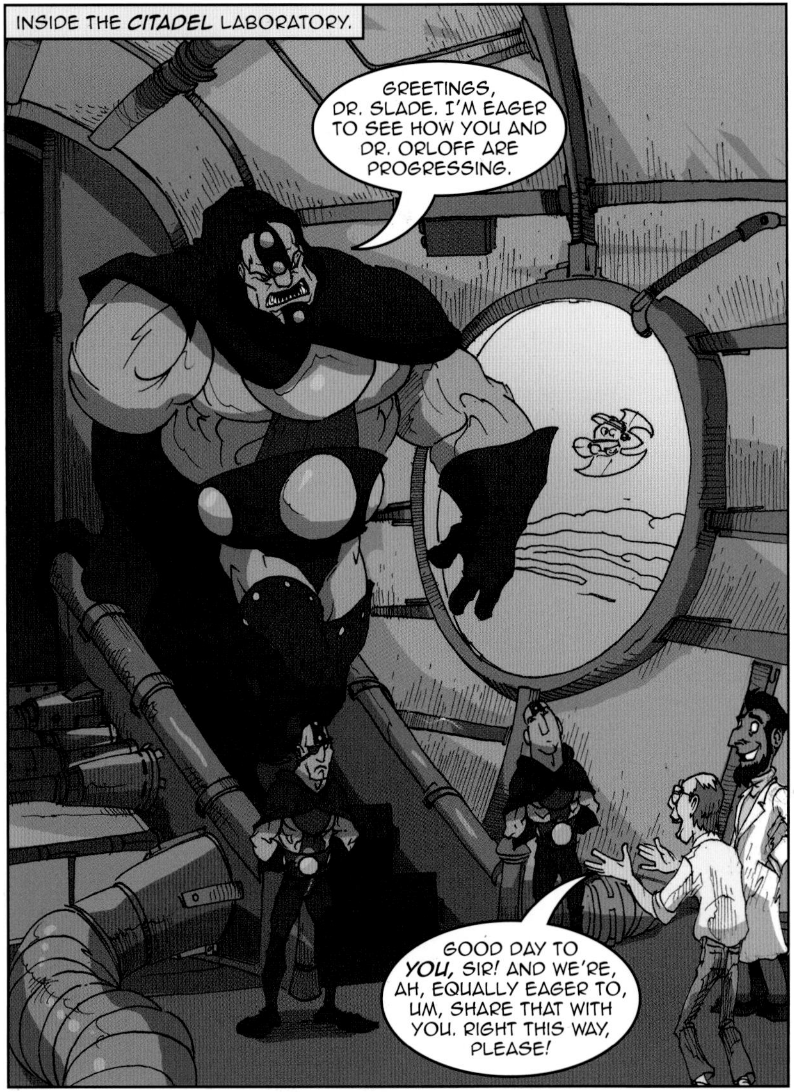
INSIDE THE CITADEL LABORATORY.
GREETINGS, DR. SLADE. I'M EAGER TO SEE HOW YOU AND DR. ORLOFF ARE PROGRESSING.
GOOD DAY TO YOU, SIR! AND WE'RE, AH, EQUALLY EAGER TO, UM, SHARE THAT WITH YOU. RIGHT THIS WAY, PLEASE!

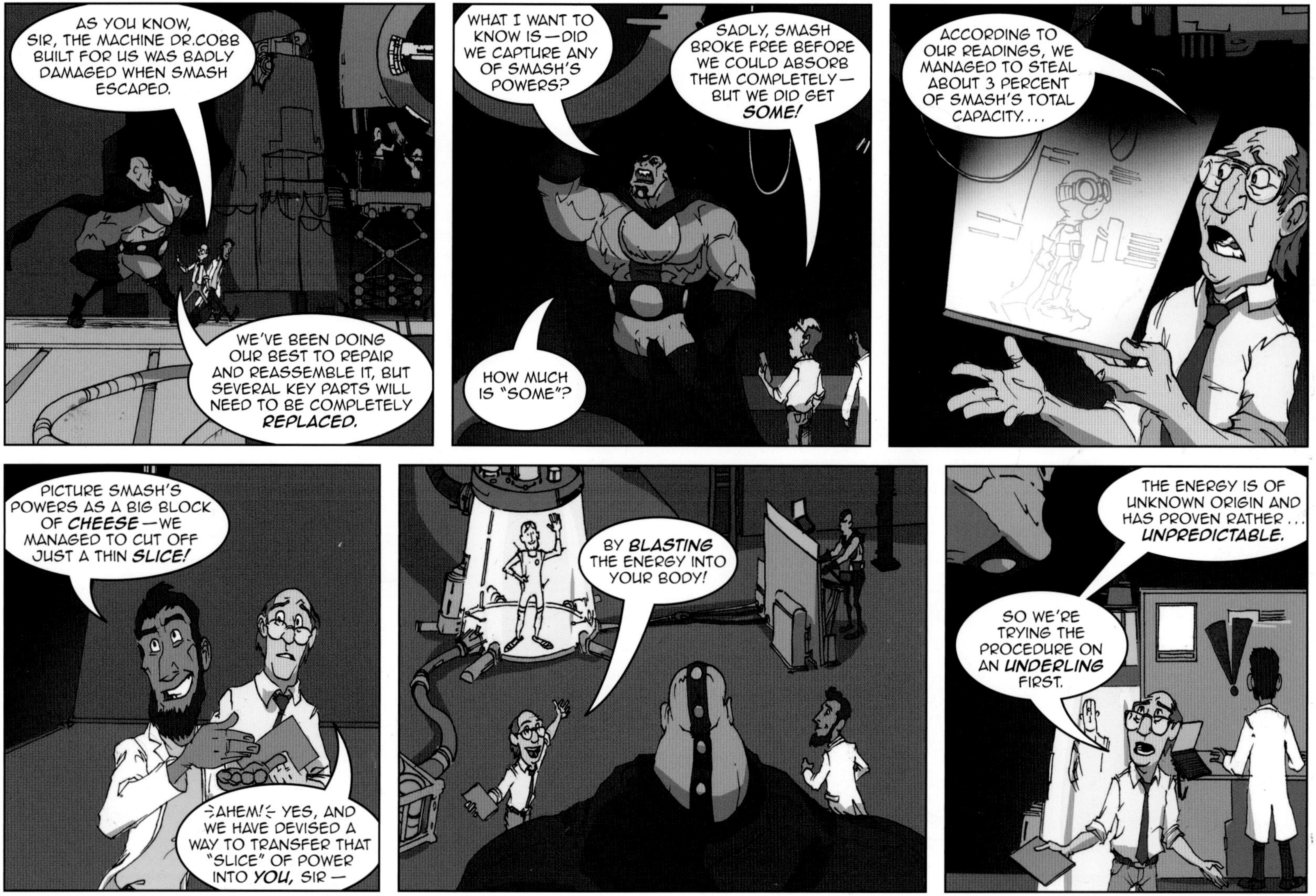
AS YOU KNOW, SIR, THE MACHINE DR.COBB BUILT FOR US WAS BADLY DAMAGED WHEN SMASH ESCAPED.
WE'VE BEEN DOING OUR BEST TO REPAIR AND REASSEMBLE IT, BUT SEVERAL KEY PARTS WILL NEED TO BE COMPLETELY REPLACED.
WHAT I WANT TO KNOW IS—DID WE CAPTURE ANY OF SMASH'S POWERS?
SADLY, SMASH BROKE FREE BEFORE WE COULD ABSORB THEM COMPLETELY—BUT WE DID GET SOME!
HOW MUCH IS "SOME"?
ACCORDING TO OUR READINGS, WE MANAGED TO STEAL ABOUT 3 PERCENT OF SMASH'S TOTAL CAPACITY. . . .
PICTURE SMASH'S POWERS AS A BIG BLOCK OF CHEESE—WE MANAGED TO CUT OFF JUST A THIN SLICE!
AHEM! YES, AND WE HAVE DEVISED A WAY TO TRANSFER THAT "SLICE" OF POWER INTO YOU, SIR—
BY BLASTING THE ENERGY INTO YOUR BODY!
THE ENERGY IS OF UNKNOWN ORIGIN AND HAS PROVEN RATHER . . . UNPREDICTABLE.
SO WE'RE TRYING THE PROCEDURE ON AN UNDERLING FIRST.

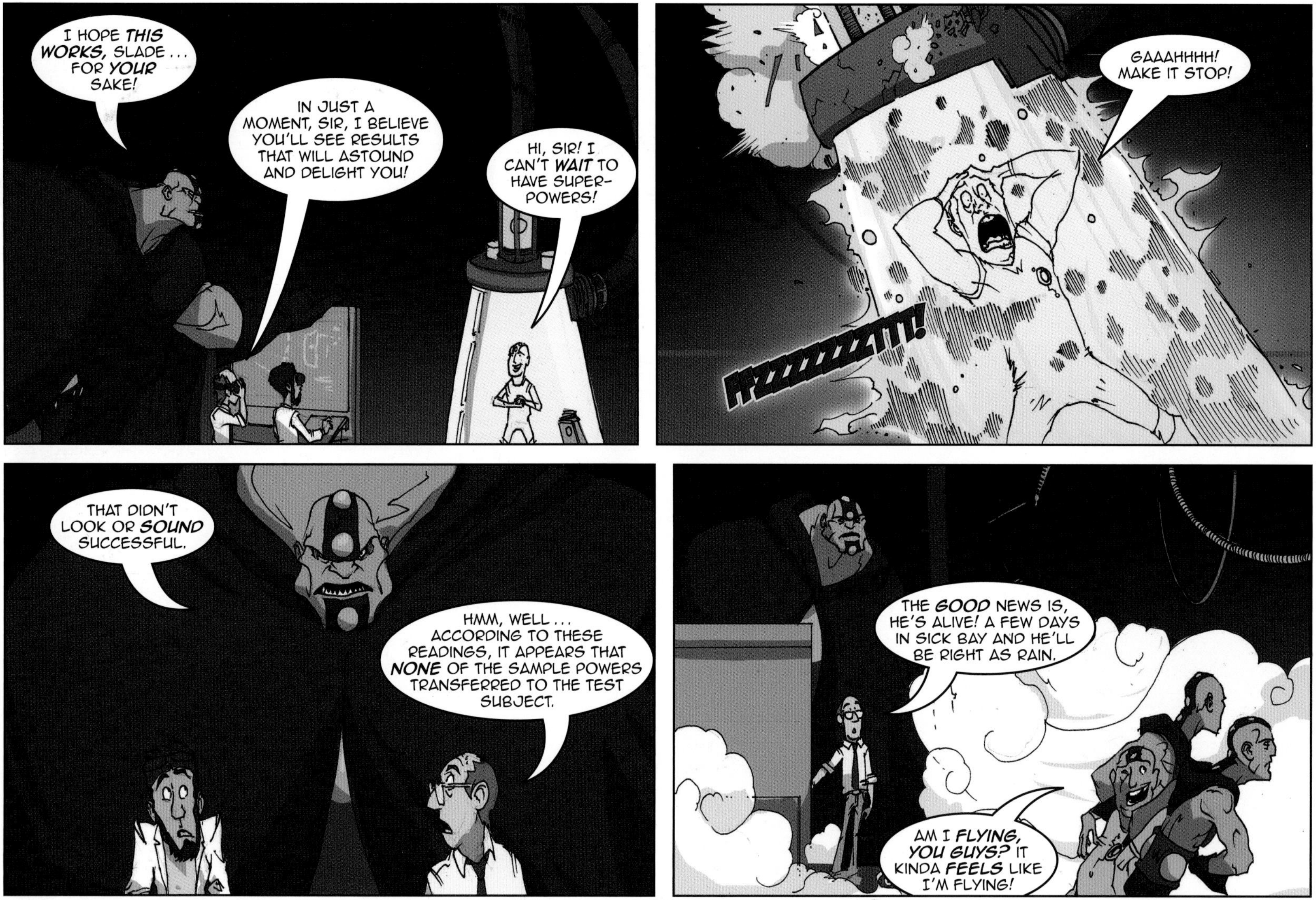
I HOPE **THIS** **WORKS,** SLADE . . . FOR **YOUR** SAKE!
IN JUST A MOMENT, SIR, I BELIEVE YOU'LL SEE RESULTS THAT WILL ASTOUND AND DELIGHT YOU!
HI, SIR! I CAN'T **WAIT** TO HAVE SUPER-POWERS!
GAAAHHHH! MAKE IT STOP!
FFZZZZZZZZTTT!
THAT DIDN'T LOOK OR **SOUND** SUCCESSFUL.
HMM, WELL . . . ACCORDING TO THESE READINGS, IT APPEARS THAT **NONE** OF THE SAMPLE POWERS TRANSFERRED TO THE TEST SUBJECT.
THE **GOOD** NEWS IS, HE'S ALIVE! A FEW DAYS IN SICK BAY AND HE'LL BE RIGHT AS RAIN.
AM I **FLYING,** **YOU GUYS?** IT KINDA **FEELS** LIKE I'M FLYING!

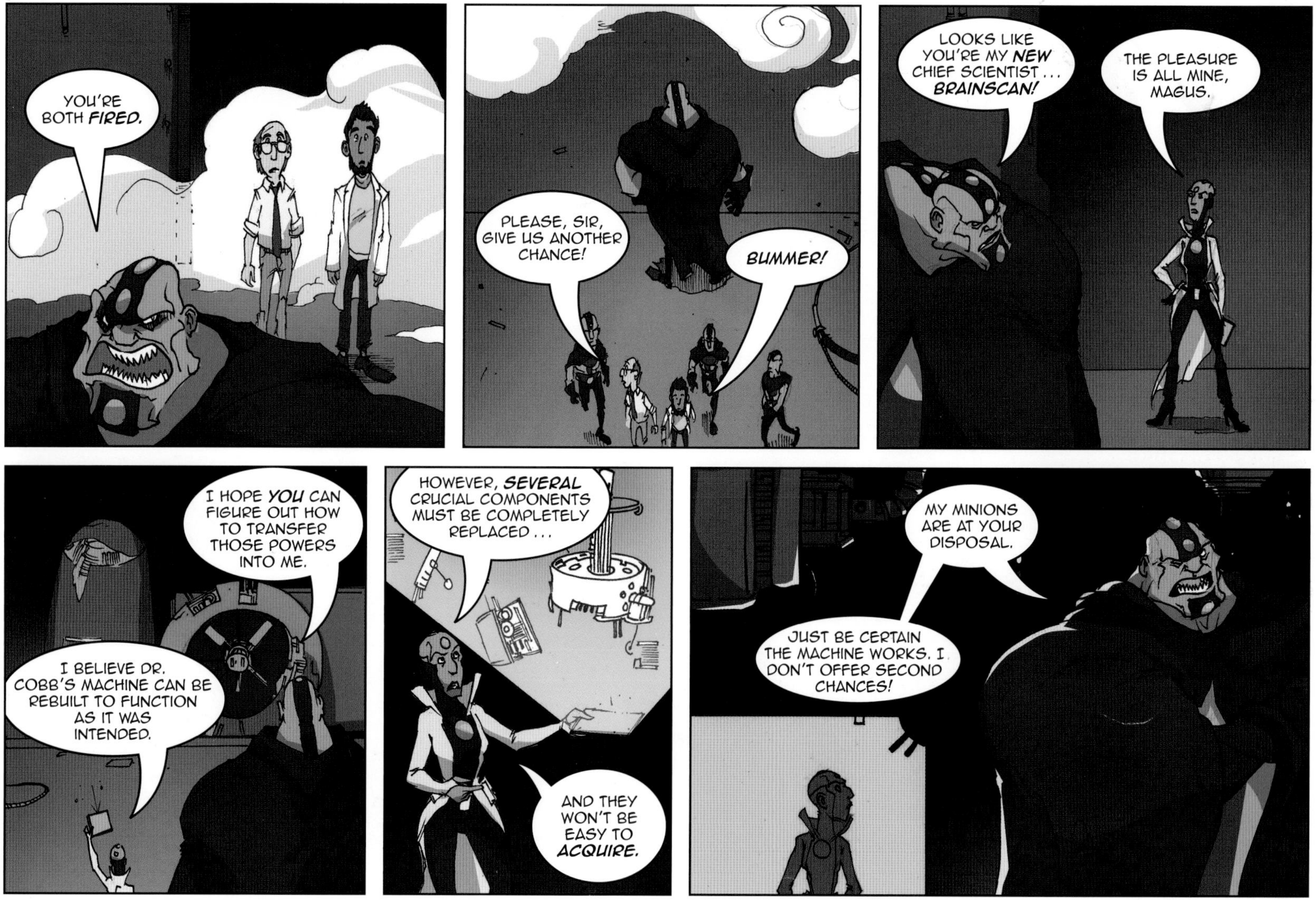
YOU'RE BOTH FIRED.
PLEASE, SIR, GIVE US ANOTHER CHANCE!
BUMMER!
LOOKS LIKE YOU'RE MY NEW CHIEF SCIENTIST . . . BRAINSCAN!
THE PLEASURE IS ALL MINE, MAGUS.
I HOPE YOU CAN FIGURE OUT HOW TO TRANSFER THOSE POWERS INTO ME.
I BELIEVE DR. COBB'S MACHINE CAN BE REBUILT TO FUNCTION AS IT WAS INTENDED.
HOWEVER, SEVERAL CRUCIAL COMPONENTS MUST BE COMPLETELY REPLACED . . .
AND THEY WON'T BE EASY TO ACQUIRE.
MY MINIONS ARE AT YOUR DISPOSAL.
JUST BE CERTAIN THE MACHINE WORKS. I DON'T OFFER SECOND CHANCES!

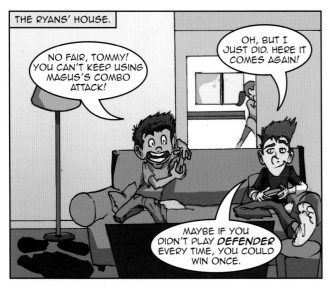

THE RYANS' HOUSE.

NO FAIR, TOMMY! YOU CAN'T KEEP USING MAGUS'S COMBO ATTACK!

OH, BUT I JUST DID. HERE IT COMES AGAIN!

MAYBE IF YOU DIDN'T PLAY *DEFENDER* EVERY TIME, YOU COULD WIN ONCE.

STOP THAT!!

YOU TAKE IT BACK!

IF HE WASN'T SUCH A LOSER, HE'D STILL BE ALIVE!

I'M *WARNING* YOU . . .

TV OFF, GUYS! COME FIX YOUR FAJITAS.

FAJITA NIGHT!!

GOODNESS, ANDREW! YOU'VE BEEN EATING LIKE A *HORSE* LATELY! YOU CAN'T BE HITTING PUBERTY *YET!*

GUESS BEING A SUPERHERO REALLY BURNS UP SOME CALORIES.

OFF TO WORK! FINISH YOUR HOMEWORK BEFORE BED, OK?

SURE THING, MOM! HAVE A GOOD NIGHT!

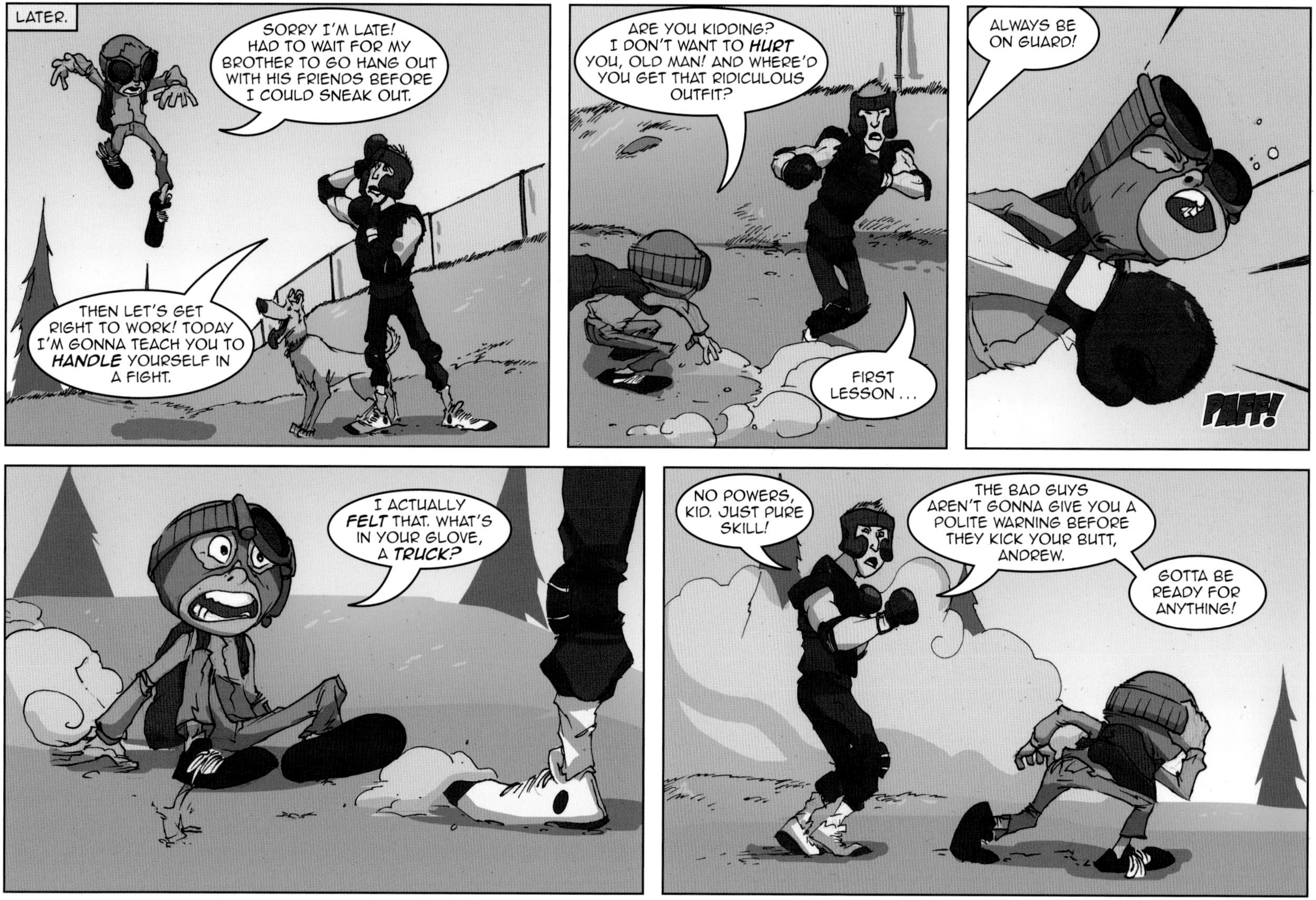
LATER.
SORRY I'M LATE! HAD TO WAIT FOR MY BROTHER TO GO HANG OUT WITH HIS FRIENDS BEFORE I COULD SNEAK OUT.
THEN LET'S GET RIGHT TO WORK! TODAY I'M GONNA TEACH YOU TO HANDLE YOURSELF IN A FIGHT.
ARE YOU KIDDING? I DON'T WANT TO HURT YOU, OLD MAN! AND WHERE'D YOU GET THAT RIDICULOUS OUTFIT?
FIRST LESSON . . .
ALWAYS BE ON GUARD!
PAFF!
I ACTUALLY FELT THAT. WHAT'S IN YOUR GLOVE, A TRUCK?
NO POWERS, KID. JUST PURE SKILL!
THE BAD GUYS AREN'T GONNA GIVE YOU A POLITE WARNING BEFORE THEY KICK YOUR BUTT, ANDREW.
GOTTA BE READY FOR ANYTHING!

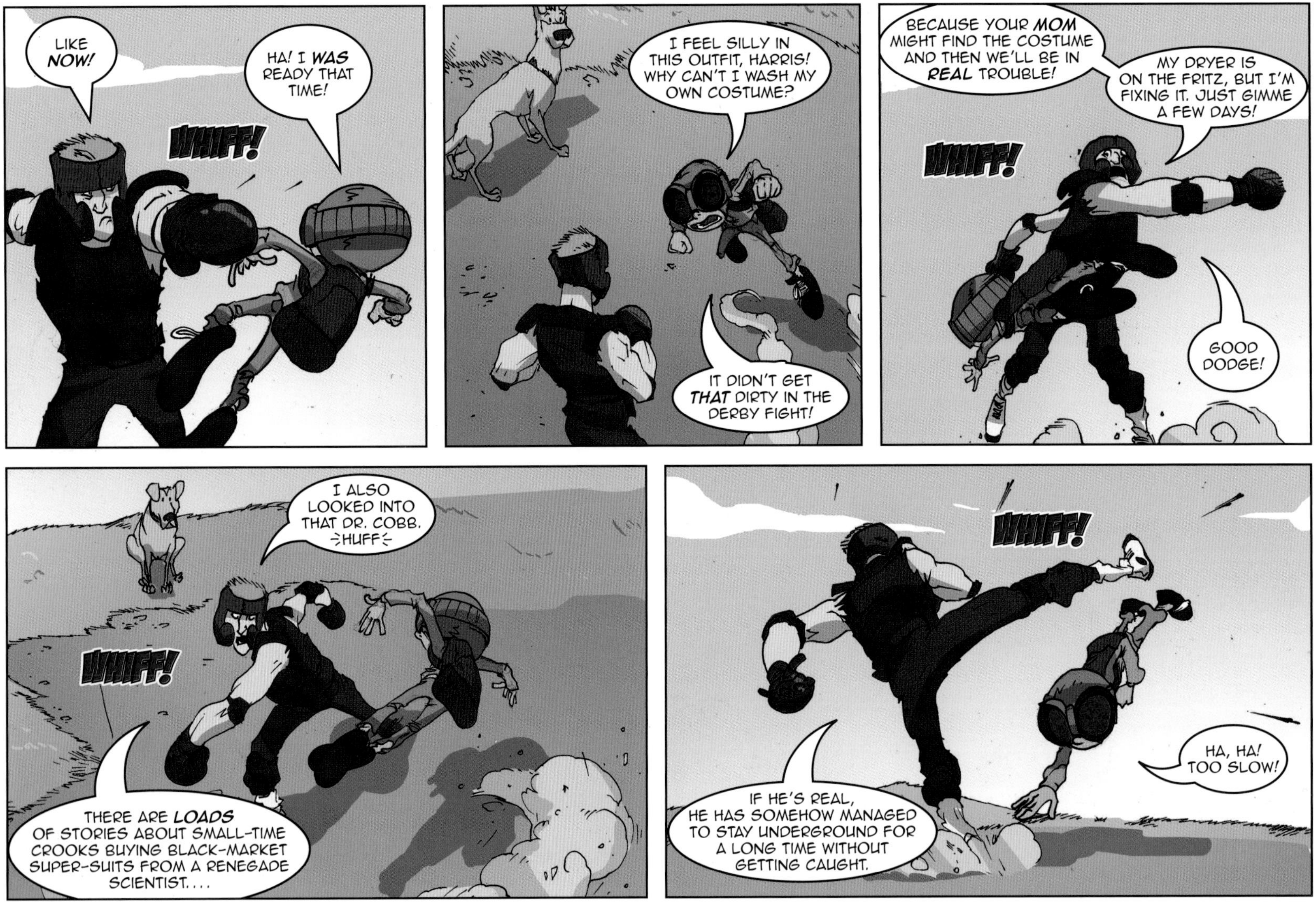

LIKE NOW!
HA! I WAS READY THAT TIME!
WHIFF!
I FEEL SILLY IN THIS OUTFIT, HARRIS! WHY CAN'T I WASH MY OWN COSTUME?
IT DIDN'T GET THAT DIRTY IN THE DERBY FIGHT!
BECAUSE YOUR MOM MIGHT FIND THE COSTUME AND THEN WE'LL BE IN REAL TROUBLE!
MY DRYER IS ON THE FRITZ, BUT I'M FIXING IT. JUST GIMME A FEW DAYS!
WHIFF!
GOOD DODGE!
I ALSO LOOKED INTO THAT DR. COBB. HUFF
WHIFF!
THERE ARE LOADS OF STORIES ABOUT SMALL-TIME CROOKS BUYING BLACK-MARKET SUPER-SUITS FROM A RENEGADE SCIENTIST. . . .
WHIFF!
HA, HA! TOO SLOW!
IF HE'S REAL, HE HAS SOMEHOW MANAGED TO STAY UNDERGROUND FOR A LONG TIME WITHOUT GETTING CAUGHT.

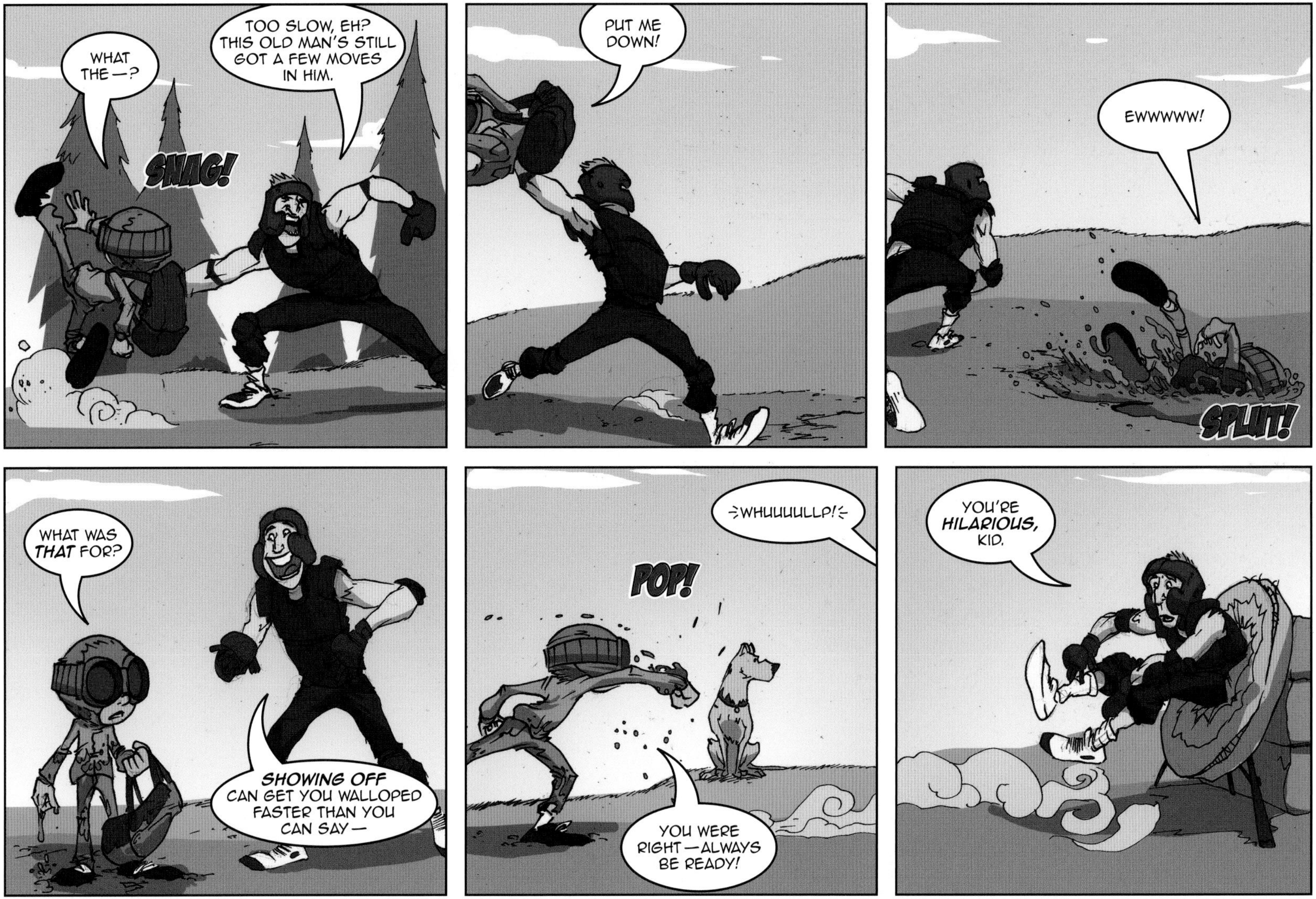
WHAT THE—?
TOO SLOW, EH? THIS OLD MAN'S STILL GOT A FEW MOVES IN HIM.
SNAG!
PUT ME DOWN!
EWWWWW!
SPLUT!
WHAT WAS *THAT* FOR?
SHOWING OFF CAN GET YOU WALLOPED FASTER THAN YOU CAN SAY—
WHUUUULLP!
POP!
YOU WERE RIGHT—ALWAYS BE READY!
YOU'RE *HILARIOUS,* KID.

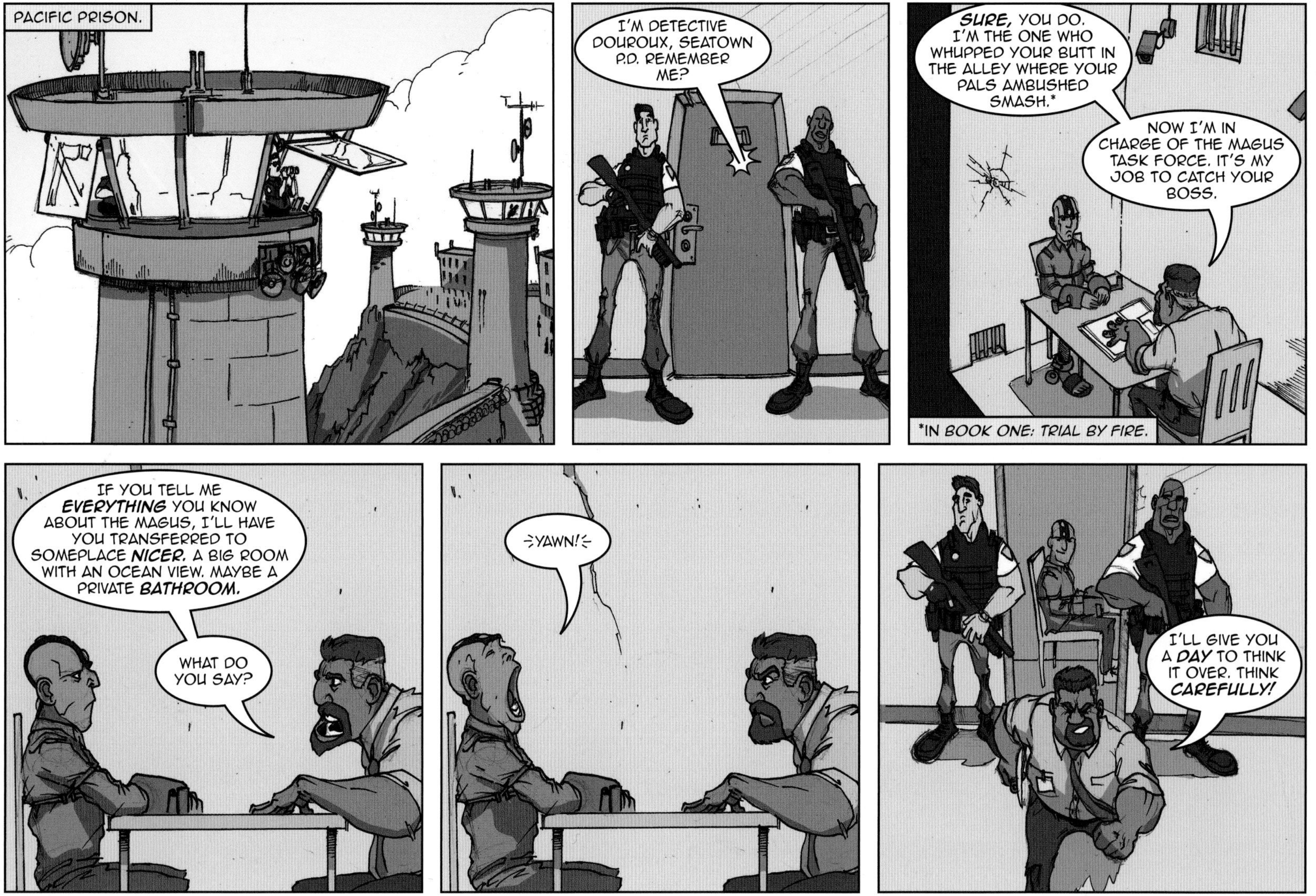
PACIFIC PRISON.
I'M DETECTIVE DOUROUX, SEATOWN P.D. REMEMBER ME?
SURE, YOU DO. I'M THE ONE WHO WHUPPED YOUR BUTT IN THE ALLEY WHERE YOUR PALS AMBUSHED SMASH.*
NOW I'M IN CHARGE OF THE MAGUS TASK FORCE. IT'S MY JOB TO CATCH YOUR BOSS.
*IN BOOK ONE: TRIAL BY FIRE.
IF YOU TELL ME EVERYTHING YOU KNOW ABOUT THE MAGUS, I'LL HAVE YOU TRANSFERRED TO SOMEPLACE NICER. A BIG ROOM WITH AN OCEAN VIEW. MAYBE A PRIVATE BATHROOM.
WHAT DO YOU SAY?
YAWN!
I'LL GIVE YOU A DAY TO THINK IT OVER. THINK CAREFULLY!

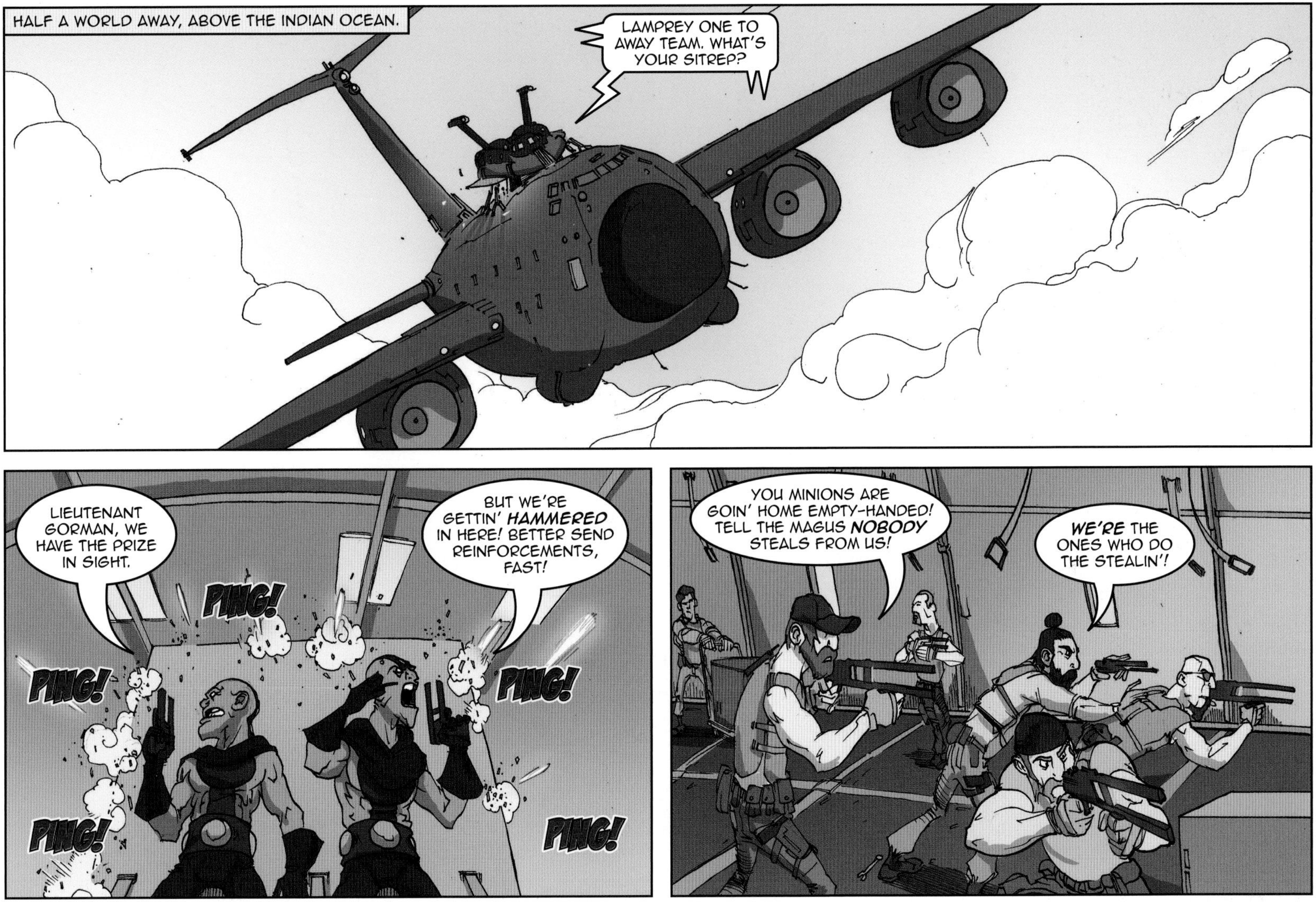
HALF A WORLD AWAY, ABOVE THE INDIAN OCEAN.
LAMPREY ONE TO AWAY TEAM. WHAT'S YOUR SITREP?
LIEUTENANT GORMAN, WE HAVE THE PRIZE IN SIGHT.
BUT WE'RE GETTIN' ***HAMMERED*** IN HERE! BETTER SEND REINFORCEMENTS, FAST!
PING!
PING!
PING!
PING!
PING!
YOU MINIONS ARE GOIN' HOME EMPTY-HANDED! TELL THE MAGUS ***NOBODY*** STEALS FROM US!
WE'RE THE ONES WHO DO THE STEALIN'!

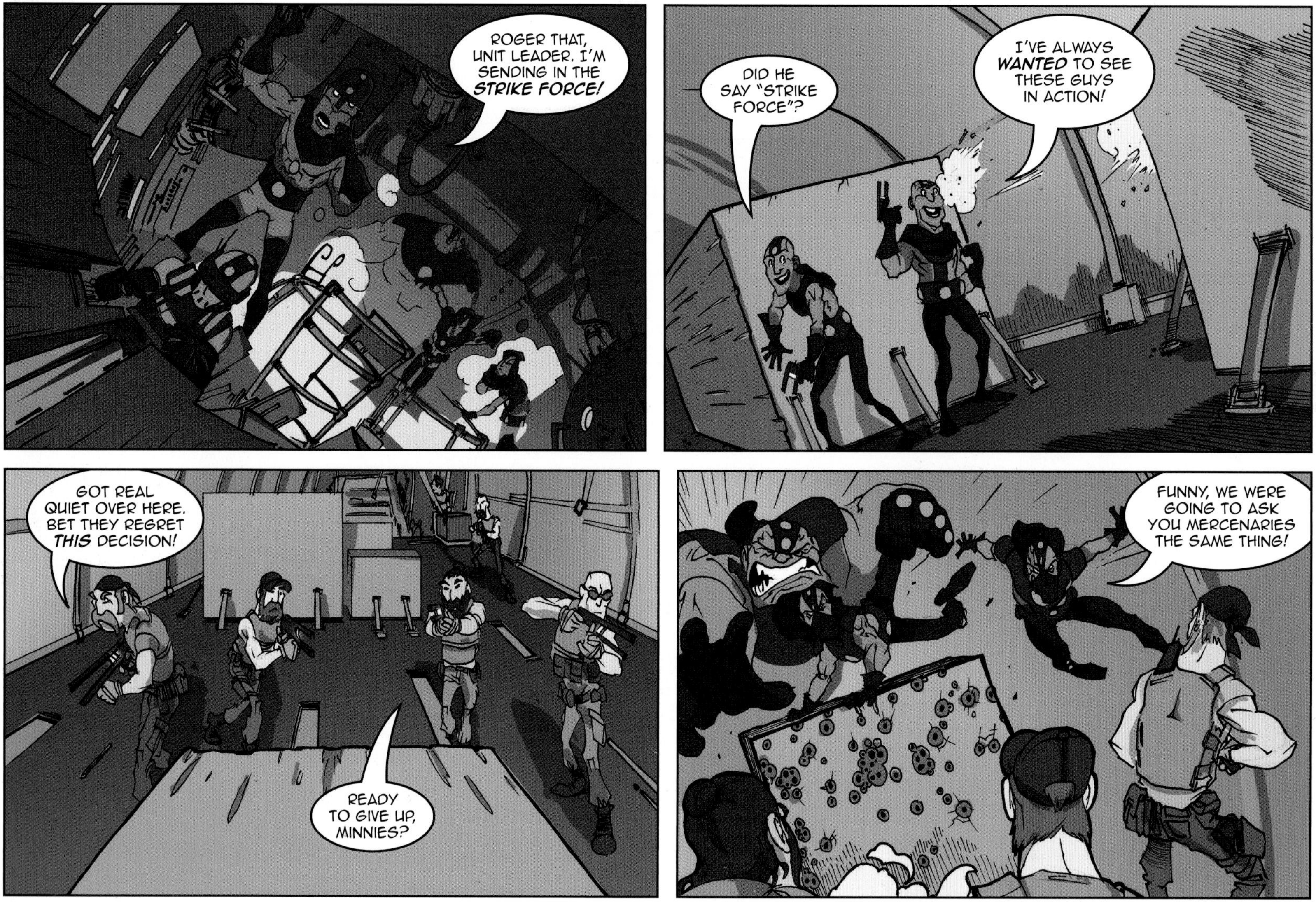
ROGER THAT, UNIT LEADER. I'M SENDING IN THE STRIKE FORCE!
DID HE SAY "STRIKE FORCE"?
I'VE ALWAYS WANTED TO SEE THESE GUYS IN ACTION!
GOT REAL QUIET OVER HERE. BET THEY REGRET THIS DECISION!
READY TO GIVE UP, MINNIES?
FUNNY, WE WERE GOING TO ASK YOU MERCENARIES THE SAME THING!

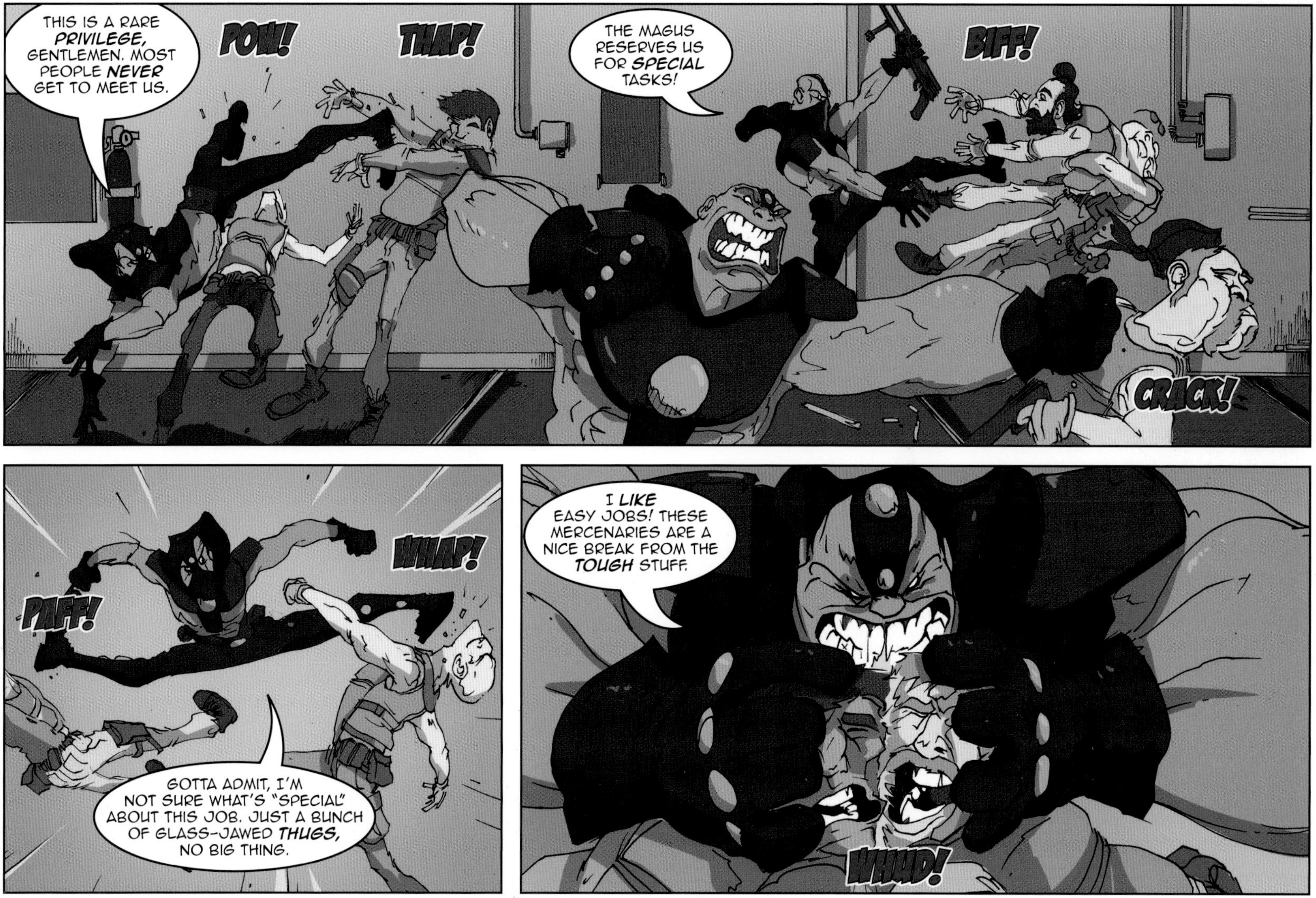
THIS IS A RARE PRIVILEGE, GENTLEMEN. MOST PEOPLE NEVER GET TO MEET US.
POW!
THAP!
THE MAGUS RESERVES US FOR SPECIAL TASKS!
BIFF!
CRACK!
WHAP!
PAFF!
GOTTA ADMIT, I'M NOT SURE WHAT'S "SPECIAL" ABOUT THIS JOB. JUST A BUNCH OF GLASS-JAWED THUGS, NO BIG THING.
I LIKE EASY JOBS! THESE MERCENARIES ARE A NICE BREAK FROM THE TOUGH STUFF.
WHUD!

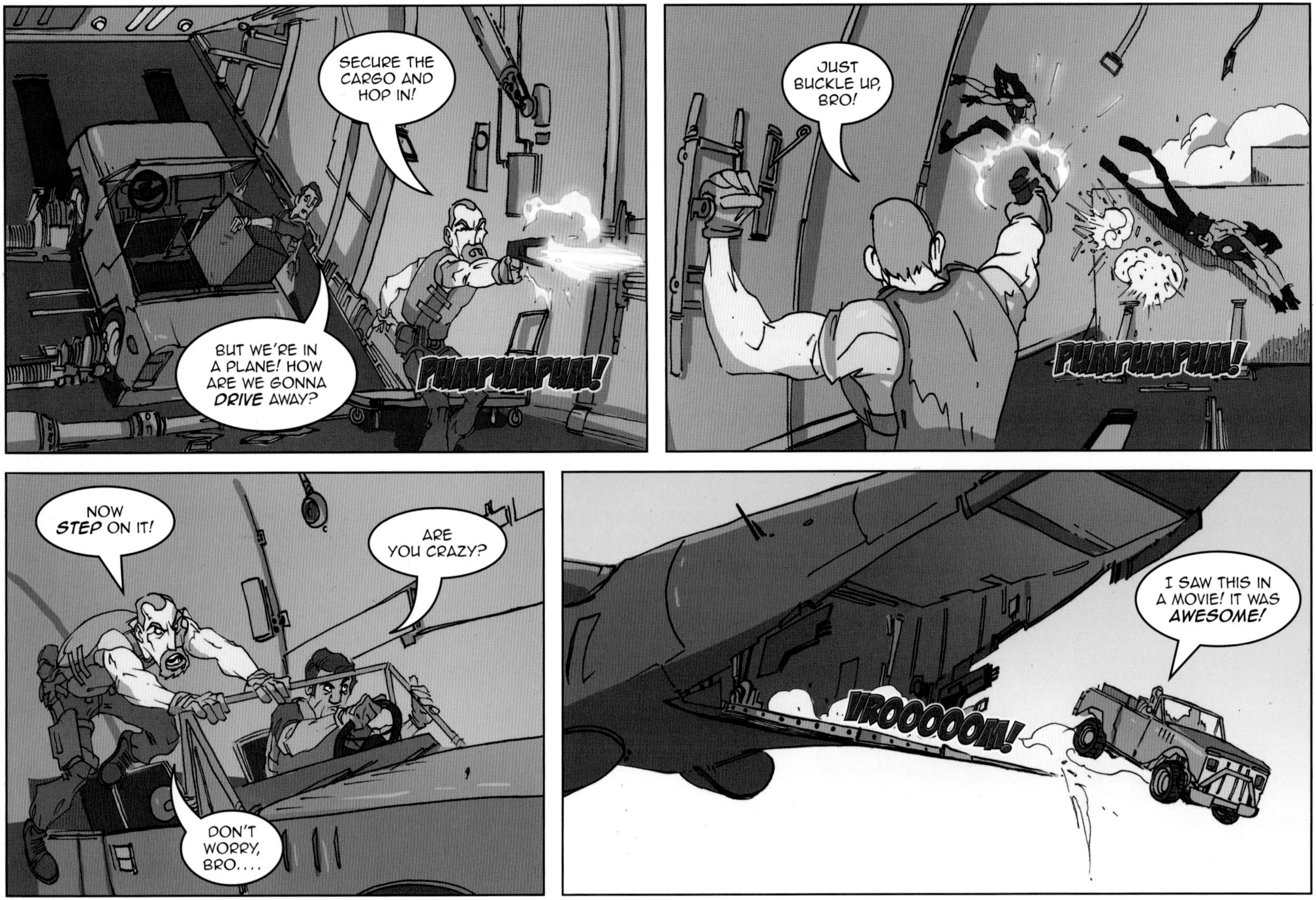
SECURE THE CARGO AND HOP IN!
BUT WE'RE IN A PLANE! HOW ARE WE GONNA DRIVE AWAY?
PUMPUMPUM!
JUST BUCKLE UP, BRO!
PUMPUMPUM!
NOW STEP ON IT!
ARE YOU CRAZY?
DON'T WORRY, BRO....
I SAW THIS IN A MOVIE! IT WAS AWESOME!
VROOOOOOM!

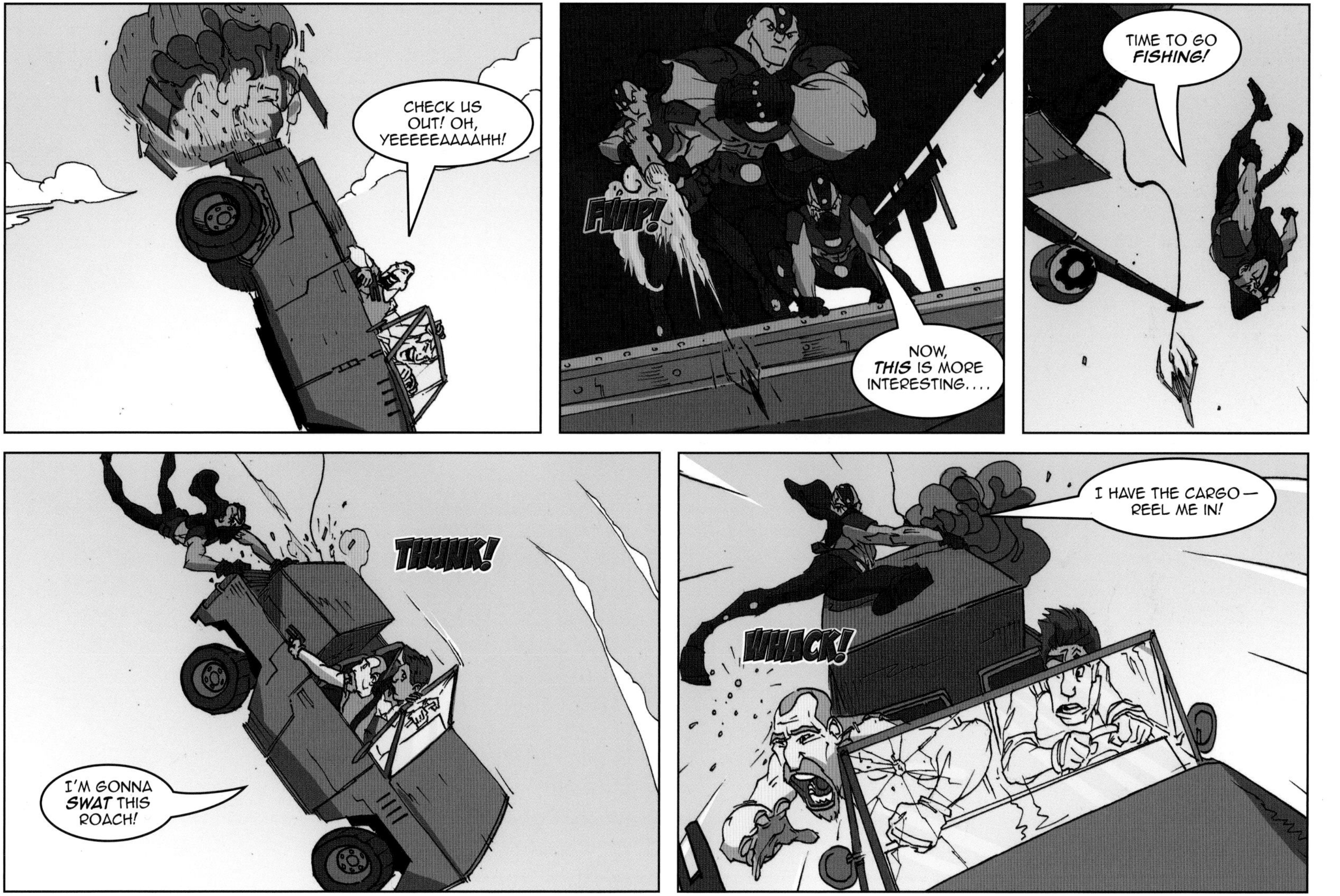
CHECK US OUT! OH, YEEEEEAAAAAHH!
FWIP!
NOW, THIS IS MORE INTERESTING. . . .
TIME TO GO FISHING!
THUNK!
I'M GONNA SWAT THIS ROACH!
I HAVE THE CARGO— REEL ME IN!
WHACK!

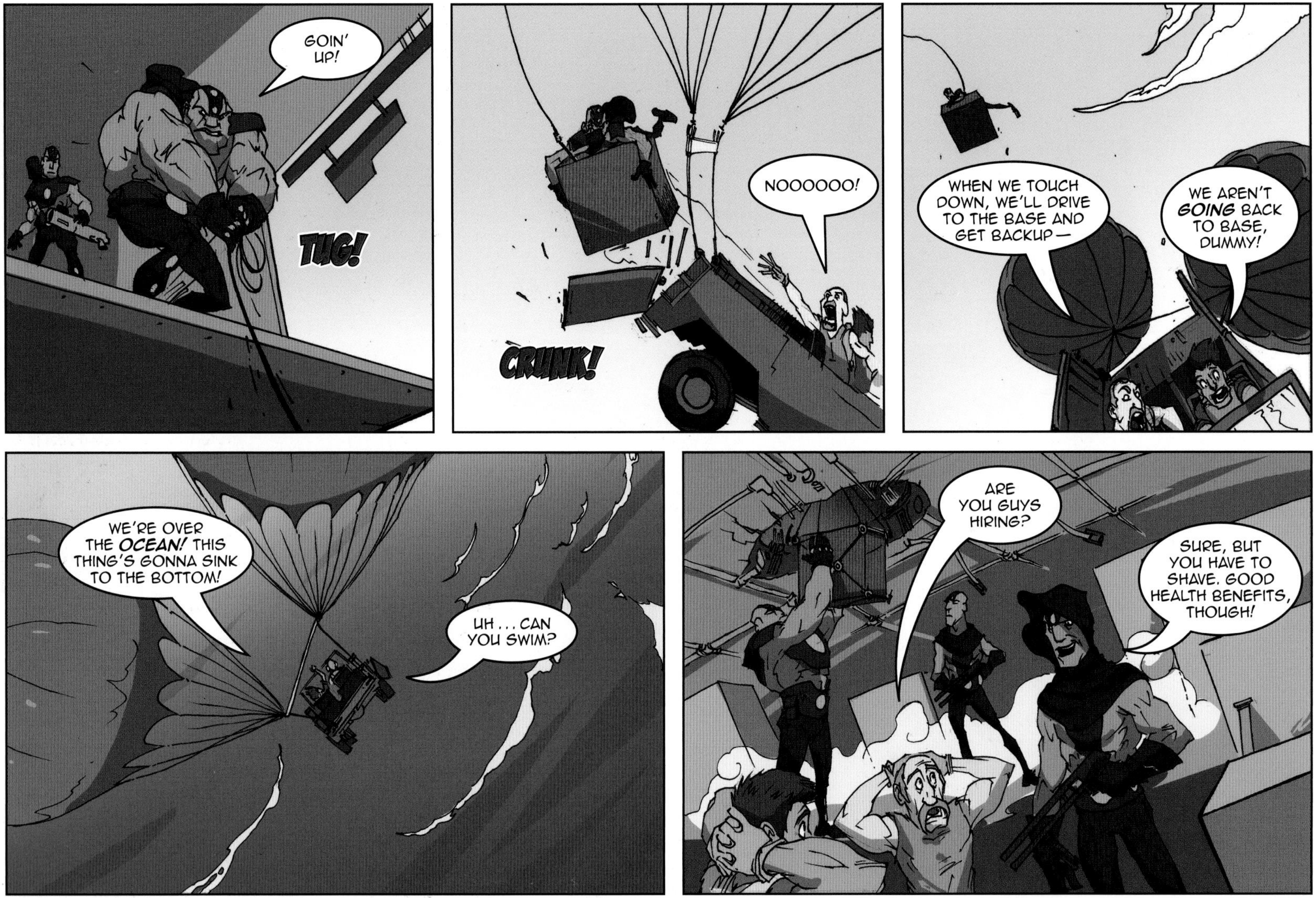
GOIN' UP!
TUG!
CRUNK!
NOOOOOO!
WHEN WE TOUCH DOWN, WE'LL DRIVE TO THE BASE AND GET BACKUP—
WE AREN'T GOING BACK TO BASE, DUMMY!
WE'RE OVER THE OCEAN! THIS THING'S GONNA SINK TO THE BOTTOM!
UH . . . CAN YOU SWIM?
ARE YOU GUYS HIRING?
SURE, BUT YOU HAVE TO SHAVE. GOOD HEALTH BENEFITS, THOUGH!

LATER.

THE STRIKE FORCE PERFORMED *ADMIRABLY,* SIR.

THE COMPONENT APPEARS UNHARMED.

WILL THIS PIECE MAKE DR. COBB'S MACHINE WORK AGAIN?

ALMOST, SIR. WE HAVE A *NEW* PROBLEM.

COBB'S MACHINE WAS DESTROYED BY AN ELECTRIC OVERLOAD. IT WAS DRAWING TOO MUCH POWER, AND WOULD HAVE SELF-DESTRUCTED SOONER OR LATER.

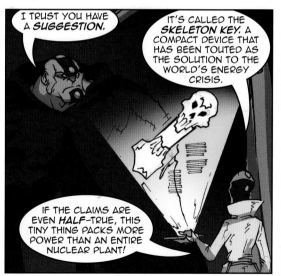

I TRUST YOU HAVE A *SUGGESTION.*

IT'S CALLED THE *SKELETON KEY.* A COMPACT DEVICE THAT HAS BEEN TOUTED AS THE SOLUTION TO THE WORLD'S ENERGY CRISIS.

IF THE CLAIMS ARE EVEN *HALF*-TRUE, THIS TINY THING PACKS MORE POWER THAN AN ENTIRE NUCLEAR PLANT!

THE DESIGNER WAS CAUGHT STEALING PROJECT FUNDS AND SENT TO PRISON.

ALBERT HAMMOND IS THE ONLY PERSON WITH ACCESS TO THE PROTOTYPE—*IF* IT TRULY EXISTS.

THEN WE MUST CONTACT HIM. . . .

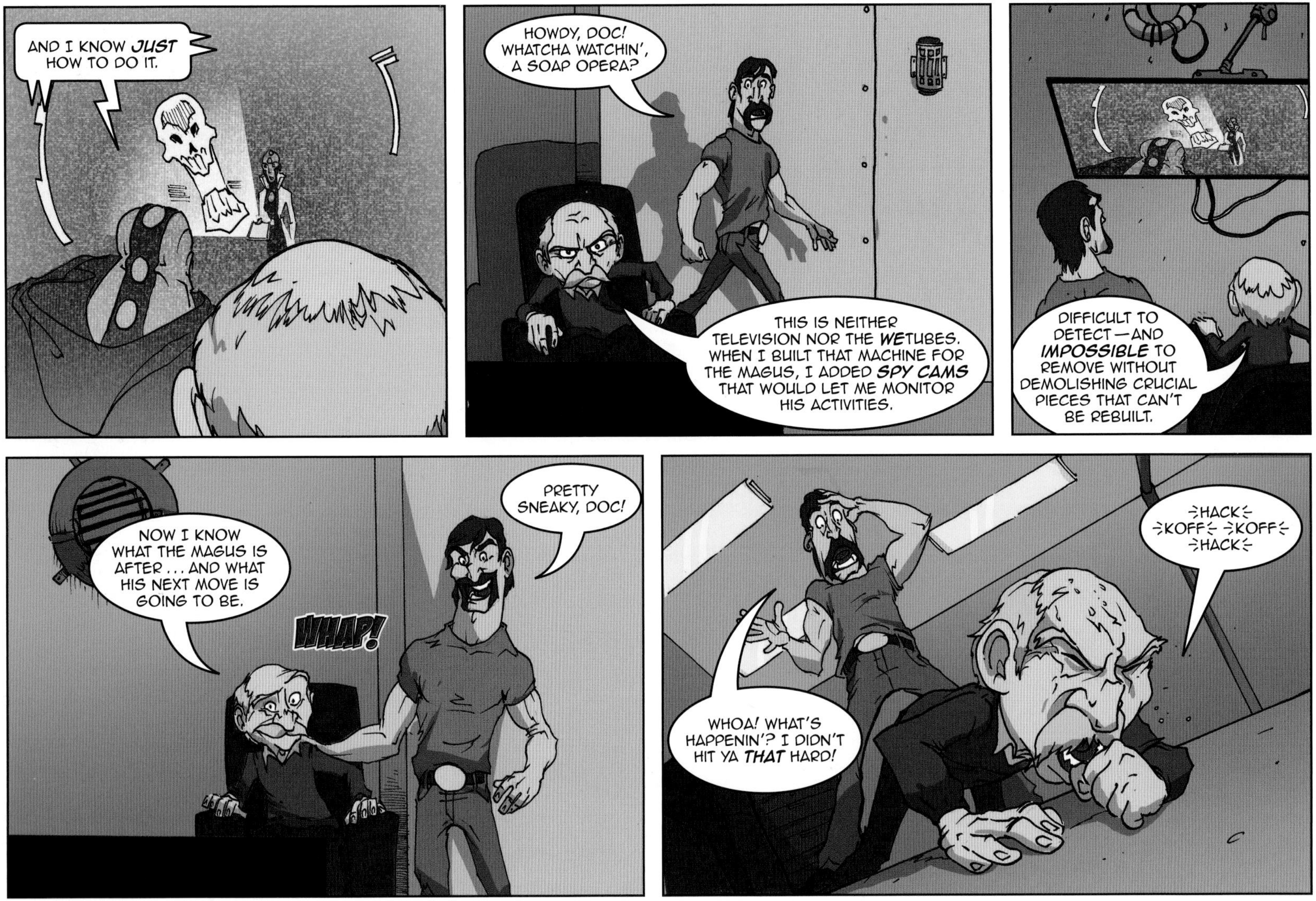
AND I KNOW JUST HOW TO DO IT.
HOWDY, DOC! WHATCHA WATCHIN', A SOAP OPERA?
THIS IS NEITHER TELEVISION NOR THE WETUBES. WHEN I BUILT THAT MACHINE FOR THE MAGUS, I ADDED SPY CAMS THAT WOULD LET ME MONITOR HIS ACTIVITIES.
DIFFICULT TO DETECT—AND IMPOSSIBLE TO REMOVE WITHOUT DEMOLISHING CRUCIAL PIECES THAT CAN'T BE REBUILT.
NOW I KNOW WHAT THE MAGUS IS AFTER . . . AND WHAT HIS NEXT MOVE IS GOING TO BE.
PRETTY SNEAKY, DOC!
WHAP!
HACK KOFF KOFF HACK
WHOA! WHAT'S HAPPENIN'? I DIDN'T HIT YA THAT HARD!

MY BODY IS *FAILING,* MR. HUSTON. ⇥KOFF⇤ I AM NOT LONG FOR THIS WORLD.

WHAT? DOC, THAT'S *AWFUL* — I HAD NO IDEA!

FEAR *NOT* ⇥HACK⇤ FOR I'LL LIVE LONG ENOUGH TO SEE YOU REPAY YOUR DEBT TO ME. VERY *SOON,* IN FACT!

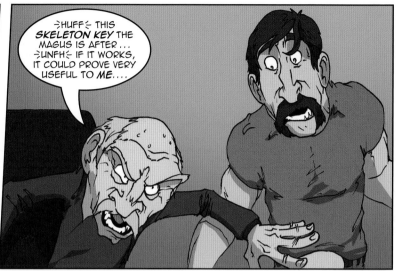

⇥HUFF⇤ THIS *SKELETON KEY* THE MAGUS IS AFTER... ⇥UNFH⇤ IF IT WORKS, IT COULD PROVE VERY USEFUL TO *ME....*

ENABLING ME TO OPERATE MY *OWN* TRANSFERENCE MACHINE... WHILE I STILL HAVE TIME!

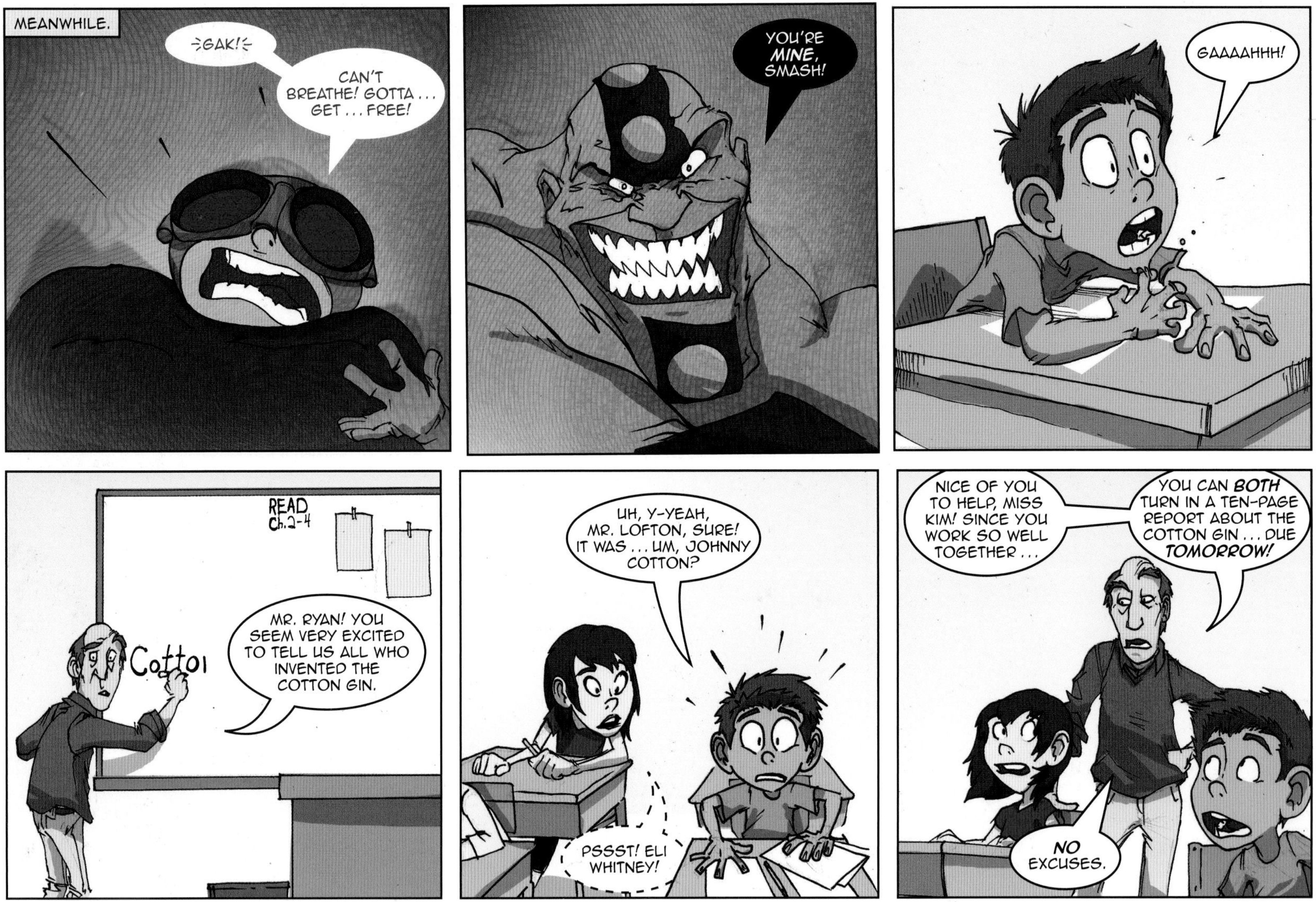
MEANWHILE.
GAK!
CAN'T BREATHE! GOTTA . . . GET . . . FREE!
YOU'RE MINE, SMASH!
GAAAAHHH!
READ Ch.2-4
Cotto
MR. RYAN! YOU SEEM VERY EXCITED TO TELL US ALL WHO INVENTED THE COTTON GIN.
PSSST! ELI WHITNEY!
UH, Y-YEAH, MR. LOFTON, SURE! IT WAS . . . UM, JOHNNY COTTON?
NICE OF YOU TO HELP, MISS KIM! SINCE YOU WORK SO WELL TOGETHER . . .
YOU CAN BOTH TURN IN A TEN-PAGE REPORT ABOUT THE COTTON GIN . . . DUE TOMORROW!
NO EXCUSES.

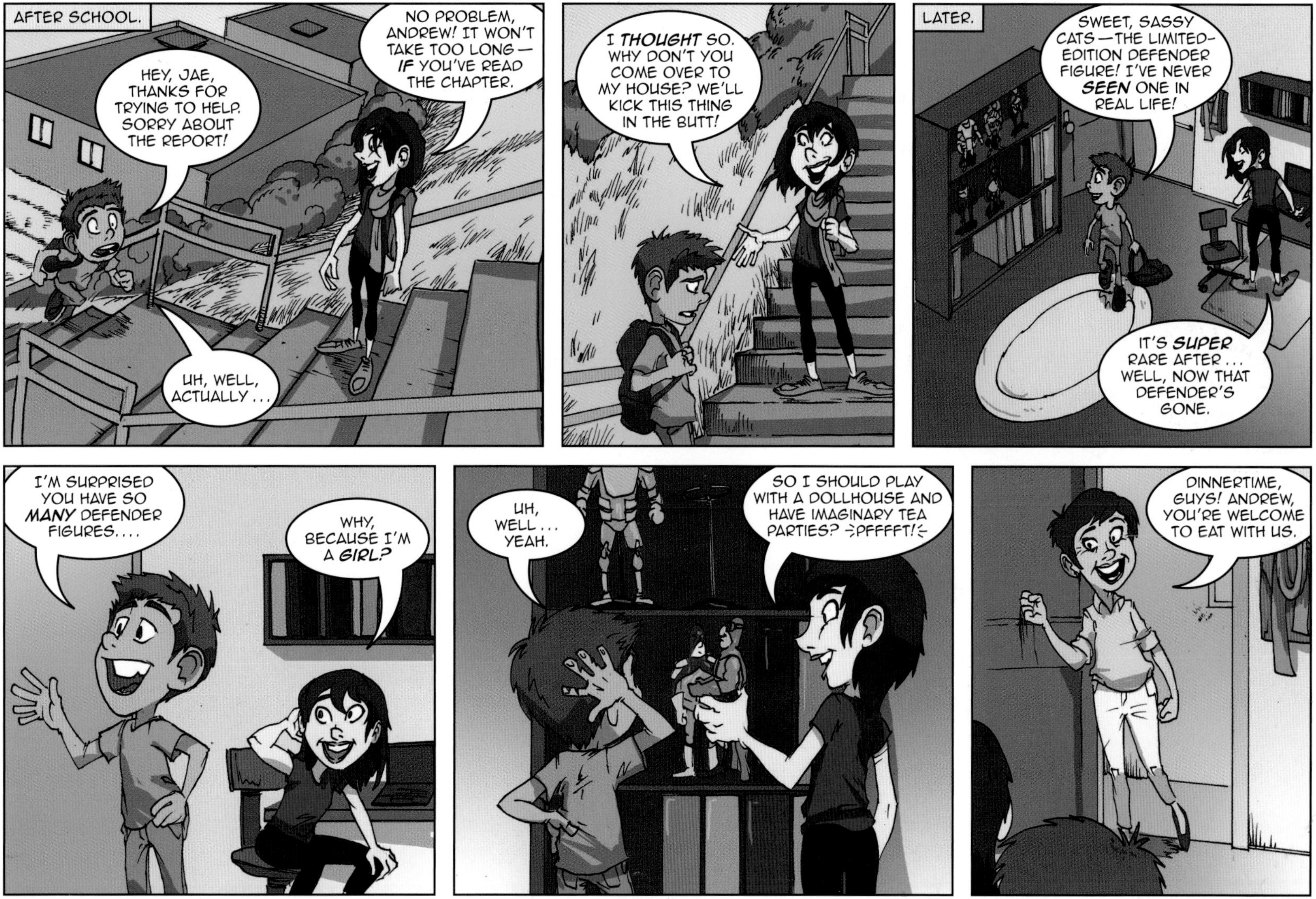
AFTER SCHOOL.
HEY, JAE, THANKS FOR TRYING TO HELP. SORRY ABOUT THE REPORT!
NO PROBLEM, ANDREW! IT WON'T TAKE TOO LONG — IF YOU'VE READ THE CHAPTER.
UH, WELL, ACTUALLY . . .
I THOUGHT SO. WHY DON'T YOU COME OVER TO MY HOUSE? WE'LL KICK THIS THING IN THE BUTT!
LATER.
SWEET, SASSY CATS — THE LIMITED-EDITION DEFENDER FIGURE! I'VE NEVER SEEN ONE IN REAL LIFE!
IT'S SUPER RARE AFTER . . . WELL, NOW THAT DEFENDER'S GONE.
I'M SURPRISED YOU HAVE SO MANY DEFENDER FIGURES. . . .
WHY, BECAUSE I'M A GIRL?
UH, WELL . . . YEAH.
SO I SHOULD PLAY WITH A DOLLHOUSE AND HAVE IMAGINARY TEA PARTIES? PFFFFT!
DINNERTIME, GUYS! ANDREW, YOU'RE WELCOME TO EAT WITH US.

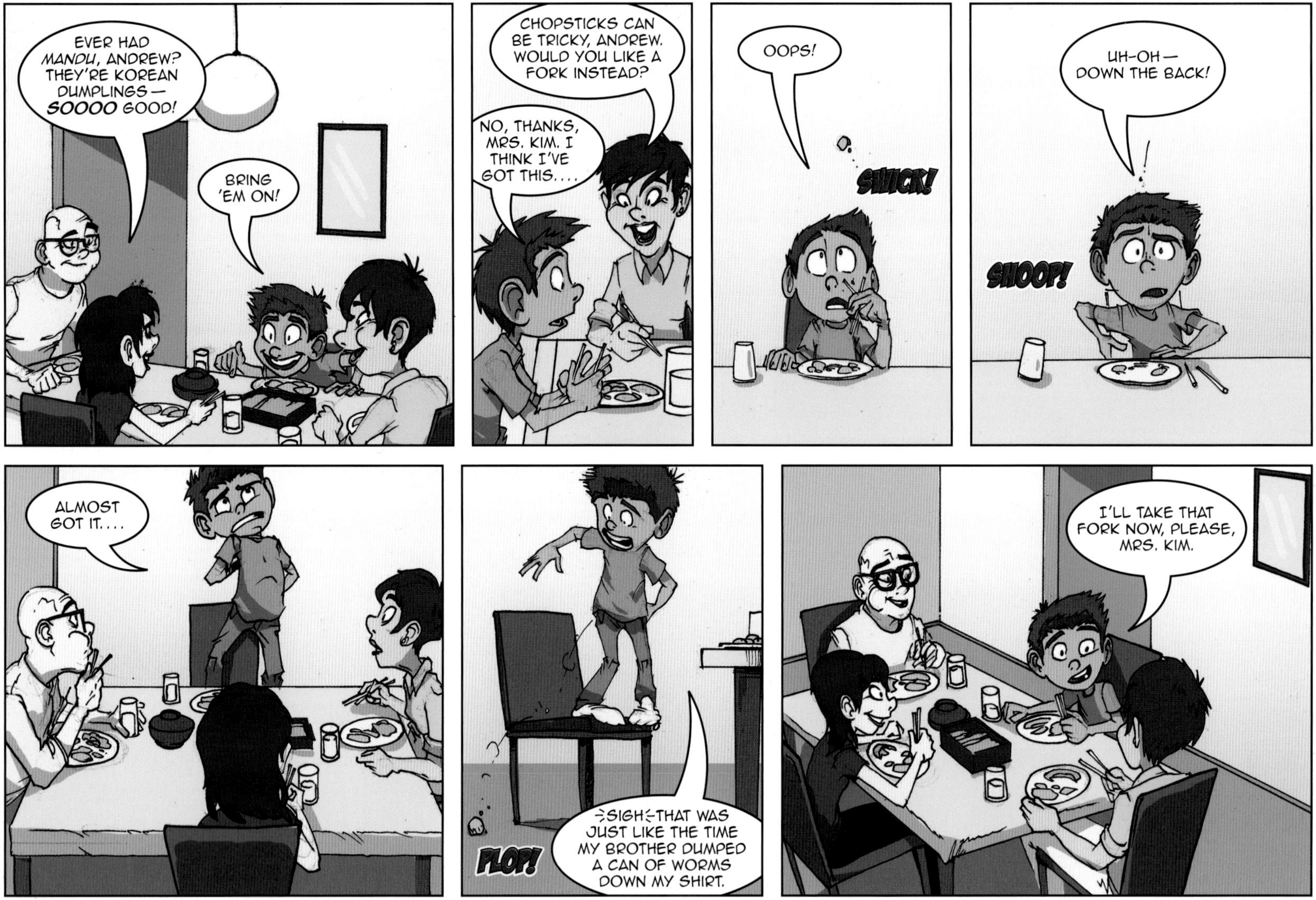

EVER HAD MANDU, ANDREW? THEY'RE KOREAN DUMPLINGS — SOOOO GOOD!
BRING 'EM ON!
CHOPSTICKS CAN BE TRICKY, ANDREW. WOULD YOU LIKE A FORK INSTEAD?
NO, THANKS, MRS. KIM. I THINK I'VE GOT THIS. . . .
OOPS!
SWICK!
UH-OH — DOWN THE BACK!
SHOOP!
ALMOST GOT IT. . . .
PLOP!
⇉SIGH⇇THAT WAS JUST LIKE THE TIME MY BROTHER DUMPED A CAN OF WORMS DOWN MY SHIRT.
I'LL TAKE THAT FORK NOW, PLEASE, MRS. KIM.

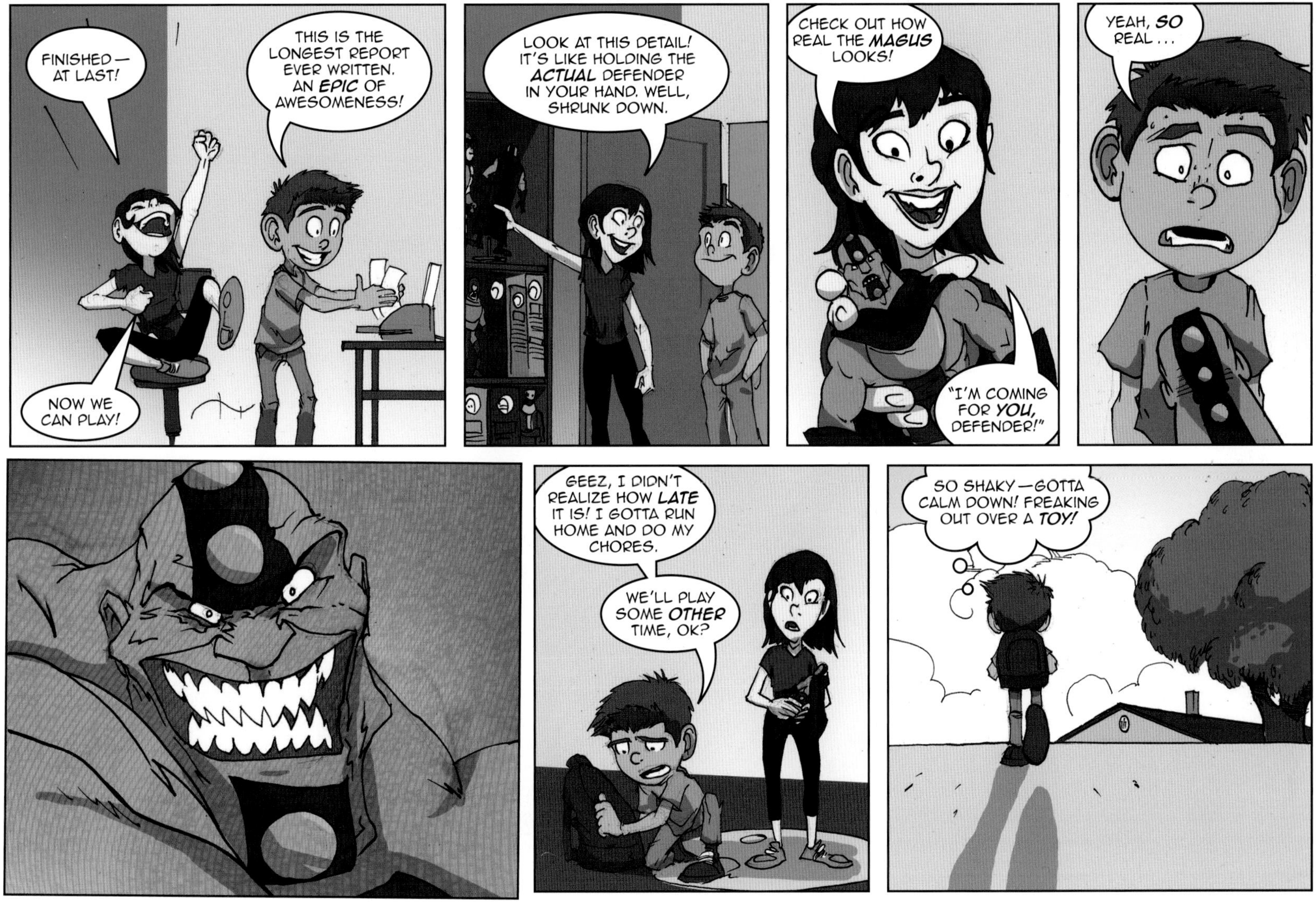
FINISHED— AT LAST!
THIS IS THE LONGEST REPORT EVER WRITTEN. AN EPIC OF AWESOMENESS!
NOW WE CAN PLAY!
LOOK AT THIS DETAIL! IT'S LIKE HOLDING THE ACTUAL DEFENDER IN YOUR HAND. WELL, SHRUNK DOWN.
CHECK OUT HOW REAL THE MAGUS LOOKS!
"I'M COMING FOR YOU, DEFENDER!"
YEAH, SO REAL . . .
GEEZ, I DIDN'T REALIZE HOW LATE IT IS! I GOTTA RUN HOME AND DO MY CHORES.
WE'LL PLAY SOME OTHER TIME, OK?
SO SHAKY—GOTTA CALM DOWN! FREAKING OUT OVER A TOY!

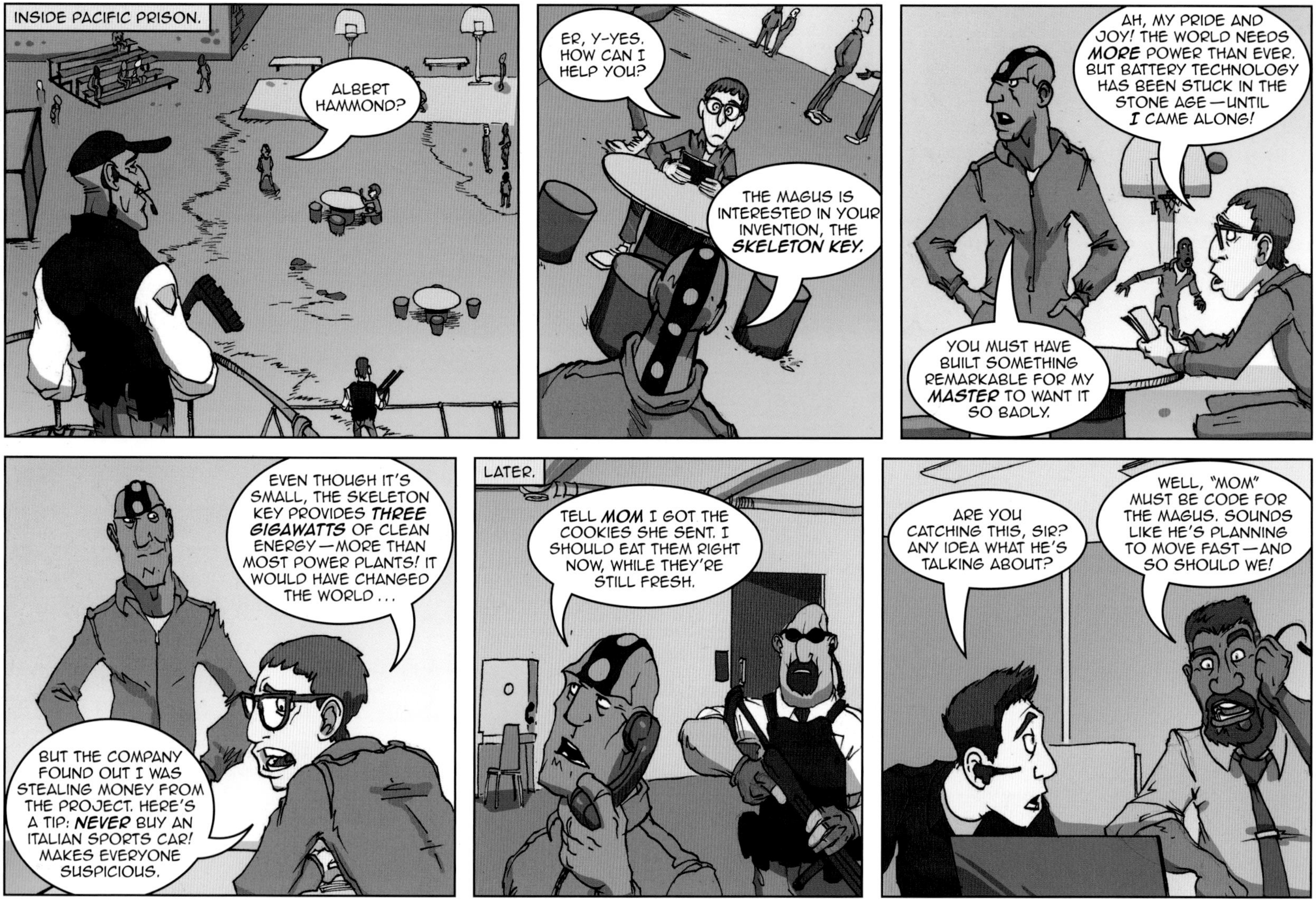
INSIDE PACIFIC PRISON.
ALBERT HAMMOND?
ER, Y-YES. HOW CAN I HELP YOU?
THE MAGUS IS INTERESTED IN YOUR INVENTION, THE SKELETON KEY.
AH, MY PRIDE AND JOY! THE WORLD NEEDS MORE POWER THAN EVER. BUT BATTERY TECHNOLOGY HAS BEEN STUCK IN THE STONE AGE—UNTIL I CAME ALONG!
YOU MUST HAVE BUILT SOMETHING REMARKABLE FOR MY MASTER TO WANT IT SO BADLY.
EVEN THOUGH IT'S SMALL, THE SKELETON KEY PROVIDES THREE GIGAWATTS OF CLEAN ENERGY—MORE THAN MOST POWER PLANTS! IT WOULD HAVE CHANGED THE WORLD . . .
BUT THE COMPANY FOUND OUT I WAS STEALING MONEY FROM THE PROJECT. HERE'S A TIP: NEVER BUY AN ITALIAN SPORTS CAR! MAKES EVERYONE SUSPICIOUS.
LATER.
TELL MOM I GOT THE COOKIES SHE SENT. I SHOULD EAT THEM RIGHT NOW, WHILE THEY'RE STILL FRESH.
ARE YOU CATCHING THIS, SIR? ANY IDEA WHAT HE'S TALKING ABOUT?
WELL, "MOM" MUST BE CODE FOR THE MAGUS. SOUNDS LIKE HE'S PLANNING TO MOVE FAST—AND SO SHOULD WE!

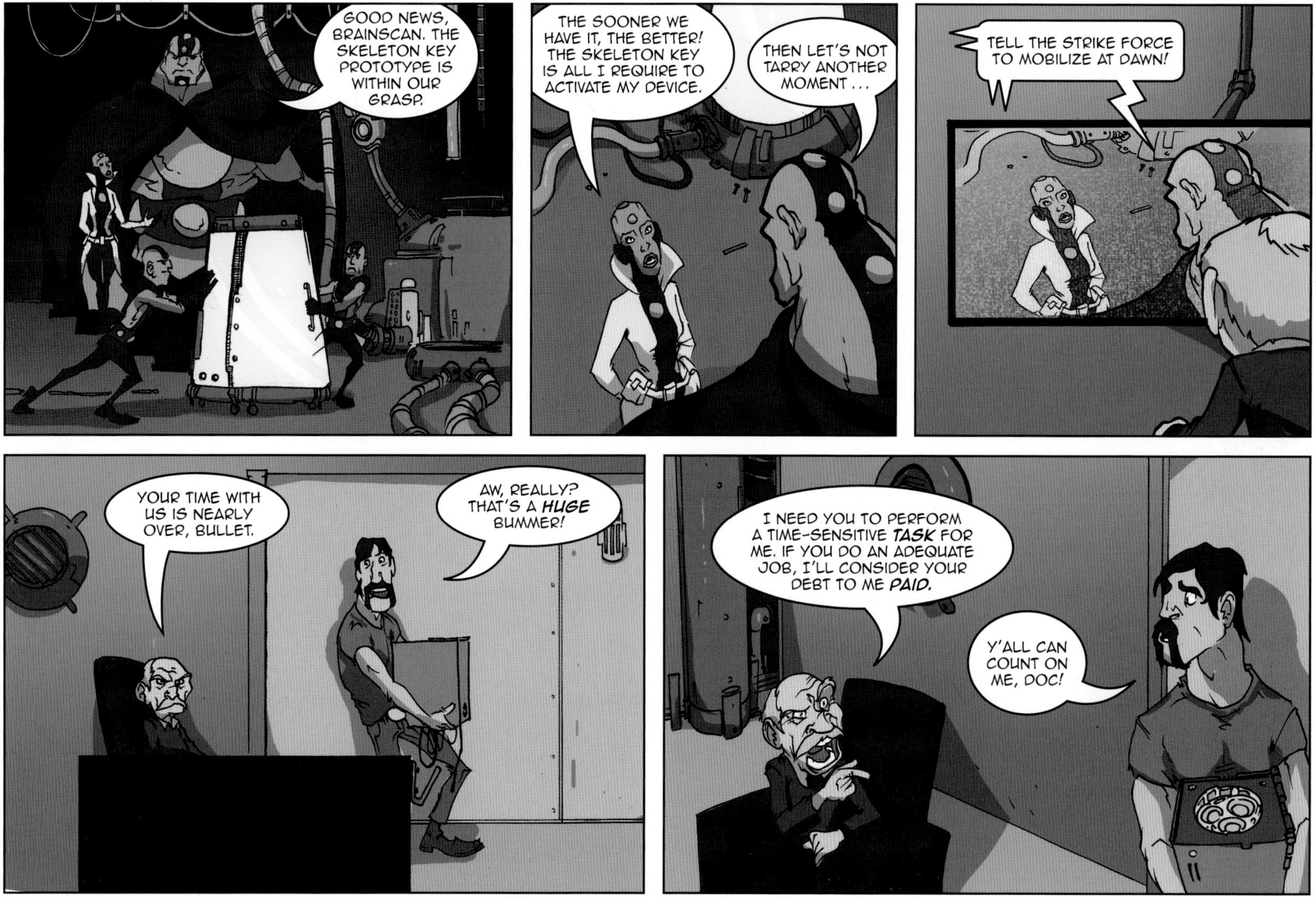
GOOD NEWS, BRAINSCAN. THE SKELETON KEY PROTOTYPE IS WITHIN OUR GRASP.
THE SOONER WE HAVE IT, THE BETTER! THE SKELETON KEY IS ALL I REQUIRE TO ACTIVATE MY DEVICE.
THEN LET'S NOT TARRY ANOTHER MOMENT . . .
TELL THE STRIKE FORCE TO MOBILIZE AT DAWN!
YOUR TIME WITH US IS NEARLY OVER, BULLET.
AW, REALLY? THAT'S A HUGE BUMMER!
I NEED YOU TO PERFORM A TIME-SENSITIVE TASK FOR ME. IF YOU DO AN ADEQUATE JOB, I'LL CONSIDER YOUR DEBT TO ME PAID.
Y'ALL CAN COUNT ON ME, DOC!

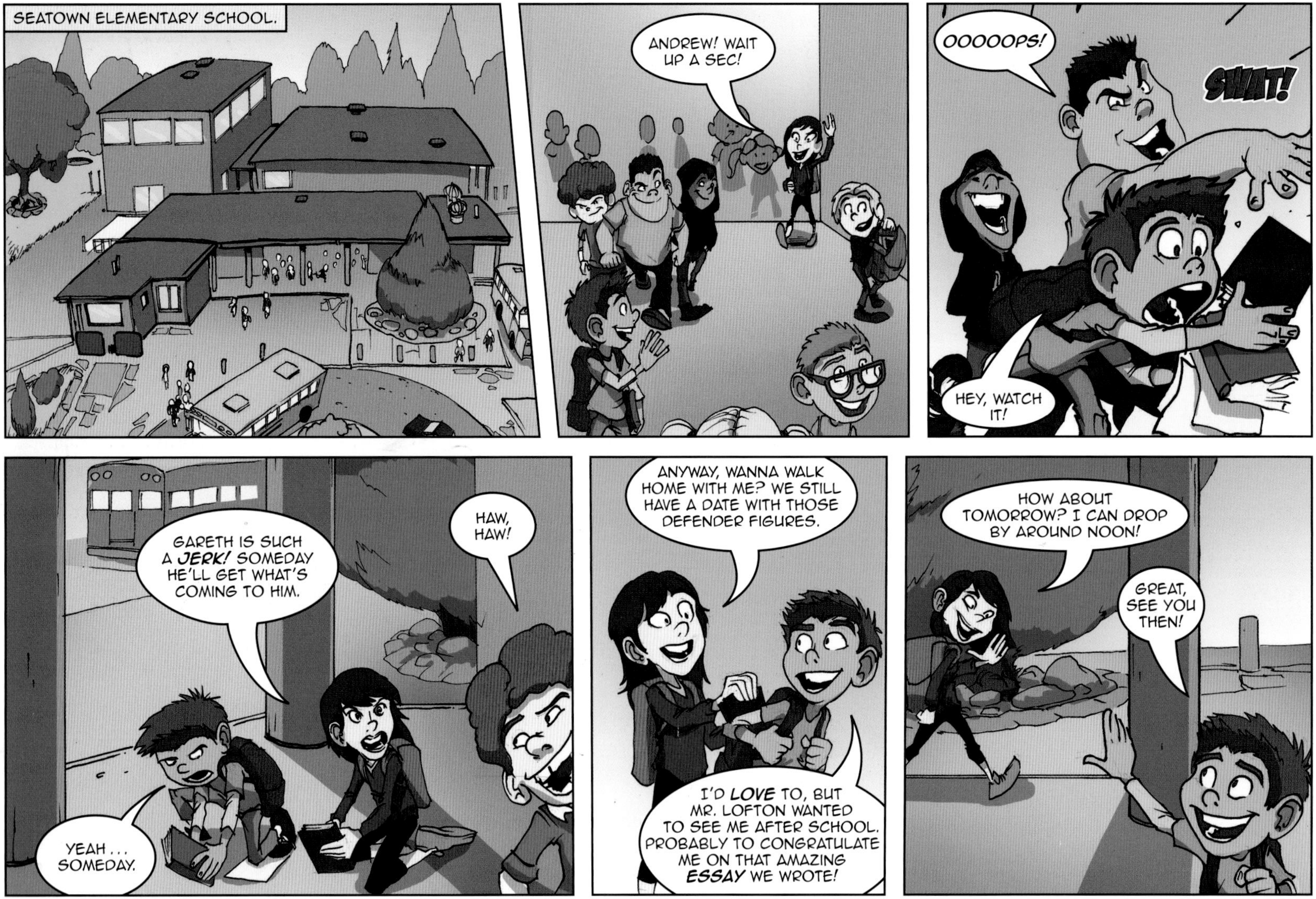
SEATOWN ELEMENTARY SCHOOL.
ANDREW! WAIT UP A SEC!
OOOOOPS!
SWAT!
HEY, WATCH IT!
GARETH IS SUCH A **JERK!** SOMEDAY HE'LL GET WHAT'S COMING TO HIM.
HAW, HAW!
YEAH . . . SOMEDAY.
ANYWAY, WANNA WALK HOME WITH ME? WE STILL HAVE A DATE WITH THOSE DEFENDER FIGURES.
I'D **LOVE** TO, BUT MR. LOFTON WANTED TO SEE ME AFTER SCHOOL. PROBABLY TO CONGRATULATE ME ON THAT AMAZING **ESSAY** WE WROTE!
HOW ABOUT TOMORROW? I CAN DROP BY AROUND NOON!
GREAT, SEE YOU THEN!

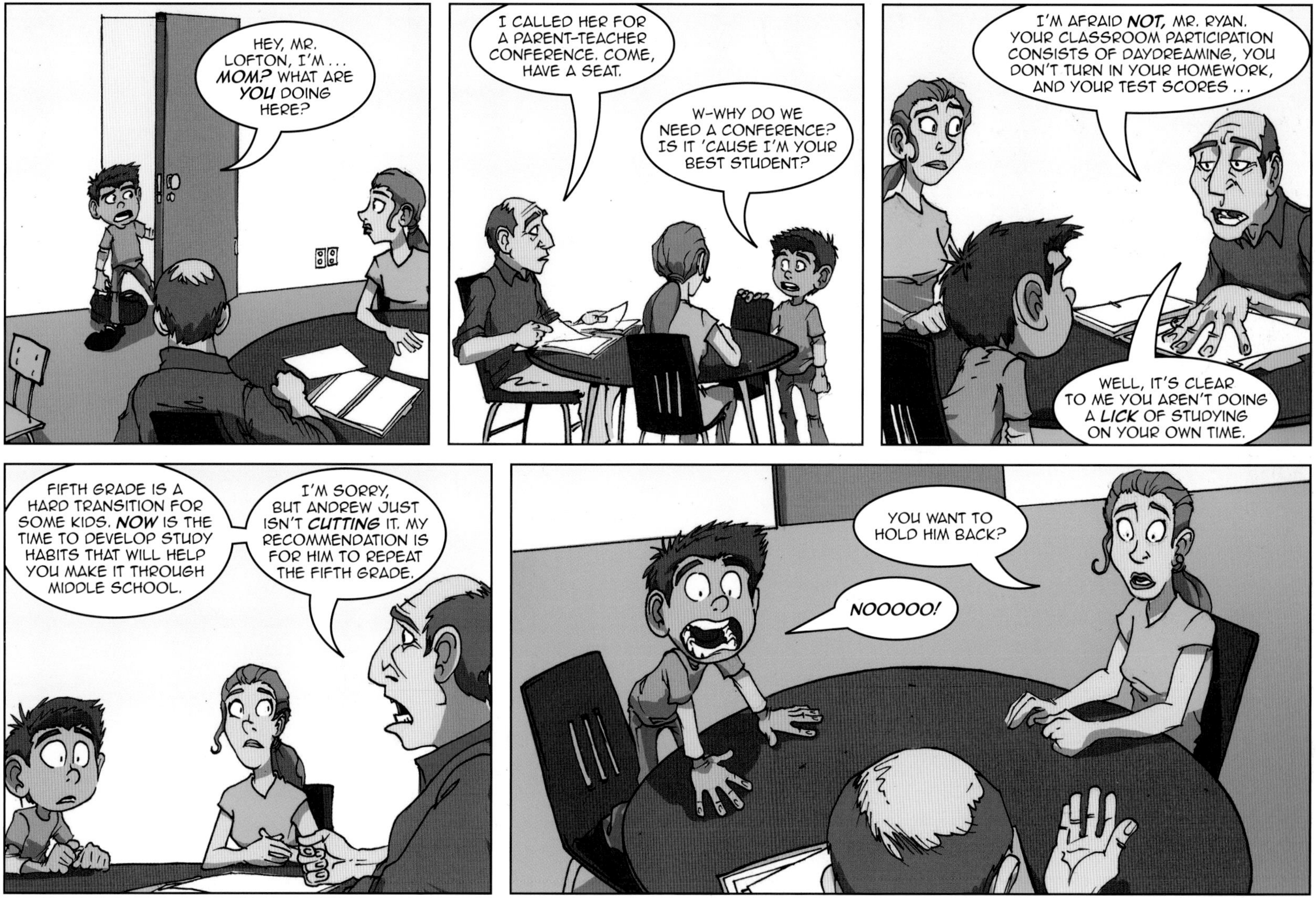

HEY, MR. LOFTON, I'M . . . MOM? WHAT ARE YOU DOING HERE?
I CALLED HER FOR A PARENT-TEACHER CONFERENCE. COME, HAVE A SEAT.
W-WHY DO WE NEED A CONFERENCE? IS IT 'CAUSE I'M YOUR BEST STUDENT?
I'M AFRAID NOT, MR. RYAN. YOUR CLASSROOM PARTICIPATION CONSISTS OF DAYDREAMING, YOU DON'T TURN IN YOUR HOMEWORK, AND YOUR TEST SCORES . . .
WELL, IT'S CLEAR TO ME YOU AREN'T DOING A LICK OF STUDYING ON YOUR OWN TIME.
FIFTH GRADE IS A HARD TRANSITION FOR SOME KIDS. NOW IS THE TIME TO DEVELOP STUDY HABITS THAT WILL HELP YOU MAKE IT THROUGH MIDDLE SCHOOL.
I'M SORRY, BUT ANDREW JUST ISN'T CUTTING IT. MY RECOMMENDATION IS FOR HIM TO REPEAT THE FIFTH GRADE.
YOU WANT TO HOLD HIM BACK?
NOOOOO!

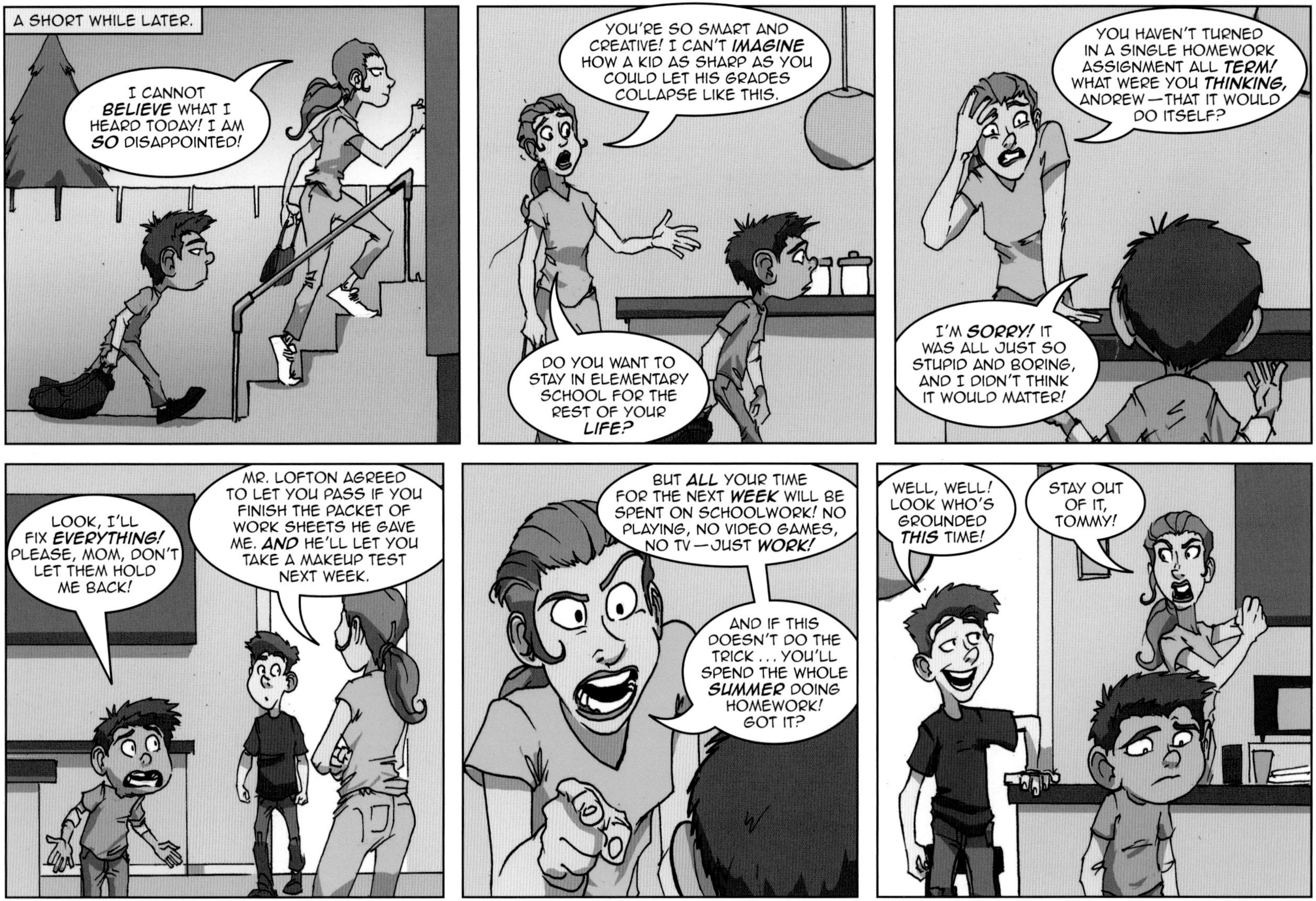
A SHORT WHILE LATER.
I CANNOT BELIEVE WHAT I HEARD TODAY! I AM SO DISAPPOINTED!
YOU'RE SO SMART AND CREATIVE! I CAN'T IMAGINE HOW A KID AS SHARP AS YOU COULD LET HIS GRADES COLLAPSE LIKE THIS.
DO YOU WANT TO STAY IN ELEMENTARY SCHOOL FOR THE REST OF YOUR LIFE?
YOU HAVEN'T TURNED IN A SINGLE HOMEWORK ASSIGNMENT ALL TERM! WHAT WERE YOU THINKING, ANDREW—THAT IT WOULD DO ITSELF?
I'M SORRY! IT WAS ALL JUST SO STUPID AND BORING, AND I DIDN'T THINK IT WOULD MATTER!
LOOK, I'LL FIX EVERYTHING! PLEASE, MOM, DON'T LET THEM HOLD ME BACK!
MR. LOFTON AGREED TO LET YOU PASS IF YOU FINISH THE PACKET OF WORK SHEETS HE GAVE ME. AND HE'LL LET YOU TAKE A MAKEUP TEST NEXT WEEK.
BUT ALL YOUR TIME FOR THE NEXT WEEK WILL BE SPENT ON SCHOOLWORK! NO PLAYING, NO VIDEO GAMES, NO TV—JUST WORK!
AND IF THIS DOESN'T DO THE TRICK . . . YOU'LL SPEND THE WHOLE SUMMER DOING HOMEWORK! GOT IT?
WELL, WELL! LOOK WHO'S GROUNDED THIS TIME!
STAY OUT OF IT, TOMMY!

PACIFIC PRISON, THE NEXT MORNING.

THANKS FOR KEEPING AN EYE OUT.

SO, HAMMOND—DO WE HAVE A *DEAL?*

LOOKS LIKE THE MONEY IS IN MY ACCOUNT. NOW I CAN BUY THAT SPORTS CAR BACK! ONCE I MAKE *PAROLE,* ANYWAY . . .

SO, THAT MEANS YOU PROBABLY WANNA KNOW WHERE THE PROTOTYPE FOR THE SKELETON KEY IS HIDDEN . . .

GUESS WHAT—I'VE HAD IT WITH ME THE WHOLE TIME!

IT PAYS TO KNOW WHICH *GUARDS* TO BRIBE—AND TO HAVE THE *MONEY* FOR PAYOFFS, OF COURSE!

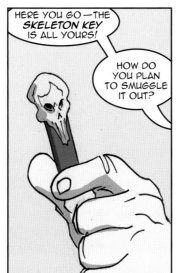

HERE YOU GO—THE *SKELETON KEY* IS ALL YOURS!

HOW DO YOU PLAN TO SMUGGLE IT OUT?

INSIDE MY *PROSTHETIC ARM*— NOT THAT ANYONE CAN TELL IT'S FAKE!

HURRY UP IN THERE! GUARDS ARE COMING.

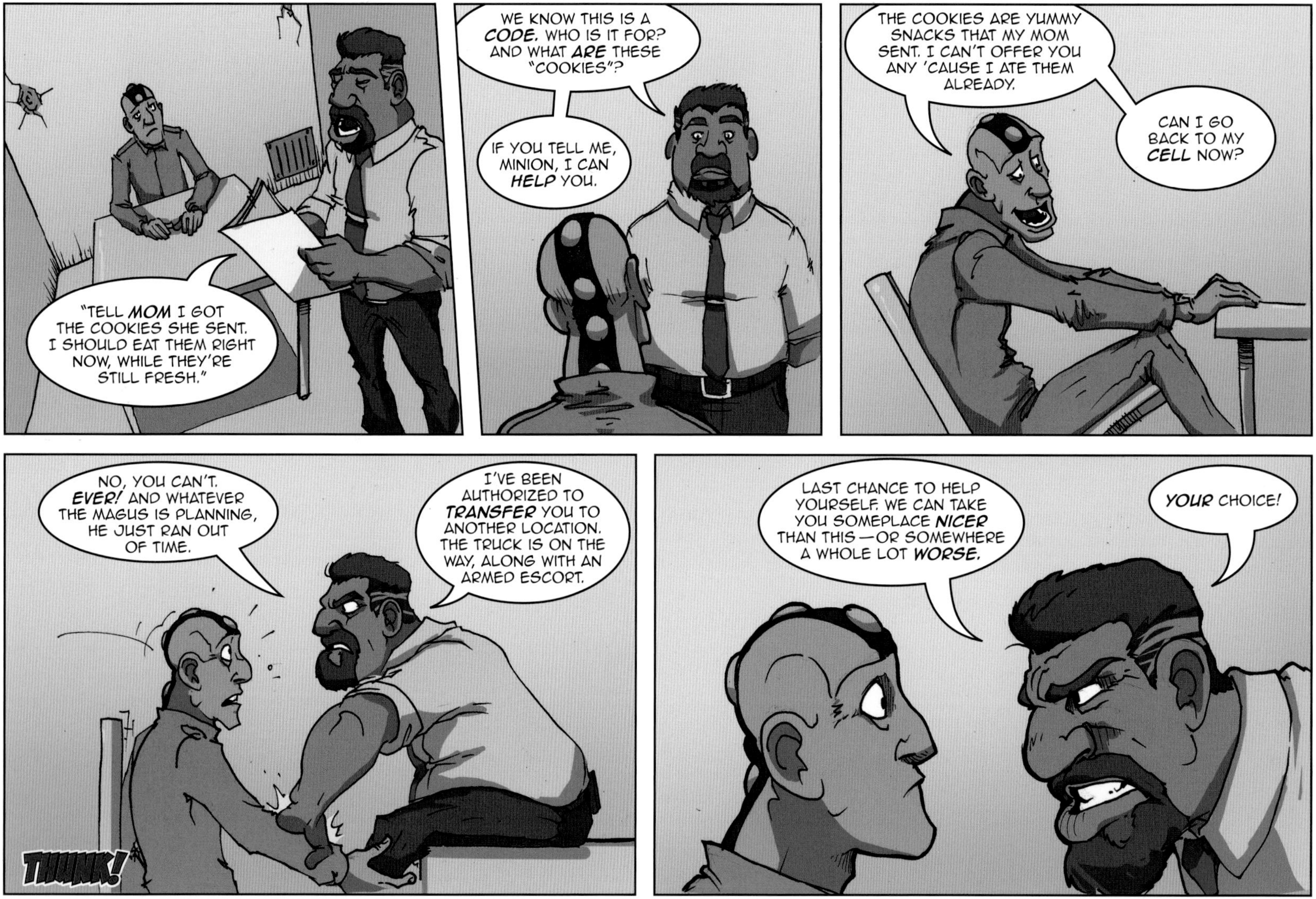
"TELL MOM I GOT THE COOKIES SHE SENT. I SHOULD EAT THEM RIGHT NOW, WHILE THEY'RE STILL FRESH."
WE KNOW THIS IS A CODE. WHO IS IT FOR? AND WHAT ARE THESE "COOKIES"?
IF YOU TELL ME, MINION, I CAN HELP YOU.
THE COOKIES ARE YUMMY SNACKS THAT MY MOM SENT. I CAN'T OFFER YOU ANY 'CAUSE I ATE THEM ALREADY.
CAN I GO BACK TO MY CELL NOW?
NO, YOU CAN'T. EVER! AND WHATEVER THE MAGUS IS PLANNING, HE JUST RAN OUT OF TIME.
I'VE BEEN AUTHORIZED TO TRANSFER YOU TO ANOTHER LOCATION. THE TRUCK IS ON THE WAY, ALONG WITH AN ARMED ESCORT.
THUNK!
LAST CHANCE TO HELP YOURSELF. WE CAN TAKE YOU SOMEPLACE NICER THAN THIS—OR SOMEWHERE A WHOLE LOT WORSE.
YOUR CHOICE!

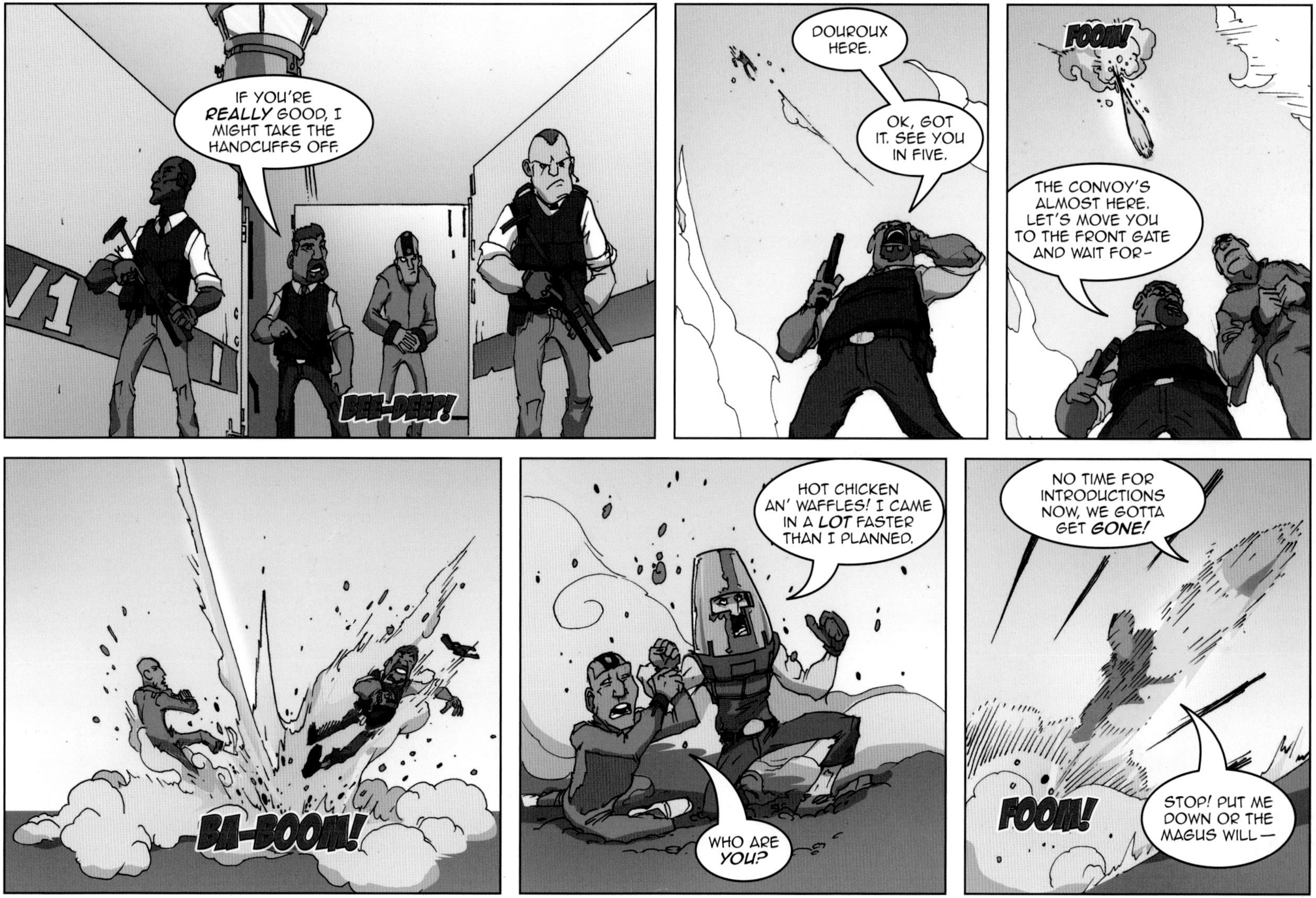
IF YOU'RE REALLY GOOD, I MIGHT TAKE THE HANDCUFFS OFF.
BEE-DEEP!
DOUROUX HERE.
OK, GOT IT. SEE YOU IN FIVE.
FOOM!
THE CONVOY'S ALMOST HERE. LET'S MOVE YOU TO THE FRONT GATE AND WAIT FOR-
BA-BOOM!
HOT CHICKEN AN' WAFFLES! I CAME IN A LOT FASTER THAN I PLANNED.
WHO ARE YOU?
NO TIME FOR INTRODUCTIONS NOW, WE GOTTA GET GONE!
FOOM!
STOP! PUT ME DOWN OR THE MAGUS WILL—

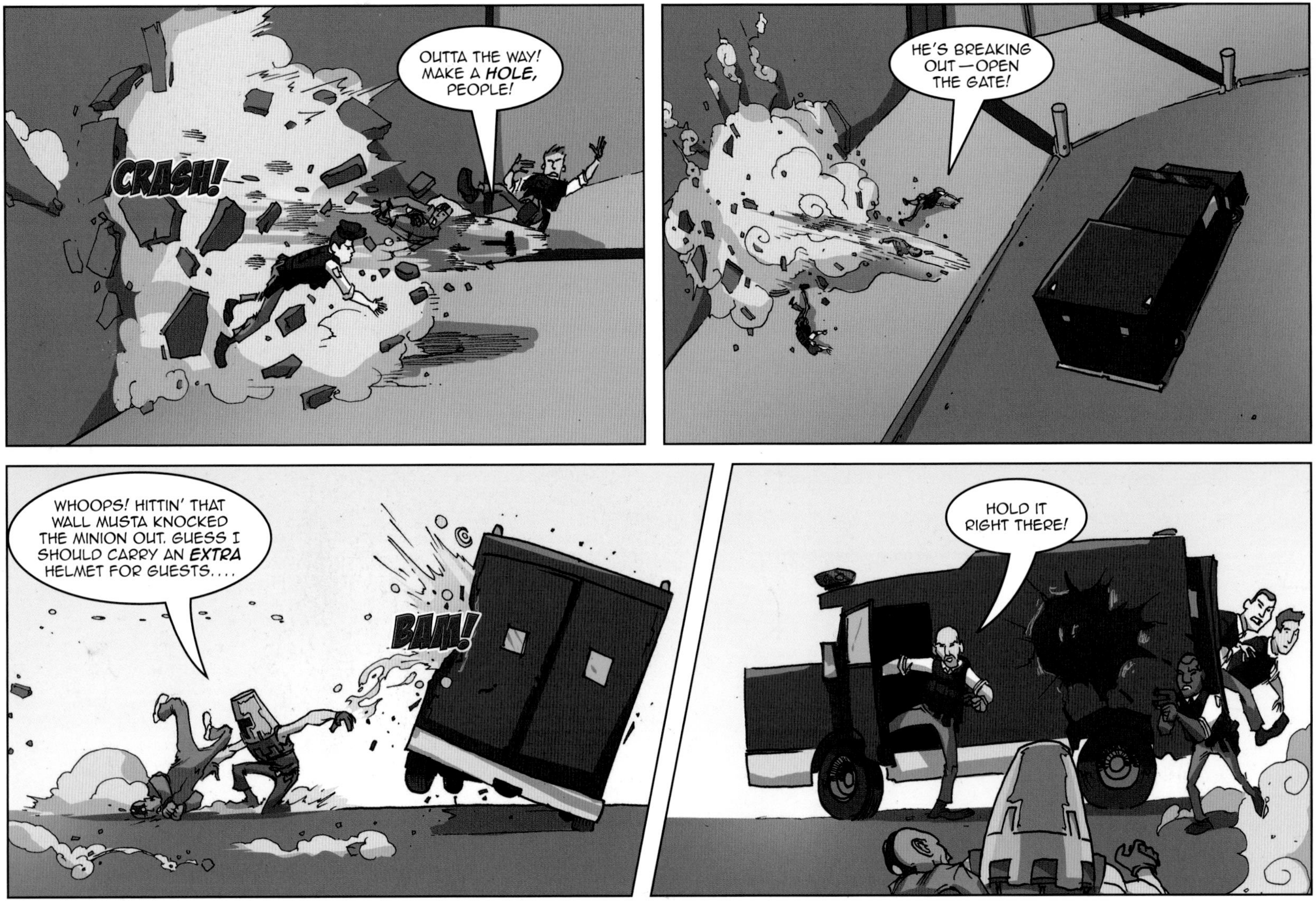
OUTTA THE WAY! MAKE A HOLE, PEOPLE!
CRASH!
HE'S BREAKING OUT—OPEN THE GATE!
WHOOPS! HITTIN' THAT WALL MUSTA KNOCKED THE MINION OUT. GUESS I SHOULD CARRY AN EXTRA HELMET FOR GUESTS....
BAM!
HOLD IT RIGHT THERE!

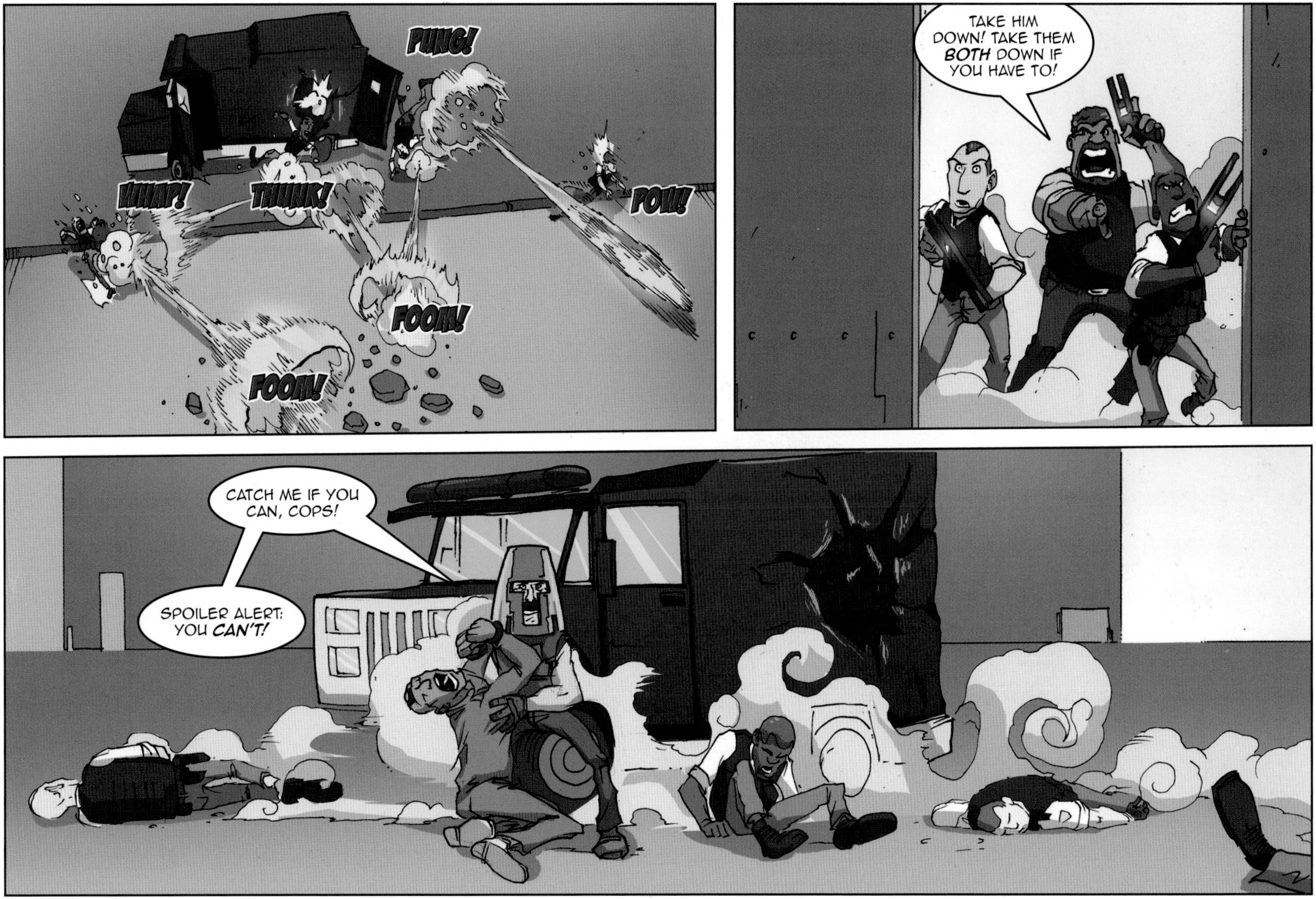
PUNG!
WHAP!
THUNK!
POW!
FOOM!
FOOM!
TAKE HIM DOWN! TAKE THEM *BOTH* DOWN IF YOU HAVE TO!
CATCH ME IF YOU CAN, COPS!
SPOILER ALERT: YOU *CAN'T!*

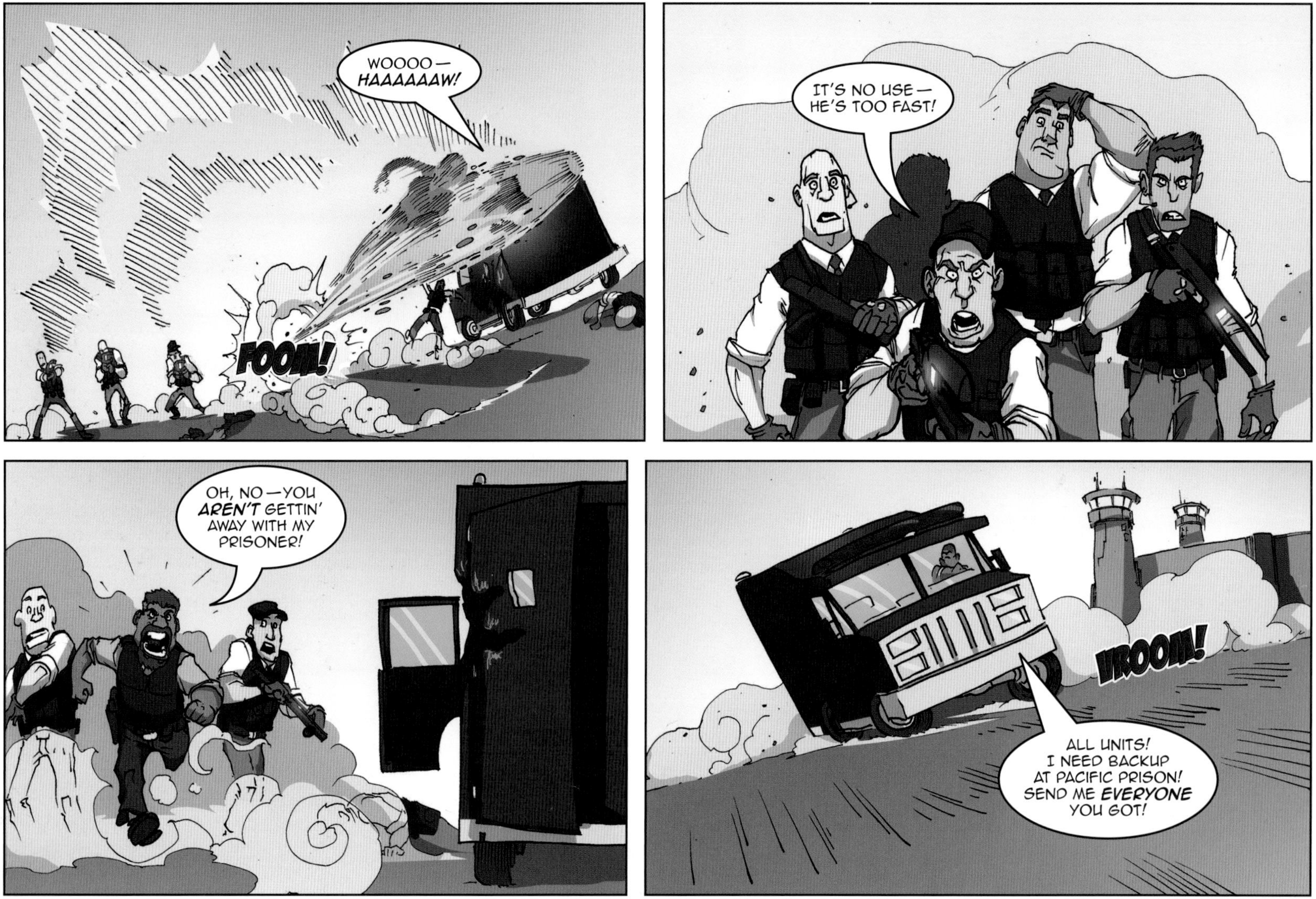
WOOOO—HAAAAAAW!
FOOM!
IT'S NO USE—HE'S TOO FAST!
OH, NO—YOU AREN'T GETTIN' AWAY WITH MY PRISONER!
VROOM!
ALL UNITS! I NEED BACKUP AT PACIFIC PRISON! SEND ME EVERYONE YOU GOT!

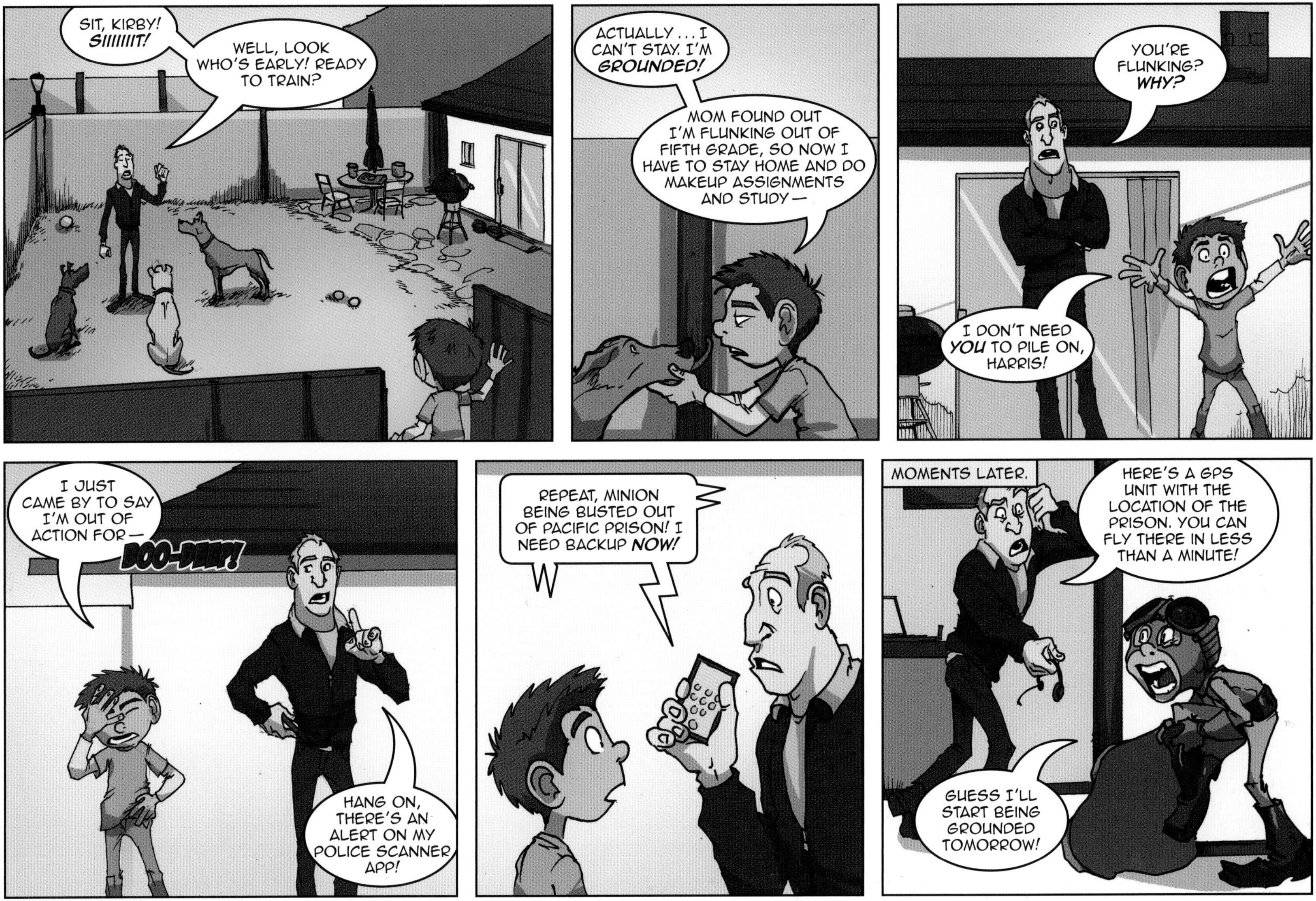

SIT, KIRBY! SIIIIIIT!
WELL, LOOK WHO'S EARLY! READY TO TRAIN?
ACTUALLY . . . I CAN'T STAY. I'M GROUNDED!
MOM FOUND OUT I'M FLUNKING OUT OF FIFTH GRADE, SO NOW I HAVE TO STAY HOME AND DO MAKEUP ASSIGNMENTS AND STUDY—
YOU'RE FLUNKING? WHY?
I DON'T NEED YOU TO PILE ON, HARRIS!
I JUST CAME BY TO SAY I'M OUT OF ACTION FOR—
BOO-DEEP!
HANG ON, THERE'S AN ALERT ON MY POLICE SCANNER APP!
REPEAT, MINION BEING BUSTED OUT OF PACIFIC PRISON! I NEED BACKUP NOW!
MOMENTS LATER.
HERE'S A GPS UNIT WITH THE LOCATION OF THE PRISON. YOU CAN FLY THERE IN LESS THAN A MINUTE!
GUESS I'LL START BEING GROUNDED TOMORROW!

IT FEELS SO GOOD TO BE SO UNSTOPPABLE! I AIN'T NEVER TAKIN' OFF THIS SUIT—
WHOOSH!
DANCIN' CRICKETS! WHO THE HECK ARE YOU GUYS?
SKRIIIIITCH!
WE'RE THE MAGUS'S STRIKE FORCE. YOU DON'T WANT US CRAWLING UP YOUR TAILPIPE!
WE'LL GIVE YOU EXACTLY ONE CHANCE TO HAND OVER THE PRISONER.
WE DON'T ASK TWICE!

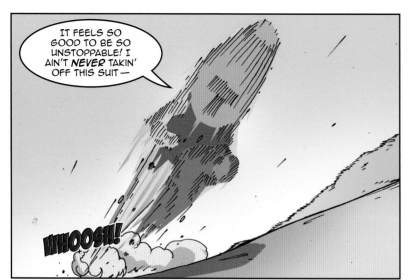

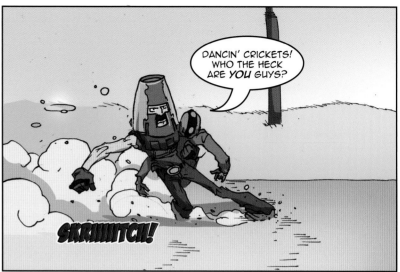

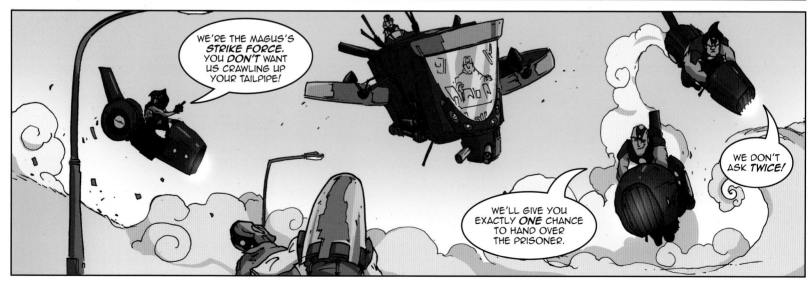

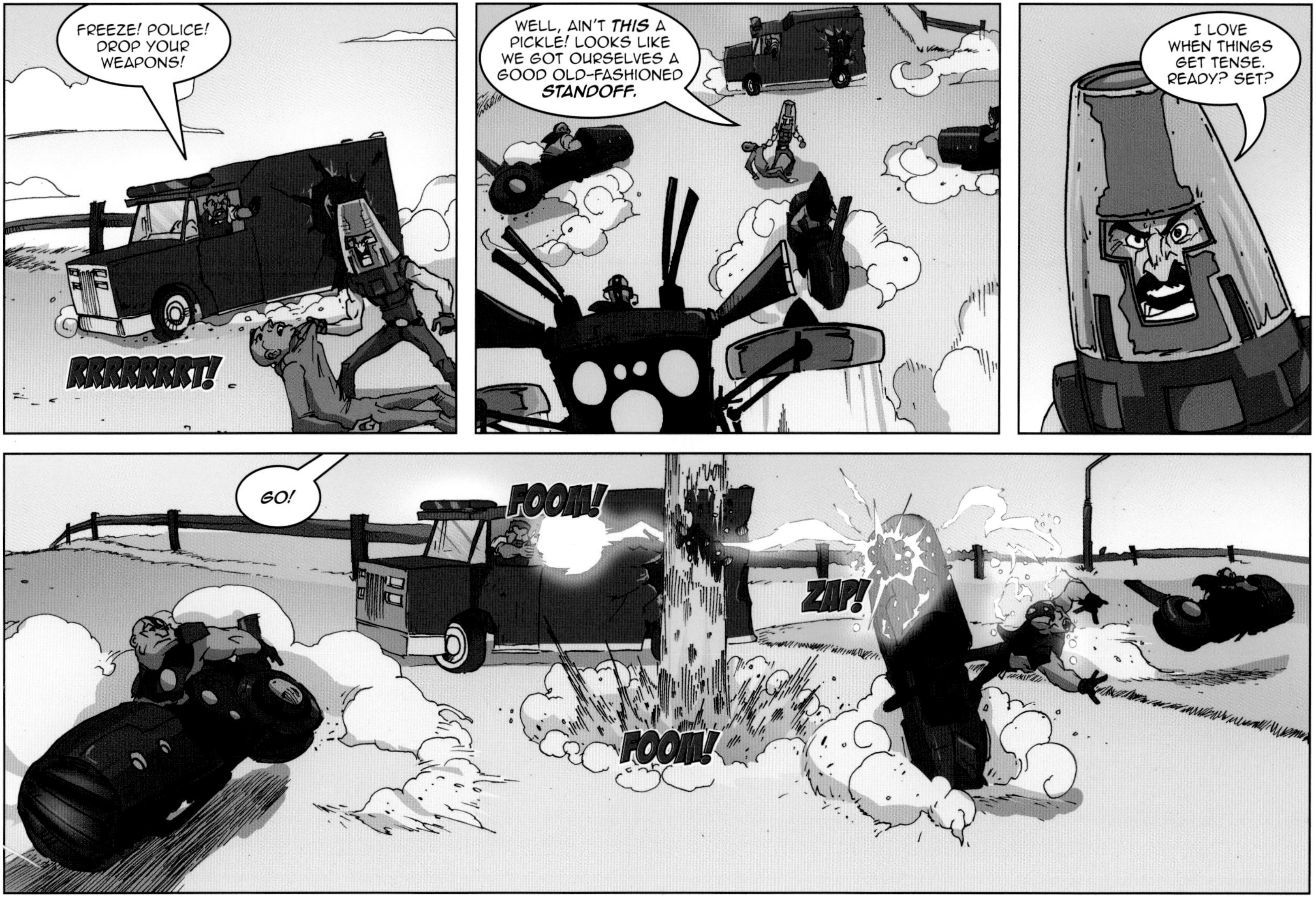
FREEZE! POLICE! DROP YOUR WEAPONS!
RRRRRRRT!
WELL, AIN'T *THIS* A PICKLE! LOOKS LIKE WE GOT OURSELVES A GOOD OLD-FASHIONED *STANDOFF.*
I LOVE WHEN THINGS GET TENSE. READY? SET?
GO!
FOOM!
ZAP!
FOOM!

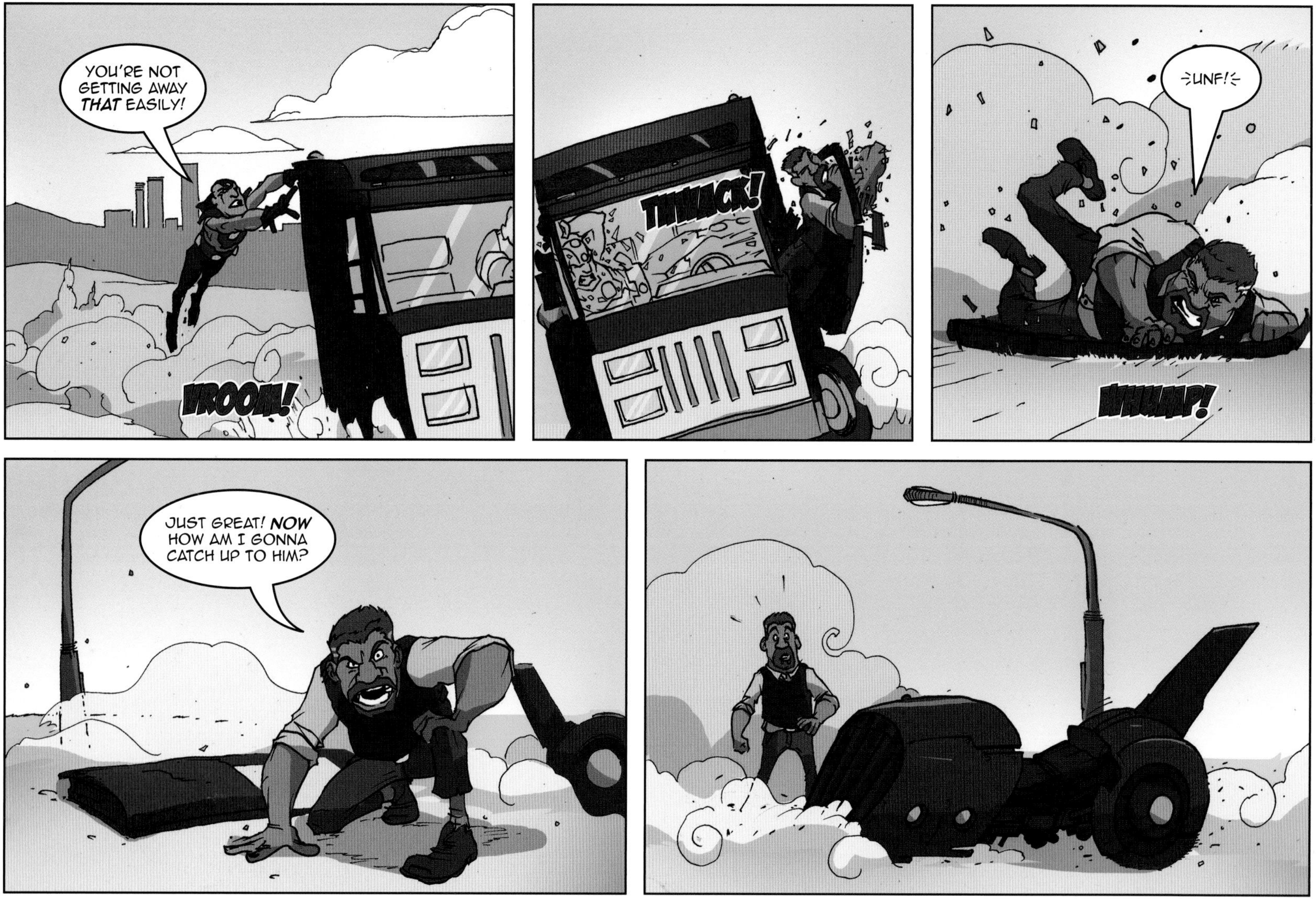
YOU'RE NOT GETTING AWAY *THAT* EASILY!
VROOM!
THWACK!
UNF!
WHUMP!
JUST GREAT! *NOW* HOW AM I GONNA CATCH UP TO HIM?

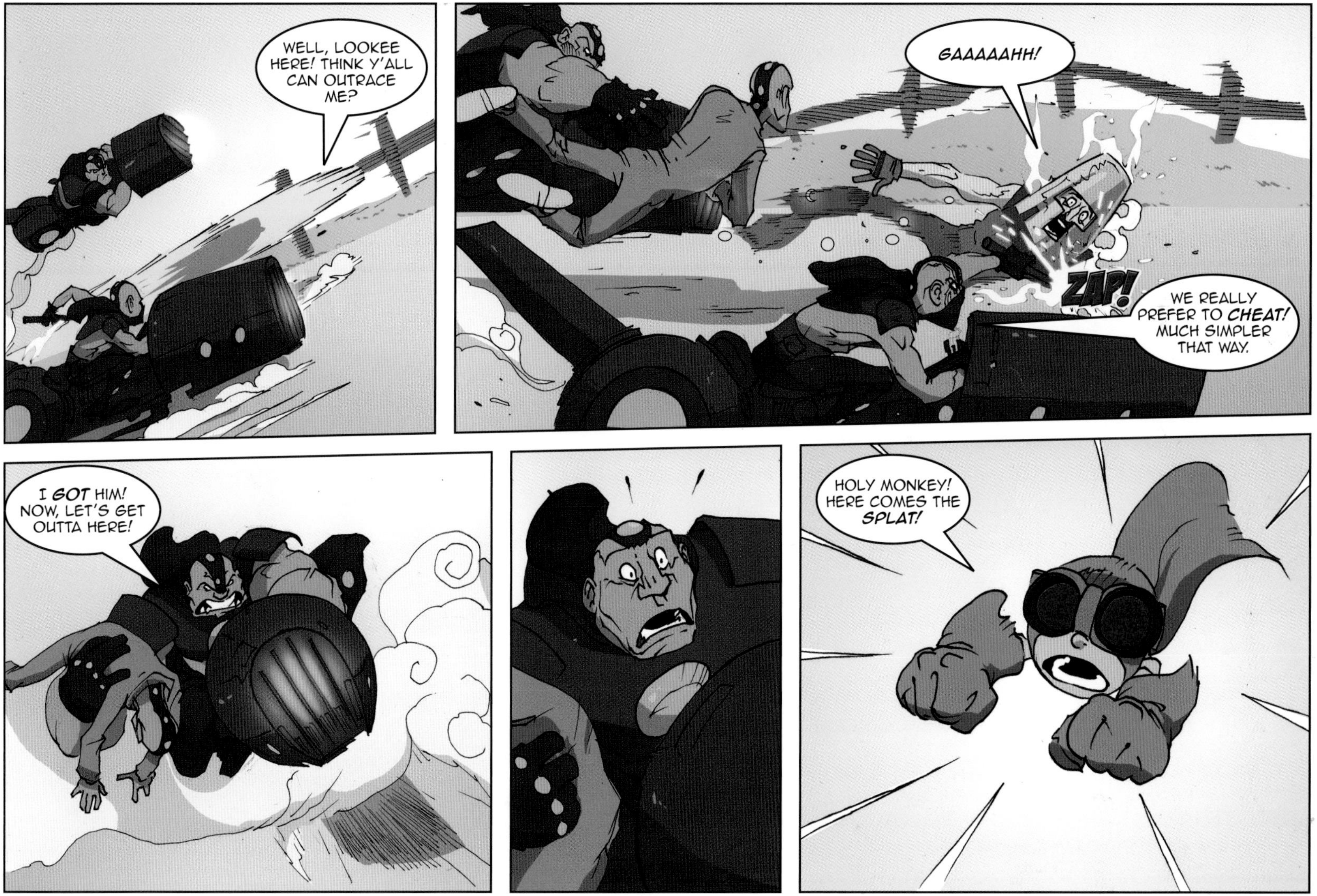

WELL, LOOKEE HERE! THINK Y'ALL CAN OUTRACE ME?
GAAAAAHH!
ZAP!
WE REALLY PREFER TO CHEAT! MUCH SIMPLER THAT WAY.
I GOT HIM! NOW, LET'S GET OUTTA HERE!
HOLY MONKEY! HERE COMES THE SPLAT!

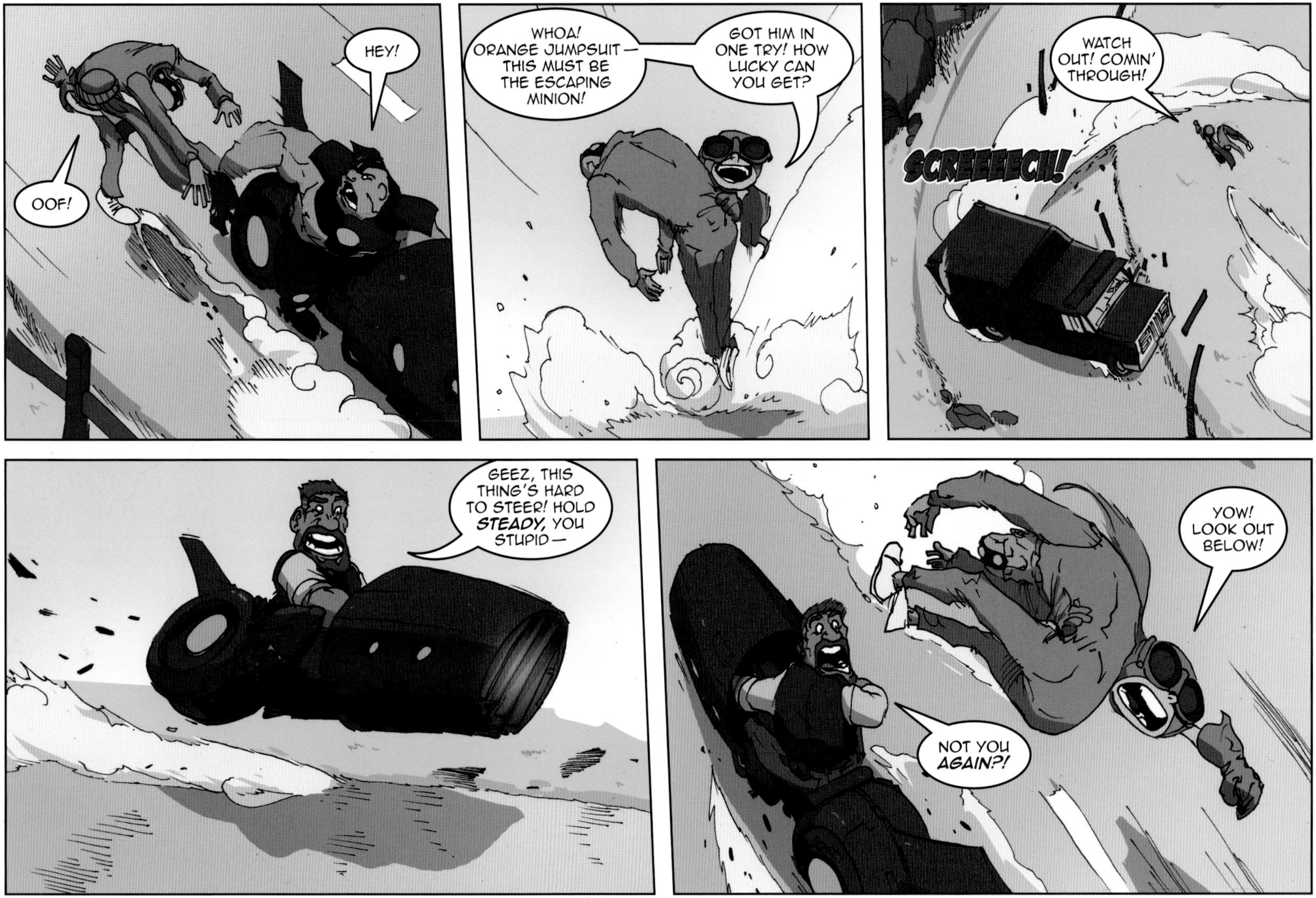
HEY!
OOF!
WHOA! ORANGE JUMPSUIT — THIS MUST BE THE ESCAPING MINION!
GOT HIM IN ONE TRY! HOW LUCKY CAN YOU GET?
WATCH OUT! COMIN' THROUGH!
SCREEEECH!
GEEZ, THIS THING'S HARD TO STEER! HOLD **STEADY,** YOU STUPID —
YOW! LOOK OUT BELOW!
NOT YOU **AGAIN?!**

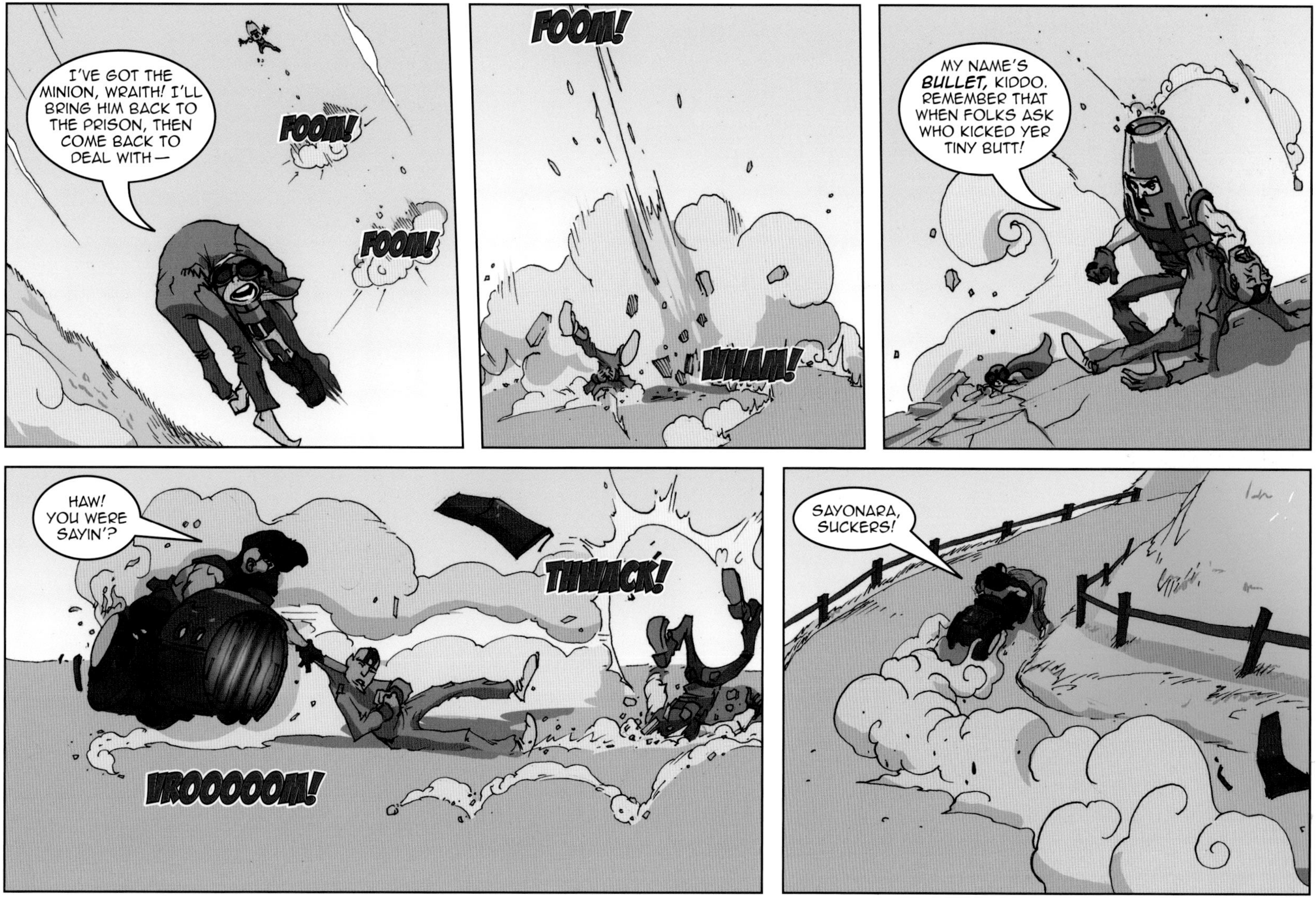
I'VE GOT THE MINION, WRAITH! I'LL BRING HIM BACK TO THE PRISON, THEN COME BACK TO DEAL WITH—
FOOM!
FOOM!
FOOM!
WHAM!
MY NAME'S **BULLET,** KIDDO. REMEMBER THAT WHEN FOLKS ASK WHO KICKED YER TINY BUTT!
HAW! YOU WERE SAYIN'?
THWACK!
VROOOOOOM!
SAYONARA, SUCKERS!

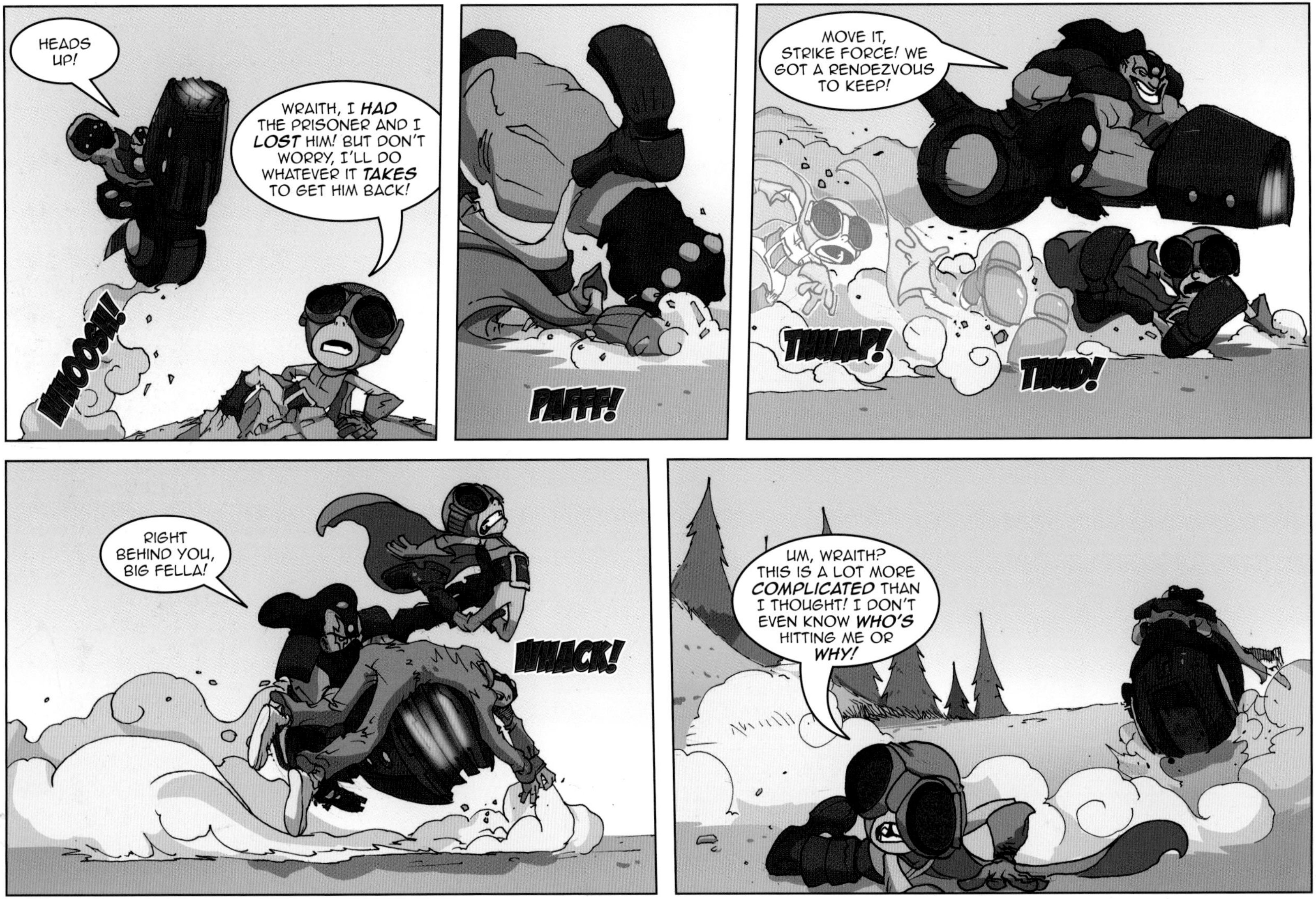
HEADS UP!
WRAITH, I HAD THE PRISONER AND I LOST HIM! BUT DON'T WORRY, I'LL DO WHATEVER IT TAKES TO GET HIM BACK!
WHOOSH!
PAFFF!
MOVE IT, STRIKE FORCE! WE GOT A RENDEZVOUS TO KEEP!
THUMP!
THUD!
RIGHT BEHIND YOU, BIG FELLA!
WHACK!
UM, WRAITH? THIS IS A LOT MORE COMPLICATED THAN I THOUGHT! I DON'T EVEN KNOW WHO'S HITTING ME OR WHY!

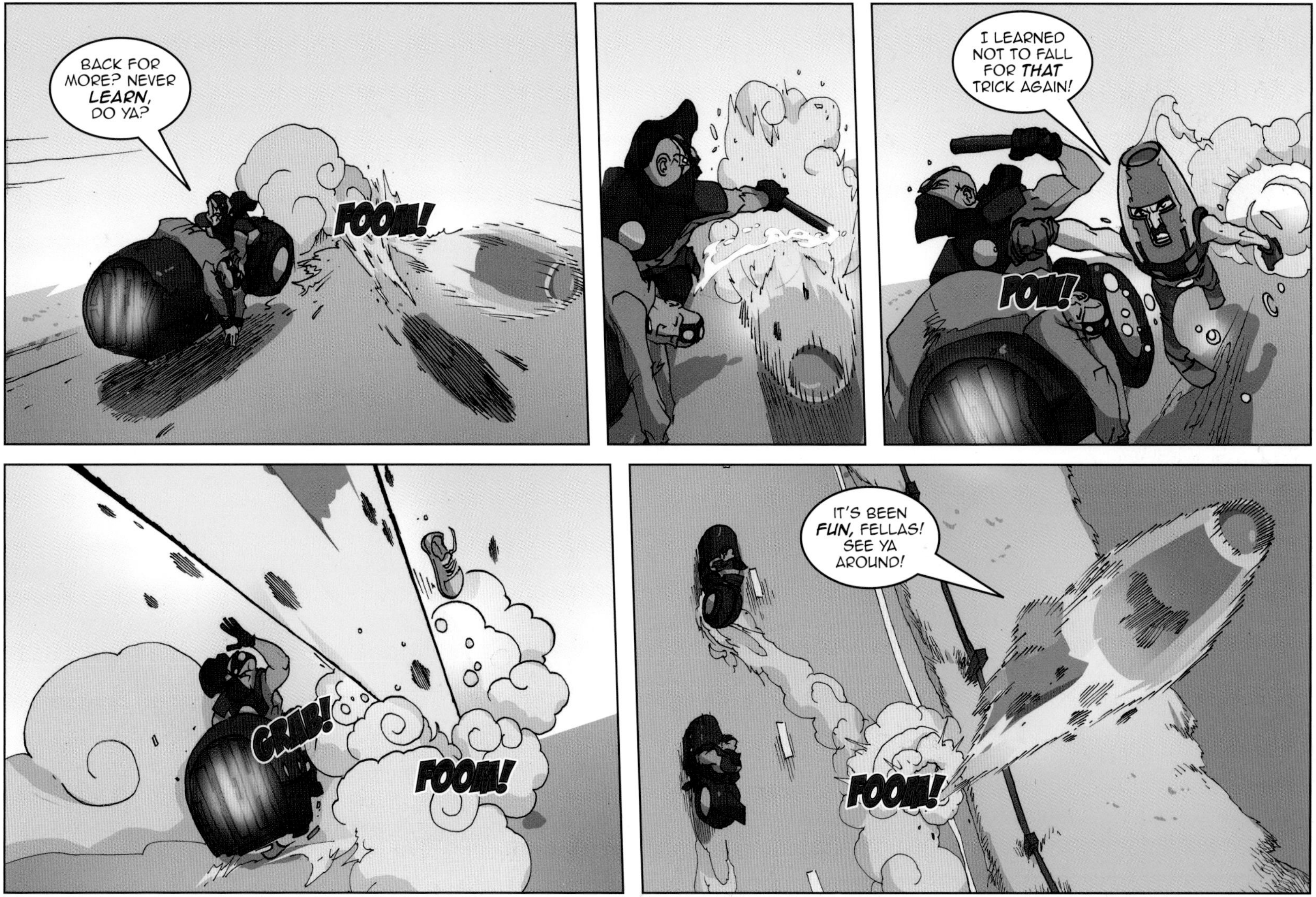
BACK FOR MORE? NEVER LEARN, DO YA?
FOOM!
I LEARNED NOT TO FALL FOR THAT TRICK AGAIN!
POW!
GRAB!
FOOM!
IT'S BEEN FUN, FELLAS! SEE YA AROUND!
FOOM!

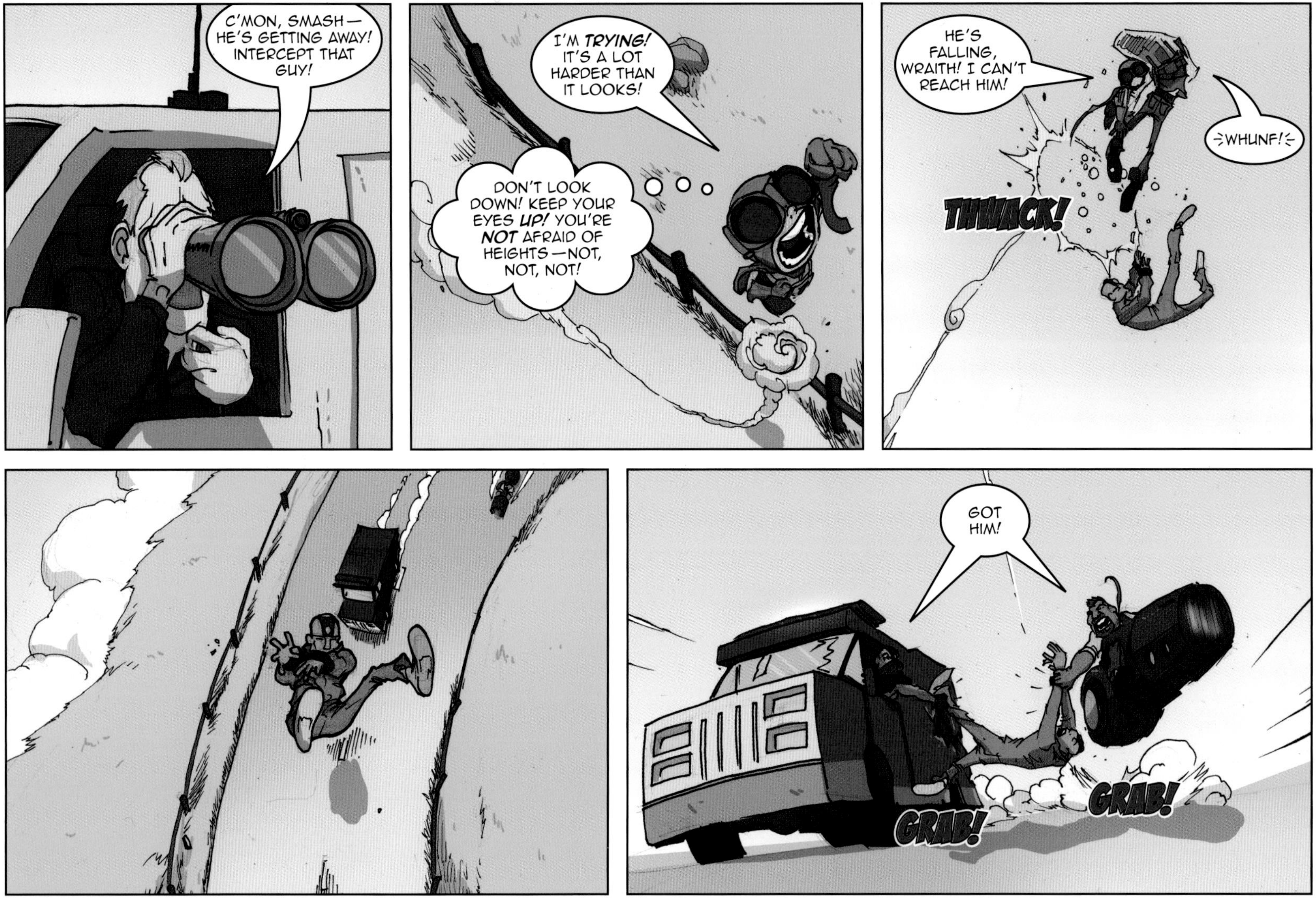
C'MON, SMASH— HE'S GETTING AWAY! INTERCEPT THAT GUY!
I'M TRYING! IT'S A LOT HARDER THAN IT LOOKS!
DON'T LOOK DOWN! KEEP YOUR EYES UP! YOU'RE NOT AFRAID OF HEIGHTS—NOT, NOT, NOT!
HE'S FALLING, WRAITH! I CAN'T REACH HIM!
WHUNF!
THWACK!
GOT HIM!
GRAB!
GRAB!

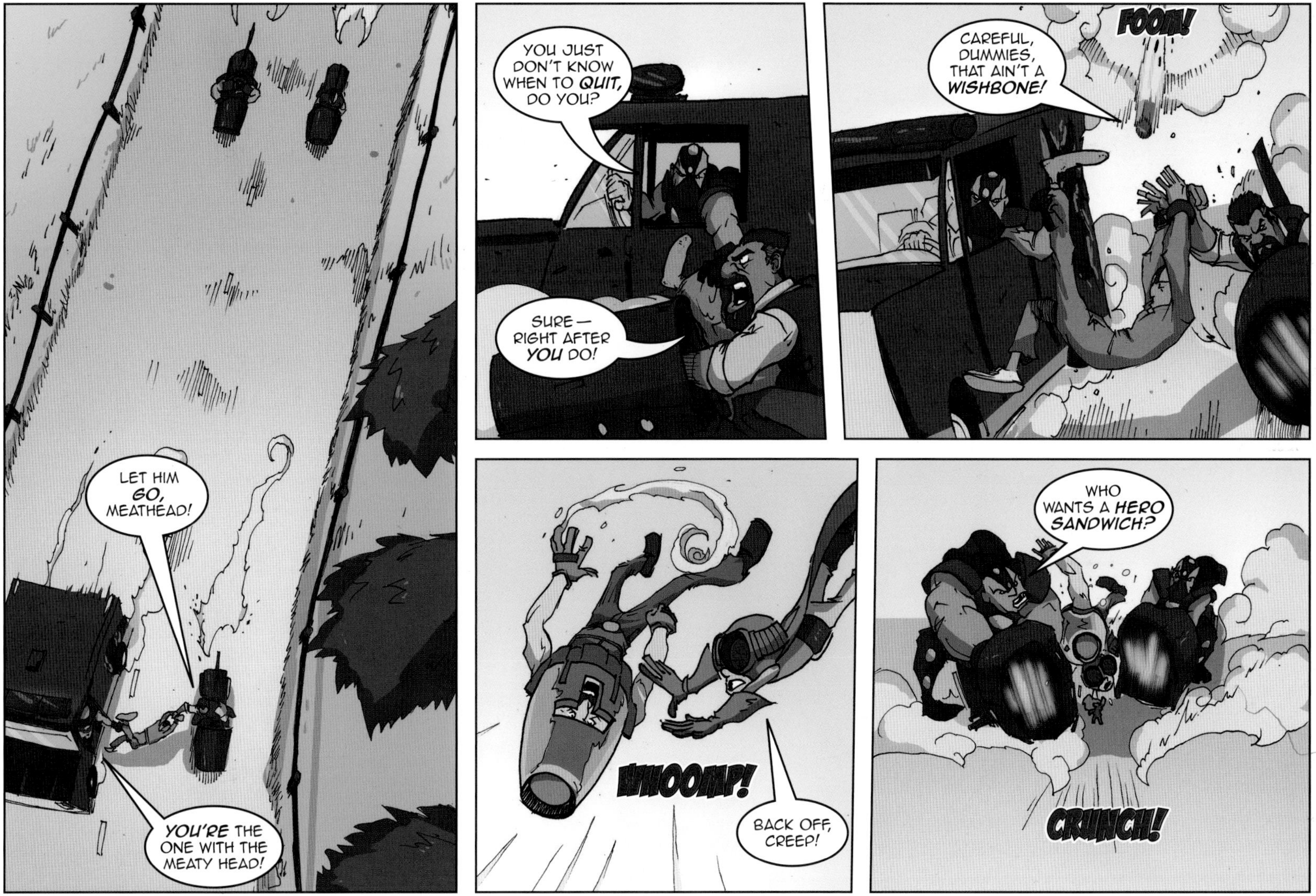
LET HIM GO, MEATHEAD!
YOU'RE THE ONE WITH THE MEATY HEAD!
YOU JUST DON'T KNOW WHEN TO QUIT, DO YOU?
SURE— RIGHT AFTER YOU DO!
FOOM!
CAREFUL, DUMMIES, THAT AIN'T A WISHBONE!
WHOOMP!
BACK OFF, CREEP!
WHO WANTS A HERO SANDWICH?
CRUNCH!

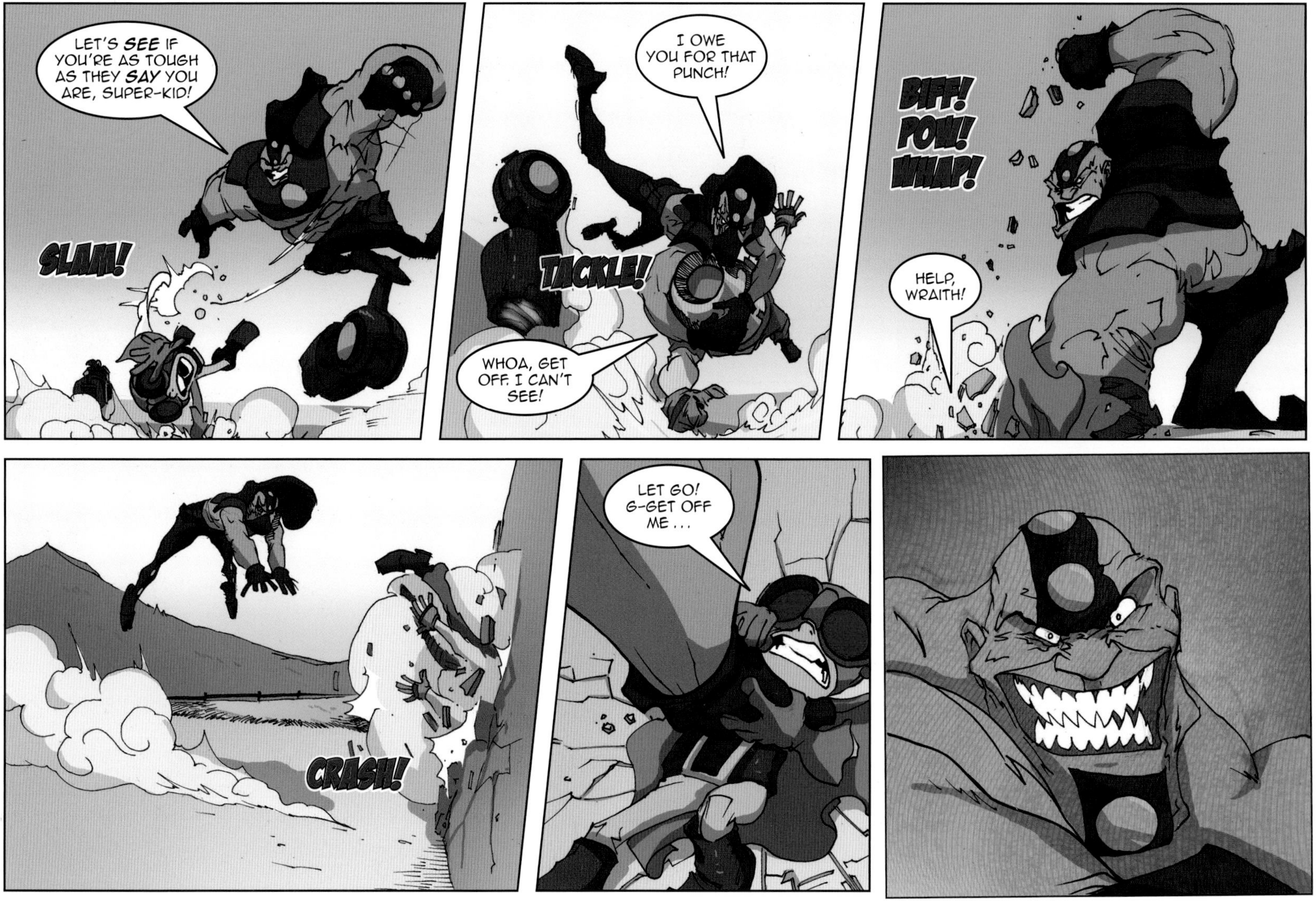
LET'S **SEE** IF YOU'RE AS TOUGH AS THEY **SAY** YOU ARE, SUPER-KID!
SLAM!
I OWE YOU FOR THAT PUNCH!
TACKLE!
WHOA, GET OFF. I CAN'T SEE!
BIFF! POW! WHAP!
HELP, WRAITH!
CRASH!
LET GO! G-GET OFF ME . . .

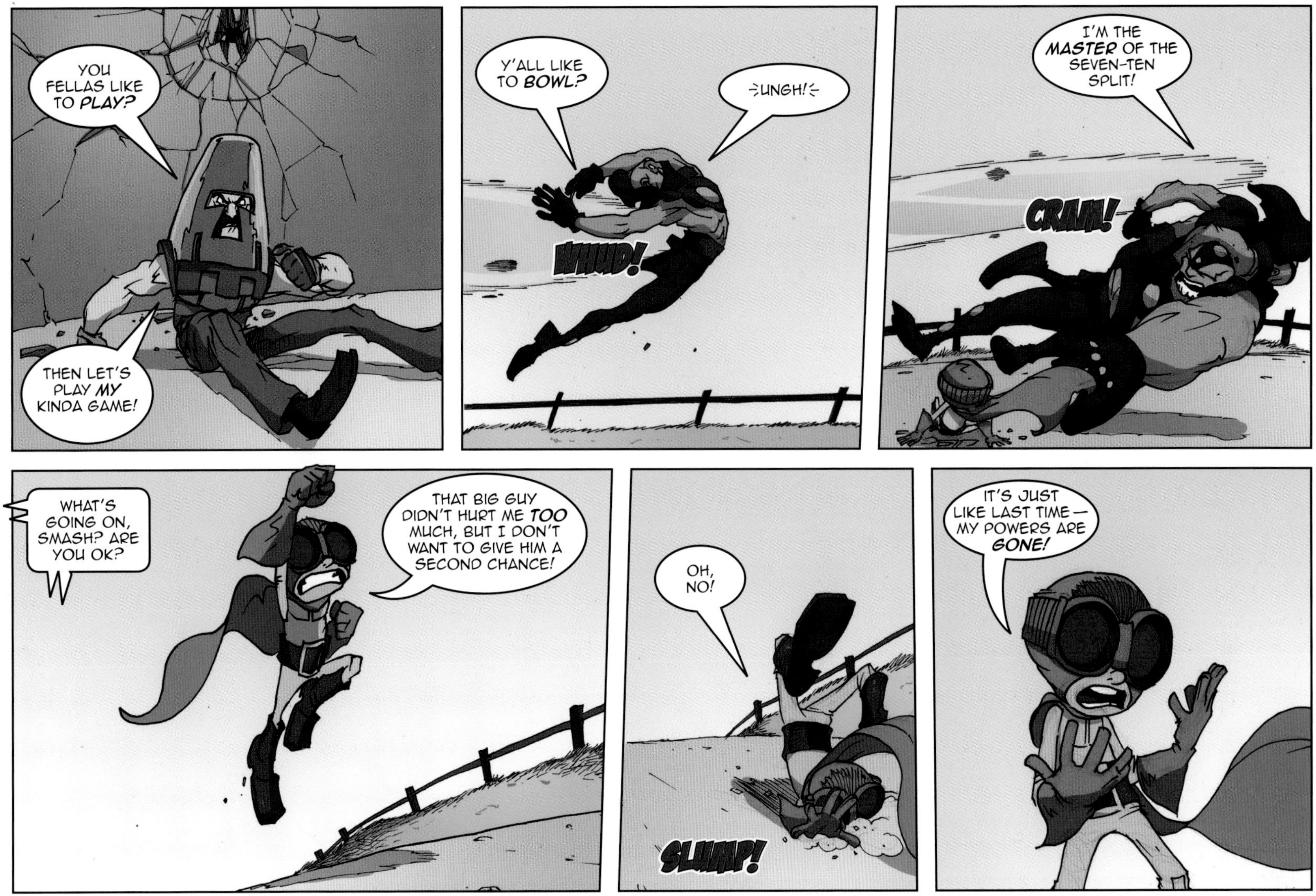
YOU FELLAS LIKE TO PLAY?
THEN LET'S PLAY MY KINDA GAME!
Y'ALL LIKE TO BOWL?
UNGH!
WHUD!
I'M THE MASTER OF THE SEVEN-TEN SPLIT!
CRAM!
WHAT'S GOING ON, SMASH? ARE YOU OK?
THAT BIG GUY DIDN'T HURT ME TOO MUCH, BUT I DON'T WANT TO GIVE HIM A SECOND CHANCE!
OH, NO!
SLUMP!
IT'S JUST LIKE LAST TIME — MY POWERS ARE GONE!

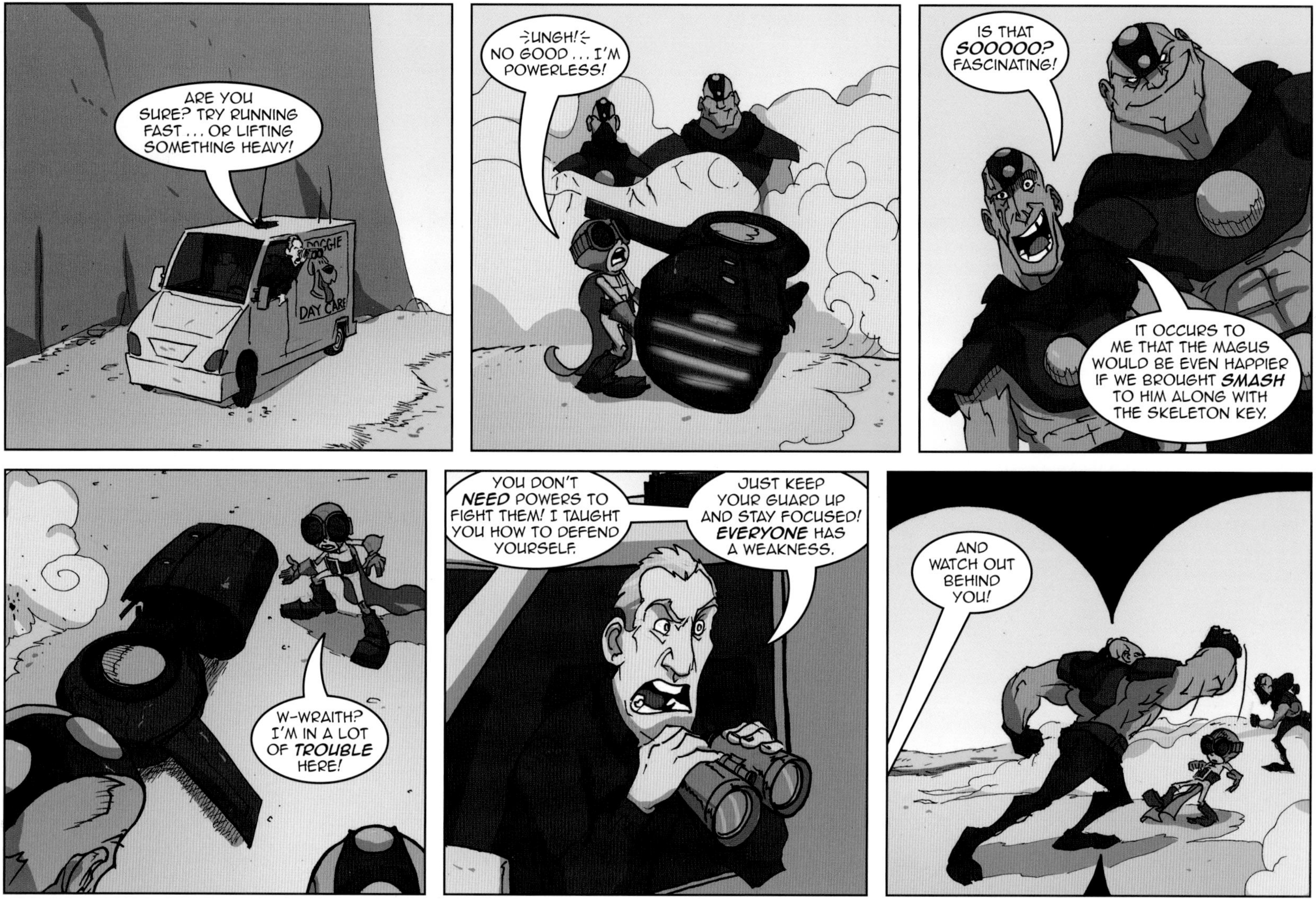
ARE YOU SURE? TRY RUNNING FAST . . . OR LIFTING SOMETHING HEAVY!
DOGGIE DAY CARE
UNGH! NO GOOD . . . I'M POWERLESS!
IS THAT SOOOOO? FASCINATING!
IT OCCURS TO ME THAT THE MAGUS WOULD BE EVEN HAPPIER IF WE BROUGHT SMASH TO HIM ALONG WITH THE SKELETON KEY.
W-WRAITH? I'M IN A LOT OF TROUBLE HERE!
YOU DON'T NEED POWERS TO FIGHT THEM! I TAUGHT YOU HOW TO DEFEND YOURSELF.
JUST KEEP YOUR GUARD UP AND STAY FOCUSED! EVERYONE HAS A WEAKNESS.
AND WATCH OUT BEHIND YOU!

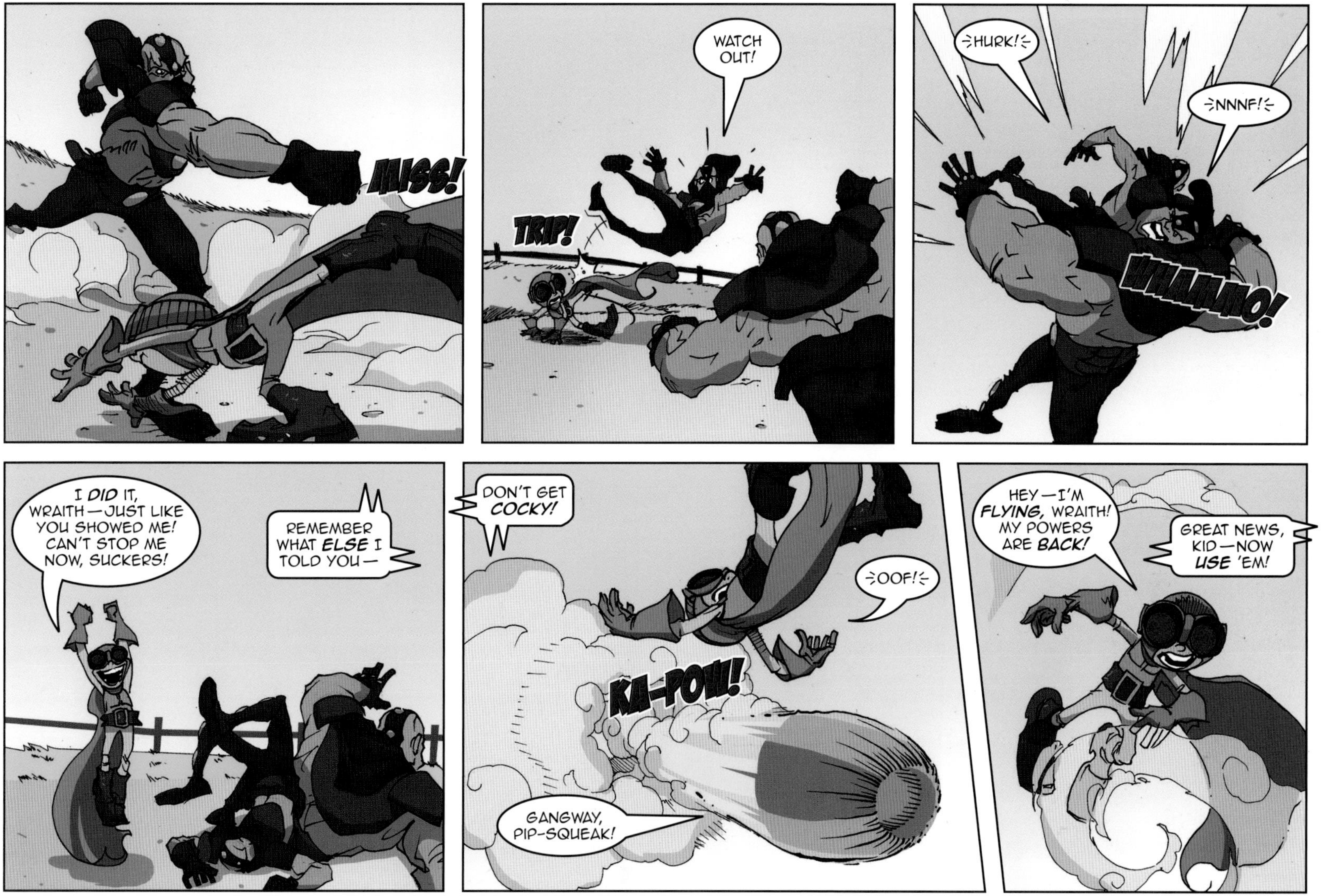
MISS!
TRIP!
WATCH OUT!
HURK!
NNNF!
WHAMMO!
I DID IT, WRAITH—JUST LIKE YOU SHOWED ME! CAN'T STOP ME NOW, SUCKERS!
REMEMBER WHAT ELSE I TOLD YOU—
DON'T GET COCKY!
OOF!
KA-POW!
GANGWAY, PIP-SQUEAK!
HEY—I'M FLYING, WRAITH! MY POWERS ARE BACK!
GREAT NEWS, KID—NOW USE 'EM!

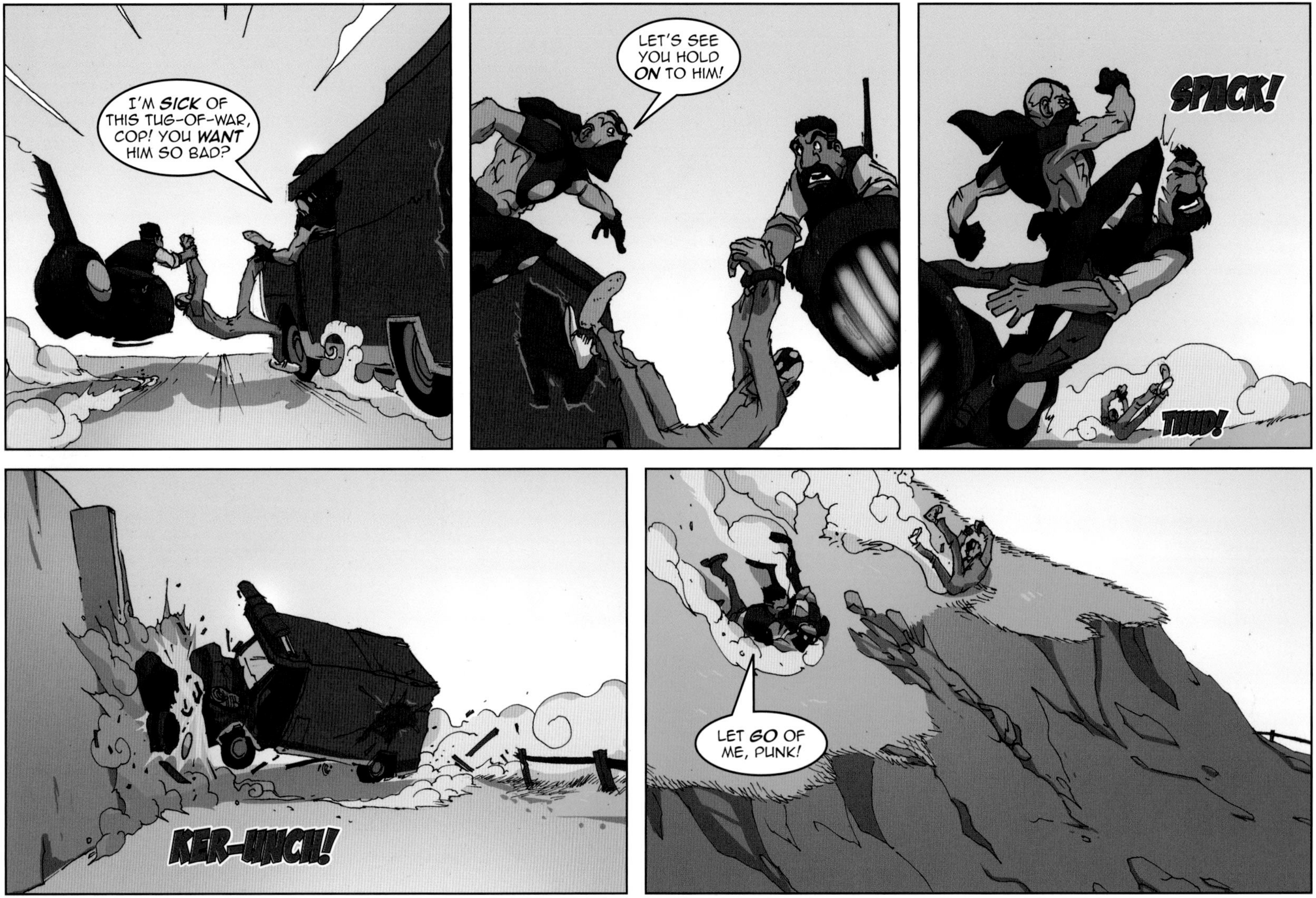
I'M SICK OF THIS TUG-OF-WAR, COP! YOU WANT HIM SO BAD?
LET'S SEE YOU HOLD ON TO HIM!
SPACK!
THUD!
KER-UNCH!
LET GO OF ME, PUNK!

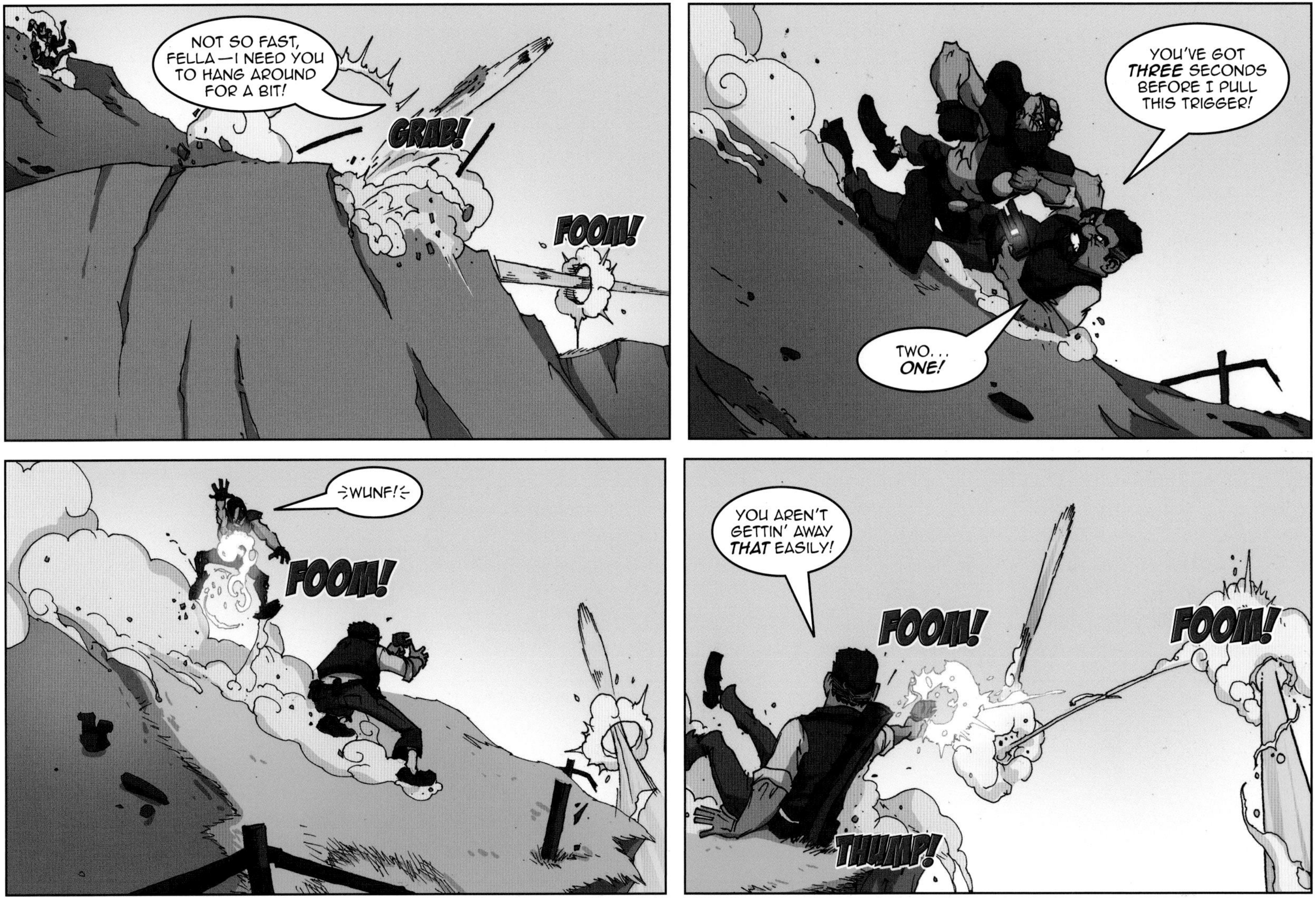
NOT SO FAST, FELLA—I NEED YOU TO HANG AROUND FOR A BIT!
GRAB!
FOOM!
YOU'VE GOT THREE SECONDS BEFORE I PULL THIS TRIGGER!
TWO. . . ONE!
WUNF!
FOOM!
YOU AREN'T GETTIN' AWAY THAT EASILY!
FOOM!
FOOM!
THUMP!

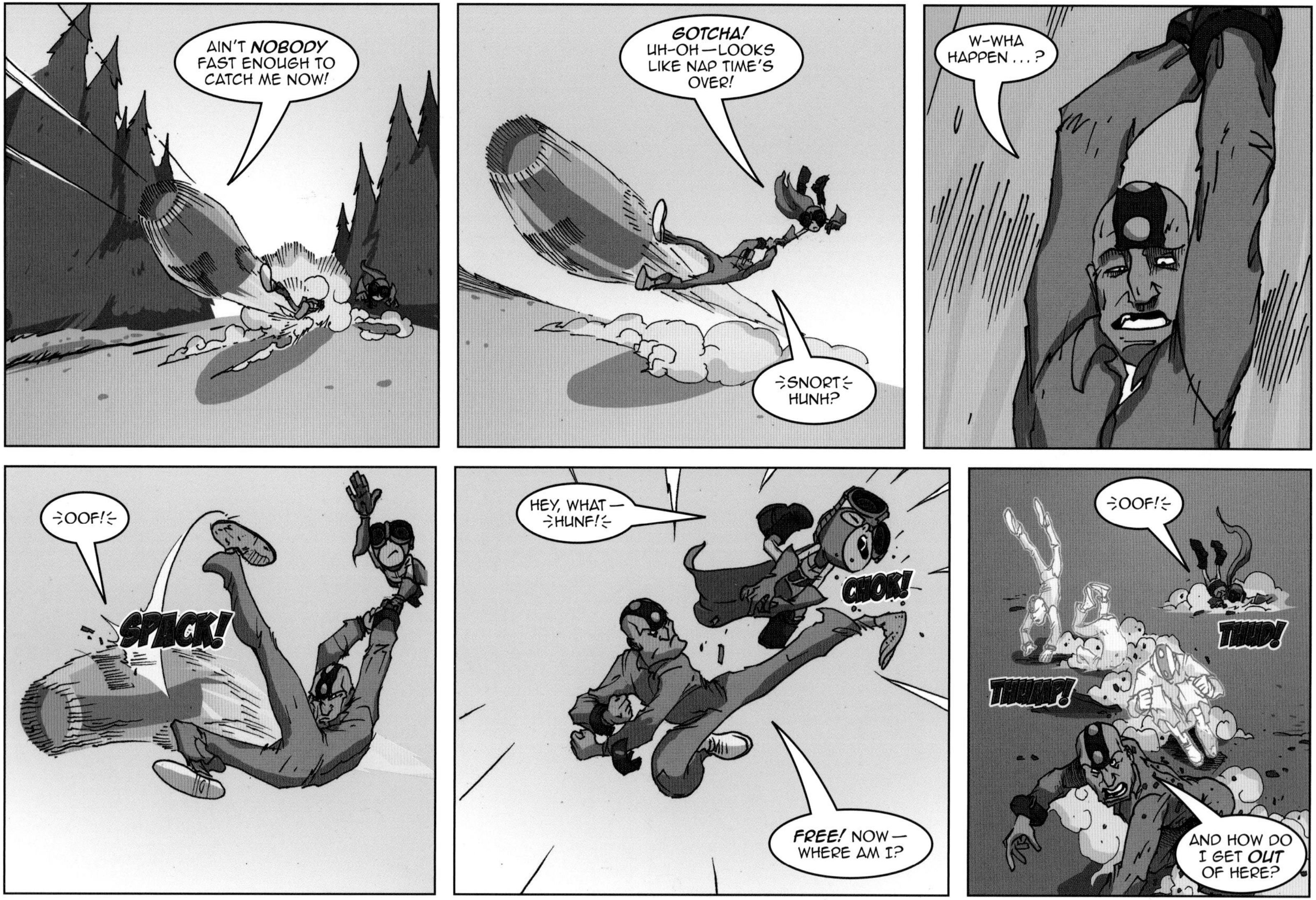
AIN'T NOBODY FAST ENOUGH TO CATCH ME NOW!
GOTCHA! UH-OH—LOOKS LIKE NAP TIME'S OVER!
SNORT HUNH?
W-WHA HAPPEN . . . ?
OOF!
SPACK!
HEY, WHAT— HUNF!
CHOK!
FREE! NOW— WHERE AM I?
OOF!
THUD!
THUMP!
AND HOW DO I GET OUT OF HERE?

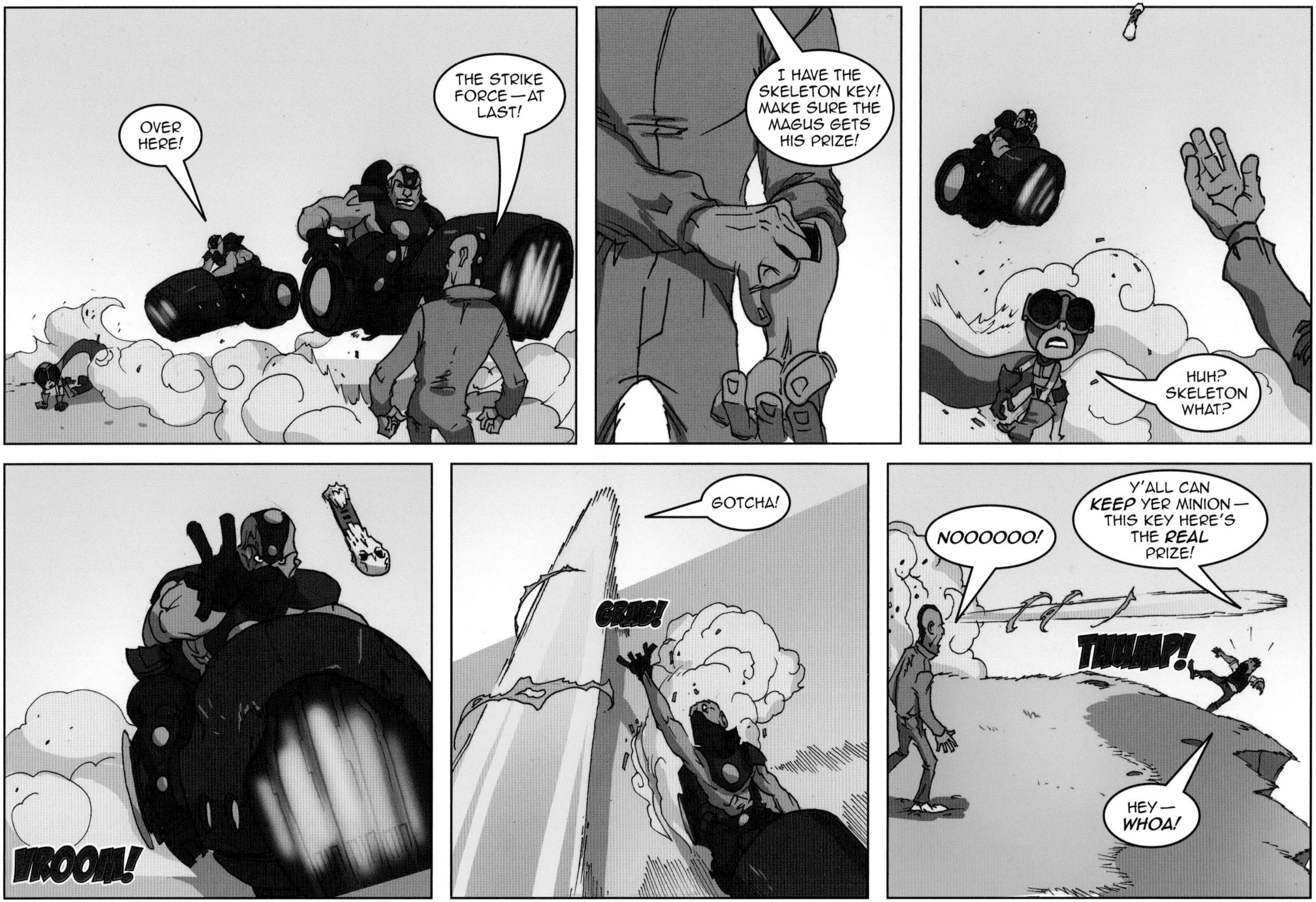
OVER HERE!
THE STRIKE FORCE—AT LAST!
I HAVE THE SKELETON KEY! MAKE SURE THE MAGUS GETS HIS PRIZE!
HUH? SKELETON WHAT?
VROOM!
GOTCHA!
GRAB!
NOOOOOO!
Y'ALL CAN KEEP YER MINION—THIS KEY HERE'S THE REAL PRIZE!
THUMP!
HEY—WHOA!

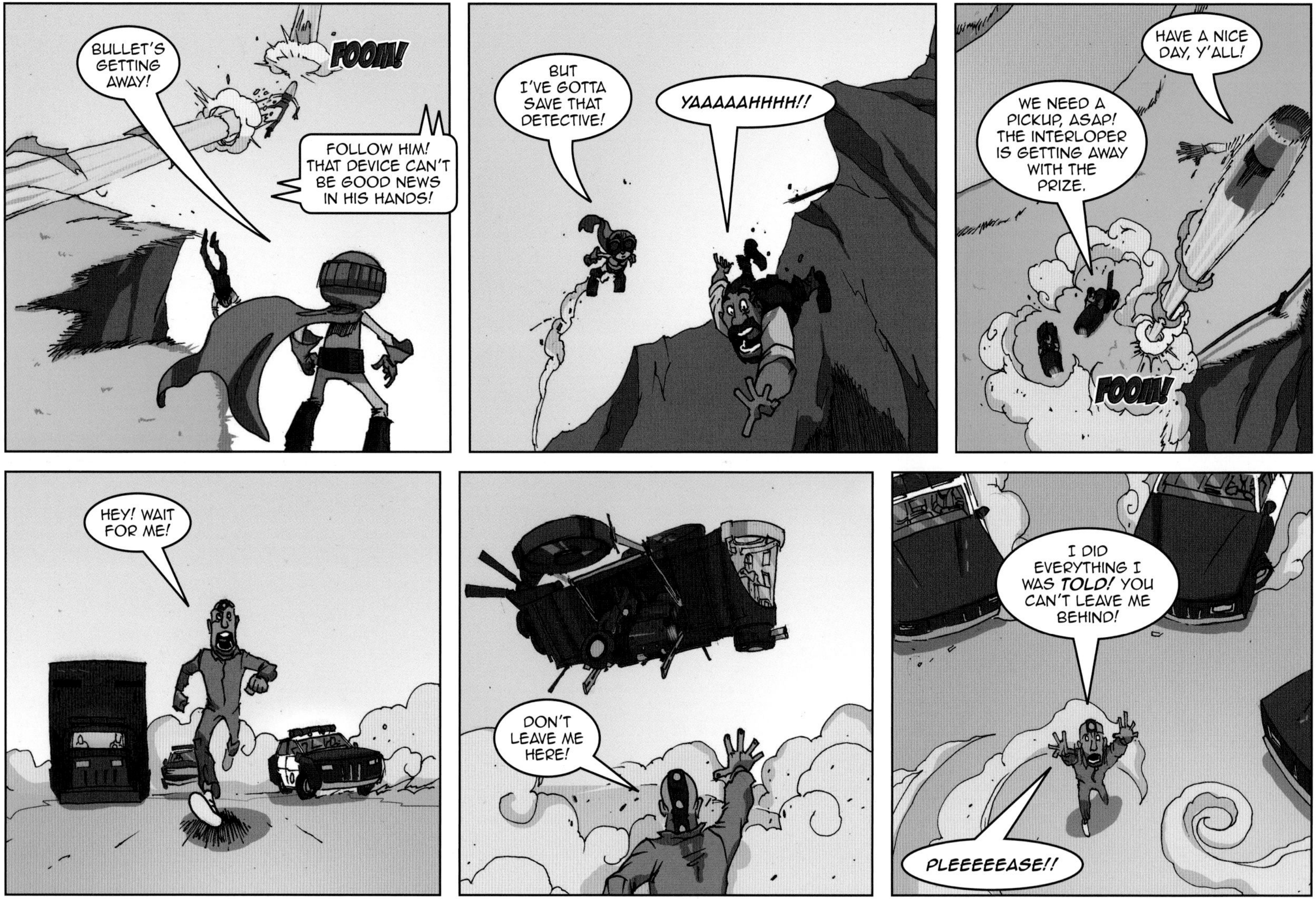
BULLET'S GETTING AWAY!
FOOM!
FOLLOW HIM! THAT DEVICE CAN'T BE GOOD NEWS IN HIS HANDS!
BUT I'VE GOTTA SAVE THAT DETECTIVE!
YAAAAAHHHH!!
HAVE A NICE DAY, Y'ALL!
WE NEED A PICKUP, ASAP! THE INTERLOPER IS GETTING AWAY WITH THE PRIZE.
FOOM!
HEY! WAIT FOR ME!
DON'T LEAVE ME HERE!
I DID EVERYTHING I WAS *TOLD!* YOU CAN'T LEAVE ME BEHIND!
PLEEEEEASE!!

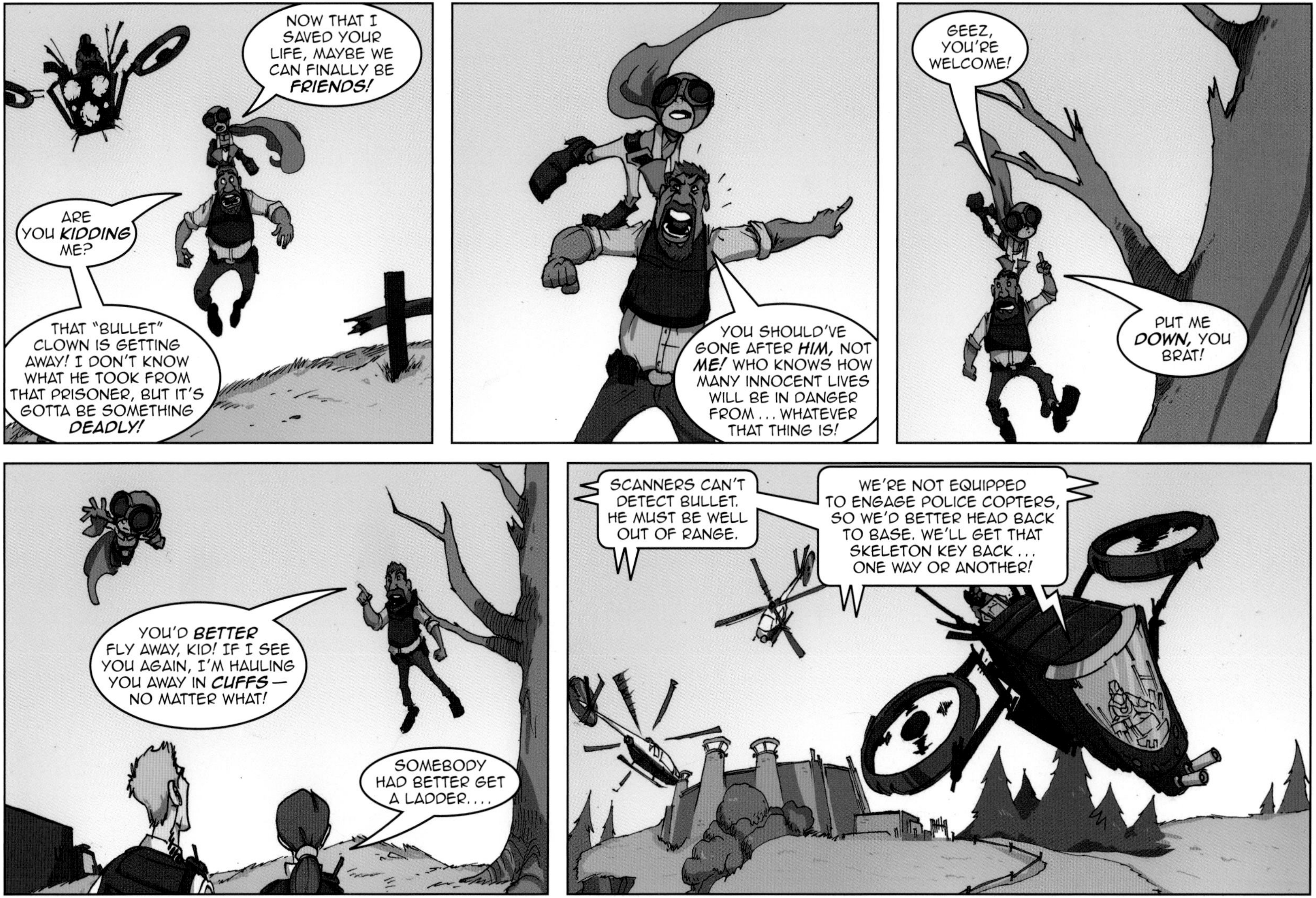
NOW THAT I SAVED YOUR LIFE, MAYBE WE CAN FINALLY BE FRIENDS!
ARE YOU KIDDING ME?
THAT "BULLET" CLOWN IS GETTING AWAY! I DON'T KNOW WHAT HE TOOK FROM THAT PRISONER, BUT IT'S GOTTA BE SOMETHING DEADLY!
YOU SHOULD'VE GONE AFTER HIM, NOT ME! WHO KNOWS HOW MANY INNOCENT LIVES WILL BE IN DANGER FROM . . . WHATEVER THAT THING IS!
GEEZ, YOU'RE WELCOME!
PUT ME DOWN, YOU BRAT!
YOU'D BETTER FLY AWAY, KID! IF I SEE YOU AGAIN, I'M HAULING YOU AWAY IN CUFFS — NO MATTER WHAT!
SOMEBODY HAD BETTER GET A LADDER. . . .
SCANNERS CAN'T DETECT BULLET. HE MUST BE WELL OUT OF RANGE.
WE'RE NOT EQUIPPED TO ENGAGE POLICE COPTERS, SO WE'D BETTER HEAD BACK TO BASE. WE'LL GET THAT SKELETON KEY BACK . . . ONE WAY OR ANOTHER!

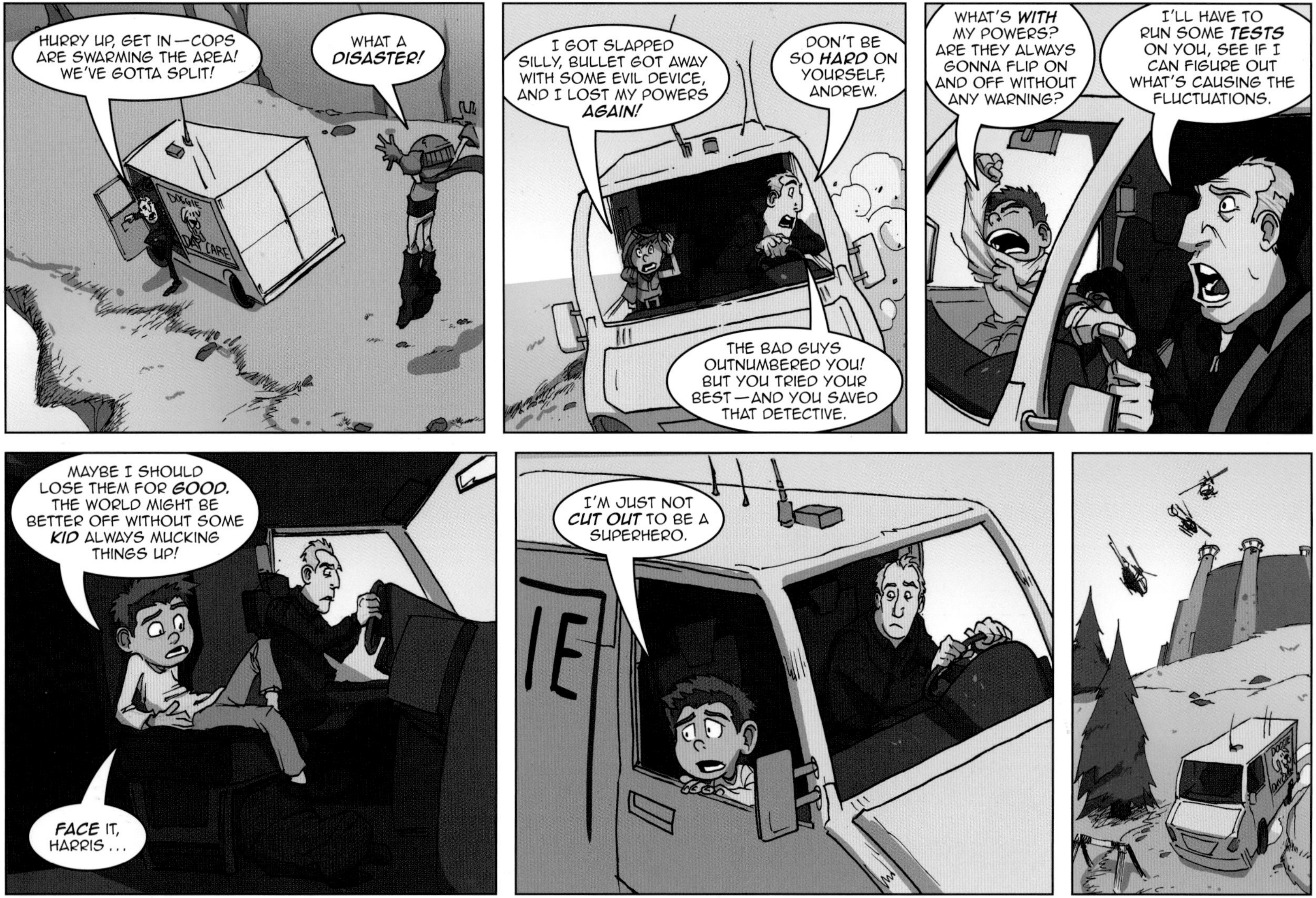
HURRY UP, GET IN—COPS ARE SWARMING THE AREA! WE'VE GOTTA SPLIT!
WHAT A *DISASTER!*
I GOT SLAPPED SILLY, BULLET GOT AWAY WITH SOME EVIL DEVICE, AND I LOST MY POWERS *AGAIN!*
DON'T BE SO *HARD* ON YOURSELF, ANDREW.
THE BAD GUYS OUTNUMBERED YOU! BUT YOU TRIED YOUR BEST—AND YOU SAVED THAT DETECTIVE.
WHAT'S *WITH* MY POWERS? ARE THEY ALWAYS GONNA FLIP ON AND OFF WITHOUT ANY WARNING?
I'LL HAVE TO RUN SOME *TESTS* ON YOU, SEE IF I CAN FIGURE OUT WHAT'S CAUSING THE FLUCTUATIONS.
MAYBE I SHOULD LOSE THEM FOR *GOOD.* THE WORLD MIGHT BE BETTER OFF WITHOUT SOME *KID* ALWAYS MUCKING THINGS UP!
FACE IT, HARRIS . . .
I'M JUST NOT *CUT OUT* TO BE A SUPERHERO.

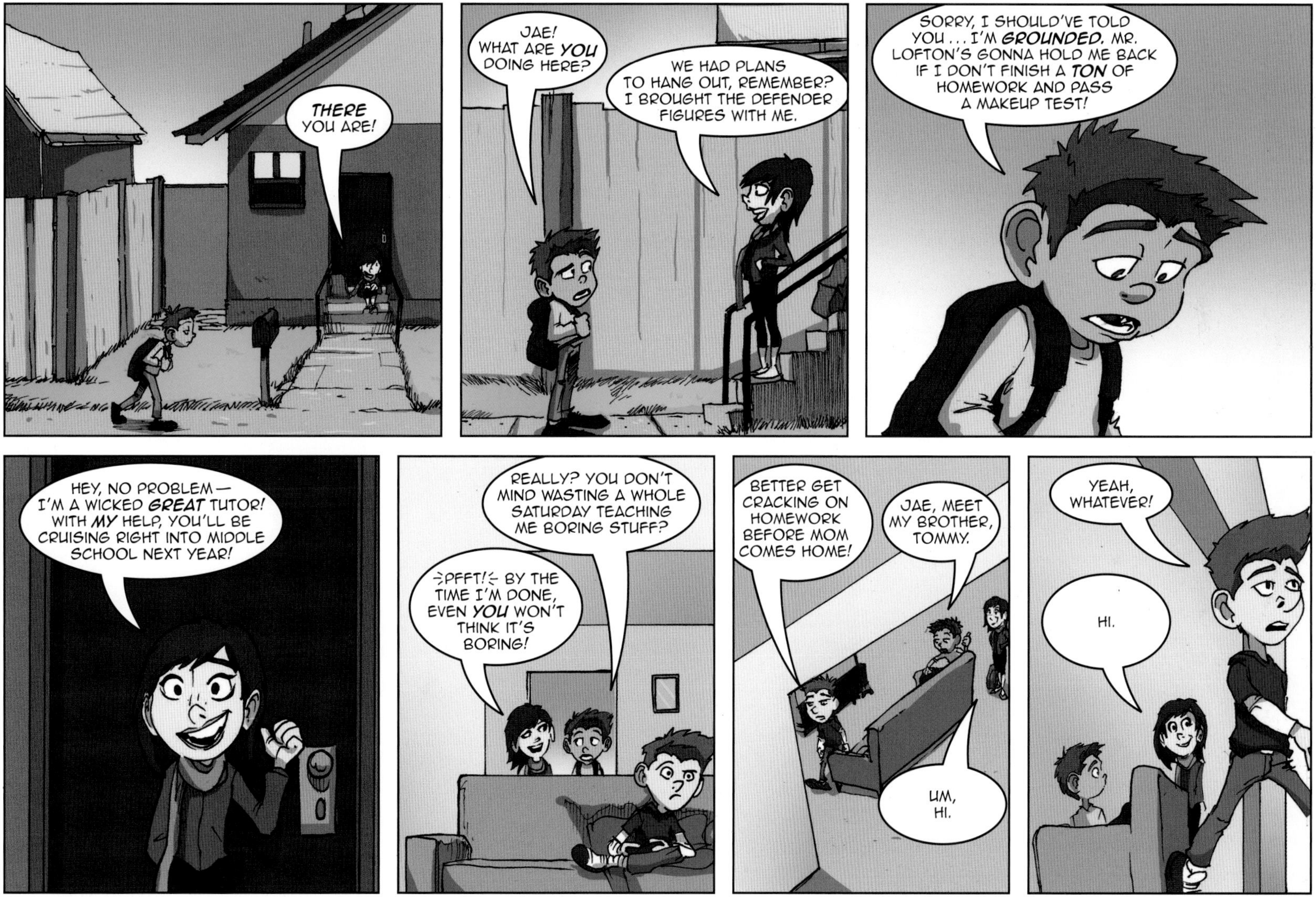
THERE YOU ARE!
JAE! WHAT ARE YOU DOING HERE?
WE HAD PLANS TO HANG OUT, REMEMBER? I BROUGHT THE DEFENDER FIGURES WITH ME.
SORRY, I SHOULD'VE TOLD YOU . . . I'M GROUNDED. MR. LOFTON'S GONNA HOLD ME BACK IF I DON'T FINISH A TON OF HOMEWORK AND PASS A MAKEUP TEST!
HEY, NO PROBLEM— I'M A WICKED GREAT TUTOR! WITH MY HELP, YOU'LL BE CRUISING RIGHT INTO MIDDLE SCHOOL NEXT YEAR!
REALLY? YOU DON'T MIND WASTING A WHOLE SATURDAY TEACHING ME BORING STUFF?
PFFT! BY THE TIME I'M DONE, EVEN YOU WON'T THINK IT'S BORING!
BETTER GET CRACKING ON HOMEWORK BEFORE MOM COMES HOME!
JAE, MEET MY BROTHER, TOMMY.
UM, HI.
YEAH, WHATEVER!
HI.

THE *CITADEL*. LATER.

BLAST IT TO HADES!

BAM!

WHEN I GET MY HANDS ON THIS "BULLET," I'LL *PULL* HIM APART—LIMB BY LIMB—AND HANG EACH PIECE ON MY WALL!

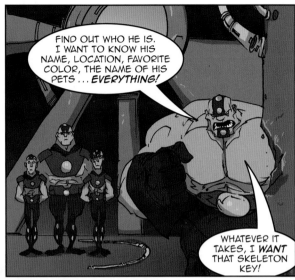

FIND OUT WHO HE IS. I WANT TO KNOW HIS NAME, LOCATION, FAVORITE COLOR, THE NAME OF HIS PETS ... *EVERYTHING!*

WHATEVER IT TAKES, I *WANT* THAT SKELETON KEY!

SIR? YOU HAVE AN INCOMING CALL.

THE CALLER CLAIMS IT'S "SUPER-URGENT."

WHO DARES TO ...? *YOU!*

HOWDY, MAGUS! MY NAME'S *BULLET*— AND I GOT AN OFFER Y'ALL CAN'T REFUSE!

SOON.

YOU HAVE AN INCOMING CALL FROM ZEKE HUSTON.

WHAT'S BEEN KEEPING YOU, MR. HUSTON? YOU WERE DUE BACK RIGHT AFTER THE BREAKOUT.

CHANGE OF PLANS, DOC....

TURNS OUT THE MINION HAD THAT SKELETON KEY ON HIM THE WHOLE TIME. AN' NOW *I* GOT IT!

I'M WILLING TO LET Y'ALL HAVE IT ... FOR THE RIGHT PRICE.

I'M GONNA HOLD ME AN *AUCTION!* HIGHEST BIDDER GETS THE SKELETON KEY.

AGAINST *WHOM* WOULD I BE BIDDING?

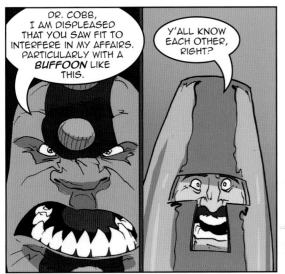

DR. COBB, I AM DISPLEASED THAT YOU SAW FIT TO INTERFERE IN MY AFFAIRS. PARTICULARLY WITH A *BUFFOON* LIKE THIS.

Y'ALL KNOW EACH OTHER, RIGHT?

YOU'RE MAKING AN UNWISE DECISION, BULLET.

YEAH, YEAH! Y'ALL ARE JUST *FULL* OF THREATS, AIN'T YA?

YOU BOTH GOT *ONE WEEK* TO MAKE YOUR FINAL BIDS. WHEN I CALL BACK, WINNER TAKES ALL!

THINK *LOTS* OF ZEROES!

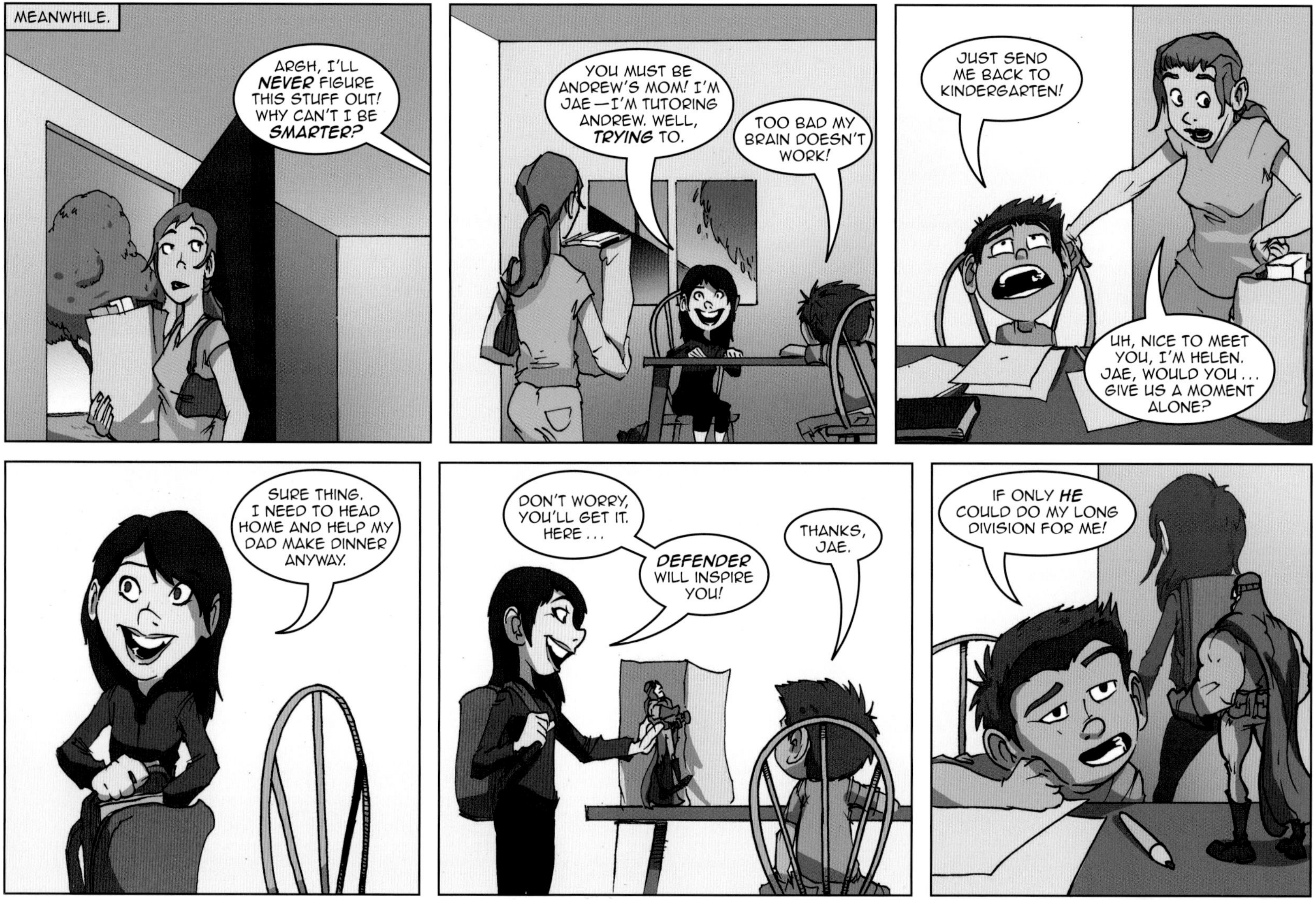
MEANWHILE.
ARGH, I'LL **NEVER** FIGURE THIS STUFF OUT! WHY CAN'T I BE **SMARTER?**
YOU MUST BE ANDREW'S MOM! I'M JAE — I'M TUTORING ANDREW. WELL, **TRYING** TO.
TOO BAD MY BRAIN DOESN'T WORK!
JUST SEND ME BACK TO KINDERGARTEN!
UH, NICE TO MEET YOU, I'M HELEN. JAE, WOULD YOU . . . GIVE US A MOMENT ALONE?
SURE THING. I NEED TO HEAD HOME AND HELP MY DAD MAKE DINNER ANYWAY.
DON'T WORRY, YOU'LL GET IT. HERE . . .
DEFENDER WILL INSPIRE YOU!
THANKS, JAE.
IF ONLY **HE** COULD DO MY LONG DIVISION FOR ME!

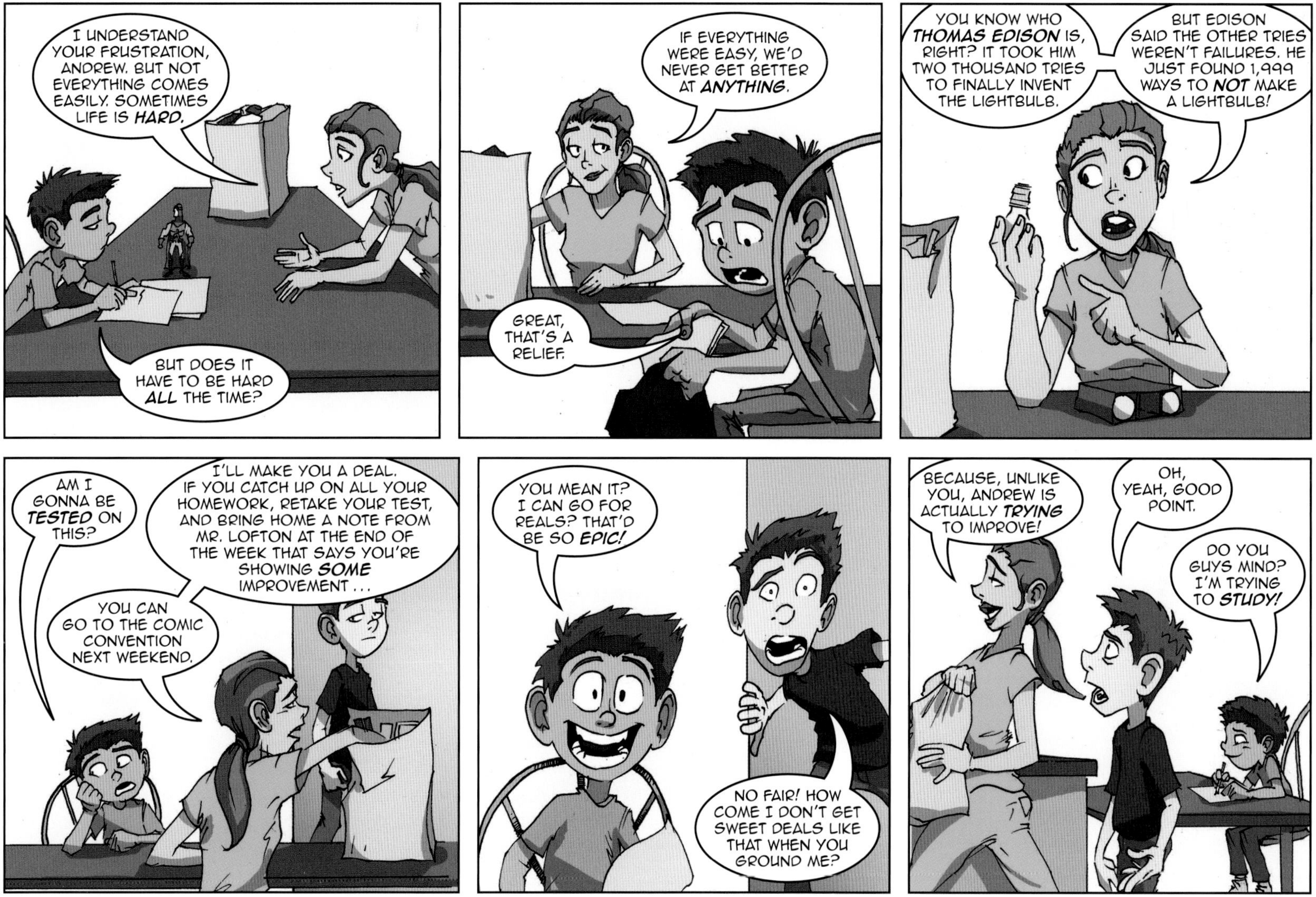
I UNDERSTAND YOUR FRUSTRATION, ANDREW. BUT NOT EVERYTHING COMES EASILY. SOMETIMES LIFE IS **HARD.**
BUT DOES IT HAVE TO BE HARD **ALL** THE TIME?
IF EVERYTHING WERE EASY, WE'D NEVER GET BETTER AT **ANYTHING**.
GREAT, THAT'S A RELIEF.
YOU KNOW WHO **THOMAS EDISON** IS, RIGHT? IT TOOK HIM TWO THOUSAND TRIES TO FINALLY INVENT THE LIGHTBULB.
BUT EDISON SAID THE OTHER TRIES WEREN'T FAILURES. HE JUST FOUND 1,999 WAYS TO **NOT** MAKE A LIGHTBULB!
AM I GONNA BE **TESTED** ON THIS?
I'LL MAKE YOU A DEAL. IF YOU CATCH UP ON ALL YOUR HOMEWORK, RETAKE YOUR TEST, AND BRING HOME A NOTE FROM MR. LOFTON AT THE END OF THE WEEK THAT SAYS YOU'RE SHOWING **SOME** IMPROVEMENT . . .
YOU CAN GO TO THE COMIC CONVENTION NEXT WEEKEND.
YOU MEAN IT? I CAN GO FOR REALS? THAT'D BE SO **EPIC!**
NO FAIR! HOW COME I DON'T GET SWEET DEALS LIKE THAT WHEN YOU GROUND ME?
BECAUSE, UNLIKE YOU, ANDREW IS ACTUALLY **TRYING** TO IMPROVE!
OH, YEAH, GOOD POINT.
DO YOU GUYS MIND? I'M TRYING TO **STUDY!**

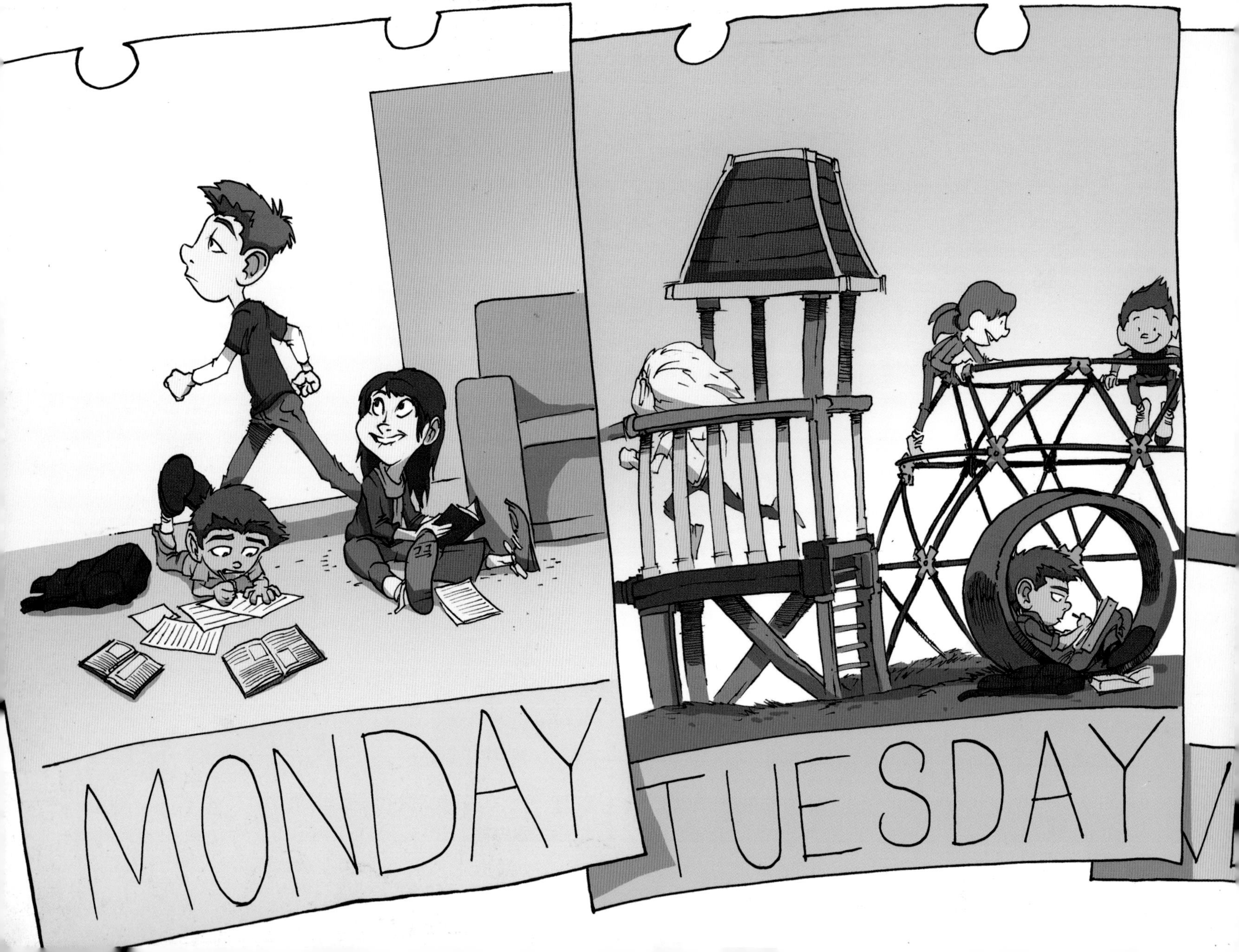
MONDAY
TUESDAY

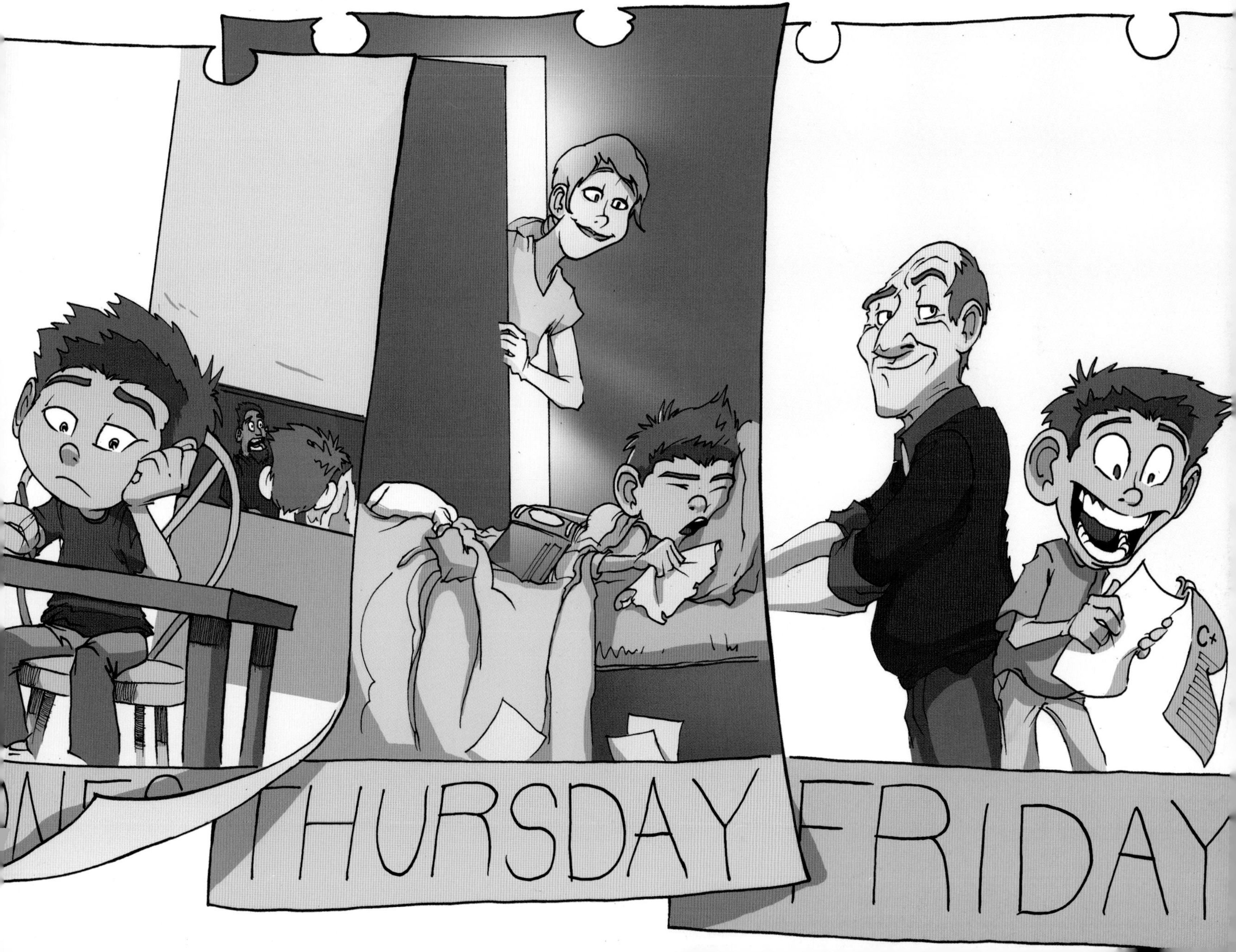
THURSDAY
FRIDAY

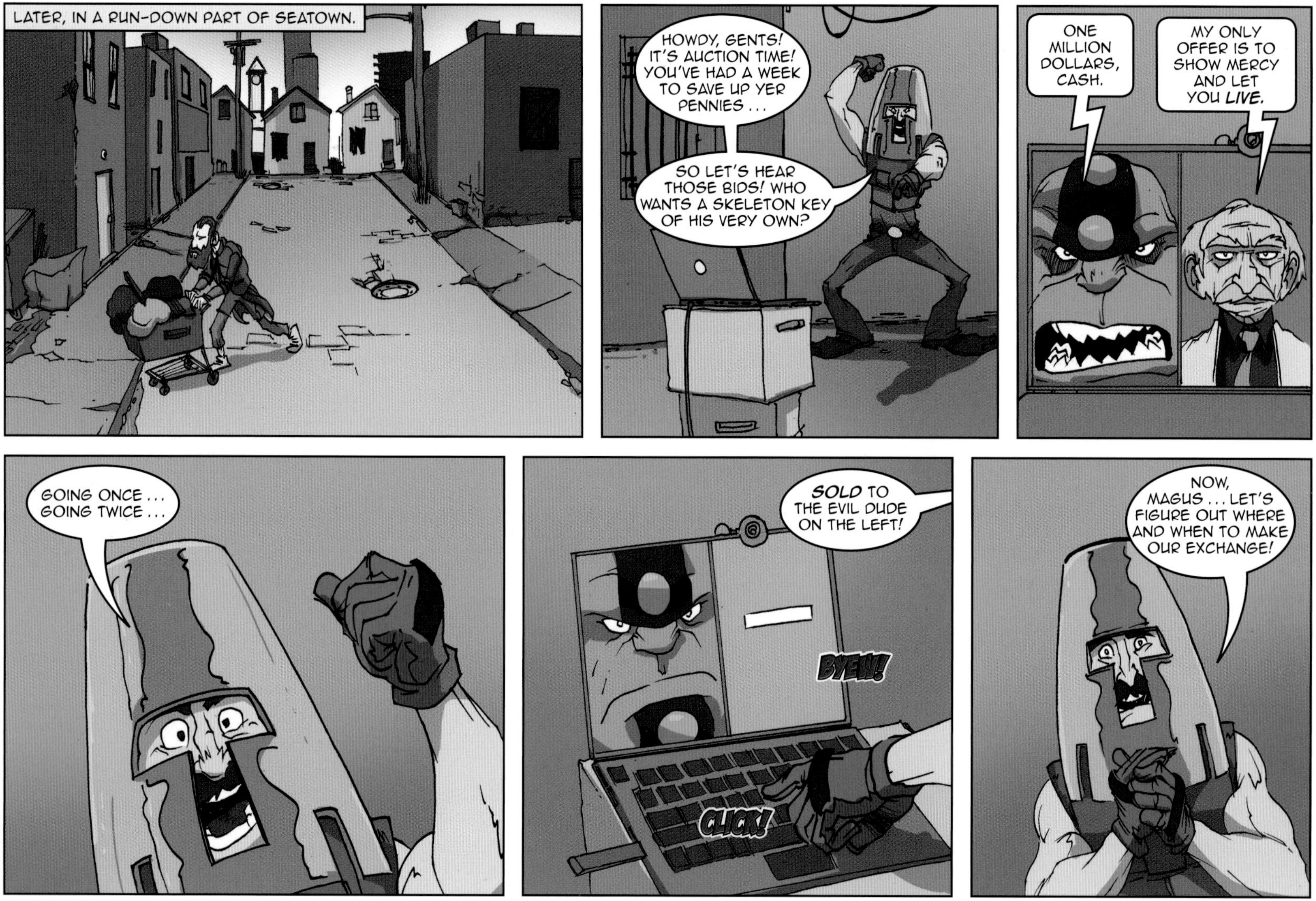
LATER, IN A RUN-DOWN PART OF SEATOWN.
HOWDY, GENTS! IT'S AUCTION TIME! YOU'VE HAD A WEEK TO SAVE UP YER PENNIES . . .
SO LET'S HEAR THOSE BIDS! WHO WANTS A SKELETON KEY OF HIS VERY OWN?
ONE MILLION DOLLARS, CASH.
MY ONLY OFFER IS TO SHOW MERCY AND LET YOU LIVE.
GOING ONCE . . . GOING TWICE . . .
SOLD TO THE EVIL DUDE ON THE LEFT!
BYEW!
CLICK!
NOW, MAGUS . . . LET'S FIGURE OUT WHERE AND WHEN TO MAKE OUR EXCHANGE!

THAT WAS . . . DISAPPOINTING.

YOUR CALL HAS BEEN DISCONNECTED.

COMPUTER, SWITCH TO SPY CAM. LET'S PEEK BEHIND THE SCENES, SHALL WE?

THE DEVICE IS READY, SIR. ALL WE NEED NOW IS THE POWER SOURCE TO ACTIVATE IT.

AND YOU SHALL HAVE IT.

THE FOOL WANTS TO MEET IN PUBLIC. HE'S CHOSEN SOME SORT OF CONVENTION, THINKING HE'LL BE SAFE IN A LARGE CROWD.

DISPATCH THE STRIKE FORCE.

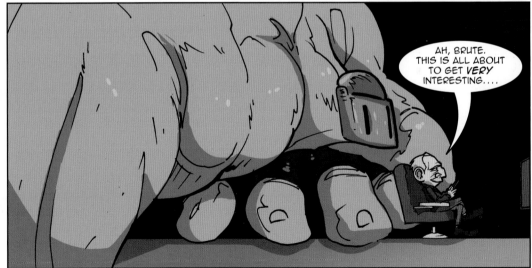

AH, BRUTE. THIS IS ALL ABOUT TO GET *VERY* INTERESTING. . . .

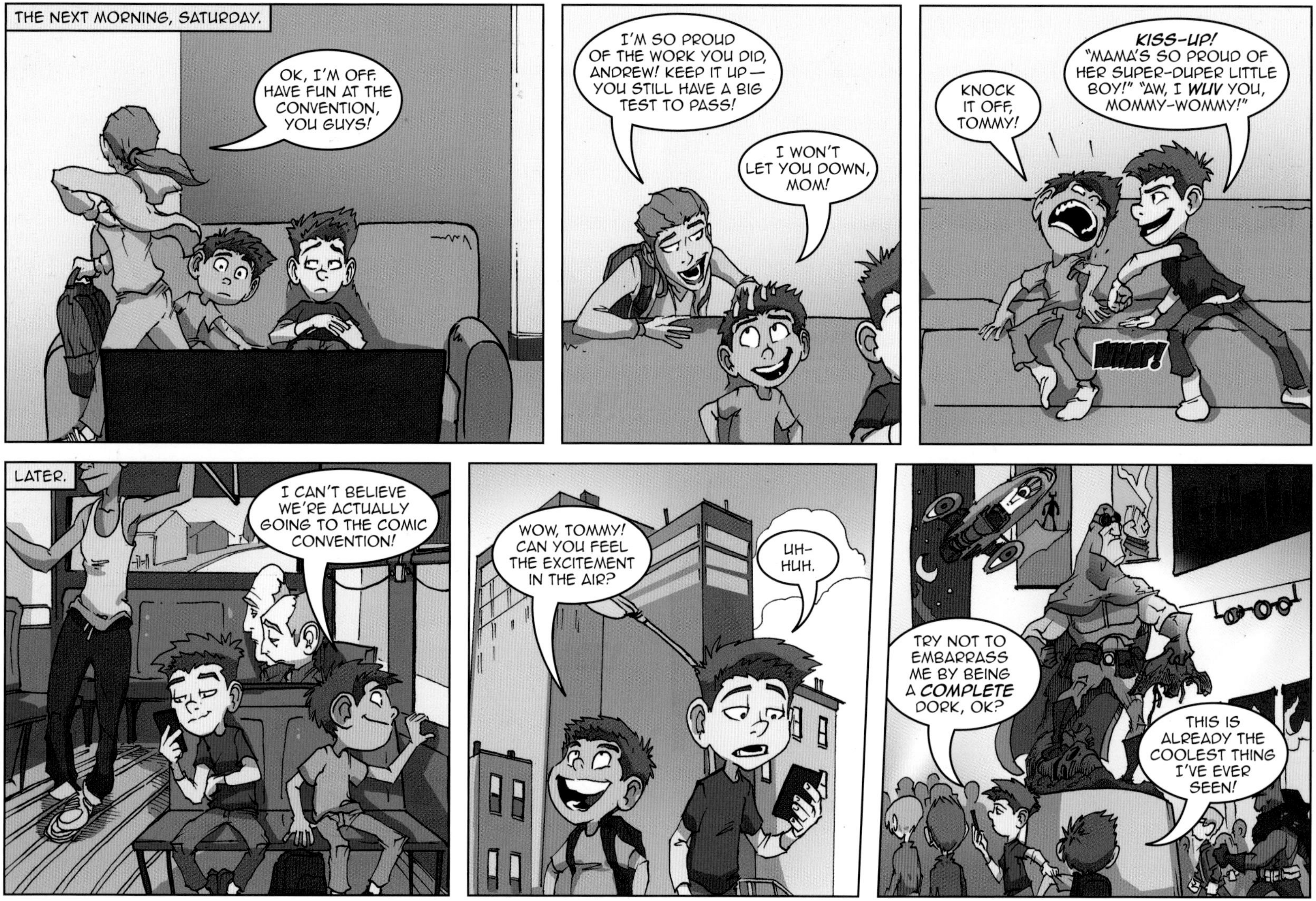

THE NEXT MORNING, SATURDAY.
OK, I'M OFF. HAVE FUN AT THE CONVENTION, YOU GUYS!
I'M SO PROUD OF THE WORK YOU DID, ANDREW! KEEP IT UP — YOU STILL HAVE A BIG TEST TO PASS!
I WON'T LET YOU DOWN, MOM!
KNOCK IT OFF, TOMMY!
KISS-UP! "MAMA'S SO PROUD OF HER SUPER-DUPER LITTLE BOY!" "AW, I WUV YOU, MOMMY-WOMMY!"
WHAP!
LATER.
I CAN'T BELIEVE WE'RE ACTUALLY GOING TO THE COMIC CONVENTION!
WOW, TOMMY! CAN YOU FEEL THE EXCITEMENT IN THE AIR?
UH-HUH.
TRY NOT TO EMBARRASS ME BY BEING A COMPLETE DORK, OK?
THIS IS ALREADY THE COOLEST THING I'VE EVER SEEN!

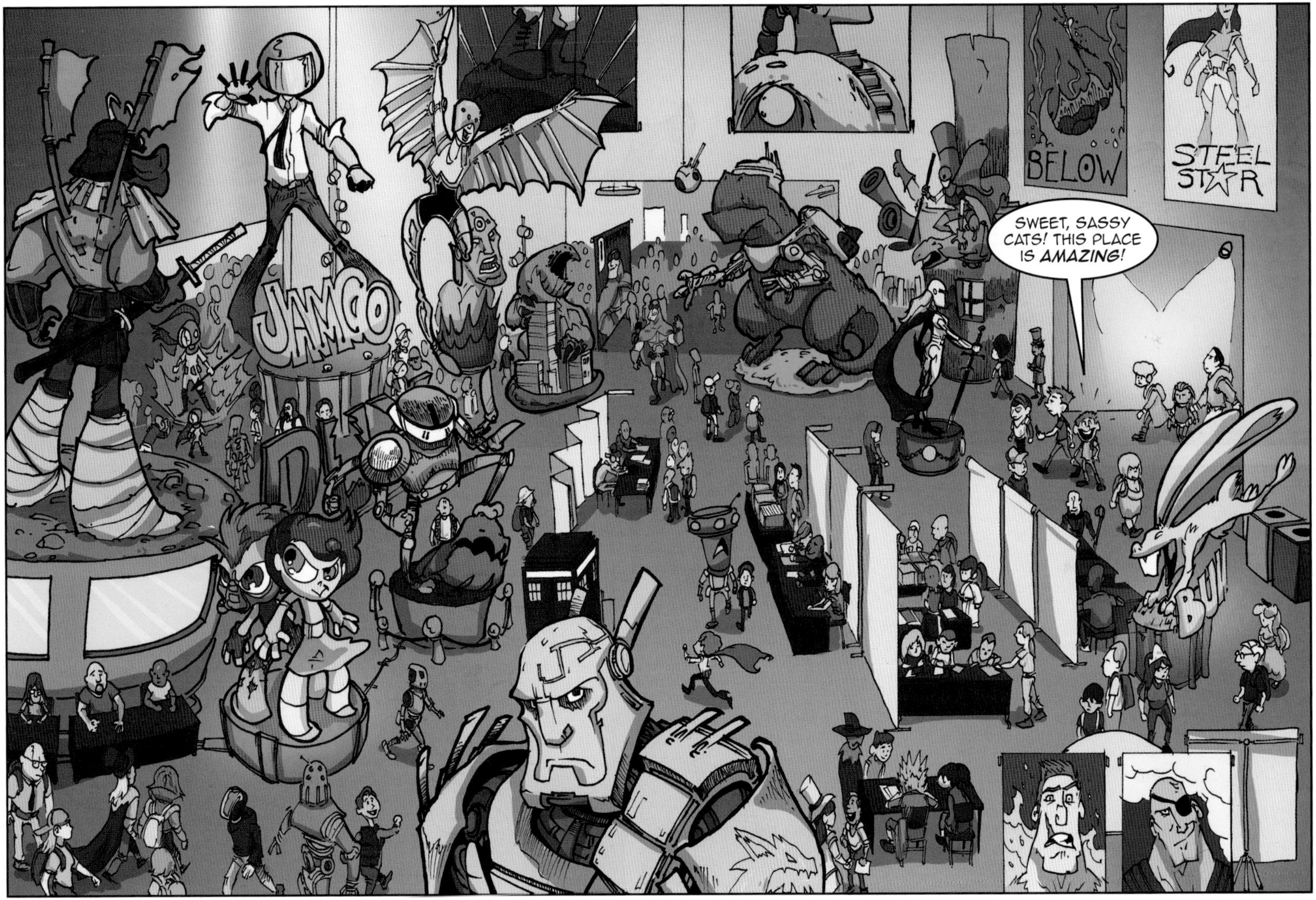
JAMCO
BELOW
STEEL STAR
SWEET, SASSY CATS! THIS PLACE IS *AMAZING*!

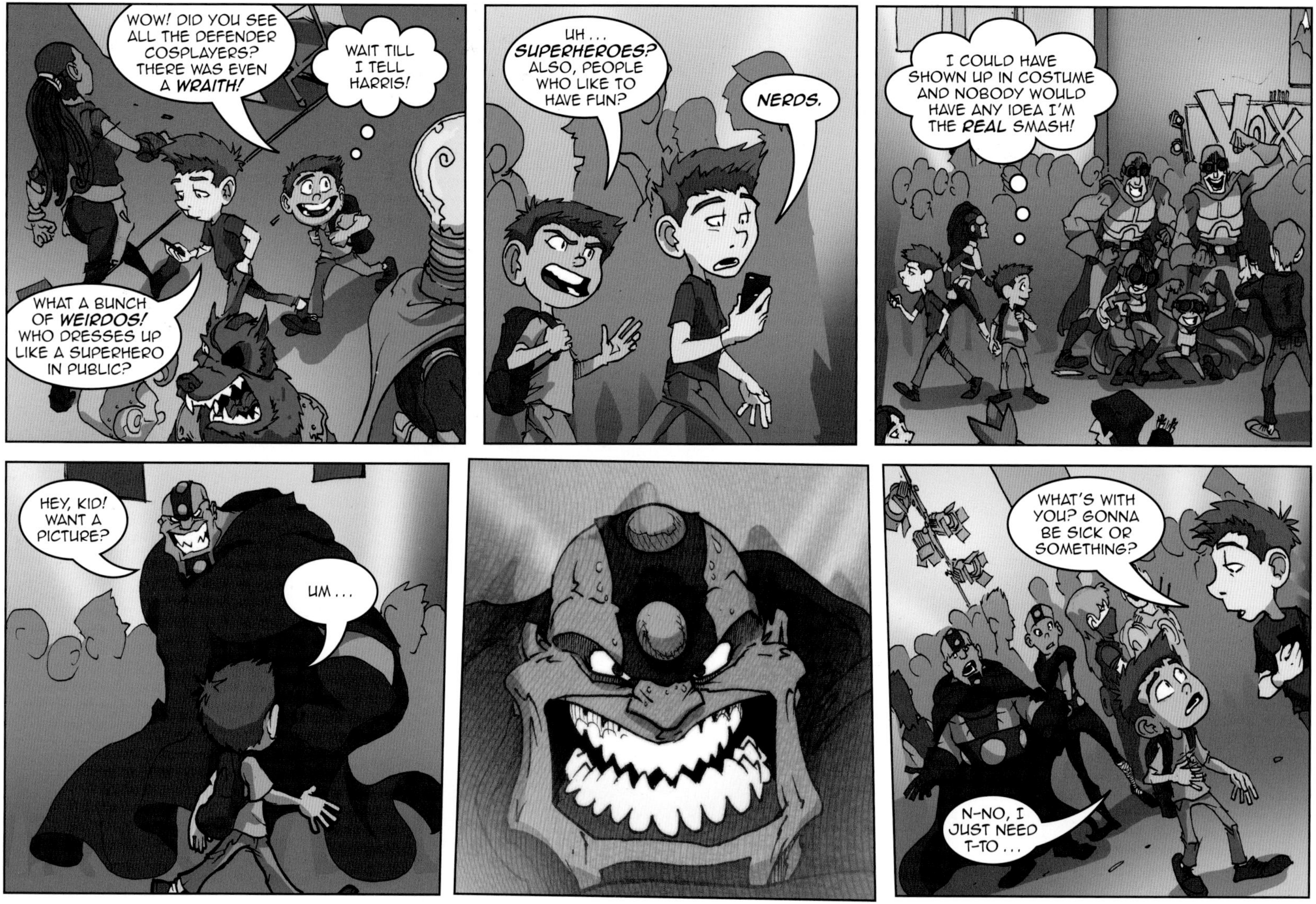
WOW! DID YOU SEE ALL THE DEFENDER COSPLAYERS? THERE WAS EVEN A **WRAITH!**
WAIT TILL I TELL HARRIS!
WHAT A BUNCH OF **WEIRDOS!** WHO DRESSES UP LIKE A SUPERHERO IN PUBLIC?
UH . . . **SUPERHEROES?** ALSO, PEOPLE WHO LIKE TO HAVE FUN?
NERDS.
I COULD HAVE SHOWN UP IN COSTUME AND NOBODY WOULD HAVE ANY IDEA I'M THE **REAL** SMASH!
HEY, KID! WANT A PICTURE?
UM . . .
WHAT'S WITH YOU? GONNA BE SICK OR SOMETHING?
N-NO, I JUST NEED T-TO . . .

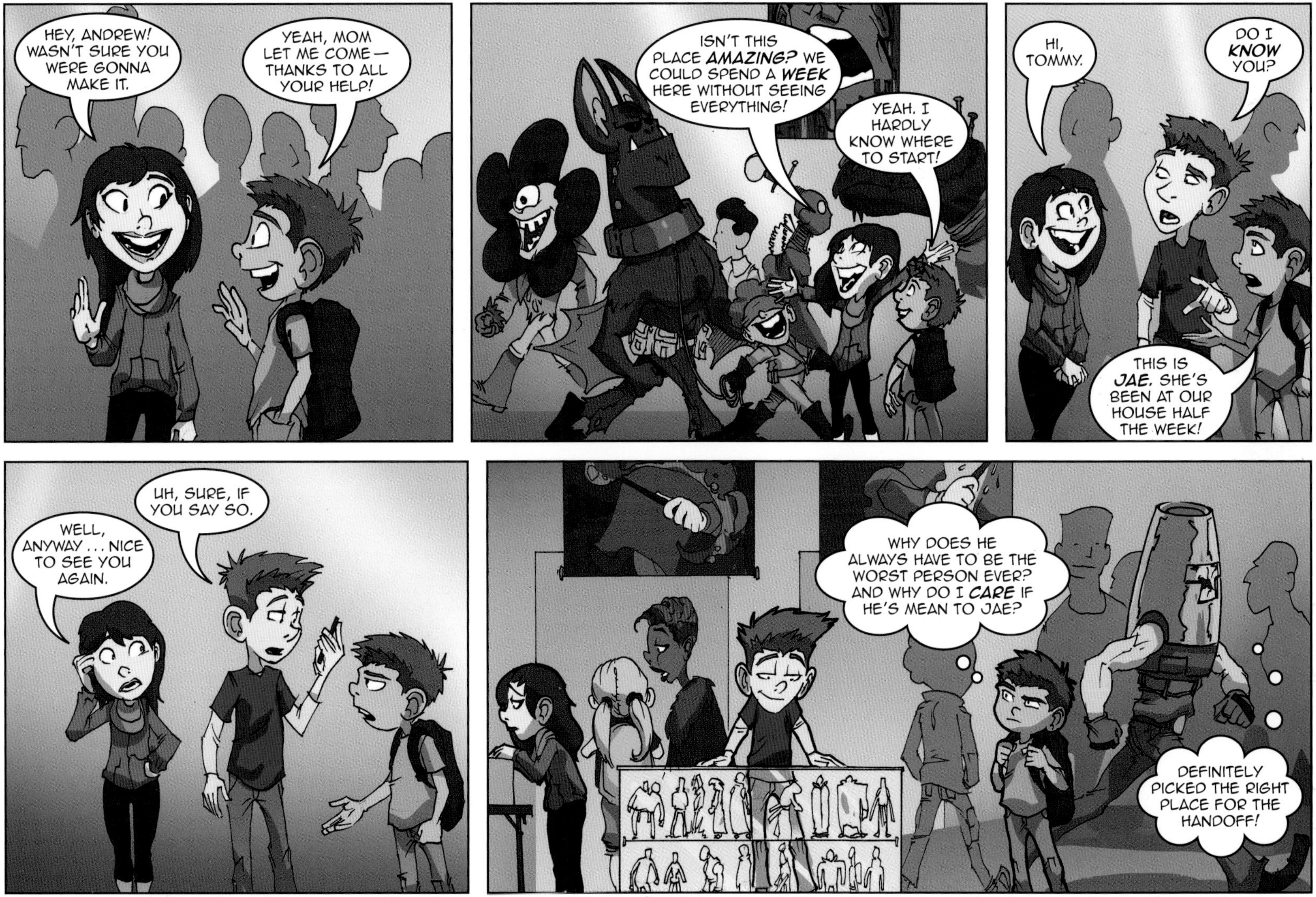

HEY, ANDREW! WASN'T SURE YOU WERE GONNA MAKE IT.
YEAH, MOM LET ME COME — THANKS TO ALL YOUR HELP!
ISN'T THIS PLACE AMAZING? WE COULD SPEND A WEEK HERE WITHOUT SEEING EVERYTHING!
YEAH. I HARDLY KNOW WHERE TO START!
HI, TOMMY.
DO I KNOW YOU?
THIS IS JAE. SHE'S BEEN AT OUR HOUSE HALF THE WEEK!
WELL, ANYWAY . . . NICE TO SEE YOU AGAIN.
UH, SURE, IF YOU SAY SO.
WHY DOES HE ALWAYS HAVE TO BE THE WORST PERSON EVER? AND WHY DO I CARE IF HE'S MEAN TO JAE?
DEFINITELY PICKED THE RIGHT PLACE FOR THE HANDOFF!

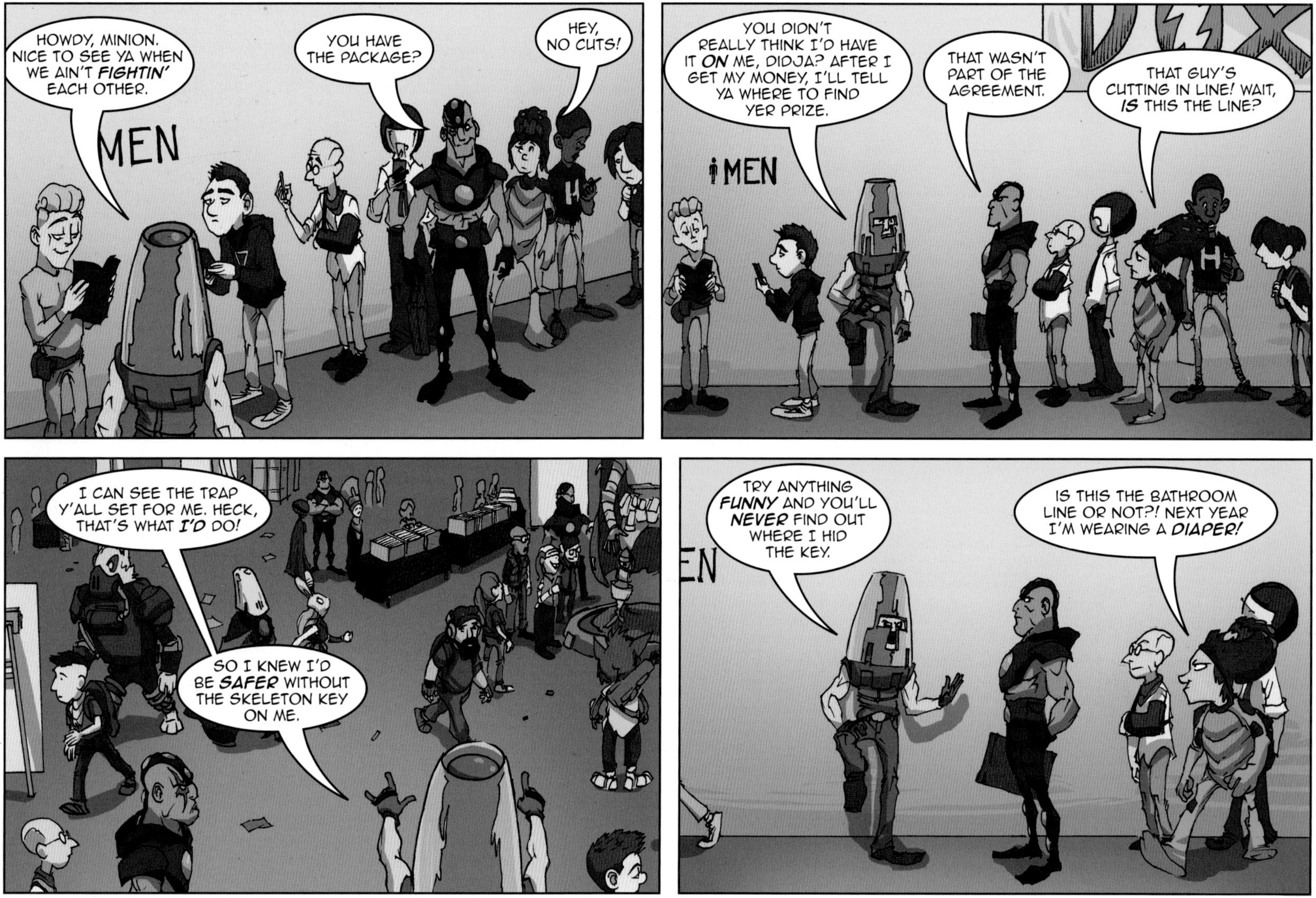
HOWDY, MINION. NICE TO SEE YA WHEN WE AIN'T **FIGHTIN'** EACH OTHER.
MEN
YOU HAVE THE PACKAGE?
HEY, NO CUTS!
YOU DIDN'T REALLY THINK I'D HAVE IT **ON** ME, DIDJA? AFTER I GET MY MONEY, I'LL TELL YA WHERE TO FIND YER PRIZE.
MEN
THAT WASN'T PART OF THE AGREEMENT.
THAT GUY'S CUTTING IN LINE! WAIT, **IS** THIS THE LINE?
I CAN SEE THE TRAP Y'ALL SET FOR ME. HECK, THAT'S WHAT **I'D** DO!
SO I KNEW I'D BE **SAFER** WITHOUT THE SKELETON KEY ON ME.
TRY ANYTHING **FUNNY** AND YOU'LL **NEVER** FIND OUT WHERE I HID THE KEY.
IS THIS THE BATHROOM LINE OR NOT?! NEXT YEAR I'M WEARING A **DIAPER!**

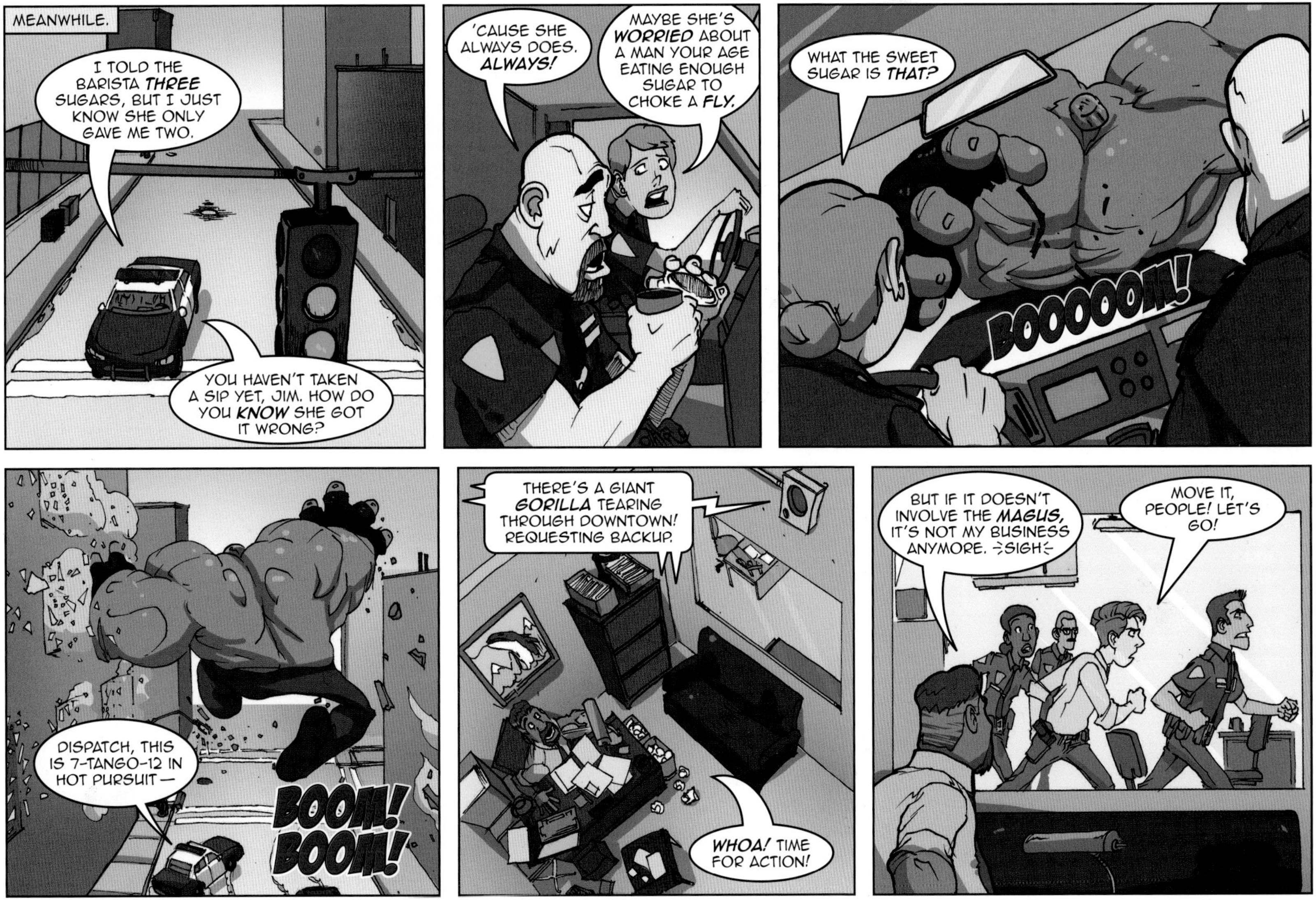
MEANWHILE.
I TOLD THE BARISTA THREE SUGARS, BUT I JUST KNOW SHE ONLY GAVE ME TWO.
YOU HAVEN'T TAKEN A SIP YET, JIM. HOW DO YOU KNOW SHE GOT IT WRONG?
'CAUSE SHE ALWAYS DOES. ALWAYS!
MAYBE SHE'S WORRIED ABOUT A MAN YOUR AGE EATING ENOUGH SUGAR TO CHOKE A FLY.
WHAT THE SWEET SUGAR IS THAT?
BOOOOOOM!
DISPATCH, THIS IS 7-TANGO-12 IN HOT PURSUIT—
BOOM! BOOM!
THERE'S A GIANT GORILLA TEARING THROUGH DOWNTOWN! REQUESTING BACKUP.
WHOA! TIME FOR ACTION!
BUT IF IT DOESN'T INVOLVE THE MAGUS, IT'S NOT MY BUSINESS ANYMORE. -SIGH-
MOVE IT, PEOPLE! LET'S GO!

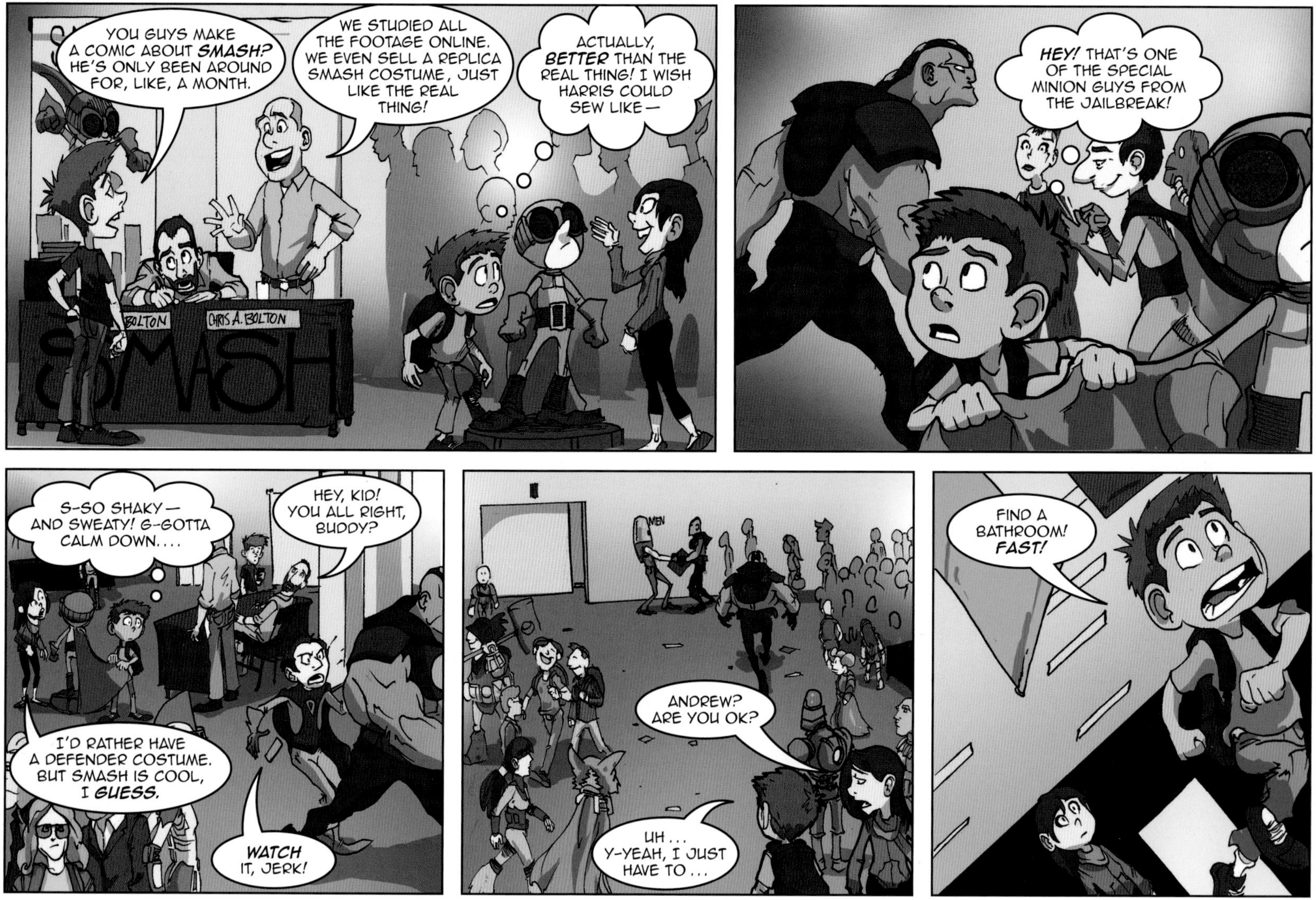
YOU GUYS MAKE A COMIC ABOUT **SMASH?** HE'S ONLY BEEN AROUND FOR, LIKE, A MONTH.
WE STUDIED ALL THE FOOTAGE ONLINE. WE EVEN SELL A REPLICA SMASH COSTUME, JUST LIKE THE REAL THING!
ACTUALLY, **BETTER** THAN THE REAL THING! I WISH HARRIS COULD SEW LIKE—
BOLTON
CHRIS A. BOLTON
SMASH
HEY! THAT'S ONE OF THE SPECIAL MINION GUYS FROM THE JAILBREAK!
S-SO SHAKY— AND SWEATY! G-GOTTA CALM DOWN....
HEY, KID! YOU ALL RIGHT, BUDDY?
I'D RATHER HAVE A DEFENDER COSTUME. BUT SMASH IS COOL, I **GUESS.**
WATCH IT, JERK!
MEN
ANDREW? ARE YOU OK?
UH... Y-YEAH, I JUST HAVE TO...
FIND A BATHROOM! **FAST!**

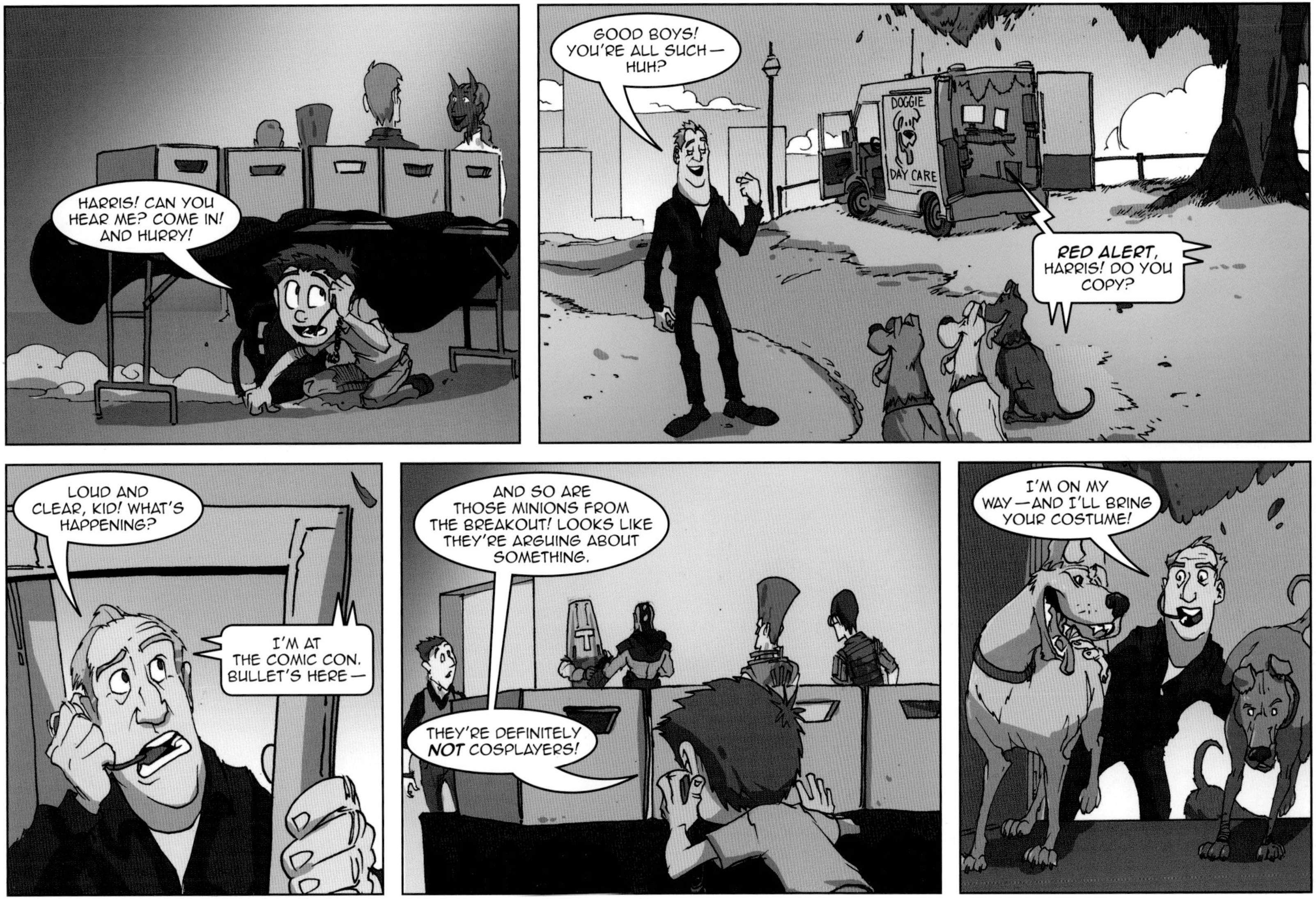
HARRIS! CAN YOU HEAR ME? COME IN! AND HURRY!
GOOD BOYS! YOU'RE ALL SUCH— HUH?
DOGGIE DAY CARE
RED ALERT, HARRIS! DO YOU COPY?
LOUD AND CLEAR, KID! WHAT'S HAPPENING?
I'M AT THE COMIC CON. BULLET'S HERE—
AND SO ARE THOSE MINIONS FROM THE BREAKOUT! LOOKS LIKE THEY'RE ARGUING ABOUT SOMETHING.
THEY'RE DEFINITELY NOT COSPLAYERS!
I'M ON MY WAY—AND I'LL BRING YOUR COSTUME!

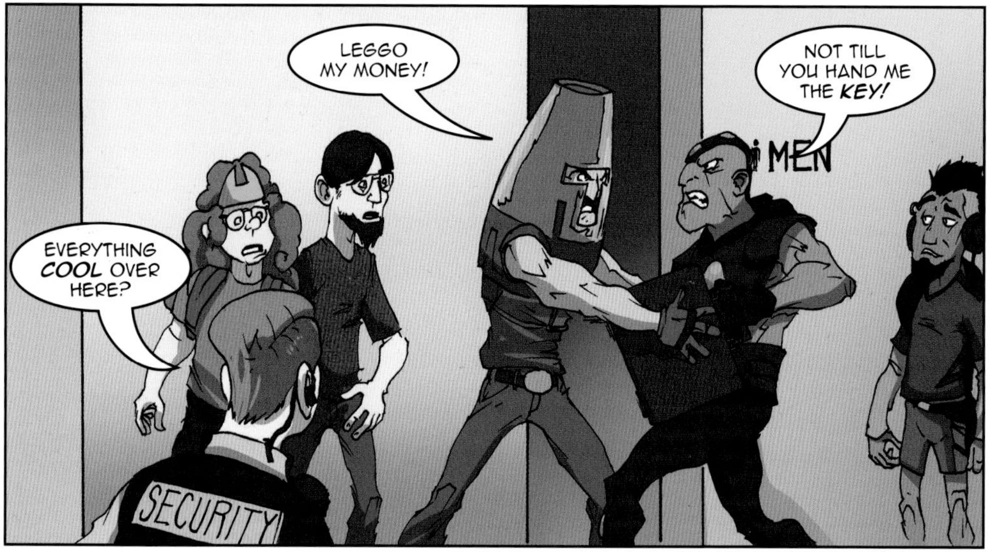
LEGGO MY MONEY!
NOT TILL YOU HAND ME THE *KEY!*
MEN
EVERYTHING **COOL** OVER HERE?
SECURITY

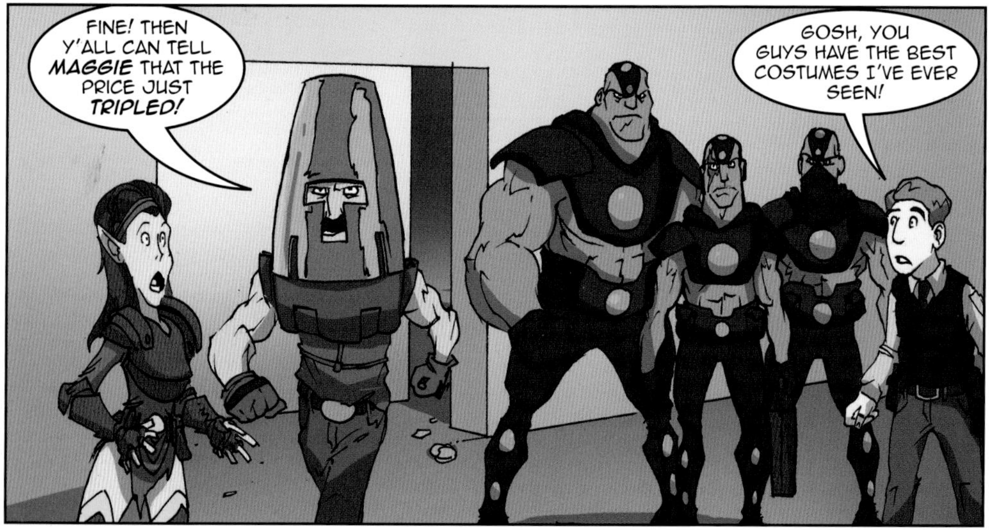
FINE! THEN Y'ALL CAN TELL **MAGGIE** THAT THE PRICE JUST **TRIPLED!**
GOSH, YOU GUYS HAVE THE BEST COSTUMES I'VE EVER SEEN!

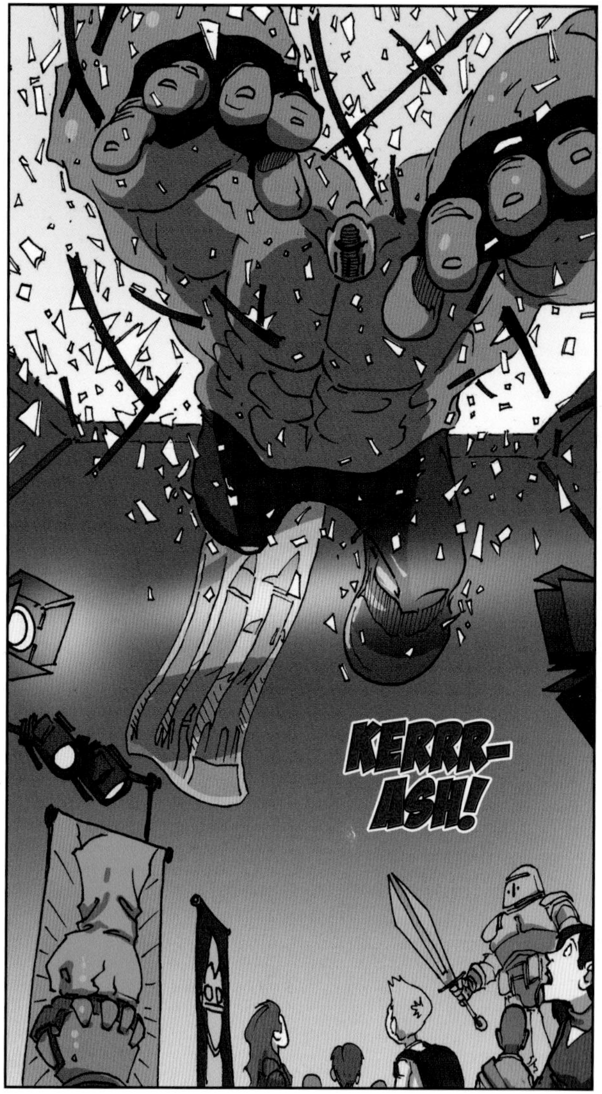
KERRR-ASH!

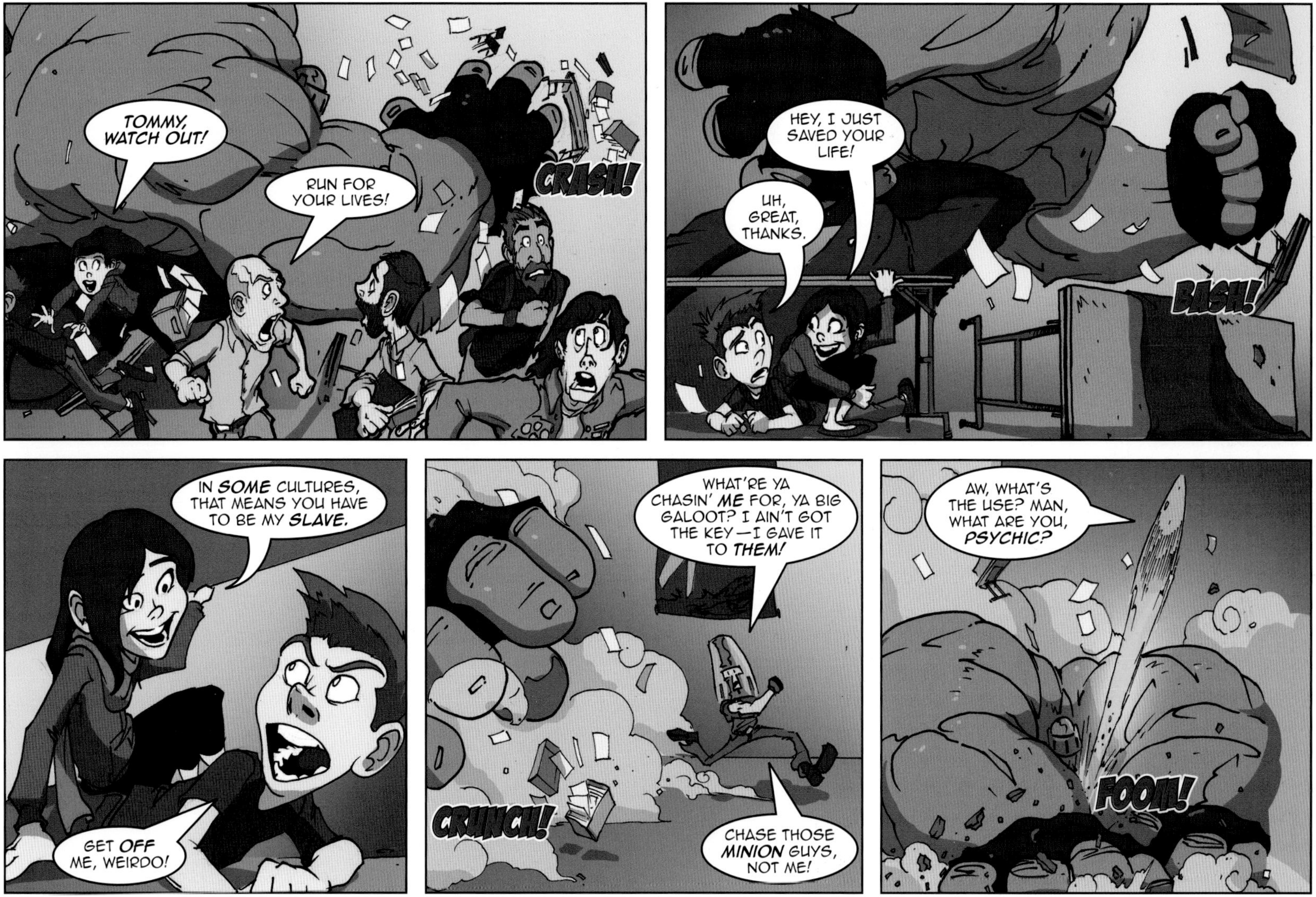
TOMMY, WATCH OUT!
RUN FOR YOUR LIVES!
CRASH!
HEY, I JUST SAVED YOUR LIFE!
UH, GREAT, THANKS.
BASH!
IN SOME CULTURES, THAT MEANS YOU HAVE TO BE MY SLAVE.
GET OFF ME, WEIRDO!
WHAT'RE YA CHASIN' ME FOR, YA BIG GALOOT? I AIN'T GOT THE KEY—I GAVE IT TO THEM!
CRUNCH!
CHASE THOSE MINION GUYS, NOT ME!
AW, WHAT'S THE USE? MAN, WHAT ARE YOU, PSYCHIC?
FOOM!

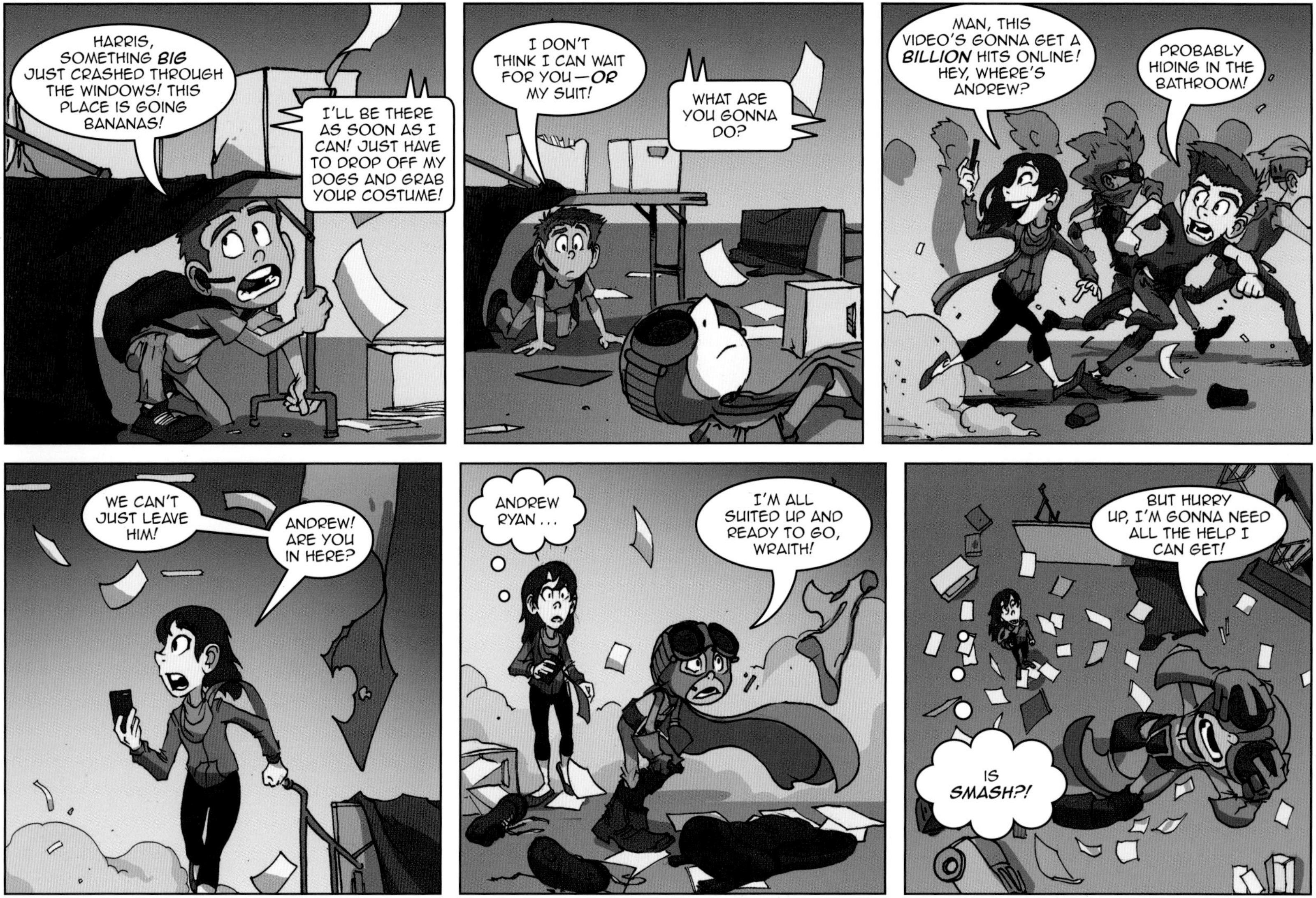
HARRIS, SOMETHING BIG JUST CRASHED THROUGH THE WINDOWS! THIS PLACE IS GOING BANANAS!
I'LL BE THERE AS SOON AS I CAN! JUST HAVE TO DROP OFF MY DOGS AND GRAB YOUR COSTUME!
I DON'T THINK I CAN WAIT FOR YOU—OR MY SUIT!
WHAT ARE YOU GONNA DO?
MAN, THIS VIDEO'S GONNA GET A BILLION HITS ONLINE! HEY, WHERE'S ANDREW?
PROBABLY HIDING IN THE BATHROOM!
WE CAN'T JUST LEAVE HIM!
ANDREW! ARE YOU IN HERE?
ANDREW RYAN . . .
I'M ALL SUITED UP AND READY TO GO, WRAITH!
BUT HURRY UP, I'M GONNA NEED ALL THE HELP I CAN GET!
IS SMASH?!

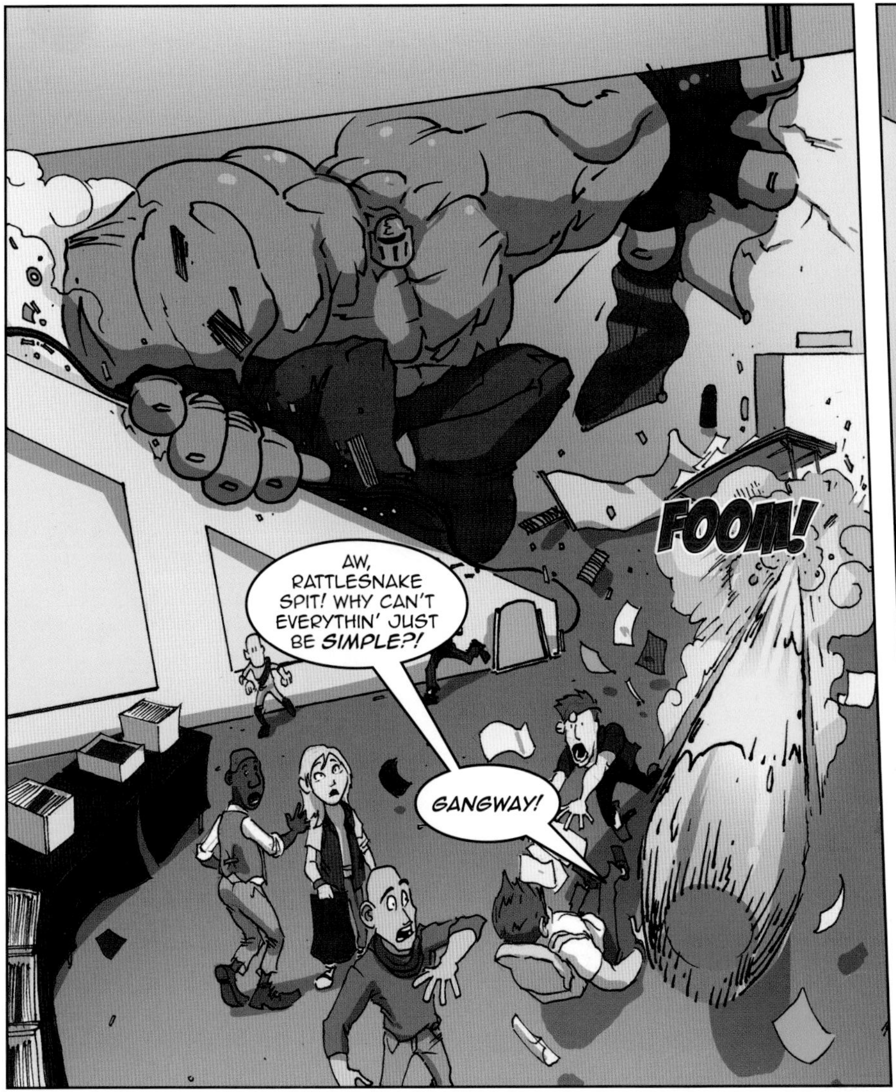
FOOM!
AW, RATTLESNAKE SPIT! WHY CAN'T EVERYTHIN' JUST BE SIMPLE?!
GANGWAY!

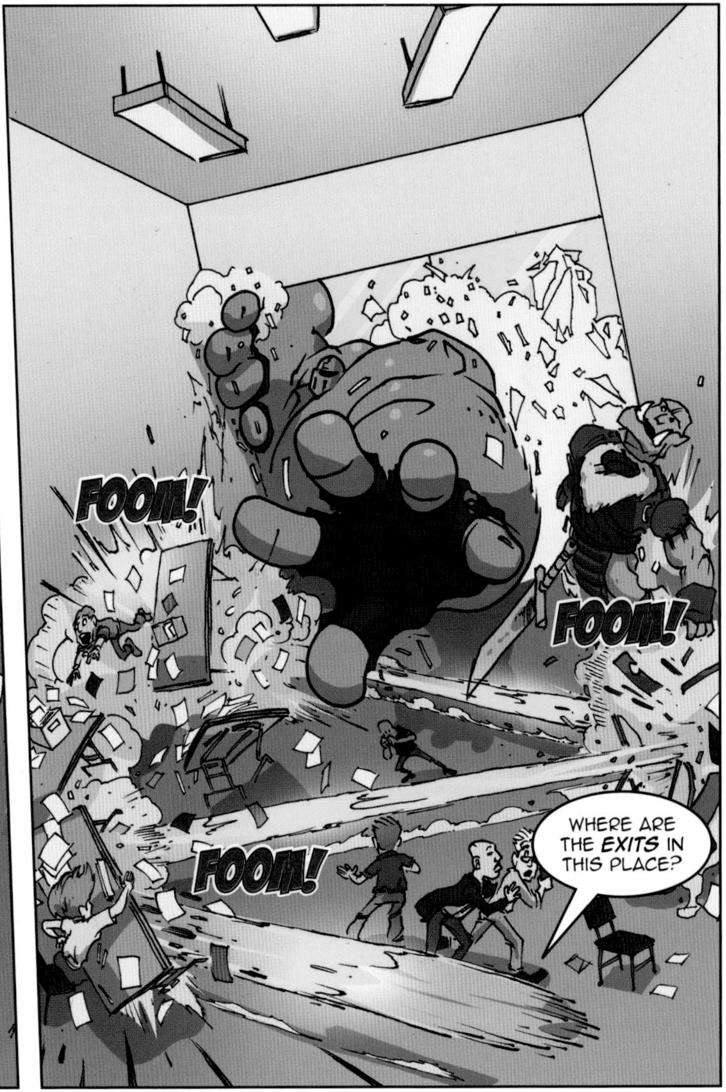
FOOM!
FOOM!
FOOM!
WHERE ARE THE EXITS IN THIS PLACE?

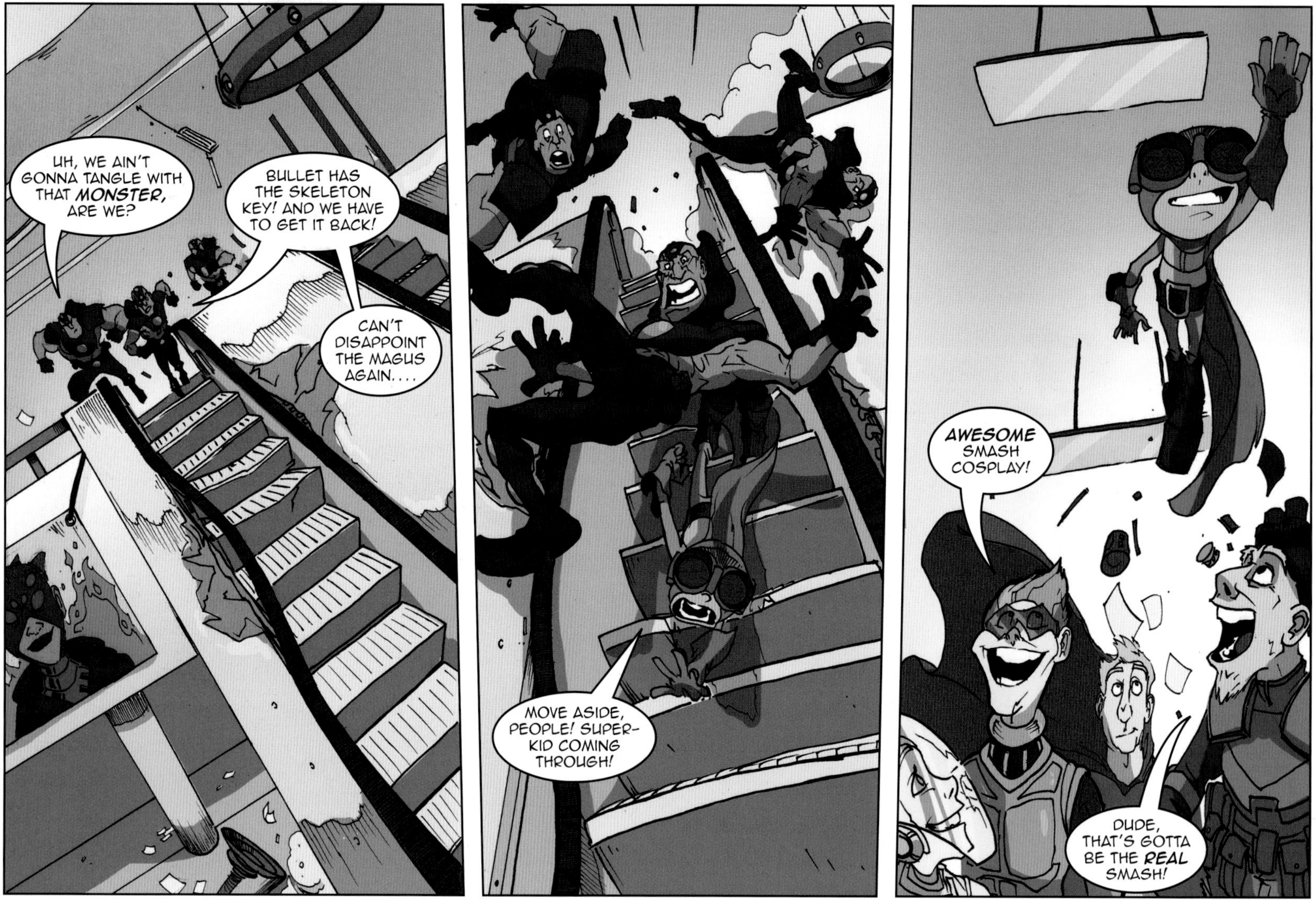
UH, WE AIN'T GONNA TANGLE WITH THAT MONSTER, ARE WE?
BULLET HAS THE SKELETON KEY! AND WE HAVE TO GET IT BACK!
CAN'T DISAPPOINT THE MAGUS AGAIN. . . .
MOVE ASIDE, PEOPLE! SUPER-KID COMING THROUGH!
AWESOME SMASH COSPLAY!
DUDE, THAT'S GOTTA BE THE REAL SMASH!

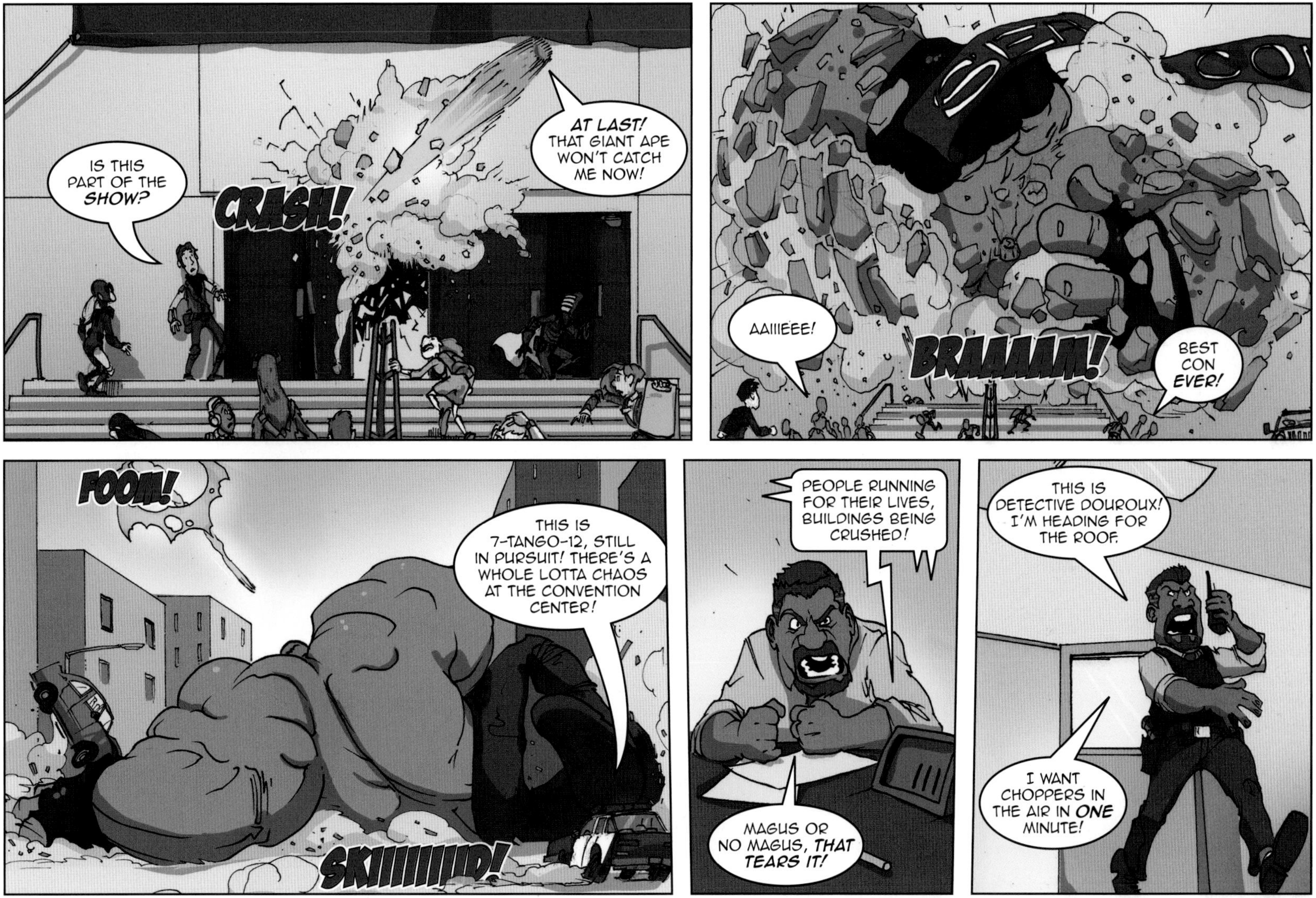
IS THIS PART OF THE *SHOW?*
CRASH!
AT LAST! THAT GIANT APE WON'T CATCH ME NOW!
AAIIIEEE!
BRAAAAM!
BEST CON *EVER!*
FOOM!
THIS IS 7-TANGO-12, STILL IN PURSUIT! THERE'S A WHOLE LOTTA CHAOS AT THE CONVENTION CENTER!
SKIIIIIIID!
PEOPLE RUNNING FOR THEIR LIVES, BUILDINGS BEING CRUSHED!
MAGUS OR NO MAGUS, *THAT TEARS IT!*
THIS IS DETECTIVE DOUROUX! I'M HEADING FOR THE ROOF.
I WANT CHOPPERS IN THE AIR IN *ONE* MINUTE!

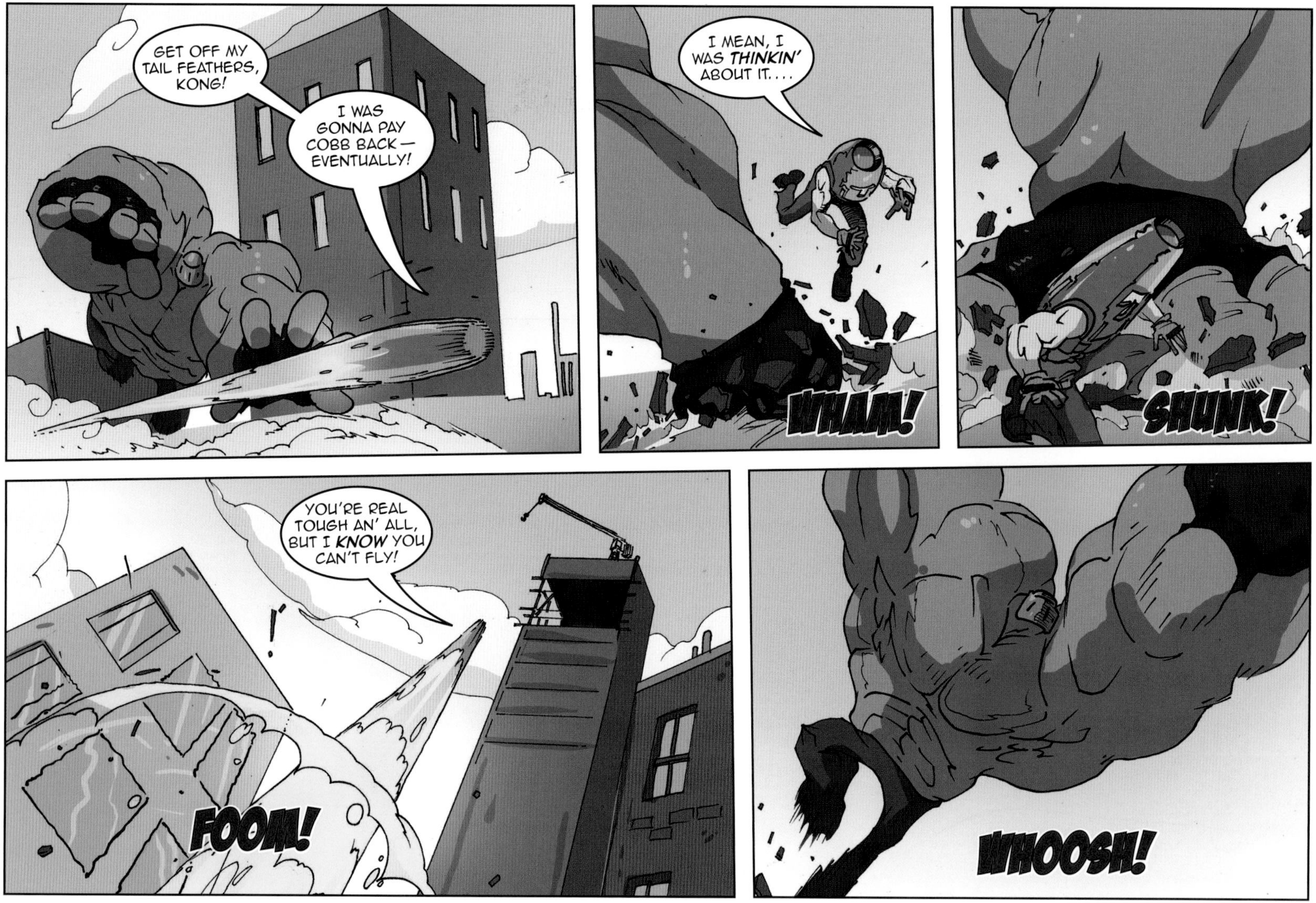
GET OFF MY TAIL FEATHERS, KONG!
I WAS GONNA PAY COBB BACK— EVENTUALLY!
I MEAN, I WAS *THINKIN'* ABOUT IT. . . .
WHAM!
SHUNK!
YOU'RE REAL TOUGH AN' ALL, BUT I *KNOW* YOU CAN'T FLY!
FOOM!
WHOOSH!

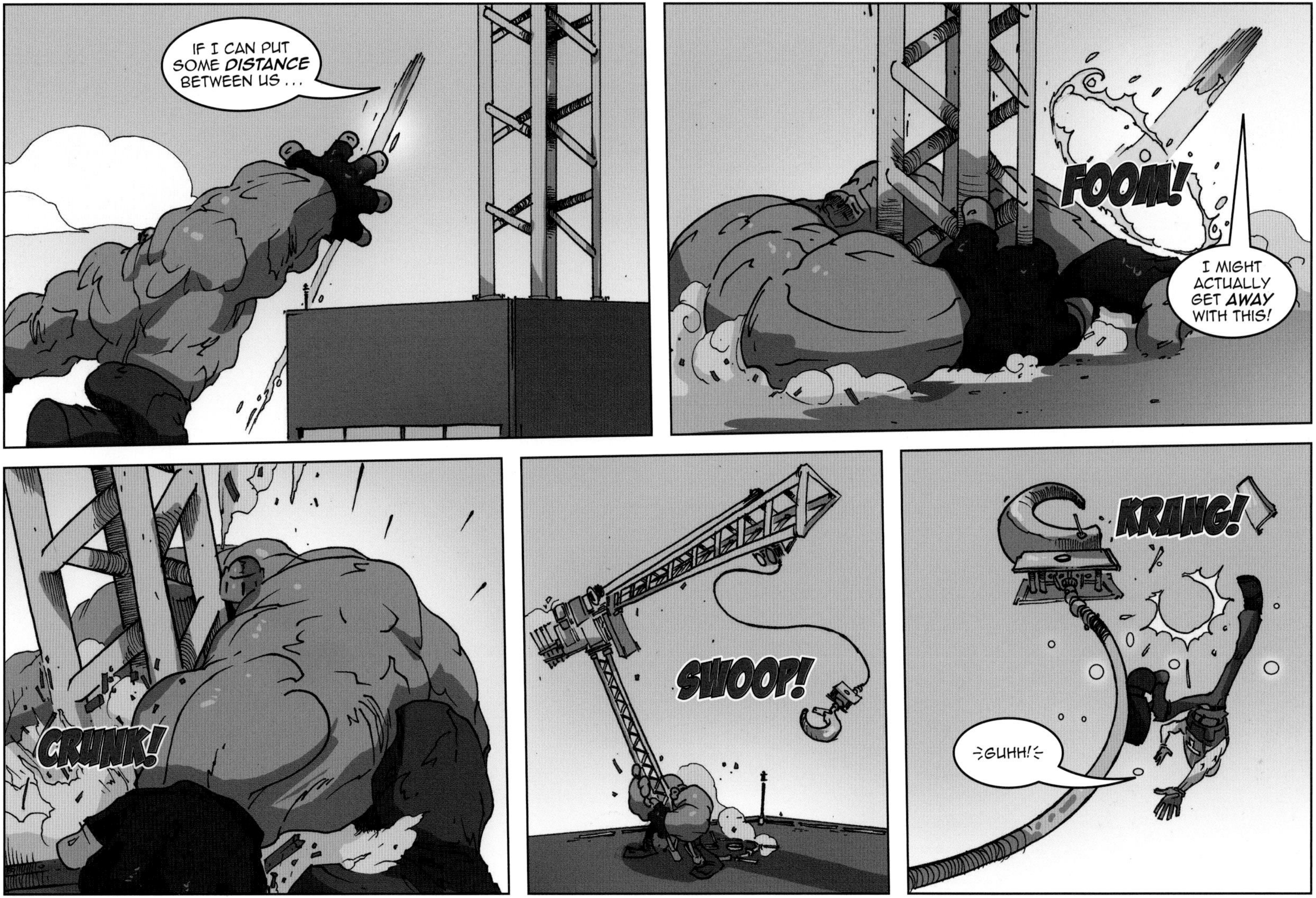
IF I CAN PUT SOME *DISTANCE* BETWEEN US . . .
FOOM!
I MIGHT ACTUALLY GET *AWAY* WITH THIS!
CRUNK!
SWOOP!
KRANG!
GUHH!

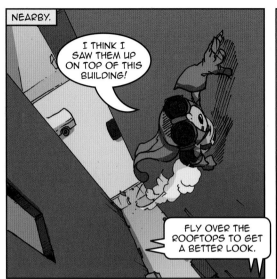

NEARBY.

I THINK I SAW THEM UP ON TOP OF THIS BUILDING!

FLY OVER THE ROOFTOPS TO GET A BETTER LOOK.

÷WHUNF!÷

THWAM!

÷NUNGH!÷

THUD!

AW, OF ALL THE STINKIN' LUCK!

GUESS THIS MUST BE THE PART WHERE —

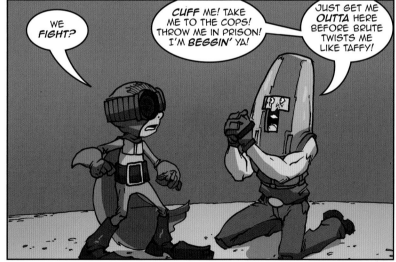

WE FIGHT?

CUFF ME! TAKE ME TO THE COPS! THROW ME IN PRISON! I'M BEGGIN' YA!

JUST GET ME OUTTA HERE BEFORE BRUTE TWISTS ME LIKE TAFFY!

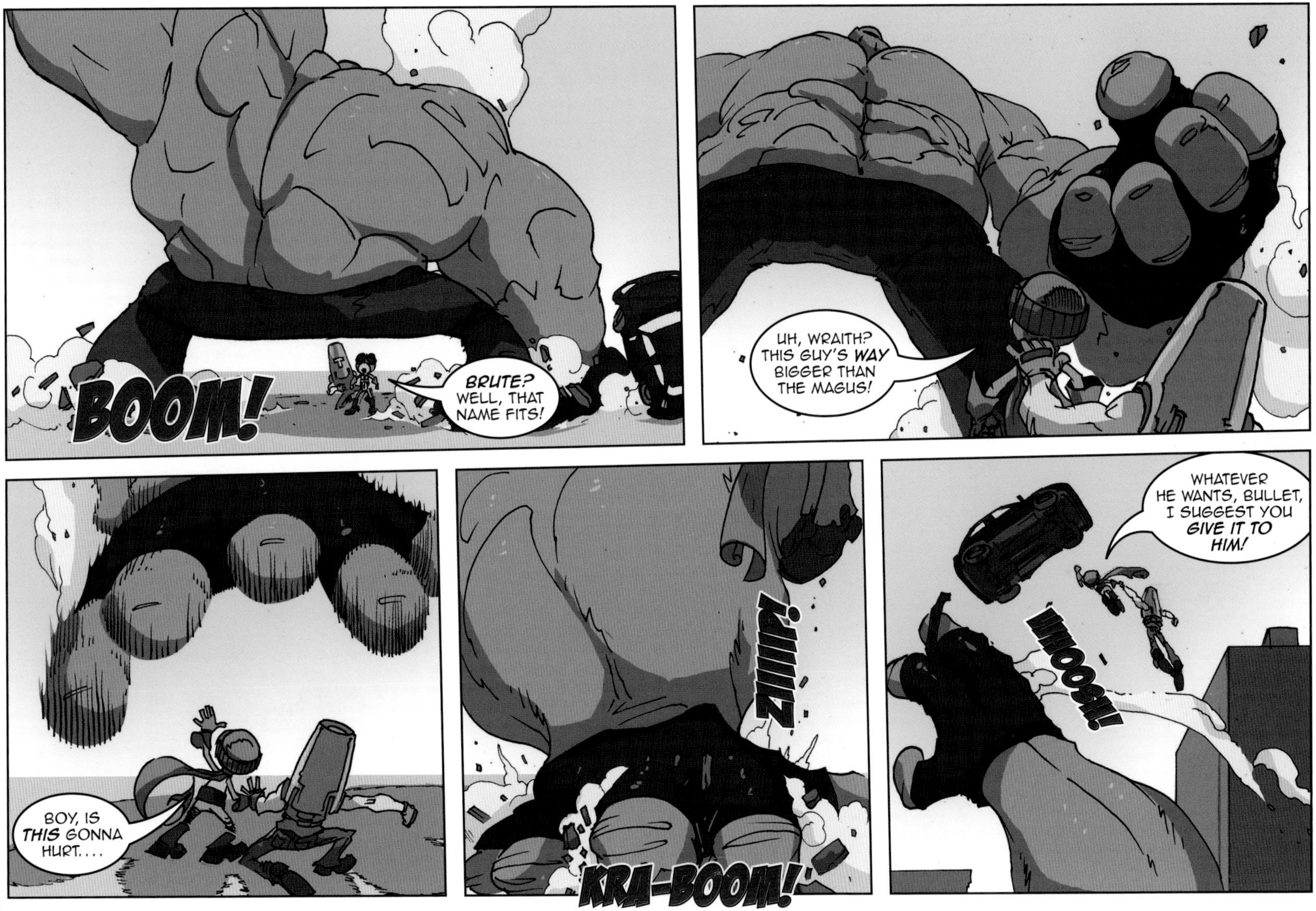
BOOM!
BRUTE? WELL, THAT NAME FITS!
UH, WRAITH? THIS GUY'S WAY BIGGER THAN THE MAGUS!
BOY, IS THIS GONNA HURT. . . .
KRA-BOOM!
WHATEVER HE WANTS, BULLET, I SUGGEST YOU GIVE IT TO HIM!
WHOOSH!

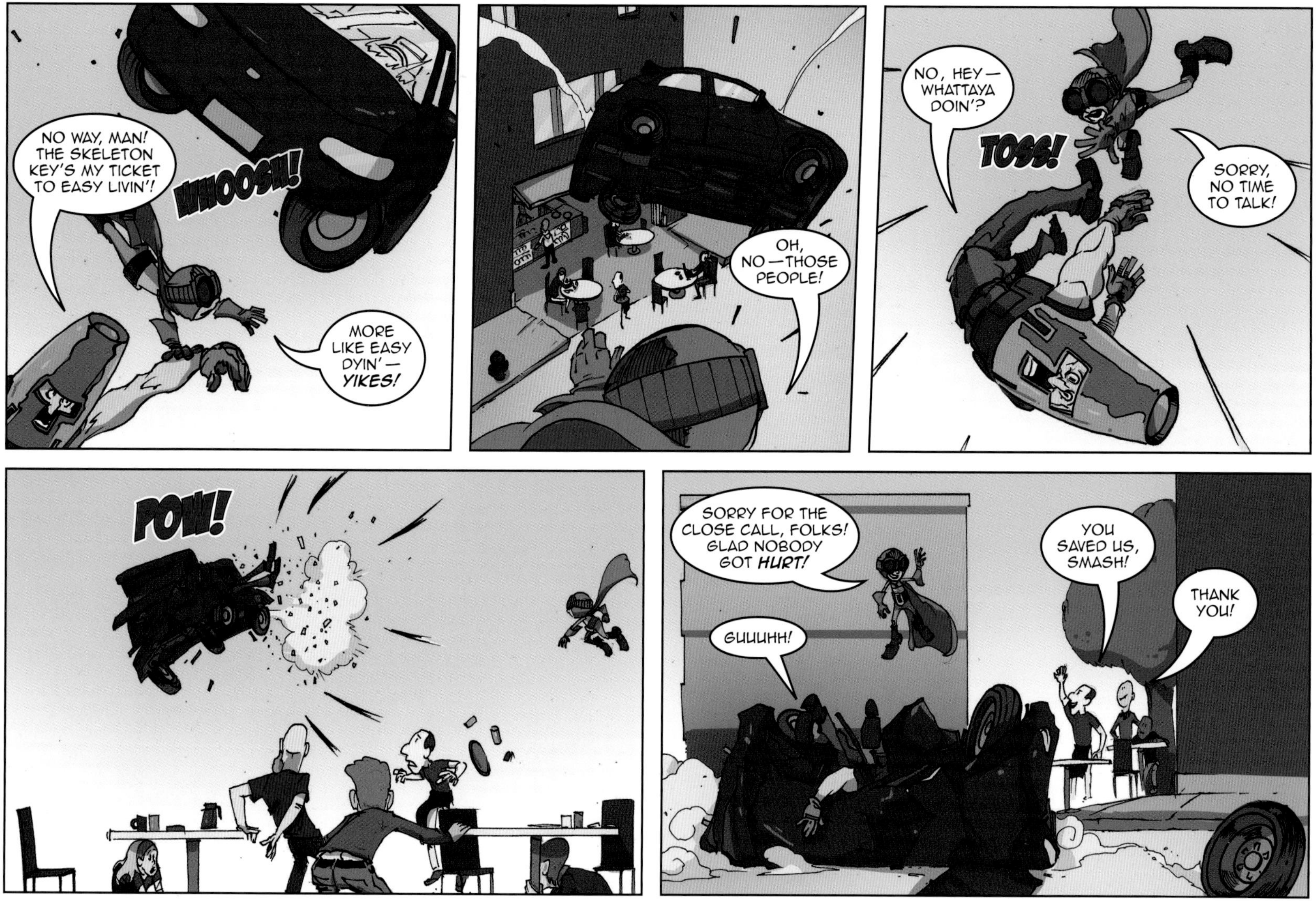
NO WAY, MAN! THE SKELETON KEY'S MY TICKET TO EASY LIVIN'!
WHOOSH!
MORE LIKE EASY DYIN'— *YIKES!*
OH, NO—THOSE PEOPLE!
NO, HEY— WHATTAYA DOIN'?
TOSS!
SORRY, NO TIME TO TALK!
POW!
SORRY FOR THE CLOSE CALL, FOLKS! GLAD NOBODY GOT *HURT!*
GUUUHH!
YOU SAVED US, SMASH!
THANK YOU!

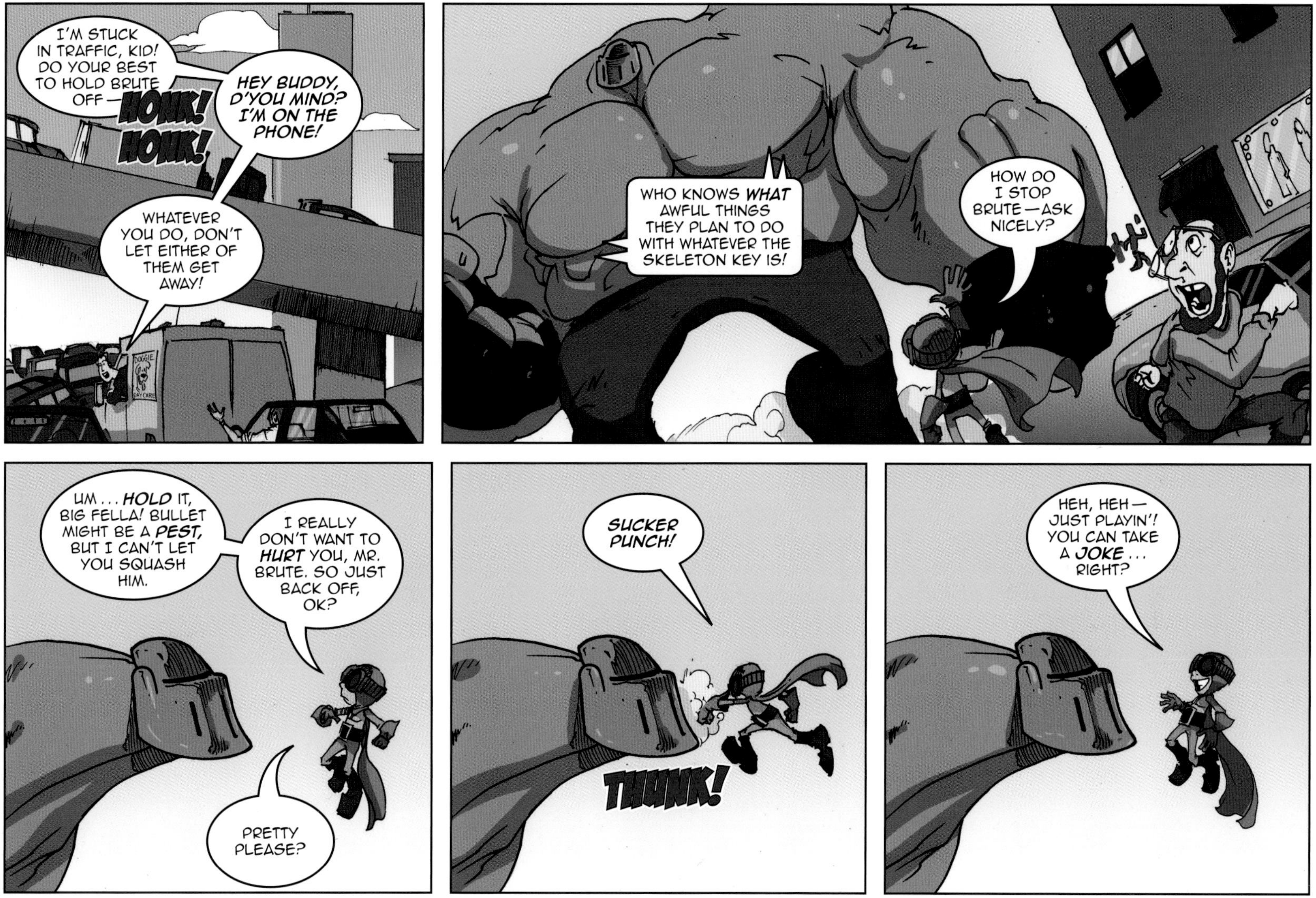
I'M STUCK IN TRAFFIC, KID! DO YOUR BEST TO HOLD BRUTE OFF—
HONK! HONK!
HEY BUDDY, D'YOU MIND? I'M ON THE PHONE!
WHATEVER YOU DO, DON'T LET EITHER OF THEM GET AWAY!
DOGGIE DAY CARE
WHO KNOWS WHAT AWFUL THINGS THEY PLAN TO DO WITH WHATEVER THE SKELETON KEY IS!
HOW DO I STOP BRUTE—ASK NICELY?
UM . . . HOLD IT, BIG FELLA! BULLET MIGHT BE A PEST, BUT I CAN'T LET YOU SQUASH HIM.
I REALLY DON'T WANT TO HURT YOU, MR. BRUTE. SO JUST BACK OFF, OK?
PRETTY PLEASE?
SUCKER PUNCH!
THUNK!
HEH, HEH—JUST PLAYIN'! YOU CAN TAKE A JOKE . . . RIGHT?

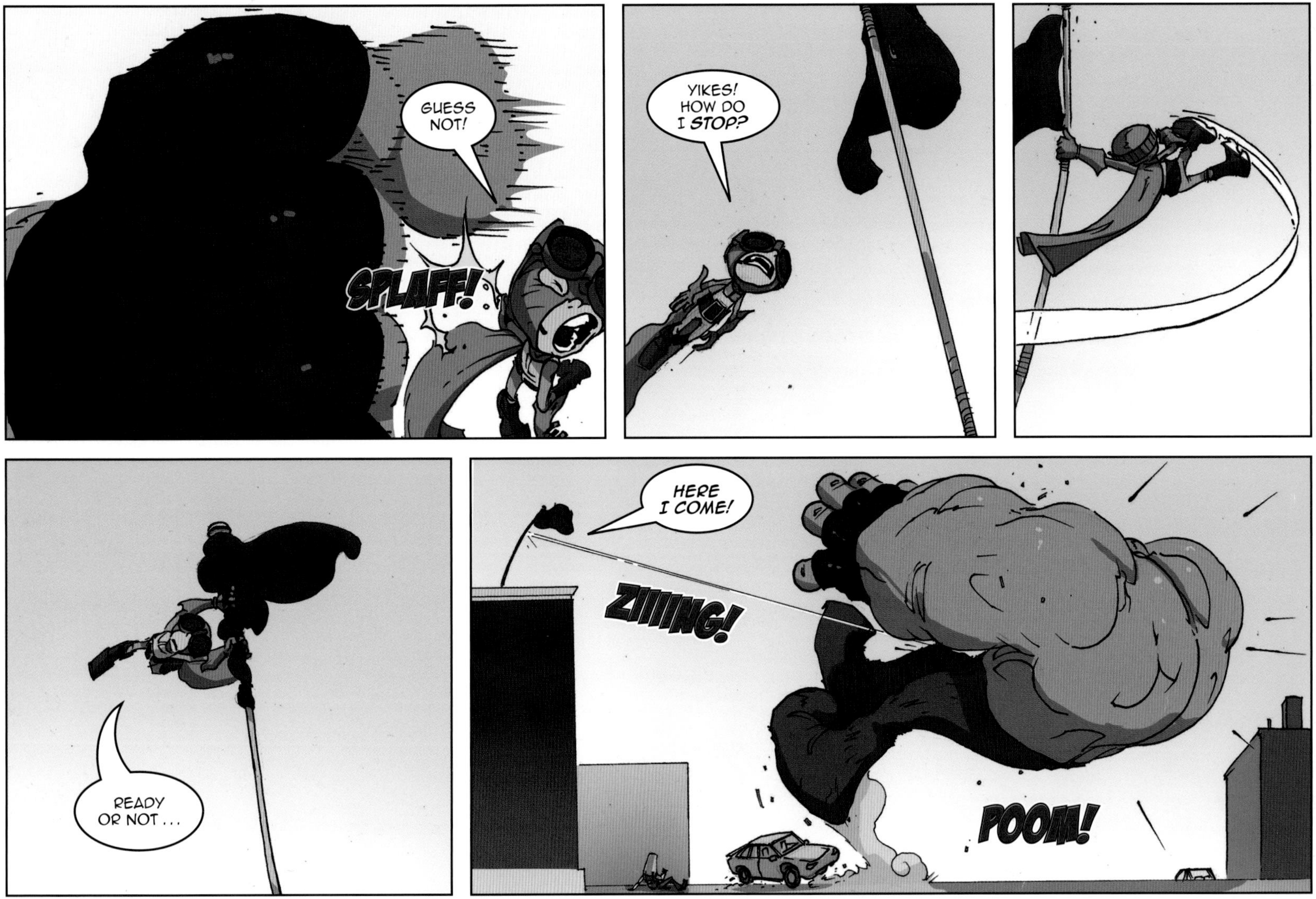
GUESS NOT!
SPLAFF!
YIKES! HOW DO I STOP?
READY OR NOT . . .
HERE I COME!
ZIIIING!
POOM!

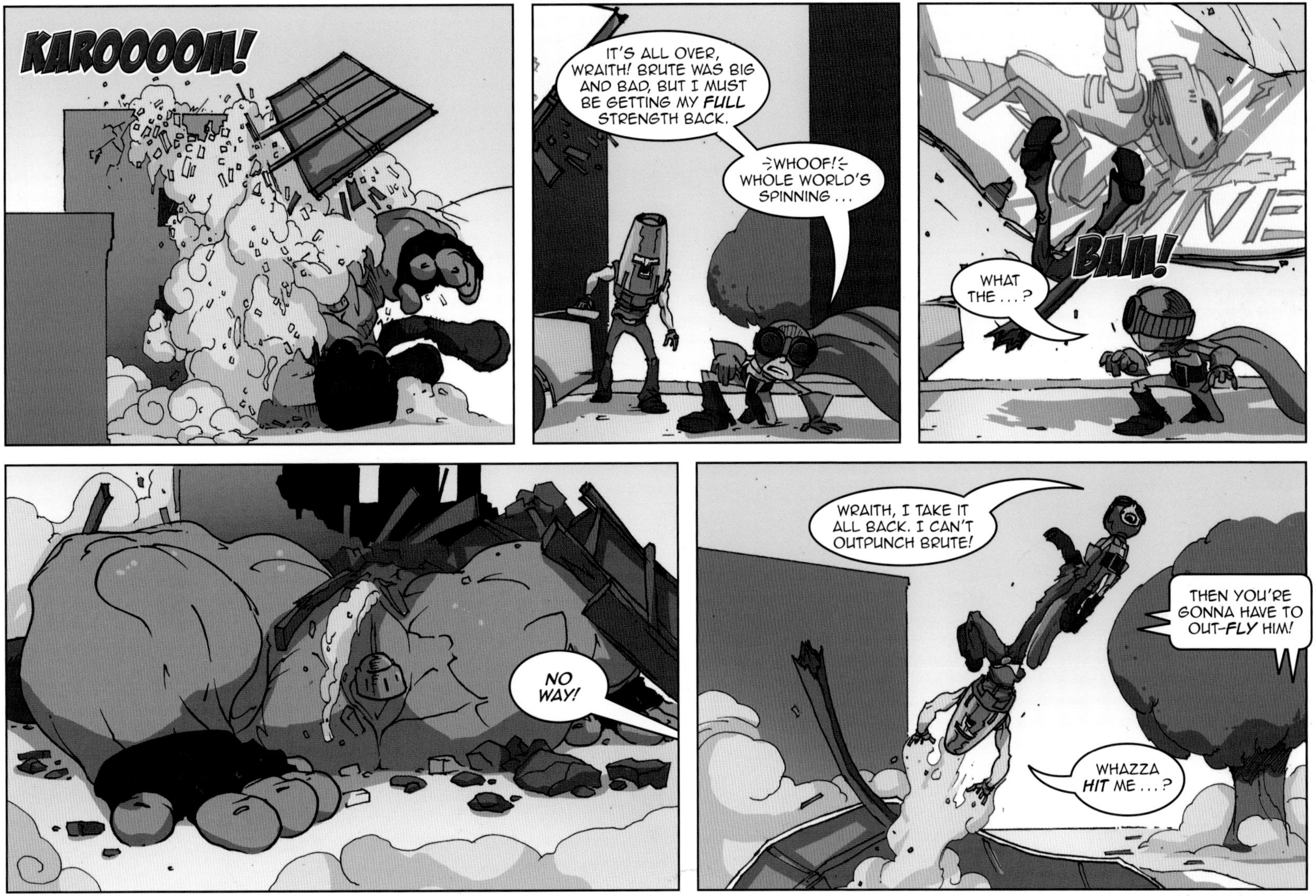
KAROOOOM!
IT'S ALL OVER, WRAITH! BRUTE WAS BIG AND BAD, BUT I MUST BE GETTING MY FULL STRENGTH BACK.
WHOOF! WHOLE WORLD'S SPINNING . . .
BAM!
WHAT THE . . . ?
NO WAY!
WRAITH, I TAKE IT ALL BACK. I CAN'T OUTPUNCH BRUTE!
THEN YOU'RE GONNA HAVE TO OUT-FLY HIM!
WHAZZA HIT ME . . . ?

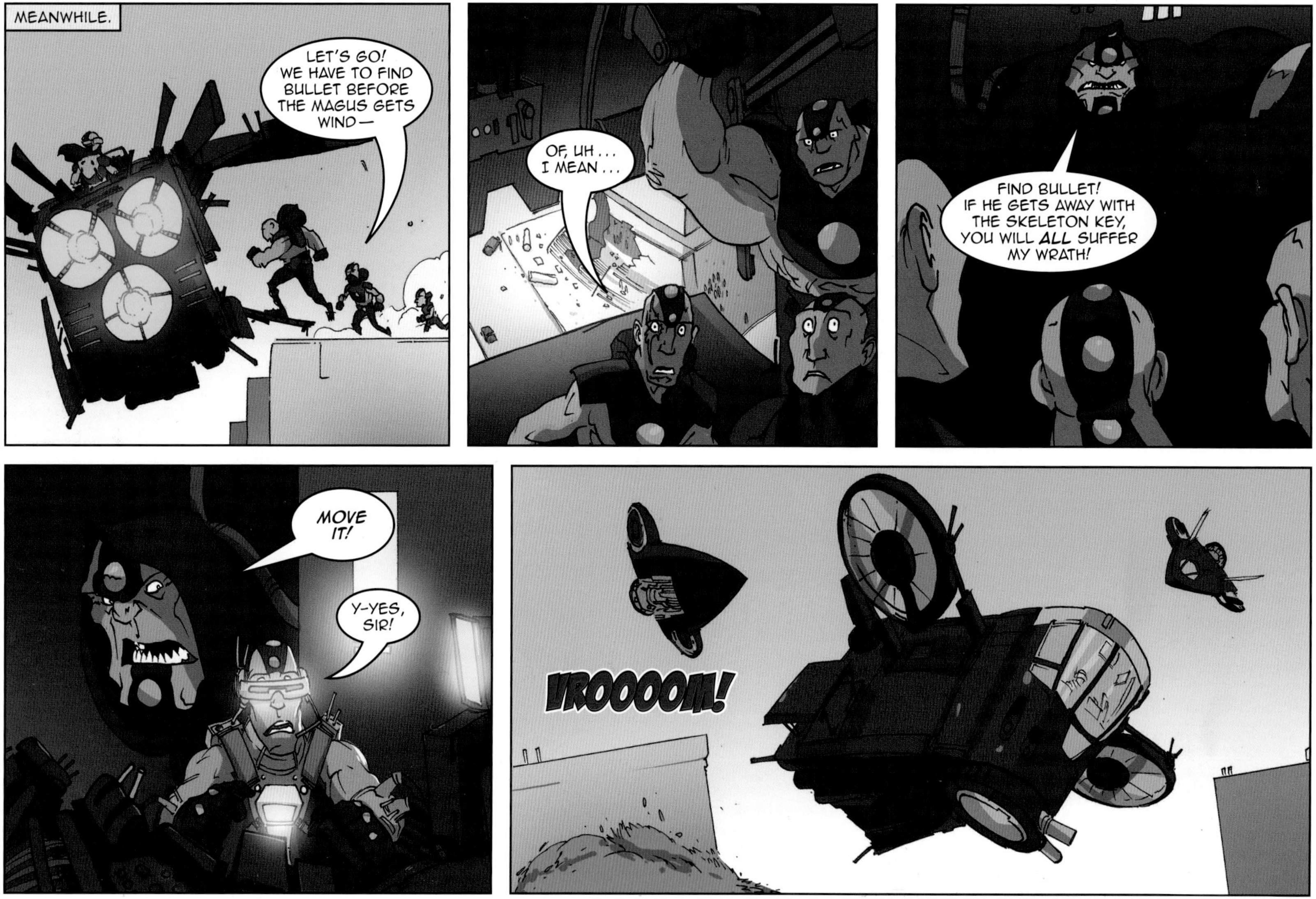
MEANWHILE.
LET'S GO! WE HAVE TO FIND BULLET BEFORE THE MAGUS GETS WIND—
OF, UH . . . I MEAN . . .
FIND BULLET! IF HE GETS AWAY WITH THE SKELETON KEY, YOU WILL ALL SUFFER MY WRATH!
MOVE IT!
Y-YES, SIR!
VROOOOOM!

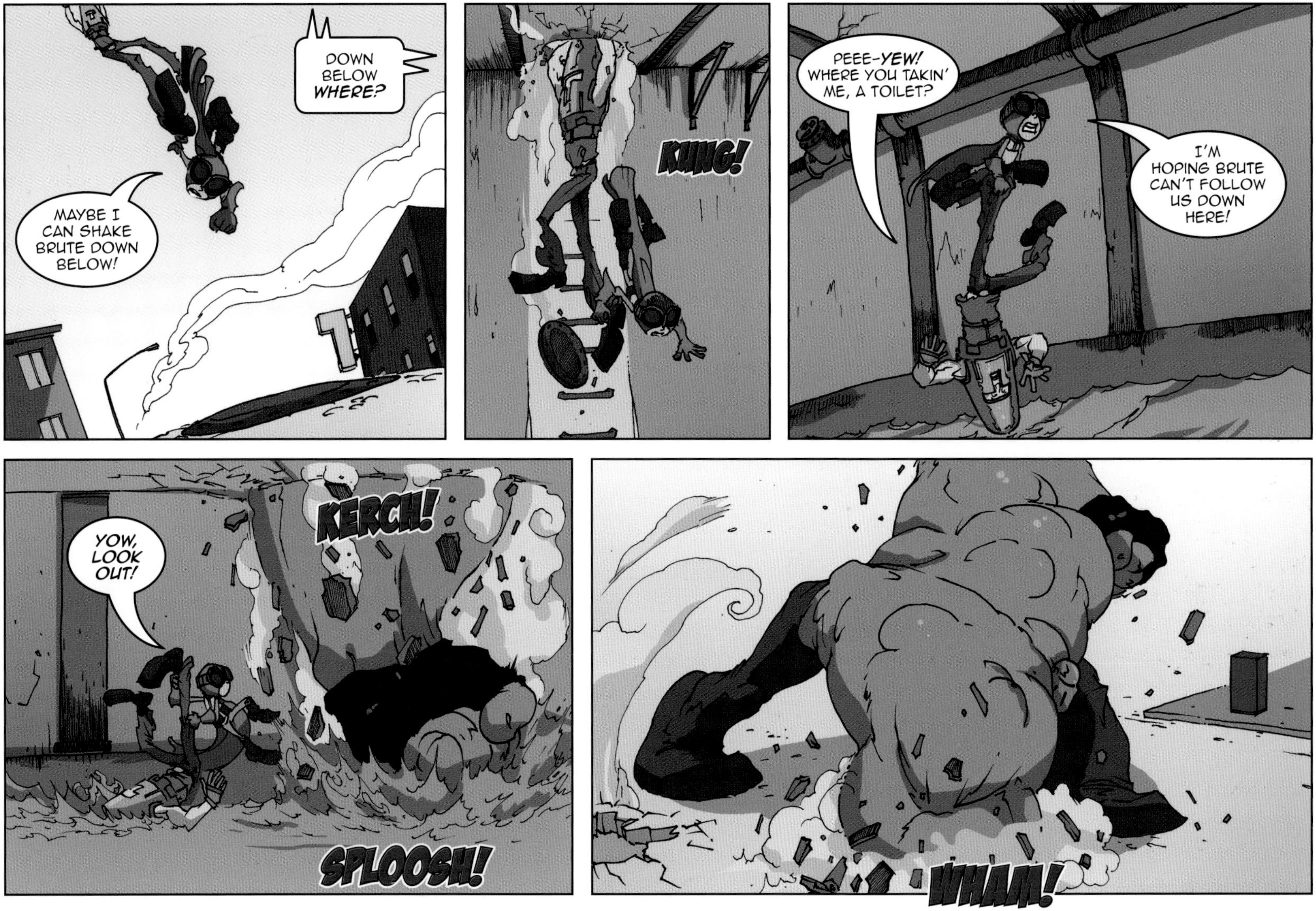
MAYBE I CAN SHAKE BRUTE DOWN BELOW!
DOWN BELOW WHERE?
KUNG!
PEEE-YEW! WHERE YOU TAKIN' ME, A TOILET?
I'M HOPING BRUTE CAN'T FOLLOW US DOWN HERE!
KERCH!
YOW, LOOK OUT!
SPLOOSH!
WHAM!

CRAM!

HOW DOES HE *DO* THAT? RADAR? PSYCHIC POWERS? BORN LUCKY?

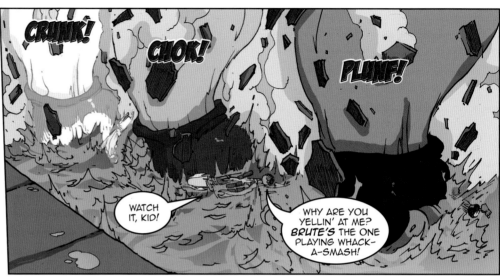

CRUNK!

CHOK!

PLUNF!

WATCH IT, KID!

WHY ARE YOU YELLIN' AT ME? *BRUTE'S* THE ONE PLAYING WHACK-A-SMASH!

BA-DUNK!

AHHH! NO TIME TO STOP!

≥UNF!≤ LET ME *GO*, YOU BIG ...!

≥NNGH!≤

HE'S TOO STRONG ... CAN'T BREAK FREE ...

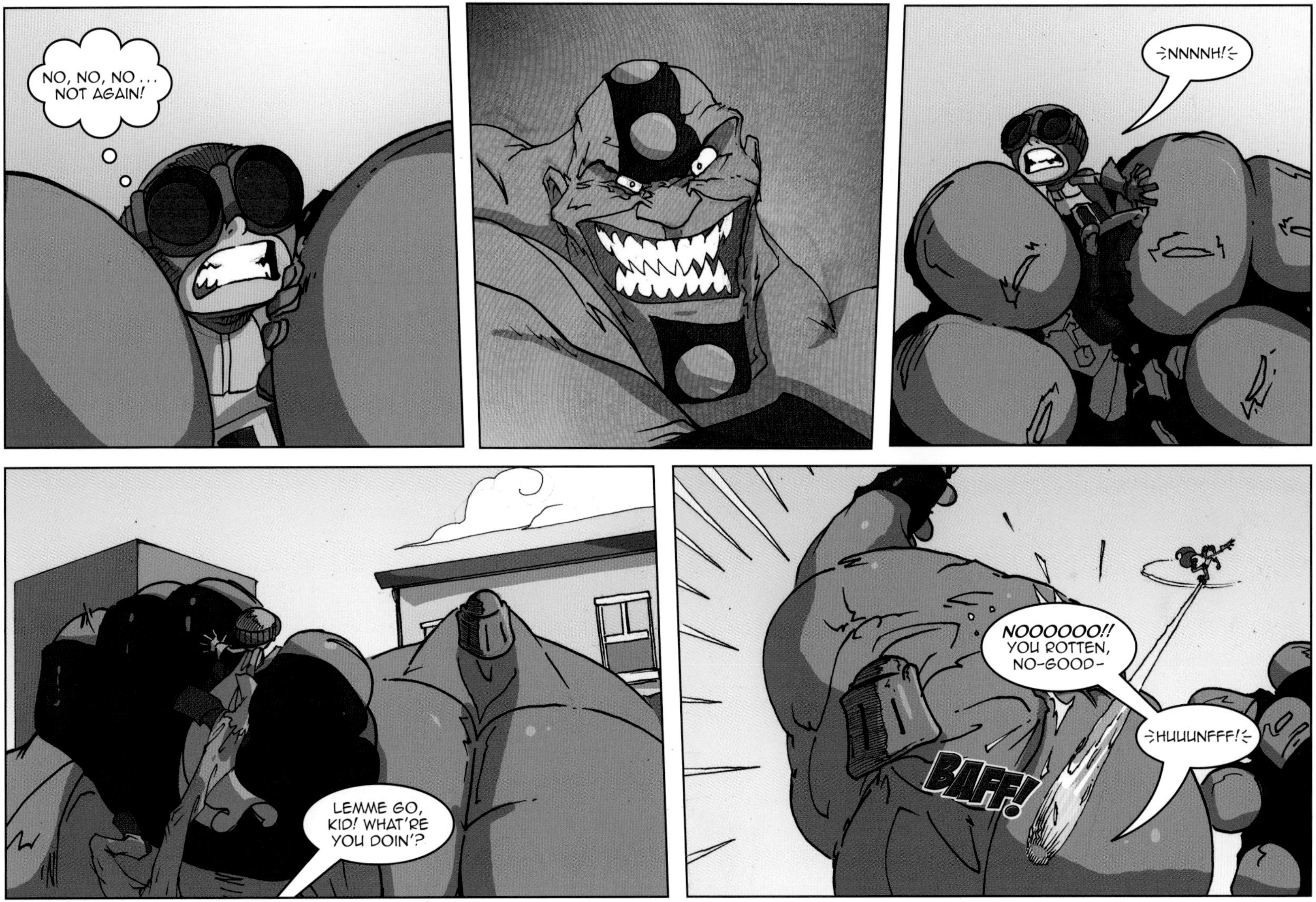
NO, NO, NO . . .
NOT AGAIN!
NNNNH!
LEMME GO, KID! WHAT'RE YOU DOIN'?
NOOOOOO!! YOU ROTTEN, NO-GOOD-
HUUUNFFF!
BAFF!

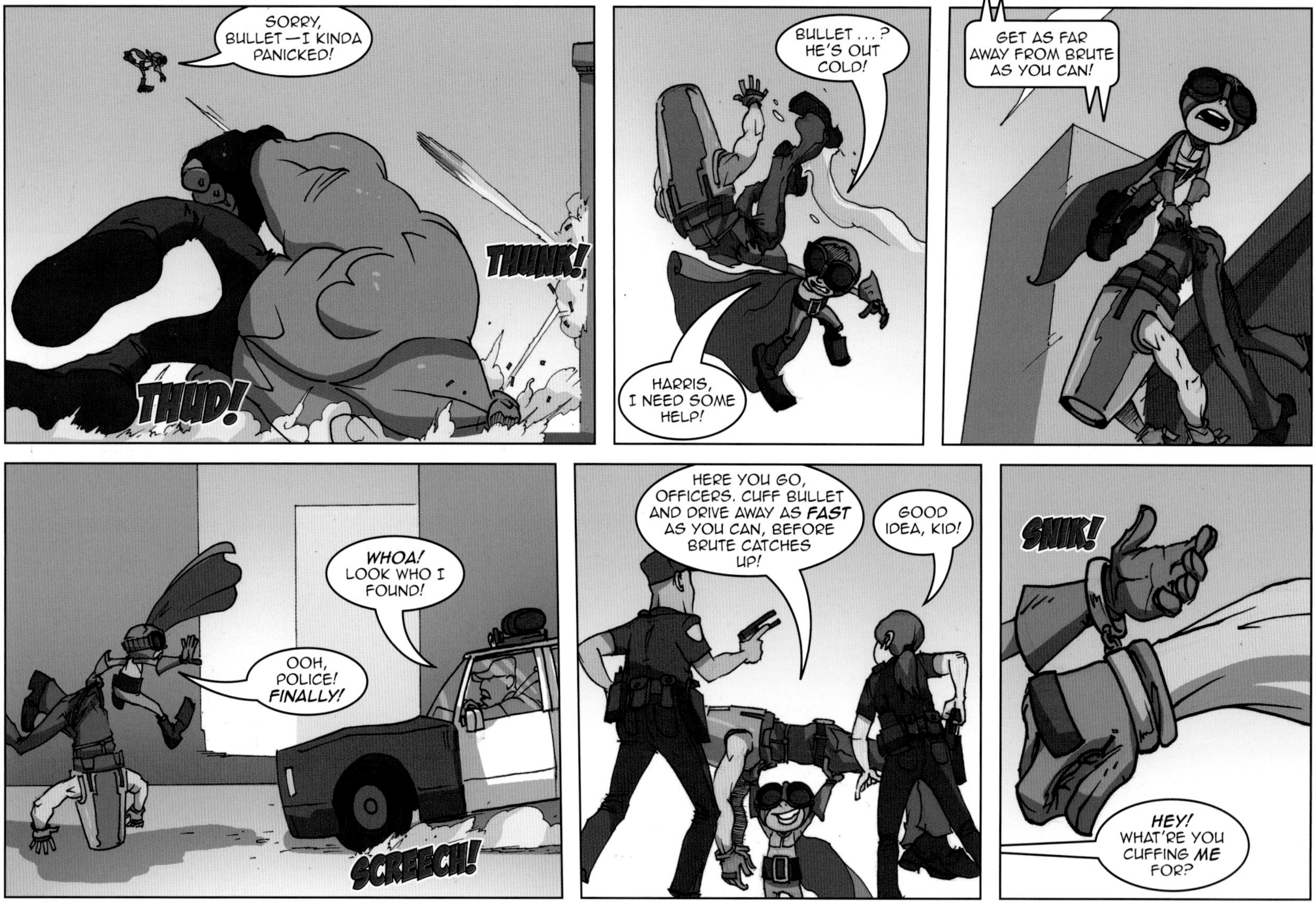
SORRY, BULLET—I KINDA PANICKED!
THUNK!
THUD!
BULLET . . . ? HE'S OUT COLD!
HARRIS, I NEED SOME HELP!
GET AS FAR AWAY FROM BRUTE AS YOU CAN!
WHOA! LOOK WHO I FOUND!
OOH, POLICE! FINALLY!
SCREECH!
HERE YOU GO, OFFICERS. CUFF BULLET AND DRIVE AWAY AS FAST AS YOU CAN, BEFORE BRUTE CATCHES UP!
GOOD IDEA, KID!
SNIK!
HEY! WHAT'RE YOU CUFFING ME FOR?

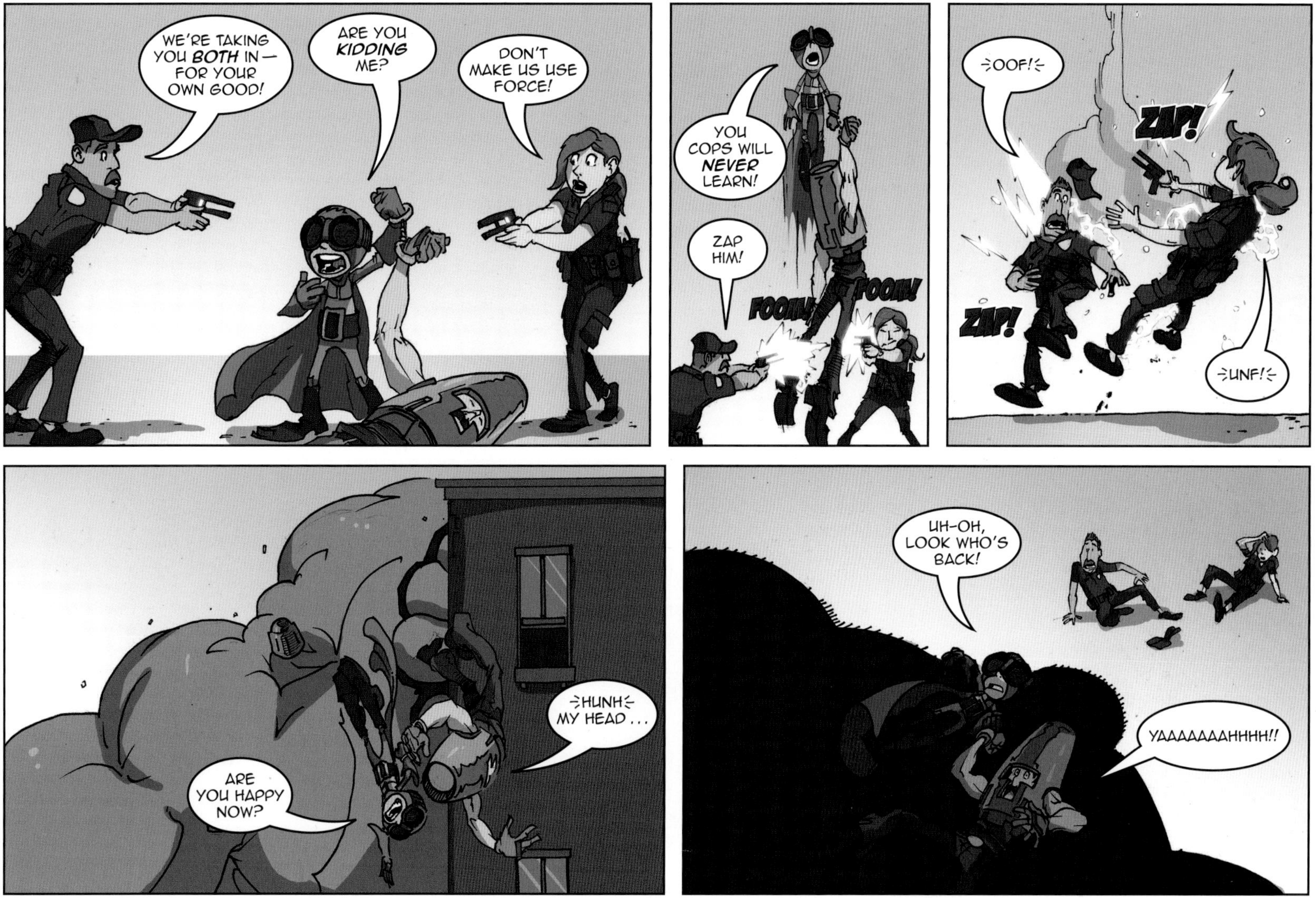
WE'RE TAKING YOU BOTH IN— FOR YOUR OWN GOOD!
ARE YOU KIDDING ME?
DON'T MAKE US USE FORCE!
YOU COPS WILL NEVER LEARN!
ZAP HIM!
FOOM!
FOOM!
OOF!
ZAP!
ZAP!
UNF!
HUNH MY HEAD . . .
ARE YOU HAPPY NOW?
UH-OH, LOOK WHO'S BACK!
YAAAAAAAHHHH!!

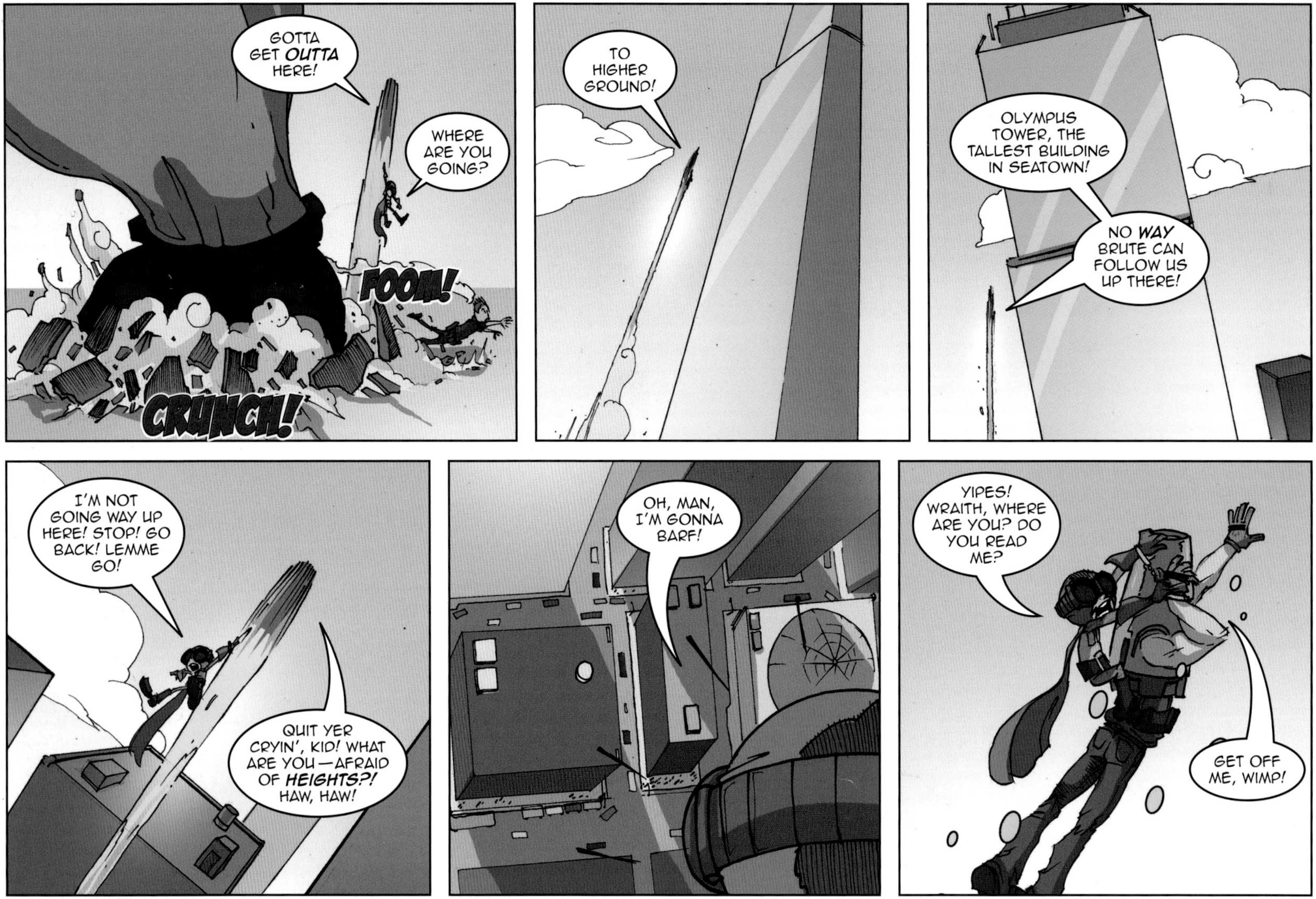
GOTTA GET OUTTA HERE!
WHERE ARE YOU GOING?
FOOM!
CRUNCH!
TO HIGHER GROUND!
OLYMPUS TOWER, THE TALLEST BUILDING IN SEATOWN!
NO WAY BRUTE CAN FOLLOW US UP THERE!
I'M NOT GOING WAY UP HERE! STOP! GO BACK! LEMME GO!
QUIT YER CRYIN', KID! WHAT ARE YOU—AFRAID OF HEIGHTS?! HAW, HAW!
OH, MAN, I'M GONNA BARF!
YIPES! WRAITH, WHERE ARE YOU? DO YOU READ ME?
GET OFF ME, WIMP!

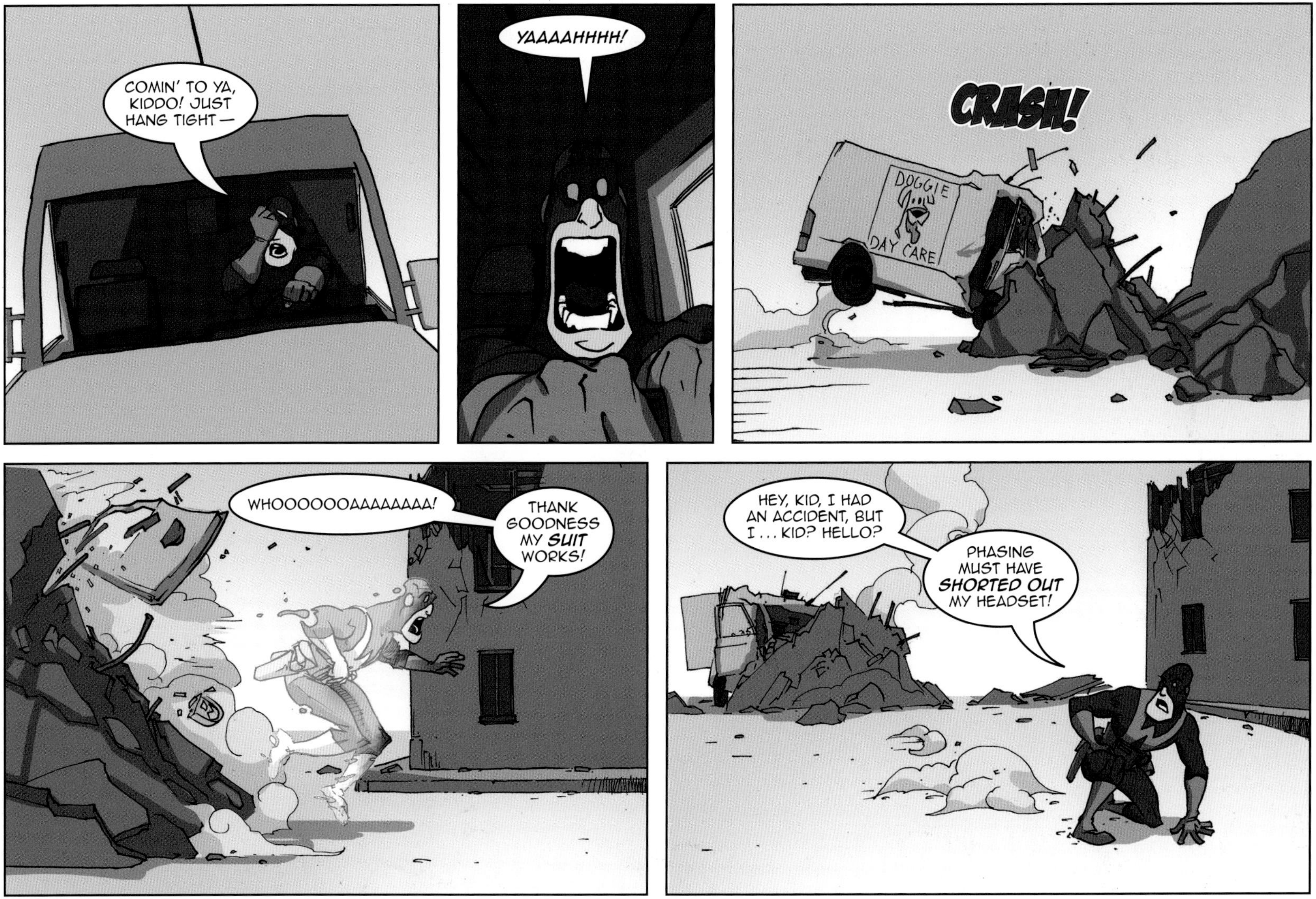
COMIN' TO YA, KIDDO! JUST HANG TIGHT—
YAAAAHHHH!
CRASH!
DOGGIE DAY CARE
WHOOOOOOAAAAAAAA!
THANK GOODNESS MY SUIT WORKS!
HEY, KID, I HAD AN ACCIDENT, BUT I . . . KID? HELLO?
PHASING MUST HAVE SHORTED OUT MY HEADSET!

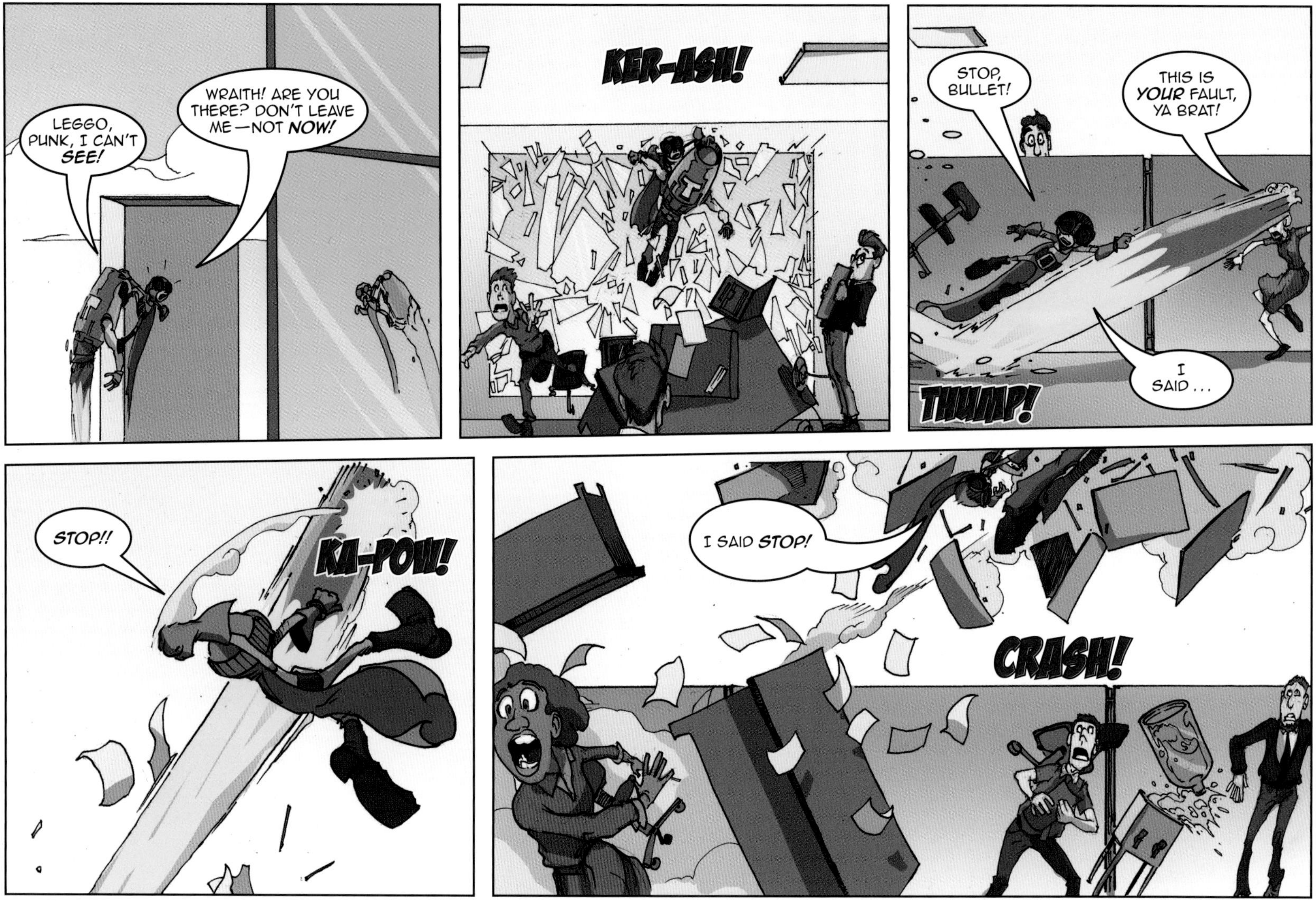
LEGGO, PUNK, I CAN'T SEE!
WRAITH! ARE YOU THERE? DON'T LEAVE ME—NOT NOW!
KER-ASH!
STOP, BULLET!
THIS IS YOUR FAULT, YA BRAT!
THUMP!
I SAID . . .
STOP!!
KA-POW!
I SAID STOP!
CRASH!

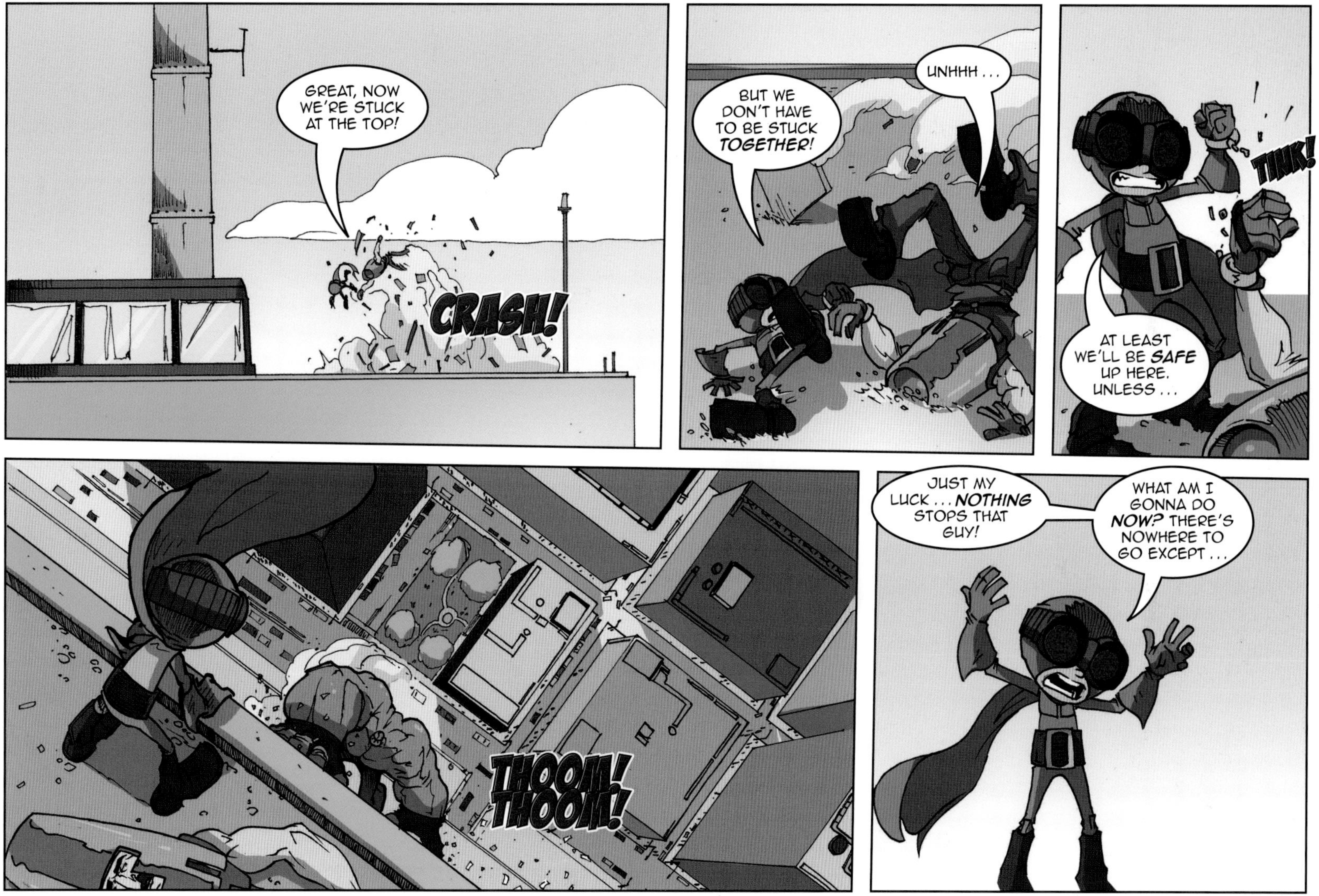
GREAT, NOW WE'RE STUCK AT THE TOP!
CRASH!
BUT WE DON'T HAVE TO BE STUCK TOGETHER!
UNHHH . . .
TINK!
AT LEAST WE'LL BE SAFE UP HERE. UNLESS . . .
THOOM! THOOM!
JUST MY LUCK . . . NOTHING STOPS THAT GUY!
WHAT AM I GONNA DO NOW? THERE'S NOWHERE TO GO EXCEPT . . .

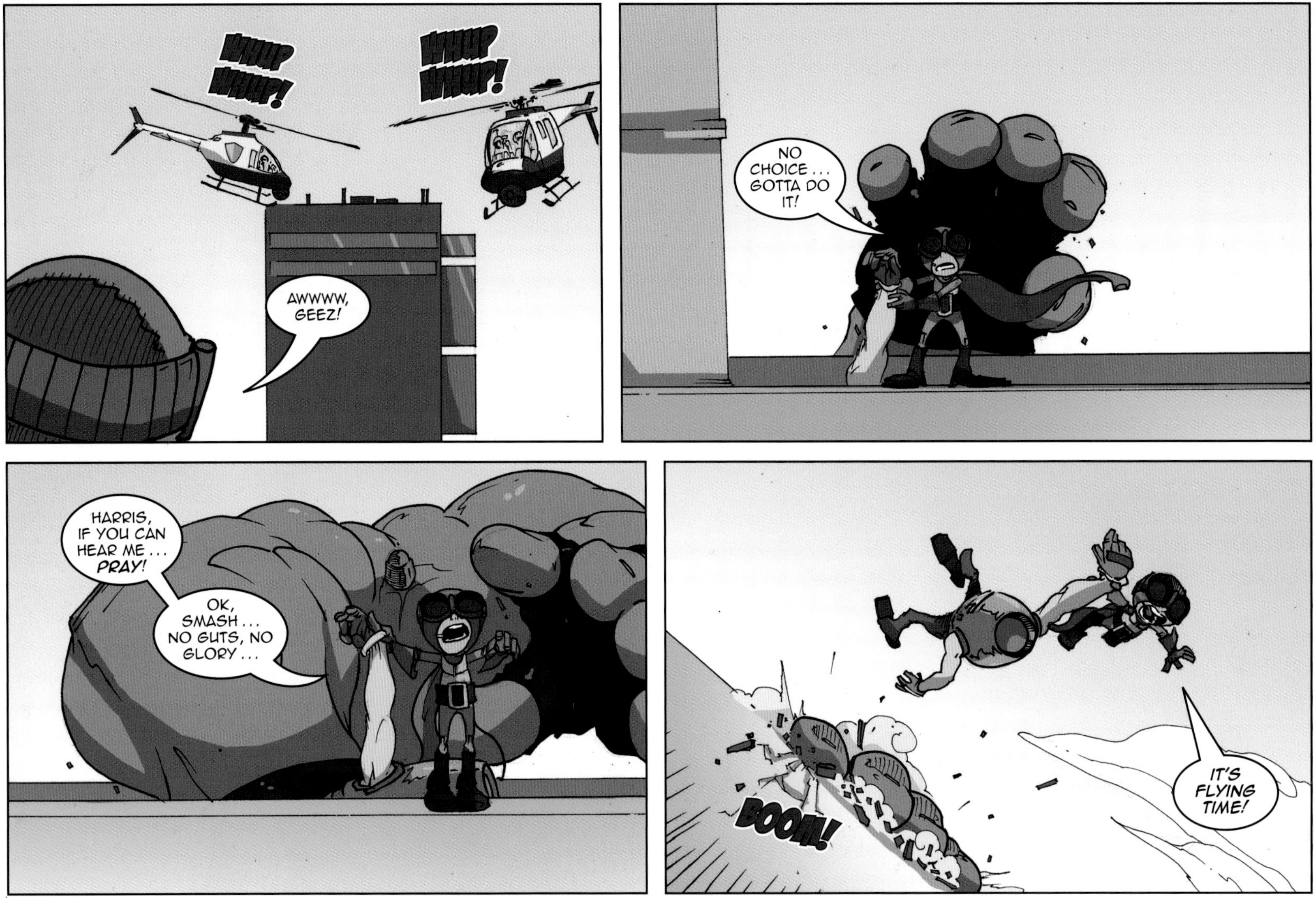
WHUP WHUP!
WHUP WHUP!
AWWWW, GEEZ!
NO CHOICE . . . GOTTA DO IT!
HARRIS, IF YOU CAN HEAR ME . . . PRAY!
OK, SMASH . . . NO GUTS, NO GLORY . . .
BOOM!
IT'S FLYING TIME!

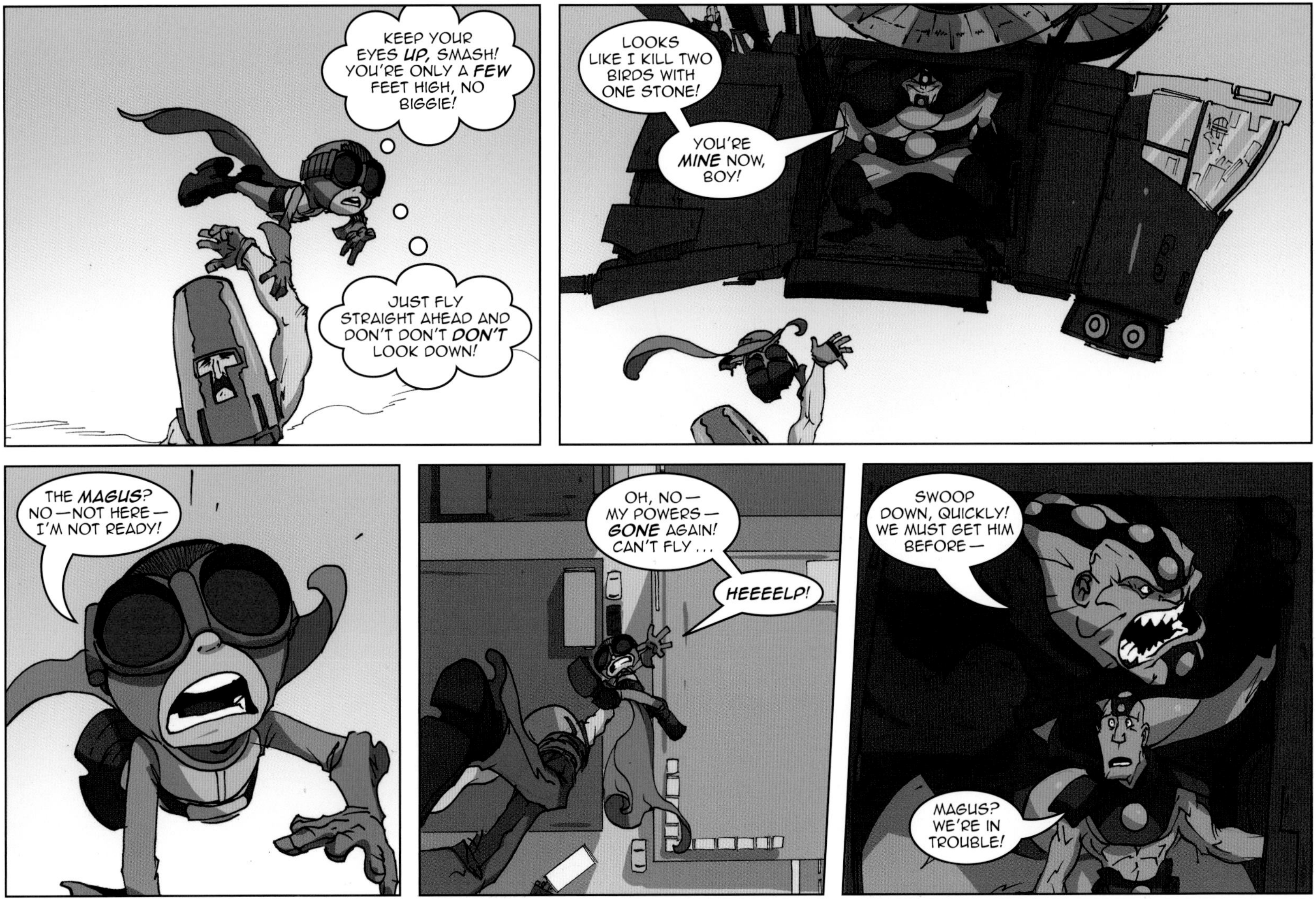
KEEP YOUR EYES *UP*, SMASH! YOU'RE ONLY A *FEW* FEET HIGH, NO BIGGIE!
JUST FLY STRAIGHT AHEAD AND DON'T DON'T *DON'T* LOOK DOWN!
LOOKS LIKE I KILL TWO BIRDS WITH ONE STONE!
YOU'RE *MINE* NOW, BOY!
THE *MAGUS*? NO—NOT HERE—I'M NOT READY!
OH, NO—MY POWERS—*GONE* AGAIN! CAN'T FLY . . .
HEEEELP!
SWOOP DOWN, QUICKLY! WE MUST GET HIM BEFORE—
MAGUS? WE'RE IN TROUBLE!

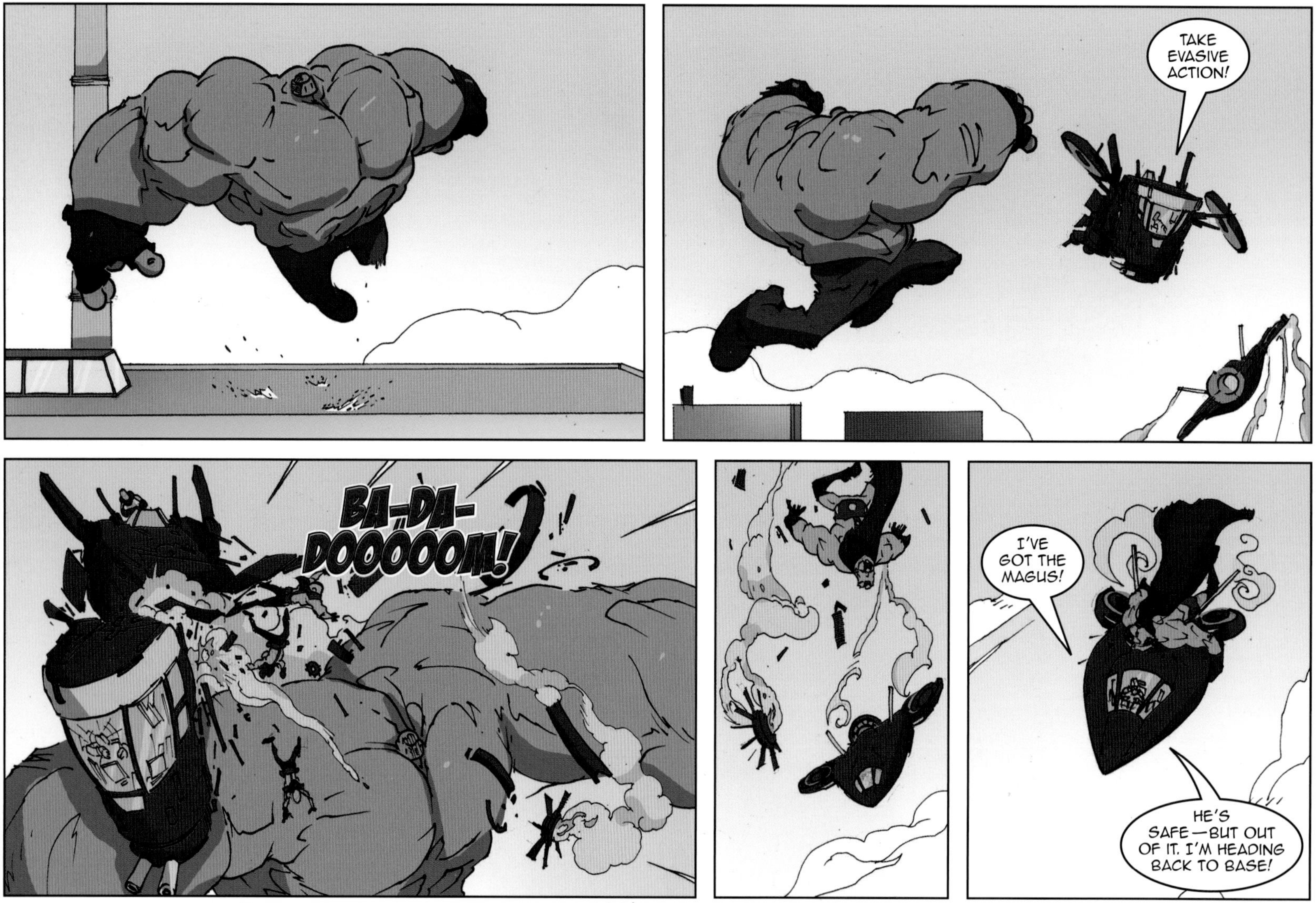
TAKE EVASIVE ACTION!
BA-DA-DOOOOOOM!
I'VE GOT THE MAGUS!
HE'S SAFE—BUT OUT OF IT. I'M HEADING BACK TO BASE!

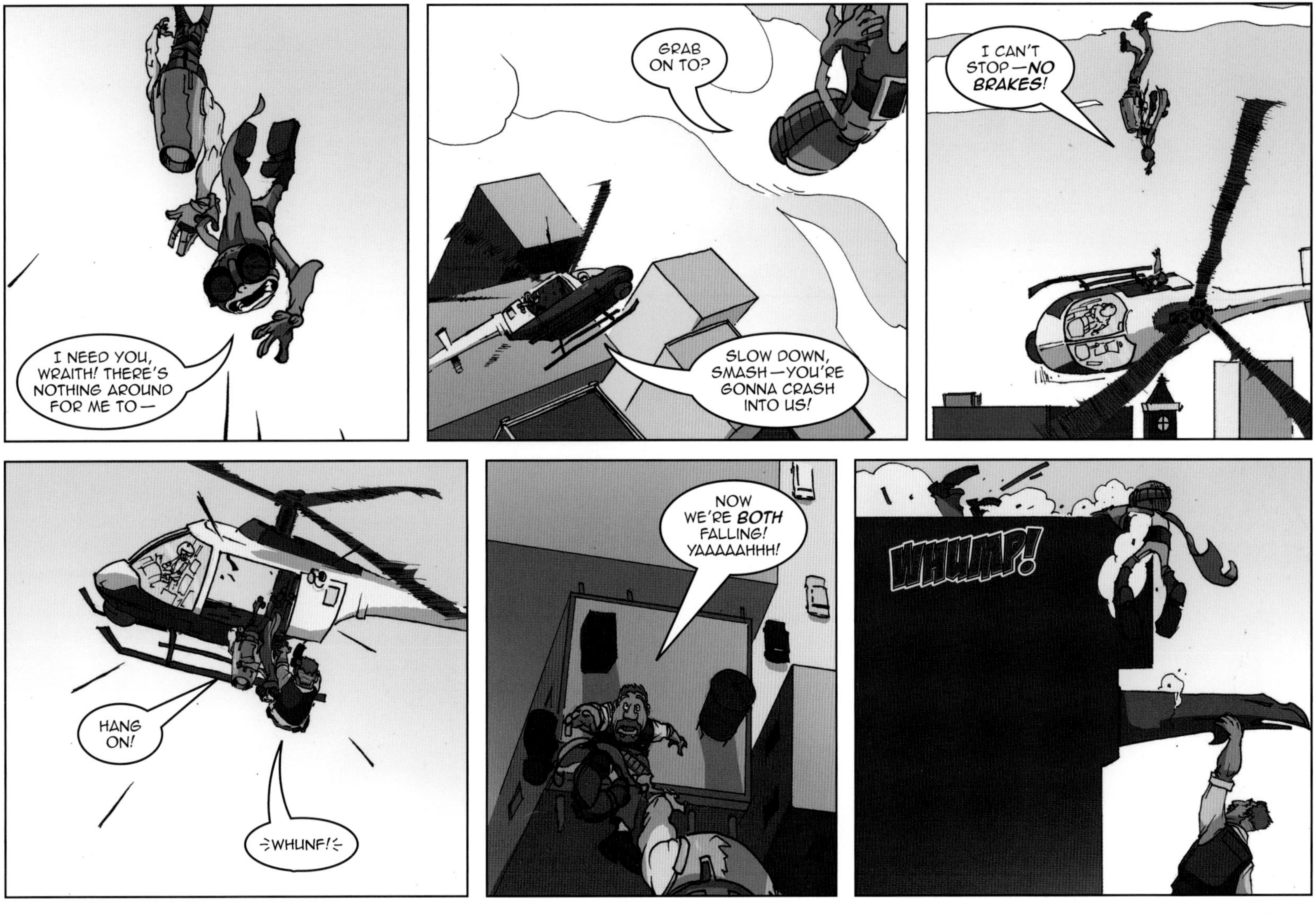
I NEED YOU, WRAITH! THERE'S NOTHING AROUND FOR ME TO—
GRAB ON TO?
SLOW DOWN, SMASH—YOU'RE GONNA CRASH INTO US!
I CAN'T STOP—**NO BRAKES**!
HANG ON!
WHUNF!
NOW WE'RE **BOTH** FALLING! YAAAAAHHH!
WHUMP!

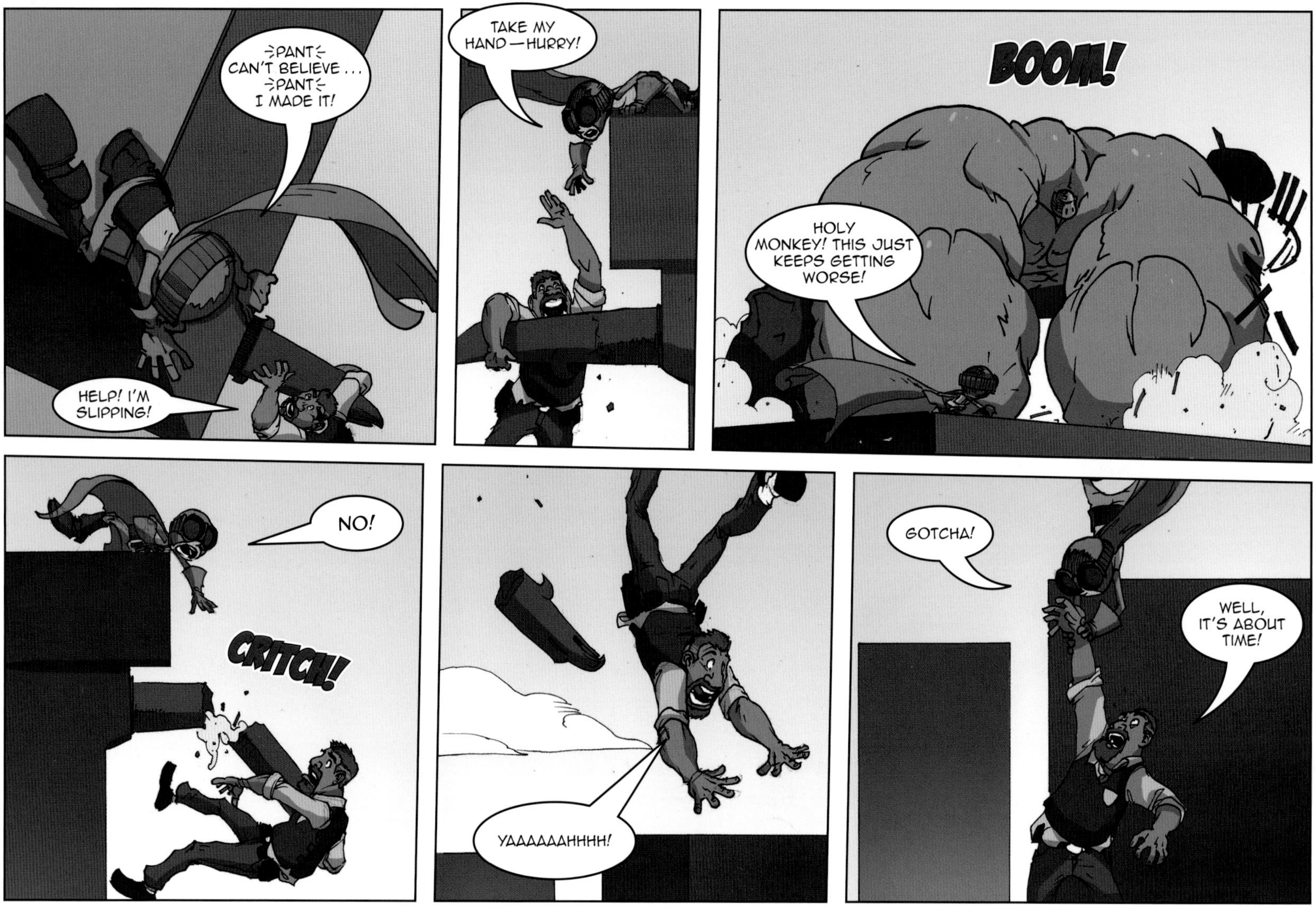

⇒PANT⇐ CAN'T BELIEVE . . . ⇒PANT⇐ I MADE IT!
HELP! I'M SLIPPING!
TAKE MY HAND—HURRY!
BOOM!
HOLY MONKEY! THIS JUST KEEPS GETTING WORSE!
NO!
CRITCH!
YAAAAAAHHHH!
GOTCHA!
WELL, IT'S ABOUT TIME!

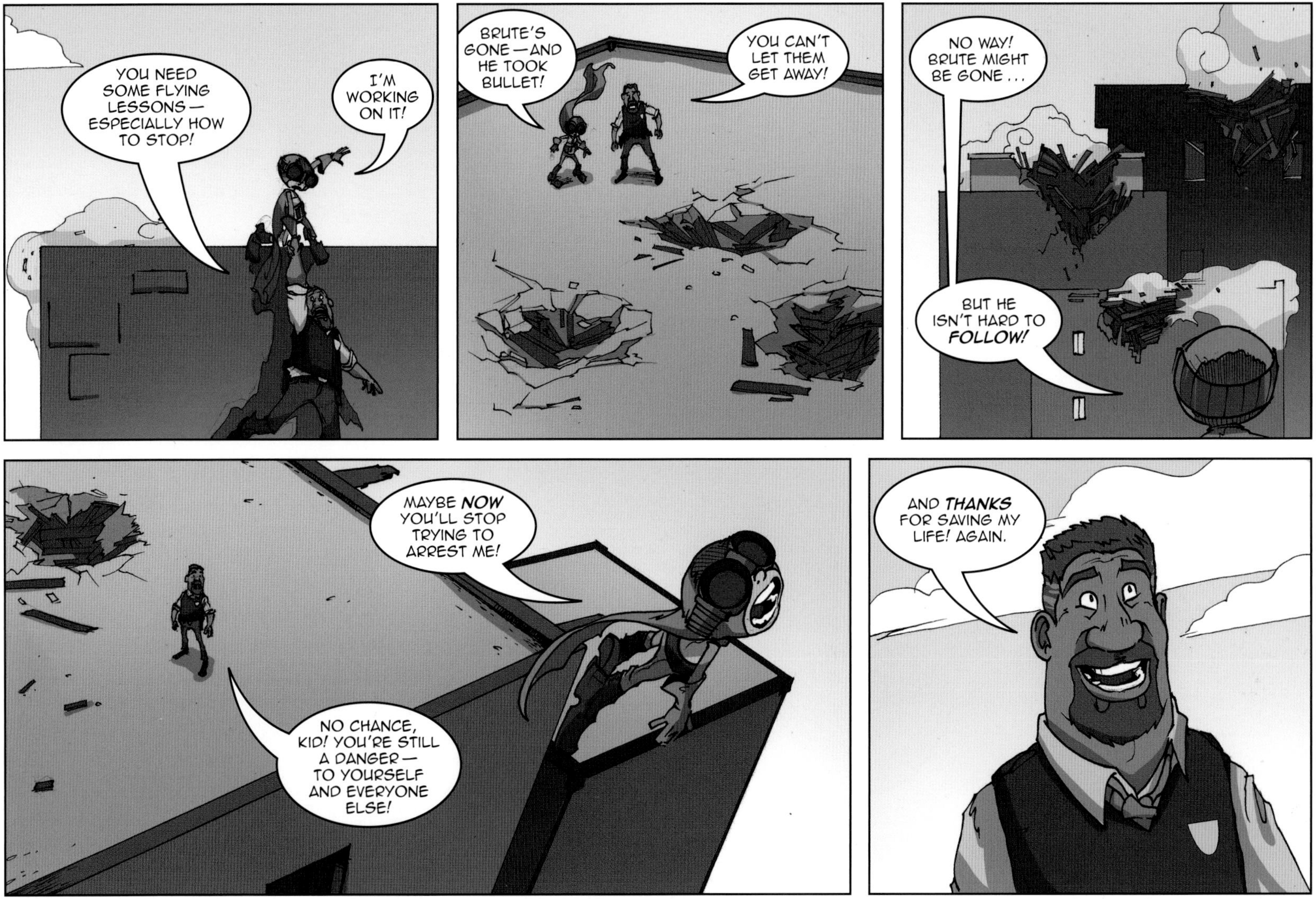

YOU NEED SOME FLYING LESSONS— ESPECIALLY HOW TO STOP!
I'M WORKING ON IT!
BRUTE'S GONE—AND HE TOOK BULLET!
YOU CAN'T LET THEM GET AWAY!
NO WAY! BRUTE MIGHT BE GONE . . .
BUT HE ISN'T HARD TO *FOLLOW!*
MAYBE *NOW* YOU'LL STOP TRYING TO ARREST ME!
NO CHANCE, KID! YOU'RE STILL A DANGER— TO YOURSELF AND EVERYONE ELSE!
AND *THANKS* FOR SAVING MY LIFE! AGAIN.

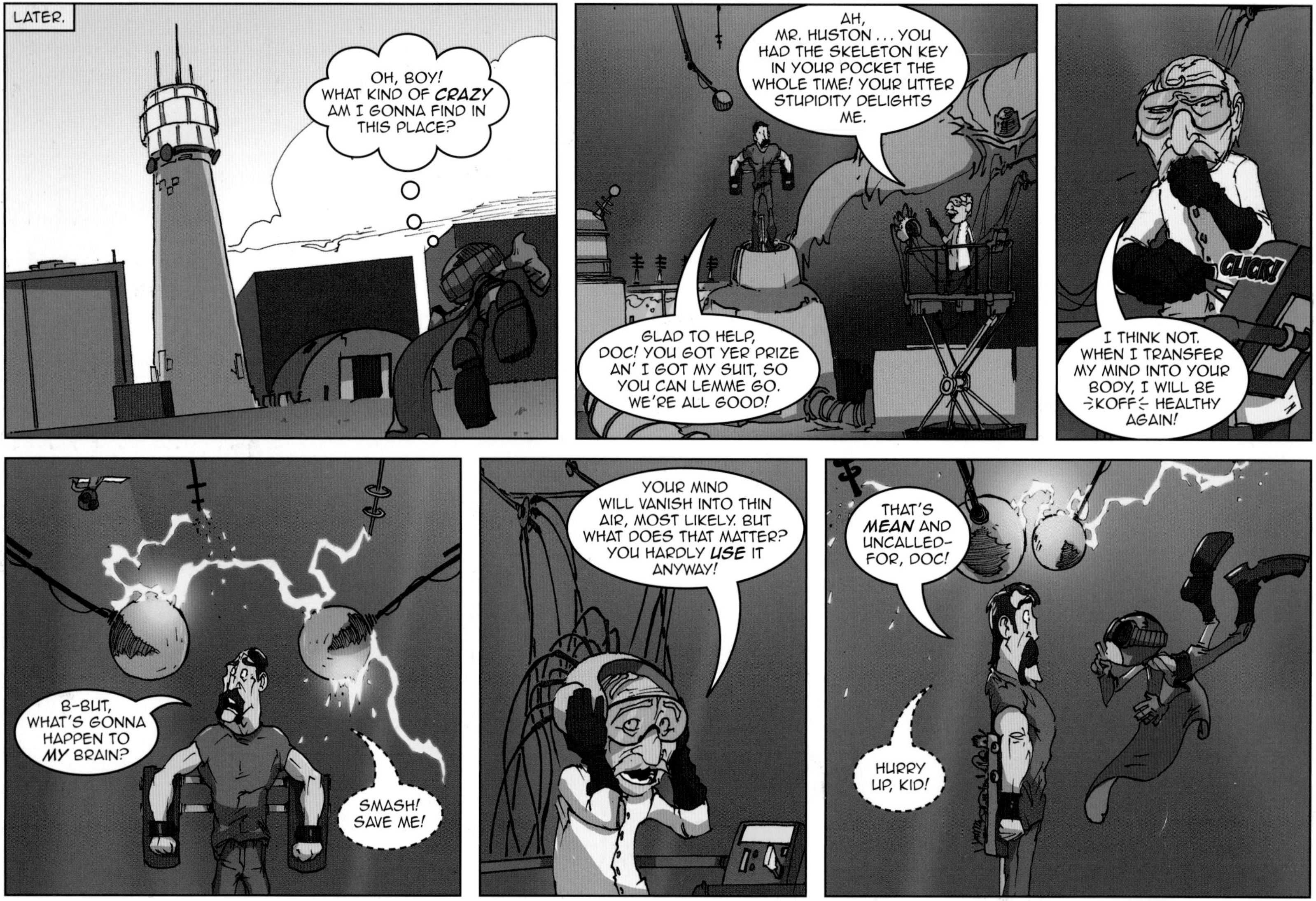
LATER.
OH, BOY! WHAT KIND OF CRAZY AM I GONNA FIND IN THIS PLACE?
AH, MR. HUSTON . . . YOU HAD THE SKELETON KEY IN YOUR POCKET THE WHOLE TIME! YOUR UTTER STUPIDITY DELIGHTS ME.
GLAD TO HELP, DOC! YOU GOT YER PRIZE AN' I GOT MY SUIT, SO YOU CAN LEMME GO. WE'RE ALL GOOD!
CLICK!
I THINK NOT. WHEN I TRANSFER MY MIND INTO YOUR BODY, I WILL BE ⇉KOFF⇇ HEALTHY AGAIN!
B-BUT, WHAT'S GONNA HAPPEN TO MY BRAIN?
SMASH! SAVE ME!
YOUR MIND WILL VANISH INTO THIN AIR, MOST LIKELY. BUT WHAT DOES THAT MATTER? YOU HARDLY USE IT ANYWAY!
THAT'S MEAN AND UNCALLED-FOR, DOC!
HURRY UP, KID!

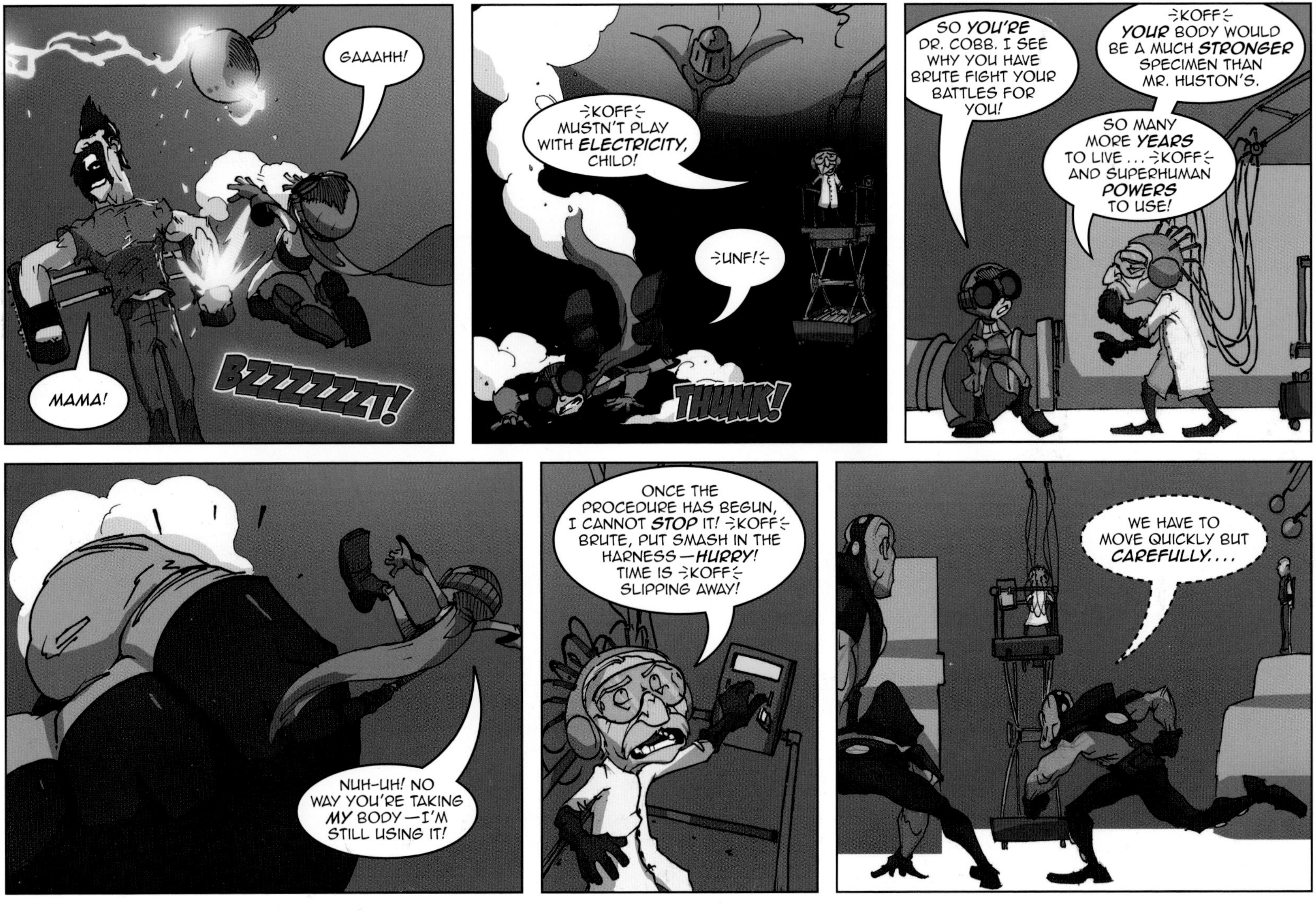
GAAAHH!
MAMA!
BZZZZZZZT!
KOFF MUSTN'T PLAY WITH ELECTRICITY, CHILD!
UNF!
THUNK!
SO YOU'RE DR. COBB. I SEE WHY YOU HAVE BRUTE FIGHT YOUR BATTLES FOR YOU!
KOFF YOUR BODY WOULD BE A MUCH STRONGER SPECIMEN THAN MR. HUSTON'S.
SO MANY MORE YEARS TO LIVE . . . KOFF AND SUPERHUMAN POWERS TO USE!
NUH-UH! NO WAY YOU'RE TAKING MY BODY—I'M STILL USING IT!
ONCE THE PROCEDURE HAS BEGUN, I CANNOT STOP IT! KOFF BRUTE, PUT SMASH IN THE HARNESS—HURRY! TIME IS KOFF SLIPPING AWAY!
WE HAVE TO MOVE QUICKLY BUT CAREFULLY. . . .

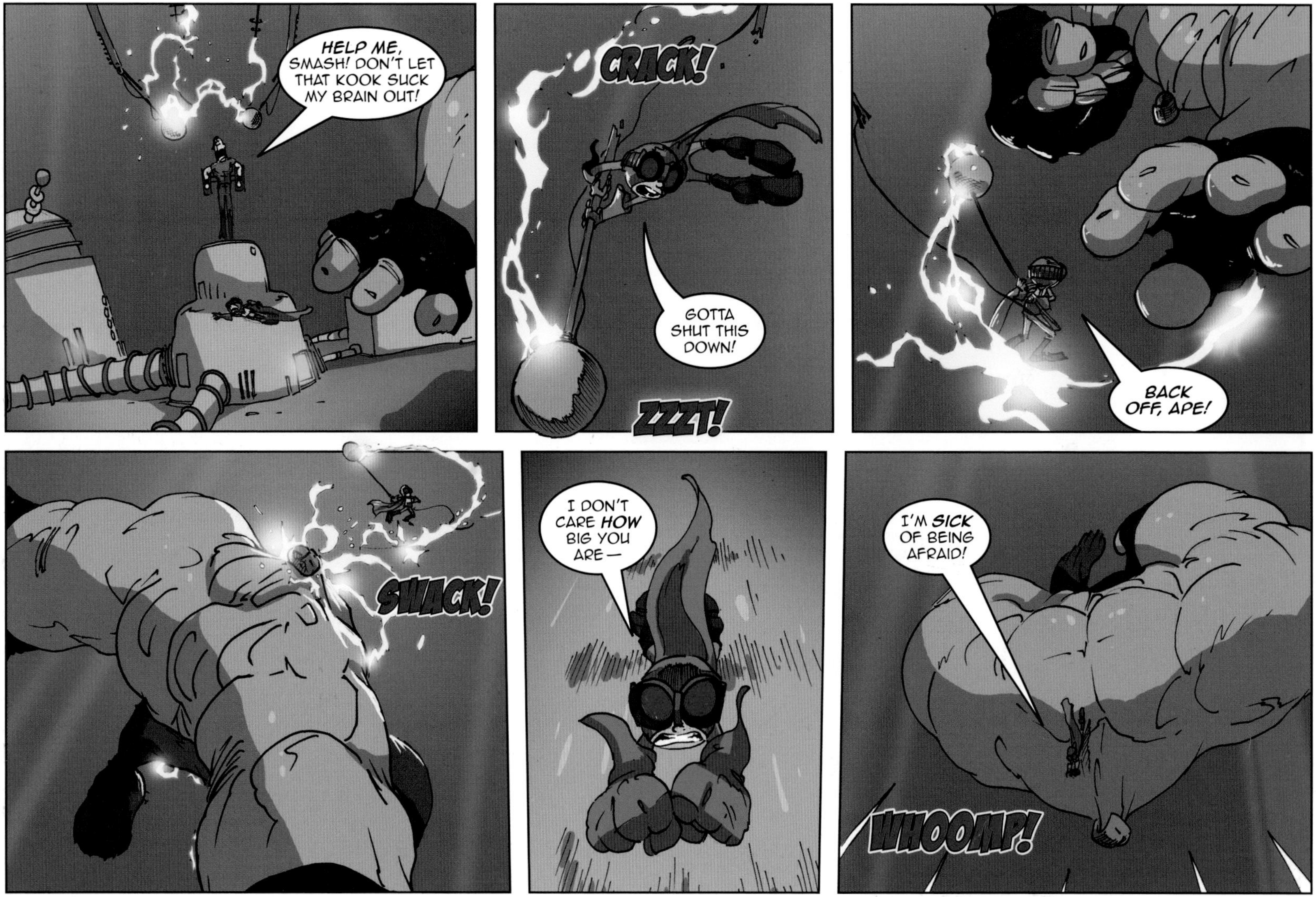
HELP ME, SMASH! DON'T LET THAT KOOK SUCK MY BRAIN OUT!
CRACK!
GOTTA SHUT THIS DOWN!
ZZZT!
BACK OFF, APE!
SWACK!
I DON'T CARE HOW BIG YOU ARE—
I'M SICK OF BEING AFRAID!
WHOOMP!

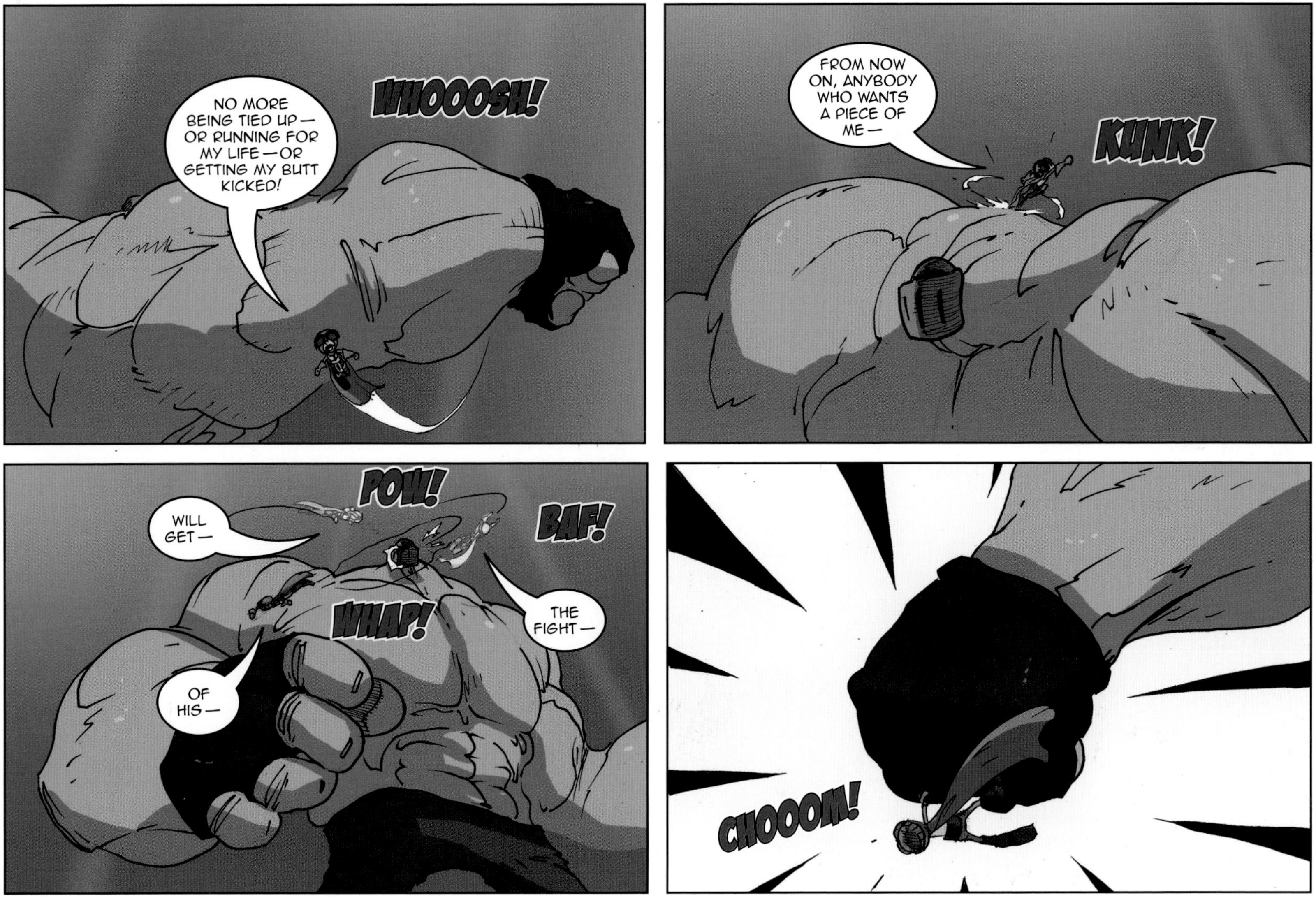
NO MORE BEING TIED UP— OR RUNNING FOR MY LIFE—OR GETTING MY BUTT KICKED!
WHOOOOSH!
FROM NOW ON, ANYBODY WHO WANTS A PIECE OF ME—
KUNK!
POW!
WILL GET—
BAF!
THE FIGHT—
WHAP!
OF HIS—
CHOOOM!

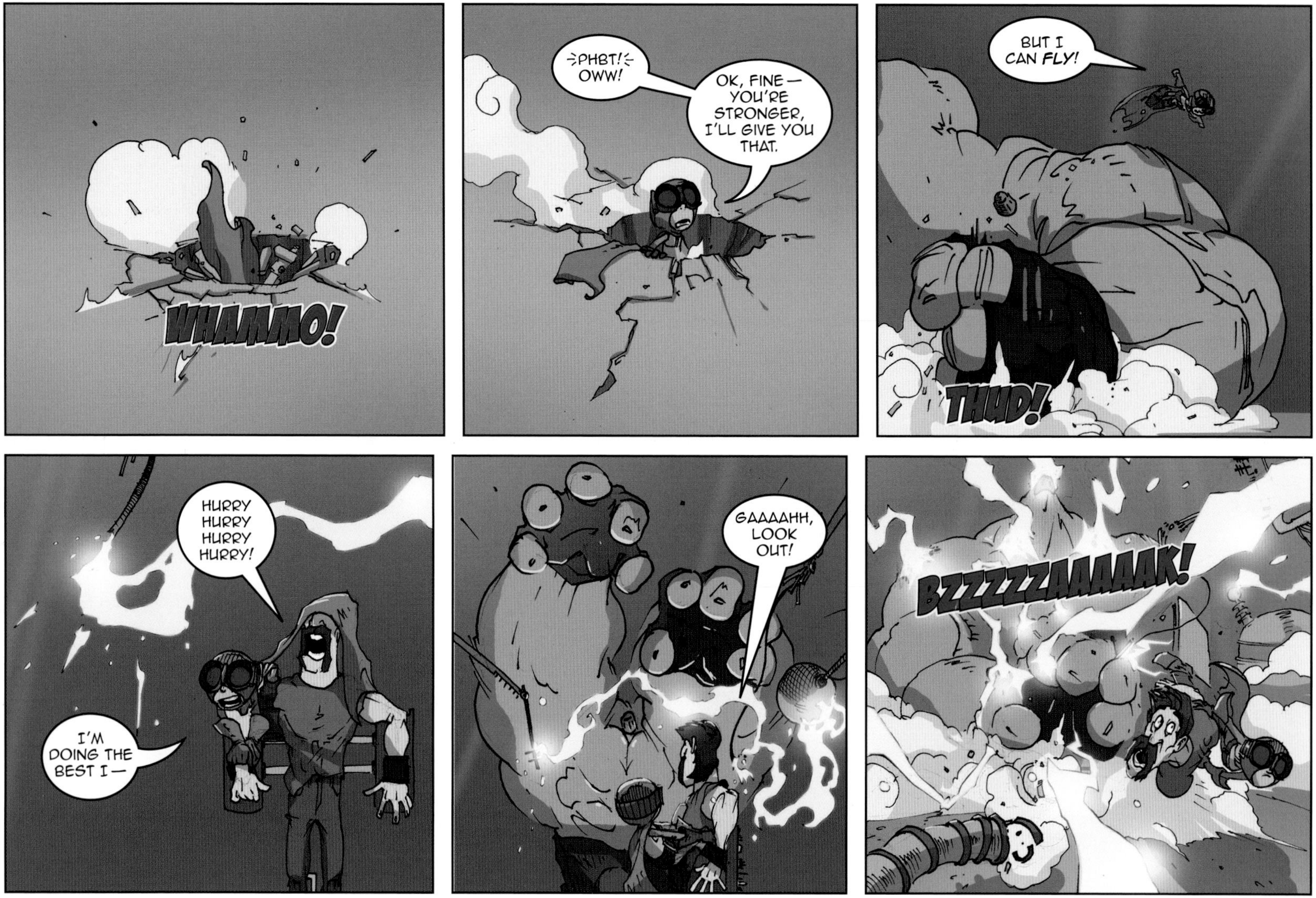
WHAMMO!
PHBT! OWW!
OK, FINE — YOU'RE STRONGER, I'LL GIVE YOU THAT.
BUT I CAN FLY!
THUD!
HURRY HURRY HURRY HURRY!
I'M DOING THE BEST I —
GAAAAHH, LOOK OUT!
BZZZZZAAAAAK!

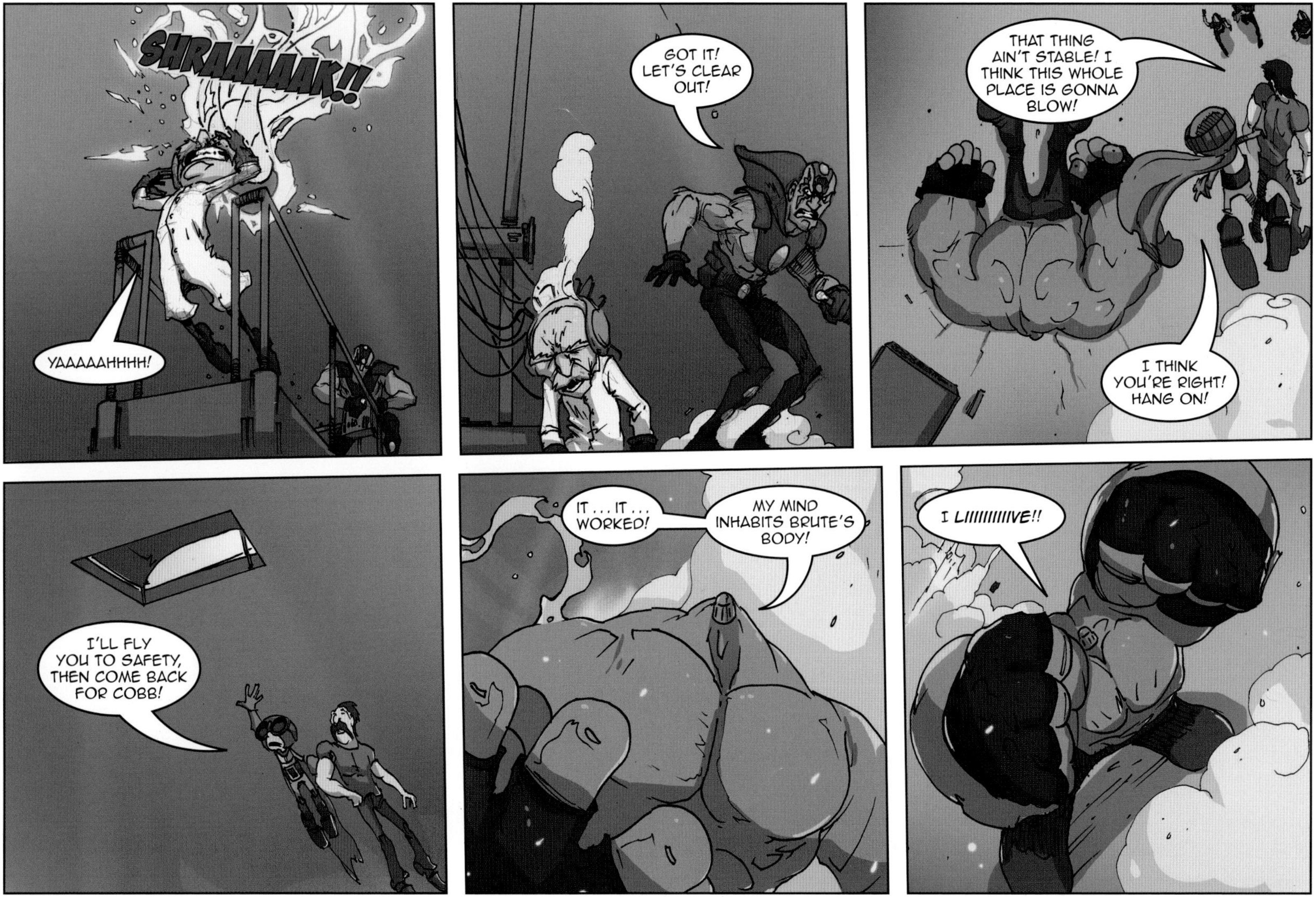
SHRAAAAAK!!
YAAAAAHHHH!
GOT IT! LET'S CLEAR OUT!
THAT THING AIN'T STABLE! I THINK THIS WHOLE PLACE IS GONNA BLOW!
I THINK YOU'RE RIGHT! HANG ON!
I'LL FLY YOU TO SAFETY, THEN COME BACK FOR COBB!
IT . . . IT . . . WORKED!
MY MIND INHABITS BRUTE'S BODY!
I LIIIIIIIIIVE!!

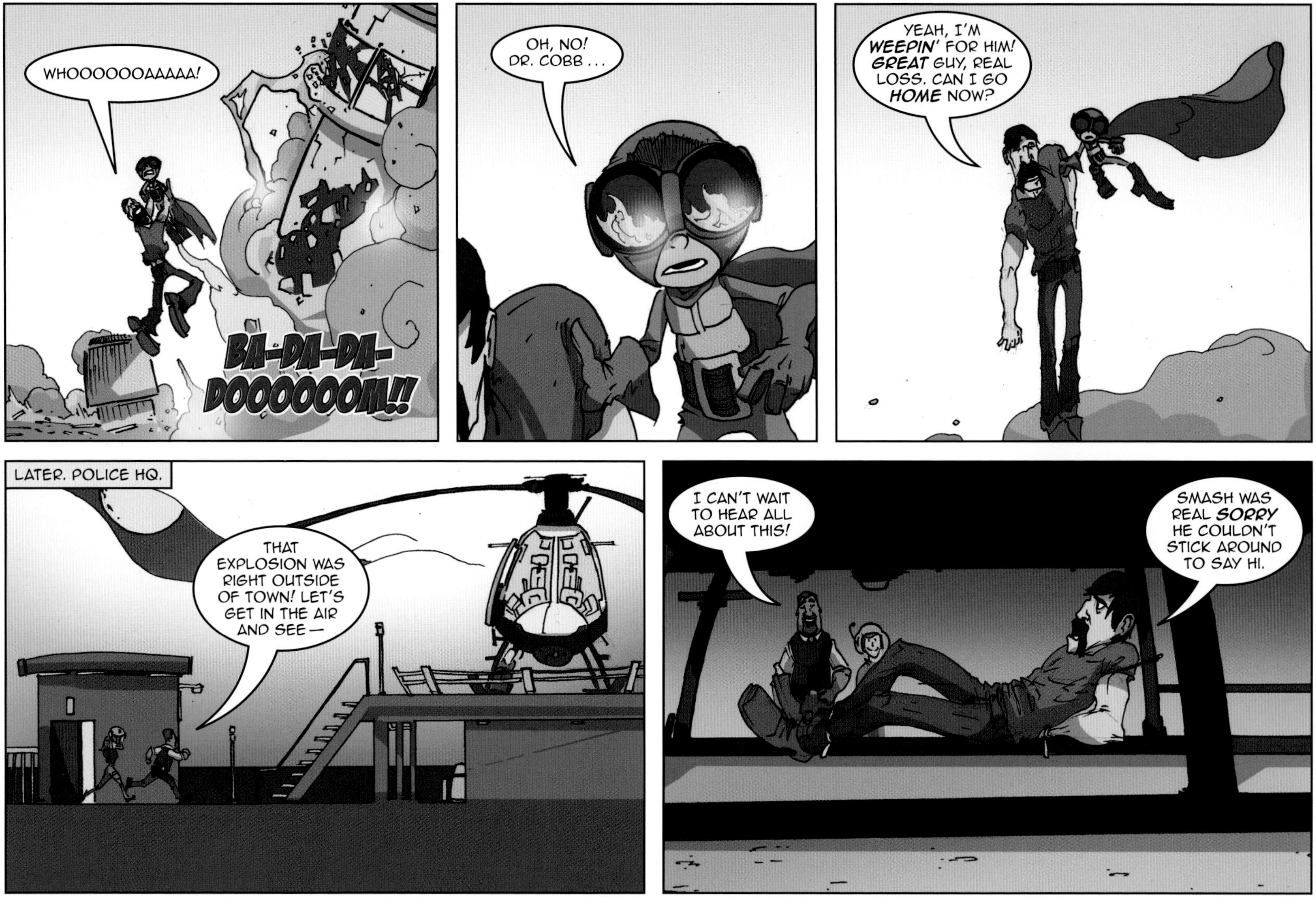
WHOOOOOOAAAAA!
BA-DA-DA-DOOOOOOM!!
OH, NO! DR. COBB . . .
YEAH, I'M WEEPIN' FOR HIM! GREAT GUY, REAL LOSS. CAN I GO HOME NOW?
LATER. POLICE HQ.
THAT EXPLOSION WAS RIGHT OUTSIDE OF TOWN! LET'S GET IN THE AIR AND SEE—
I CAN'T WAIT TO HEAR ALL ABOUT THIS!
SMASH WAS REAL SORRY HE COULDN'T STICK AROUND TO SAY HI.

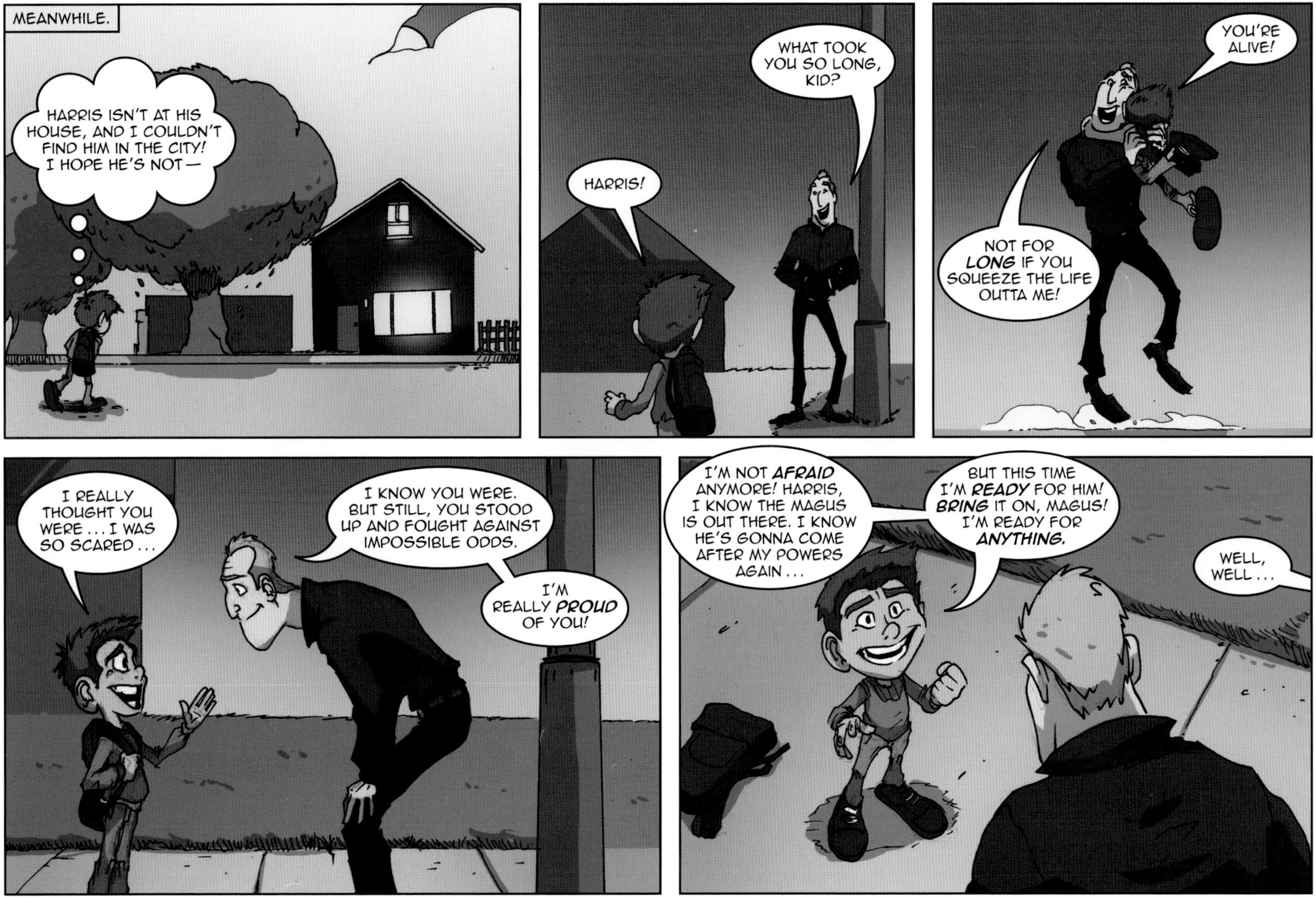
MEANWHILE.
HARRIS ISN'T AT HIS HOUSE, AND I COULDN'T FIND HIM IN THE CITY! I HOPE HE'S NOT—
WHAT TOOK YOU SO LONG, KID?
HARRIS!
YOU'RE ALIVE!
NOT FOR LONG IF YOU SQUEEZE THE LIFE OUTTA ME!
I REALLY THOUGHT YOU WERE . . . I WAS SO SCARED . . .
I KNOW YOU WERE. BUT STILL, YOU STOOD UP AND FOUGHT AGAINST IMPOSSIBLE ODDS.
I'M REALLY PROUD OF YOU!
I'M NOT AFRAID ANYMORE! HARRIS, I KNOW THE MAGUS IS OUT THERE. I KNOW HE'S GONNA COME AFTER MY POWERS AGAIN . . .
BUT THIS TIME I'M READY FOR HIM! BRING IT ON, MAGUS! I'M READY FOR ANYTHING.
WELL, WELL . . .

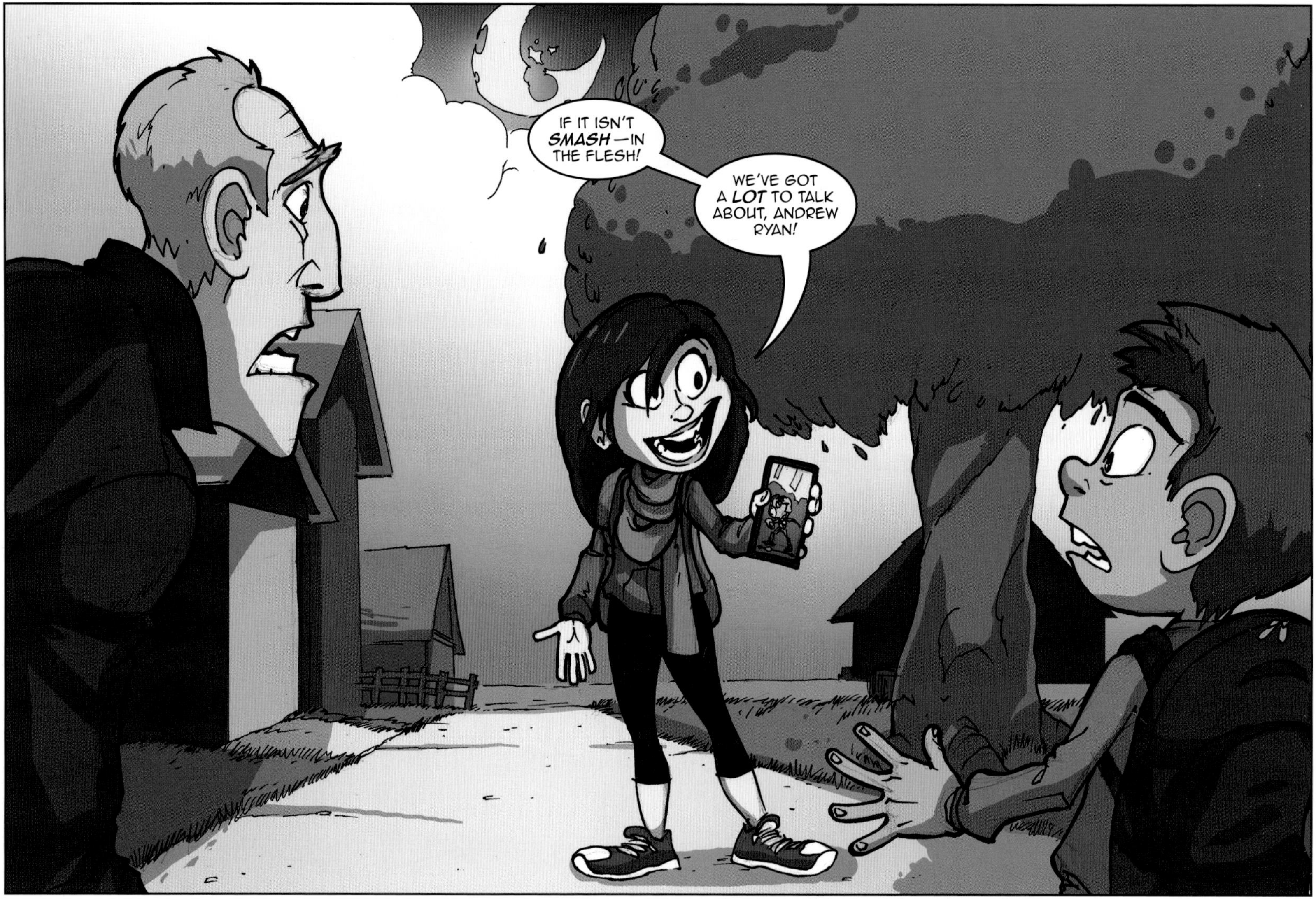
IF IT ISN'T **SMASH**—IN THE FLESH!
WE'VE GOT A **LOT** TO TALK ABOUT, ANDREW RYAN!

THE *CITADEL*. DAWN.

THE SKELETON KEY—AT LAST!

WELL DONE, STRIKE FORCE.

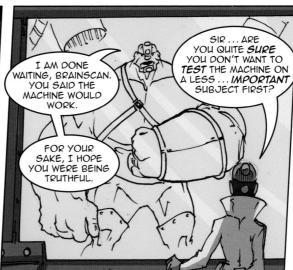

I AM DONE WAITING, BRAINSCAN. YOU SAID THE MACHINE WOULD WORK.

FOR YOUR SAKE, I HOPE YOU WERE BEING TRUTHFUL.

SIR... ARE YOU QUITE *SURE* YOU DON'T WANT TO *TEST* THE MACHINE ON A LESS... *IMPORTANT* SUBJECT FIRST?

HERE GOES...

CLICK!

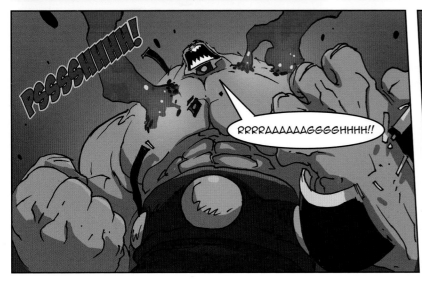

PSSSSHHHH!

RRRRAAAAAAGGGGHHHH!!

SIR! ARE YOU OK? SIR?

NO...

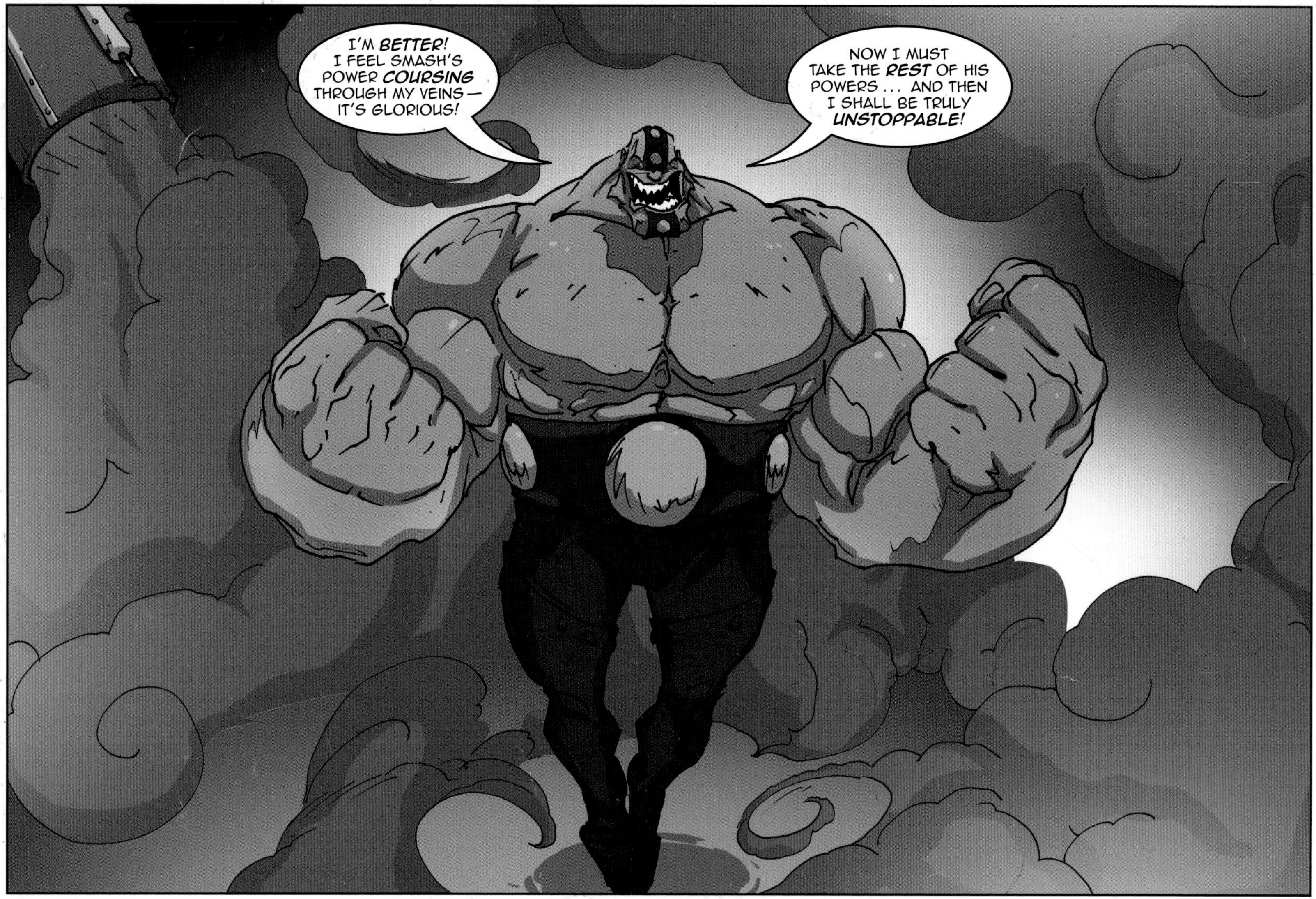
I'M BETTER! I FEEL SMASH'S POWER COURSING THROUGH MY VEINS— IT'S GLORIOUS!
NOW I MUST TAKE THE REST OF HIS POWERS . . . AND THEN I SHALL BE TRULY UNSTOPPABLE!

ACKNOWLEDGMENTS

IT TAKES A LOT OF PEOPLE TO MAKE A BOOK LIKE THIS COME TOGETHER. WE'RE HUGELY INDEBTED TO THE HARDWORKING SMASH TEAM AT CANDLEWICK PRESS—IN PARTICULAR, OUR BRILLIANT EDITOR, MARY LEE DONOVAN, WHOSE INPUT ALWAYS MAKES OUR WORK BETTER, AND NATHAN PYRITZ, WHO OVERSEES THE BOOKS' DESIGN WITH ASTOUNDING PATIENCE, HELPFUL FEEDBACK, AND GREAT IDEAS.

WE ALSO WANT TO THANK OUR AGENT, BERNADETTE BAKER-BAUGHMAN FROM THE VICTORIA SANDERS AGENCY, WHO DESERVES A SUPERHERO COSTUME OF HER OWN, AS WELL AS OUR WHOLE FAMILY—MOM, DAD, BIG G (THE REAL-LIFE DETECTIVE DOUROUX), AND OUR BROTHERS AND STEPSISTER—FOR THEIR CONSTANT LOVE AND ENCOURAGEMENT. AND HUGE THANKS TO JUSTINE HERNANDEZ FOR THE FANTASTIC COLORING JOB.

CHRIS: SPECIAL THANKS TO MY WONDERFUL FRIENDS WHO HAVE BEEN SO SUPPORTIVE THROUGHOUT THE CREATION OF THIS BOOK: ELIZABETH DEAN, SHEILA ASHDOWN, LEVI BUCHANAN, CYNTHIA LOPEZ, MELISSA KAISER, RYAN DIXON, CRAIG FITZPATRICK, AND JENNIFER STEWART. MY BIGGEST THANKS OF ALL GOES TO CHRISTINA MACKIN, WHO HAS NEVER STOPPED ENCOURAGING AND BELIEVING IN ME AND WHO MAKES EVERYTHING BETTER.

KYLE: SPECIAL THANKS TO MY WIFE, JAMIE—NOT ONLY FOR HER LOVE AND GUIDANCE BUT ALSO FOR BRINGING OUR BEAUTIFUL DAUGHTER INTO THIS WORLD. MORE THANKS TO JAMIE'S ENTIRE FAMILY FOR ALWAYS BELIEVING IN SMASH AND ENCOURAGING MY ART, AND TO ALAN FERGUSON FOR HIS CONSTANT MORAL SUPPORT.